D1478695

HIS VERY SILENCE
SPEAKS

Though wounded and scarred, his very silence
speaks in terms more eloquent than words of the
desperate struggle against overwhelming odds, of
the hopeless conflict, and heroic manner in which all
went down that day.

General Orders No. 7, Colonel Samuel D. Sturgis,
commanding officer of the Seventh U.S. Cavalry,
Fort Abraham Lincoln,
Dakota Territory, April 10, 1878

Lieutenant E. S. Godfrey, a participant in the battle, reported that on the march to the Little Big Horn, at lunch time "when the haversacks were opened, the horses usually stopped grazing and put their noses near their riders' faces and asked very plainly to share the hardtack. . . . The old soldier was generally willing to share with his beast." (Drawing by Don D. Moore, done especially for this book, author's collection.)

HIS VERY SILENCE
SPEAKS

Comanche—The Horse Who Survived Custer's Last Stand

Elizabeth Atwood Lawrence

WAYNE STATE UNIVERSITY PRESS   DETROIT   1989

93 92 91 90 89   5 4 3 2 1

Library of Congress Cataloging-in-Publication Data

Lawrence, Elizabeth Atwood, 1929–
   His very silence speaks : Comanche—the horse who survived Custer's last
stand / Elizabeth Atwood Lawrence.
      p.   cm.
   Bibliography: p.
   Includes index.
   ISBN 0–8143–2196–8 (alk. paper). — ISBN 0–8143–2197–6 (pbk. : alk.
paper)
   1. Comanche (Horse) 2. Little Big Horn, Battle of the, 1876. 3. Keogh,
Myles Walter, 1840–1876. 4. Cavalry horses—Montana—Biography.
I. Title.
E83.876.L34   1989
973.8′2—dc19   89–5612
                                                     CIP

Done with the assistance of a
Fund established by Thelma Gray James
of Wayne State University for the
publication of Folklore and English Studies.

For Bob, Priscilla, and Mark
with love,

and to the memory of
the horses
who have served so faithfully

A warrior is not delivered by his
great strength.
The war horse is a vain hope for
victory,
and by its great might it cannot save.
Psalms 33:16–17

Contents

Illustrations

Illustrations

"He Screamed Like a Comanche," painting by Thomas H.
    Swearingen
"Comanche," drawing by Ernest L. Reedstrom
"Bringing Water from the River," sketch by Thomas H.
    Swearingen
"Comanche," painting by Charles O. Kemper
Comanche and his bond to Keogh, painting by Pat Hammack
"Silent Horse on a Silent Field," painting by Thomas H.
    Swearingen
"The Empty Saddle," ink drawing by Mrs. P. A. Haynes
Comanche as a Morgan gelding, painting by Jeanne Mellin
"Get Comanche!" painting by James E. Connell
Captain Myles Keogh on Comanche, bronze by Rogers Aston
Clay figure of Comanche
"The Spotted Horse Returns Alone," painting by Brummet
    Echohawk

Preface

Many of my major interests and areas for research converge on the subject of this book. As a veterinarian and a person with a lifetime of interaction with horses, it is natural that when I became a Battle of the Little Big Horn enthusiast, my focus would be on the horses who participated in that event, most especially Comanche. As a cultural anthropologist, I have been involved with Plains Indian studies, focusing on traditional attitudes toward nature which contrast with those of Judaeo-Christian teachings. I have researched the role of the horse within Plains society, past and present, and have devoted considerable attention to animals as symbols as they affect human perceptions and actions.

A combination of my training in veterinary medicine, animal behavior, and anthropology, my particular field for research and teaching is human-animal relationships, with a specialty in analysis of interactions between people and horses. Using this background to explore dimensions in the Comanche story that have not been elucidated previously, and taking account of available evidence, it is possible to reconstruct something about the life of a cavalry mount in Comanche's time and about the relationships that existed between cavalrymen and their horses. From recent scientific findings about the role of animals in society, it has been learned that under certain conditions animals can have healing effects upon people, psychologically as well as physically. Some broad parallels can be drawn with Comanche, who survived to become a factor in helping to ameliorate the national grief which followed the terrible losses sustained in the Custer disaster.

My aim is not only to update Comanche's history by documenting recent events in his museum existence, but also to illuminate the broader significance of the horse through analysis of the many metaphoric roles assigned to him. As the story of the cavalry horse unfolds, much is revealed about the way symbols operate in human thought, and the manner in which legends grow and

13

develop. Comanche, as a focus for Indian-white conflict, serves to crystallize some of the sharp differences in societal values which led to the tragic military confrontation that made him famous.

In gathering material about Comanche, I consulted written sources and traveled to many places that were or are associated with the horse. In all of these places, I carried out extensive personal interviews with people who were involved with the horse, and I used my data from informants to supplement and expand material obtained from published works. Numerous research trips were made to the Custer Battlefield National Monument in Montana, site of the Battle of the Little Big Horn, and to the Dyche Museum of Natural History at the University of Kansas in Lawrence, where the horse's remains are preserved. Visits were also made to all the western forts where Comanche was once stationed. Archival material was gathered from various libraries and historical societies throughout the United States. Tracing the life of the horse's rider, Myles Keogh, took me to areas in New York state where Keogh often stayed and where he was buried. I also visited Ireland to use the library which holds some of Keogh's letters and to see his birthplace, family homes, and sites associated with his early years in that country. I went to Tennessee to meet and talk with the composer of a song about Comanche. I also traveled to the hometowns of native Americans who took part in the protest centering on Comanche in the 1970s to discuss that experience with them. I journeyed to England to visit the contemporary counterpart of Comanche, Sefton (a mount of the Queen's Household Cavalry who was wounded by the enemy in the line of duty) and to learn more about people's reaction to the injured horse who, like Comanche, became a national hero.

In compiling data about Comanche, I have scrupulously chosen to consult primary sources whenever possible, even when this was difficult, and have relied heavily upon letters, most of which have not been published previously. Quotations are used throughout in preference to paraphrasing because they always convey intended meaning more accurately. Through diligent searching over many years, a great amount of information about Comanche has come to light—often in unexpected places—and is presented here. The surprising abundance of evidence of the horse's pervasive influence is in itself important. Inclusiveness is essential, for every detail, no matter how small (or humorous), adds a vital dimension to expand not just the totality of knowledge about the horse, but more importantly, with analysis, contributes to the understanding of the deeper meanings the animal has assumed in the popular mind and in society.

Preface

In a letter written in 1950 to express appreciation to a person for sending articles about Comanche for the university archives, the director of the Museum of Natural History at the University of Kansas wrote: "We thank you very much for this material which will be put in the Comanche file, which file I am confident will be used one day to write an exhaustive account of Comanche." In fulfilling this prediction, and in bringing together the many diverse facets of Comanche's life and meaning in one volume, I have recounted the story of this remarkable horse as completely as possible—in all its fascinating dimensions.

Interpretive historiography goes beyond factual accounts of occurrences to comprise a meaningful creative synthesis. The purpose of this book is not merely to present details which constitute another summary of the celebrated horse's life. Rather, the focus is on exploring the wider meaning and symbolism with which the figure of Comanche has become imbued at different times, after the Custer Battle and throughout the years since the celebrated horse was preserved following his death in 1891. The significance of Comanche's actual life, though interesting in itself, has been far surpassed after his death by the influence he continues to exert upon human ideas, through the lore and legend which has surrounded him, and the powerful and often-changing image he has represented following his own era and into modern times.

Acknowledgments

I owe a deep debt of gratitude to numerous people associated with different aspects of Comanche's story. My very special thanks go to Tom Swearingen, Exhibits Director of the Dyche Museum of Natural History at the University of Kansas, who has served as the horse's dedicated caretaker for over thirty years. His friendship and his enthusiastic willingness to share his knowledge are appreciated beyond measure. I want to express appreciation to Museum Director Philip S. Humphrey and Associate Director for Membership and Public Relations Cathy Dwigans, who provided invaluable assistance with this project, giving freely of their time and resources. Robert Mengel and Ann Schlager added some fascinating dimensions of Comanche's museum life from their particular perspectives.

I am most grateful to Neil Mangum, former Chief Historian at Custer Battlefield National Monument, for his help. I could not have followed the story of Sefton first-hand without the exceptional kindness of Brigadier Gerald D. M. Landy, OBE, who paved the way and gave not only his knowledge and time, but also his friendship. My thanks go to veterinarians Brigadier John Spurry and Major Noel Carding for their gracious hospitality. I want to acknowledge with much appreciation the help of Kathleen Nye Smith, Louis Hieb, Bruce Liddic, Roberta Cheney, David Dary, Murray Wax, Frances Bandy, Duane Valentry, Gary Keogh, and Bob Lee. I am extremely grateful to Ona Mzhickteno Fleming, Marty Kreipe, Nanette Roubideaux Swope, Kathryn Redcorn Block, Clara Sue Kidwell, and Wanda Wahnee Purdy. Special thanks go to Bonnie Beaver, Ron Kilgour, Andrew Fraser, Katherine Houpt, and Marthe Kiley-Worthington, colleagues consulted for their scholarly expertise in the field of equine behavior.

With gratitude, I acknowledge the assistance provided by the Brigham Young University Library, the Lilly Library of Indiana University, the Kansas State Historical Society, the State Historical Society of North Dakota, the Montana Historical Society, the Wyoming State Archives Museums and Historical Department, the Walt Disney Archives, and the National Library of Ireland. I am deeply appreciative for use of the University of Kansas Archives, the files of the Custer Battlefield National Monument, and the files of the U. S. Cavalry Museum at Fort Riley. Mark Lawrence, Priscilla Lawrence, Robert Lawrence, Jay Smith, Ellen Mueller, Charles Hall, and Lynn Wilke were particularly generous in supplying references. Others who contributed in this regard are Everett Miller, Richard Hardorff, Ray Meketa, Kenneth Hammer, Frank Mercatante, and Donald Westfall.

I acknowledge with appreciation the following poets, publishers, and agents for allowing me to quote from or reprint poems relating to Comanche: "The Custer Mystery" by J. K. Ralston by permission of Marjorie Walter; "Look Past the Stars" by Catherine E. Berry by permission of the *Denver Post*; "To the Last Man" by Vaun Arnold and "Comanche" by Robert E. Haggard by permission of the University of Kansas Archives; "Old Comanche" by William V. Wade by permission of William Wade Weeden; "Comanche" by G. T. Lanigan by permission of Custer Battlefield National Monument; "Talk T' Me" by Ben Mayfield by permission of Jay Smith, editor of the *Little Big Horn Associates Research Review*; "Comanche" by Audrey Hazell by permission of Frank Mercatante; "Comanche" by Gary Gildner by permission of the author; "Comanche! Oh Comanche!" and "The Far West's Race with Death" by F. A. Lydic by permission of the author. I want to express my appreciation to all the owners and creators of art works and photographs who graciously allowed their portrayals of Comanche to be reproduced in this book. Their names are listed with the illustrations.

Bob, Priscilla, and Mark were helpful and supportive in countless ways and to them I am most grateful, as always.

Introduction

This is the story of Comanche, the United States Cavalry horse who survived the battle known as Custer's Last Stand, June 25, 1876. A complete review of known facts about this horse's life, based upon information from the sparse available first-hand sources, would consist of only the briefest of narratives. For, after the early accounts revealing contemporary knowledge about him were written, little else representing new material could, with any accuracy, be added to the various repetitive writings published about Comanche over the years.

Biographical facts about the flesh-and-blood horse who interacted with people in the context of frontier America serve as the essential background for an understanding of the real saga of Comanche, with all its expanded dimensions. Following his survival of the battle which made him famous, the solicitous care the horse received, his unique retirement status, and his preservation after death depended upon his evocation of human emotion and upon the symbolic meaning he attained. The lore and legend which have grown up around Comanche were, and still are, based upon the horse's actual history, but owe their tenacity and power to the human feelings and perceptions which represent responses to that history. Respect and admiration for him as a noble war horse and appreciation for the qualities he represented conferred lasting popularity and fame. Comanche is still praised for fidelity and cherished for his innocence. People continue to empathize with his plight at the Little Big Horn and to identify with his legendary endurance. During the horse's life, and later in retrospect, various thoughts, emotions, and motivations have frequently been attributed to Comanche. Even as a museum specimen, he is unashamedly anthropomorphized by surprising numbers of individuals. Comanche is very infrequently referred to as "it" and is still spoken of as though he were alive by almost everyone who mentions him. In short, it is not utility, but rather sentiment, that

18

makes Comanche a hero. And it is the strength of that sentiment, which involves both the human relationship to horses in general and a specific relationship to this particular horse, that created the phenomenon of his widespread importance in the public mind.

The early chapters of this book provide the factual information needed to understand how Comanche gained his reputation as America's most famous military horse. Brief descriptions of the Battle of the Little Big Horn and of the portion of that battle known as Custer's Last Stand are provided for readers unfamiliar with these events, but are not intended to be all-inclusive. Many complex factors underlie the extraordinary amount of interest evoked by the Custer Battle, including, of course, the flamboyant and controversial nature of the General himself. A potent source of fascination lies in the fact that there were no human survivors of Custer's immediate command. Not only does this element give an ever-appealing sense of mystery to the event, but it also provides a special niche for Comanche, as the enduring survivor. Of course, other horses lived through the battle, and their stories— so far as they are known or believed—are recorded here along with Comanche's. But none was ever honored like Keogh's mount.

Though some biographical details about Comanche are documented, many others are speculative. The horse's early life, like his ancestry and breeding, can never be determined. Even after he became famous, careful records about Comanche were seldom kept, and much of his history is unknown. Information about his whereabouts at specific times is often lacking, and dates and locations for many of his photographs are uncertain. But the way in which various people have filled in details about the horse reveals a great deal about the connection between wishful thinking and hearsay and what is alleged to be history. One of Comanche's characteristics that has always stimulated special interest is his color. Strangely, even among people who saw the living horse and those who view his remains today, there is disagreement. In this confusion, one can see the fascinating process at work in which people may attribute characteristics to the mount according to their own perceptions and unconscious associations. As will become evident, Comanche's color warrants particular attention because it serves not only to distinguish him and endow him with certain traits as an individual, but also links him to his past—to the American mustang, and even to the history of his species.

In this book, the life of Comanche up to the time of the Custer Battle is traced by the recorded movements of Troop I of the

19

Seventh Cavalry to which his owner belonged. The question as to how Keogh came to name his mount, an event that is deeply entrenched in Comanche historiography, is an example of the difficulties involved in sorting out fact from legend, not only in the case of the horse, but indeed regarding the famous battle itself. Edward S. Luce, Comanche's main biographer, gave details of the naming which he presumably drew from official Seventh Cavalry records to which he had access. These documents (which if available would clear up many mysteries) are not in existence today as far as I can determine. One cannot help but wonder why the army would keep accounts of such relatively minor occurrences as the wounding of an ordinary cavalry horse in a skirmish, his resultant naming, and the injuries he received in subsequent engagements. At the time, Keogh's mount was just one of many and was not yet famous. Of course, it is possible that such records were made and later destroyed. Whatever the case may be, it is the novelists' versions of such events, embellishing on ideas gleaned from Luce's book, as well as from Barron Brown's work, that have been incorporated into what authors write and most readers naively accept as history on Comanche. This process is all the more astounding because stories intended for juvenile readers have been and still are used as sources for "facts" cited about the horse.

Despite the fiction that has often passed as history, it is possible to draw from first-hand accounts (such as participants' diaries) in order to reconstruct what life may have been like for Comanche and other cavalry horses on the march to the Little Big Horn. I have gone into detail concerning the question of the condition of the Seventh Cavalry horses as a factor in the outcome of the battle. This issue is discussed in depth for reasons beyond its contribution to knowledge about cavalry horses during the Indian Wars. For one of the most fascinating aspects of the study of Comanche and his fellow war mounts is that it reveals the human tendency to manipulate various agents, whether people or animals —in this case horses—for the purpose of corroborating a particular point of view. Horses are used as vehicles of expression for opinions about Custer and other officers, about Indians, and about ideologies at stake at the Little Big Horn.

The discovery and recognition of Comanche following the battle and the making of the decision to spare him from the mercy killing that was routine for badly wounded animals reveal that the recognition of his significance came almost instantaneously. The fact that many men vied for the honor of being known as his discoverer and claimed responsibility for preventing him from being destroyed on the field speaks for the glory that was perceived to devolve upon the person associated with the horse in those vital ways. It was Comanche's rider, Captain Myles W. Keogh, of course, who drew a large measure of his own fame, posthumously, from the mount who survived him. (Yet his life in itself reads like a romantic adventure novel.) Though it cannot be proven, the captain may have had a strong bond with Comanche, a possibility to which I have devoted considerable attention. Even more interesting and important than speculation about the literal truth of that bond, however, is consideration of why belief in such an affective interrelationship is so firmly embedded in the horse's legend. By symbolizing the physical and mental closeness that is unique to the horse-rider status, Keogh and Comanche have become, it seems, an archetypal representation of the universal human desire for unity with the animal world.

Relationships between cavalrymen and their mounts, a subject which generally has received little previous attention from scholars, is explored in Chapter 14. In order to gain understanding of the horses' contribution to such relationships, I have examined relevant aspects of equine behavior in the light of recent scientific evidence. Although undoubtedly many human interactions with horses in the military were strictly utilitarian and even involved abuse, numerous first-hand testimonies from soldiers indicate great feelings of warmth for their animal partners in battle. It is significant that John Keegan, an acknowledged expert in the field of war studies, wrote that by 1916 the horse

> had disappeared from the battlefield, though to the regret of almost every soldier—even infantry officers speak lovingly of their horses—and temporary work in the transport section of infantry regiments was eagerly sought after by the men, who seemed to find in caring for animals an outlet for the gentler emotions to which they could give no expression among their fellows. (1987a:246)

Comanche's bond with his rider and his own remarkable strength and endurance are two prime factors believed to be responsible for his survival. His wounds and scars, making his recovery that much more miraculous, became (and still remain) objects of interest to the admiring public. His return to health is generally credited to hardiness and to the exceptional care that was provided. Relative to his recovery, in Chapter 6, I have suggested on the basis of available evidence the kind of medical treatments the horse would have received. The subject of equine veterinary care during the Indian Wars, about which so little is known, involves mention of John Honsinger, a veterinarian who was killed during a Seventh Cavalry expedition in 1873. Though he was not con-

21

nected with Comanche in a direct way, his story sheds light on the subject of relationships with horses in that context.

The 1878 "General Orders No. 7" regarding Comanche are indeed remarkable, and undoubtedly represent the only example of such a citation for a military horse. By means of these orders, Colonel Samuel D. Sturgis, commander of the Seventh Cavalry, established full retirement status for Comanche and set forth a defined ceremonial and symbolic role for him as a survivor, which gave the horse a nearly sacred status within the army and in the eyes of the general population. Sturgis' grief for his son who was killed with Custer must be taken into account in order to understand the genesis of the officer's actions and the meaning he attributed to the horse.

History shows that, following a comfortable retirement, Comanche began to decline in health only after losing his caretaker, Gustave Korn, who was killed at Wounded Knee in 1890. There is irony in the fact that Comanche (though of course he did not take part) was present at Wounded Knee, an engagement in which a great number of Indians were killed and which is often referred to as "the Seventh's Revenge." So Comanche's life came full circle from Indian victory to Indian defeat, and he died as twilight fell on the way of life of his former enemies.

Chapter 7 deals with the first episode in his existence as a mounted specimen: when he was exhibited at the 1893 World's Columbian Exposition in Chicago. This event is closely tied to the horse's association with Indian-white relationships and marked the beginning of a symbolic role related to the clash of cultures that was to vary with changing times. The context of that fair— the ideas and attitudes expressed in connection with American "progress"—has a great deal to do with the meanings attributed to Comanche as a relic of the Indian Wars. Further, this context forms a basis for understanding the new symbolism which Comanche attained in the 1970s.

In Chapter 10, all facets of the topic of Comanche and the Indians are explored. Through testimony from contemporary people who were directly involved with the mounted horse, it becomes evident that Comanche in recent times has served as an educational tool, stimulating thought about racial issues and bringing about the eventual resolution of controversies based on outdated meanings. Tracing the history of Comanche as an atypical museum piece raises the whole question of the intended purpose and function of museum exhibits, particularly the role of mounted animals and the display of cultural objects as curios. Though it is beyond the scope of this book to arrive at answers, the important thing is to raise the right questions, and such questions are implicit in Comanche's story. In a similar vein, recent surveys of visitors to zoos have determined that people generally gain little education from their experience in viewing the animals. Hopefully, museum visitors fare better. In 1974, the coordinator of public education at Dyche Hall indicated that "the museum is slowly getting away from public education by use of stuffed exhibits. It offers classes for adults, children, and families. It sponsors field trips and slide shows," and "some live exhibits are planned" (Schuyler 1974:5). Of course, Comanche is a unique display! Many of the 120,000 yearly visitors to the Dyche Museum in Lawrence go there particularly to see him.

Tom Swearingen, Exhibits Director at the museum, is fond of pointing out that the famous Comanche "has had more battles fought over him than he was in." The history of these "battles" for possession of the stuffed horse is extremely significant, for it reveals a great deal about people's perceptions of what the animal stands for and the importance that is attached to him. The question as to whether or not Comanche's remains belong at Custer Battlefield, even if that transfer were possible, raises key points about his role as a relic and brings into focus the larger issue of how best to interpret history for public education. The attention Comanche's figure has commanded over the years as the museum's best "drawing card" continues into the present day. Intense interest is evidenced by the enormous amount of attention devoted to the horse during a recent mishap in which he was damaged by a flood. News about the incident was flashed across the country. No efforts were spared in repair and renovation operations for the display that well may be the most popular tourist attraction in Kansas.

Chapters 12 and 13 deal with articles, books, novels, stories, poems, films, paintings, drawings, sculpture, and songs about Comanche. All of these, to greater or lesser degree, have helped to shape and perpetuate the history and legend of the famous survivor, from the time of the Custer Battle through the present day. Analysis of these works enables one to trace the many elements that comprise the horse's story and to better understand its widespread appeal.

Some of the meanings attributed to Comanche become evident throughout the text, and are discussed briefly as they are delineated. Chapter 14 contains a fuller explanation of the horse's significance and symbolism. The influence of Custer's Last Stand is still pervasive. Hardly a week goes by without a newspaper reporter, sports commentator, or television comedian making reference to that event as a prime example of utter disaster. The horse who survived that battle against all odds, however, has surmounted defeat by means of qualities such as devotion and endurance, traits with which people strongly identify. Some of the same characteristics are attributed to Sefton, the contemporary British horse whose story is in many ways a parallel to Comanche's. This modern-day counterpart of Keogh's mount provided me with an extraordinary opportunity to add deeper dimensions to the understanding of the Comanche phenomenon through first-hand study of a horse who survived his battle wounds to live on as a celebrated figure in our own time.

With the centennial of Comanche's death approaching, one can only hope that he will continue to communicate silent messages that will enlighten us into the twenty-first century. Rather than being considered as an isolated example of one horse who participated in a specific battle at a certain time, Comanche should now take his place in a more universal context. From his remarkable saga much can be learned not only about symbolism, legends, and the vagaries of historiography, but also about the human relationship to animals, cultural differences in perceptions of humankind's status with regard to nature, the American frontier ethos, racism, and even the futility of war.

Chapter 1

Comanche the Survivor

He is the favored of the gods. (Canetti 1973:228)

The status of hero is often conferred upon a survivor. This process operates in the case of animals, as well as people, and is vividly demonstrated by the life history of the United States cavalry mount known as Comanche. Ridden into battle by Captain Myles W. Keogh on June 25, 1876, during a military engagement between the Seventh Cavalry and warriors mainly of the Sioux and Cheyenne tribes, Comanche is undoubtedly the most famous war horse in American history. General Robert E. Lee's beloved mount, Traveller, was also a celebrity, but he had a less dramatic history in the sense that both man and horse lived through the Civil War and retired together. Even on a worldwide scale, probably only Alexander the Great's celebrated steed Bucephalus rivals Comanche's fame. However, Bucephalus died in battle while his master lived on, and thus the horse's glory is not associated with survival.

Custer's Last Stand, a battle in which there were no human survivors among the United States forces, is an event that is deeply etched into American consciousness, and has never ceased to be a source of fascination both nationally and throughout many areas of the world. As one scholar phrased it, "the Custer fight will long remain the apotheosis of the adventurous American spirit" (Miller 1971:71). Though actually part of a larger two-day military engagement known as the Battle of the Little Big Horn, it is the portion of the battle fought by Lieutenant Colonel (Brevet Major General) George Armstrong Custer and his immediate command which has been imbued with epic grandeur. This episode, in which Custer and the five troops of the Seventh under his personal leadership—about 225 men in all—were annihilated by hostile Indians, has provided an archetypal metaphor for total defeat. But it is a defeat that in the popular mind is associated with glory, a defeat experienced by heroes who, though surrounded by overwhelming numbers of enemies and impossible circumstances, still fought courageously to the death.

The Little Big Horn battle represents the dramatic climax to many years of escalating hostility between Indians and whites on the American continent, resulting from inevitable conflicts over land and disputes emanating from two vastly different ideologies and ways of life. The Sioux were particularly bitter about the invasion of their sacred Black Hills in 1874 by a reconnaissance expedition with Custer in command. By 1875, a year before the United States was to celebrate its one hundredth anniversary as a nation, it was generally accepted that the westward advancement of the frontier meant that the natives must give way to the technologically superior white civilization bent on subjugating or destroying them. By that time, the vast majority of Indians already had been forcibly placed upon designated reservations. On the Great Plains, however, there were still some tribespeople, especially among the Sioux and Cheyenne, who rejected the idea of permanent reservation confinement and refused to give up traditional nomadic life. These "hostiles" (as the nonreservation natives were called) who would not (or could not) return to the reservation by January 31, 1876, became subject to military action by the government.

As a result of failure to comply with this specification, United States army plans, directed by Lieutenant General Philip H. Sheridan, called for a summer military campaign in which three columns would converge on the area of what is now southeastern Montana, near the valley of the Little Big Horn River, where most of the resisting Indians were believed to be camped. Accordingly, Colonel John Gibbon led a march east from Fort Ellis in western Montana, General George Crook proceeded north from Fort Fetterman in Wyoming, and Brigadier General Alfred Terry marched west from Fort Abraham Lincoln, North Dakota. Under Terry's command was the Seventh Cavalry, led by General Custer, the bold and flamboyant Civil-War-hero-turned-Indian-fighter, whose exploits had become legendary, and whose pride and zealous confidence in his regiment made him believe the Seventh Cavalry could defeat any Indian tribe on the Plains.

According to the plan for trapping the hostile Indians in the vicinity of the Little Big Horn Valley, Custer and the Seventh

26

Cavalry would march up the Rosebud, cross the Wolf Mountains, and move to the Indian encampment from the south. Terry would go with Gibbon, ascend the Big Horn, and enter the valley from the north. Although plans called for concerted military action on June 26, Custer, when he realized his troops had already been discovered by Indians, was convinced the enemy would flee and escape his grasp. So on June 25, in a resultant series of actions and underlying motivations which would continue to be controversial forever (and which can never be completely understood), Custer decided to attack at once. Courageous and confident of victory, Custer proceeded to divide his fighting force into three segments, assigning three companies to the command of Captain Frederick Benteen, three to Major Marcus Reno, and five companies to his own command. Ultimately, the troops under Reno, attacked by large numbers of warriors, were able to reach some high bluffs surrounding the valley. There, joined by the men under Benteen, they were besieged by Indians for two days, and, though sustaining heavy losses, avoided annihilation. As is well-known, however, the fate of Custer was death. He and all the men of his command died in a fierce struggle that has been estimated to have lasted no longer than one hour. Their bodies, and those of many of their horses, were discovered by members of Gibbon's column on the morning of June 27. The hostile Indians, representing the largest gathering of Indians ever assembled together on the Plains, had by then departed. Though winning this battle, the Indians' stunning victory at the Little Big Horn only served to hasten the loss of their hold upon their land and their way of life. Their power would forever be broken by the enemies they had defeated.

In addition to the dramatic irony that the Indians' greatest victory also tragically spelled their doom, many reasons can be cited to explain the extraordinary amount of interest that has been evoked by the Custer Battle—from the day when news of it was first announced to a stunned world through the present time. A severe blow was dealt to national pride when a foe viewed by most people as untrained and uncivilized could sustain a military victory over United States forces, especially over the famous Seventh Cavalry led by West Point graduate George Armstrong Custer. Young, exuberant, and dashing, the golden-haired Indian fighter was loved by many with an intensity only equalled by the hatred of his enemies. He was controversial in his own time and has become increasingly so as the years have passed. Still lionized as well as vilified by scholars who probe his life and times, the questions and paradoxes surrounding him and his actions at the

Little Big Horn only deepen with ensuing years. The tragedy of his death at a young age and the heroic image evoked by his last desperate struggle before succumbing to the onslaught of a so-called "savage" foe serve to capture the imagination. The fact that there were no human survivors of Custer's command at the Last Stand causes a continuing aura of mystery to surround the event. Despite conjectures, Custer's plans, actions, motivations, and feelings on that day can never be known. If the General himself or anyone in his command had lived, the battle certainly would not hold the same fascination that it does. Over the years, there have been many claimants to survivorhood; yet, none has been accepted by authoritative sources as legitimate. Closest contenders have been Curly, a Crow Indian scout in Seventh Cavalry service who actually left Custer before the fighting started, and Frank Finkel, whose escape story has been considered the most plausible (Ellison 1983; Kuhlman 1972).

Comanche has gained considerable fame through general recognition as the sole authentic survivor of Custer's Last Stand, in spite of the fact that some other mounts lived through that event. Before proceeding with Comanche's story, an account will be given of what is known about these other horses who, for various reasons, never became true rivals of Keogh's mount. Details about these animals are relevant for what they reveal about the cavalrymen's attitude toward horses and about the importance attributed to equine survivors, as well as about the factors that ultimately made Comanche's status unique.

It is well documented that a number of cavalry horses survived the Custer Battle. Some of these mounts may have wandered away to die or to suffer an unknown fate. Several horses were mercifully shot by troopers who found them too badly injured to make recovery possible (Stewart 1980:474). (Following the battle at least one severely wounded Indian pony was also the object of a soldier's humane concern, being shot in order to spare the pitiful animal a slow death [Burdick 1940:54]. See Chapter 14.) An undetermined number of Seventh Cavalry horses were undoubtedly taken by victorious Indians, for horses bearing that regiment's brand were found in September of 1876 in a Sioux encampment (Bourke 1891:371). John Finerty reported that the gauntlets belonging to Captain Keogh, Comanche's rider, as well as five Seventh Cavalry horses, were "among the prizes secured" on that occasion (1970:283–84). Although the great Sioux leader, Sitting Bull, had warned his tribesmen not to take horses and other "spoils" following the Battle of the Little Big Horn, the "excitement of victory" caused many warriors to disobey (Vestal 1932:177).

One of the most noteworthy equine survivors was a gray horse with the Seventh Cavalry brand which was purchased in 1879 at Wood Mountain, Canada, by Superintendent James M. Walsh of the Northwest Mounted Police. Presumed to have been captured by the Sioux during the Custer Battle, the horse was brought to Canada with the Indians who had fled northward after their victory. Walsh wrote to General Terry, offering to return the horse to the Seventh Cavalry. "But," he added, "of the many relics I have seen of the battle on the Little Big Horn, none have taken my fancy like this old trooper, and having been for years an admirer of the gallant Custer, and having conversed with the principal chiefs who took part in that memorable battle, to be permitted to keep this old trooper, which has come so strangely into my hands, would be a great pleasure." In response, Major Walsh received word from Washington that the Secretary of War had authorized him to retain the horse (Turner 1950, I:449–50). Named "Custer," the gray became Walsh's personal saddle mount and lived many years treated as a war hero (MacEwan 1978:27). Purportedly, Sitting Bull remembered the horse and was pleased that his friend Walsh possessed it (MacEwan 1973:176–77). When told about this horse, Major Reno said he thought it might have been "the gray that we lost two days after the battle." He also believed the gray Walsh wrote about "might be one of the horses which belonged to Custer's column. A number of animals belonging to that command fell into the hands of the Indians" (Utley 1972:409–10).

Major Walsh's horse as a "relic" of the Custer Battle evoked much interest, and it was inevitable that this equine survivor would be confused with Comanche and its ownership wrongly attributed to Custer. Responding to a letter of inquiry which identified Walsh's gray in those mistaken terms, J. P. Turner of the Royal Canadian Mounted Police wrote on March 4, 1942:

> And now about this damned horse of yours. There's not so very much on record about the unsuspecting animals which that damned glory hunter, Custer, took with him into the valley of the Little Big Horn on that fatal day in 1876. I could tell you a whole lot more about Custer than about Comanche, though I am satisfied the latter was the better character of the two and more worthy of a niche in the halls of fame. If ever a man got what was coming to him on the frontier, the "Long-hair" was that man. But enough; let's look at the horseflesh.
>
> I think I told you that Custer had two favorite mounts—Vic and Dandy. He usually rode the former, and, when not messing among Indians, bestowed Dandy upon Mrs. Custer, who was quite a horse-woman. All accounts of the Custer fight say that only one living

thing survived from Custer's column. That was the horse Comanche ridden by Captain Keogh. A large number of horses, however, were rounded up after the action and swept away by the Sioux. These were from the command of Reno, Benteen and others no doubt. Comanche was found lying on the battlefield still alive but horribly mutilated. He must have been good stuff, for he stood the journey to Fort Lincoln, headquarters of the 7th Cavalry, and, by careful nursing got back on his feet to be a soldier's pet for many years. It is ridiculous to say that he ever reached Canada, either with or without the Sioux. In fact, when he died at an old age, a taxidermist fixed him up and I believe he is still on exhibit somewhere in the States.

Among the horses brought northward by the Sioux in 1876 and 1877, was one captured by a young lad, the son of Chief Lame Deer. He was a grey gelding, about 12 years old. After Col. Irvine had visited Sitting Bull's Camp at Pinto Horse Butte northwest of Wood Mountain Post, in June, 1877, he wrote to his sister in Quebec saying "I saw one poor old grey horse with E7 branded on his hip, which of course meant E troop, 7th Cavalry. I could not help patting the poor old fellow. An Indian was sitting on his back. Few if any of the Indians have horses of any size, but in this camp you saw the large American horses that they got from the Custer fight."

Not long afterwards, Major Walsh purchased the grey gelding above referred to.

The letter goes on to describe Walsh's desire to keep the horse, his correspondence with General Terry, and his obtaining permission to own the "old trooper." Turner explains "I believe Walsh had the horse for a number of years and gave him the best of care until he passed along," and ends with the assurance "I feel convinced that this is the horse that started the story relayed to you" about the survivor of the Custer Battle. As a postscript, Turner resolves the controversy with finality by stating "Comanche was not a grey horse" (The University of Kansas Archives; hereafter designated UK Archives).

The belief that Comanche was gray in color is an error that occurs in some early sources. A newspaper report of Comanche's death in 1891, for example, called him "a large gray" (He's Joined His Command 1891). In an 1897 issue of *The Outlook*, Comanche was referred to as "a powerful gray," a designation that was perpetuated in a 1928 *Cavalry Journal* article (Ultimus 1928:257). In his 1926 newspaper editorial Major General Malin Craig wrote that Comanche, whose photograph accompanied the article, was "just a plain troop horse, . . . a big powerful grey, nearly sixteen hands high" (1926). This mistake was challenged, then soon corrected, when the newspaper "asked Brigadier General Edward S. Godfrey, a lieutenant in the Seventh Cavalry under Custer, to give his description, and he said 'Captain Myles K. [sic] Keogh's horse, Comanche, was a medium sized claybank' " (UK Archives).

There are indications that Custer's own horse, Vic, which he rode into battle at the Little Big Horn, was one of the surviving animals taken by Indians. According to Lieutenant Godfrey, a battle participant, "Vic was a sorrel, with four white feet and legs and a blaze in the face" (Partoll 1939:277), though John Burkman, who cared for the horse, remembered Custer's mount as having only "three white stockinged legs" (Wagner 1934: 94). Writing in 1896, Godfrey stated "I have heard that he [Vic] had been identified in the possession of some Indian in the hostile camp after they went into the British possessions" following the battle (Partoll 1939:277).

Indeed Sitting Bull, when talking with his biographer about the Custer Battle, related that "Many stories are current about Custer's horse, also. One day, not long after this fight, White Bull drove his ponies to water. At the watering-place he saw a fine sorrel in the bunch of Sounds-the-Ground-as-He-Walks, a Santee, and a son of Inkpaduta. White Bull asked if it was a good horse. The Santee answered, 'I know it is a good horse, for it used to be Long Hair's' " (Vestal 1932:175). Corroborating information was provided by Samuel Charger, a Sioux who wrote in his chronology of the Sioux Indians:

> The elder son of Inkpaduta captured General Custer's horse and gave it to his younger brother. One day while we were going into the mountain country some of the warriors chased an antelope and Stamps the Ground, who was on this sorrel horse, ran down the antelope and shot it. Everybody knew this horse must be the horse that Custer used to ride, as he rode a sorrel which was said to be a fast horse. Walking-in-the-Clouds later had the horse back. My uncle, Tall Ghost, traded two horses to Walking-in-the-Clouds for the sorrel horse and when he fled into Canada he sold the horse to a Canadian officer and probably Custer's horse died in Canada. (1928:3)

And in an interview given by Iron Hail, a warrior who participated in the fight at the Little Big Horn, he, too, mentions that years later a Santee Sioux named Walks Under The Ground was riding an army sorrel that had once belonged to the "head man" in the Custer Battle, whom the Sioux boasted he had killed (Echohawk 1956:47–48). A Sioux participant in the Battle of the Little Big Horn, Foolish Elk, who was highly regarded as a reliable witness, told his interviewer, Walter Camp, in 1908 that following the battle General Custer's horse "had been recognized among the captured animals." Mistakenly referring to the surviving mount as "Dandy," he, nevertheless, identified the horse as sorrel with white face and white feet (Hammer 1976:197, 200).

Until these reports came to light, it was generally assumed that Custer's mount had died in battle with his master on the knoll destined to be named "Custer Hill." In an interview with Walter M. Camp in the early 1900s, Lieutenant Edgerly, a Little Big Horn participant, stated that Vic was killed in the battle (Hammer 1976:58). Lieutenant McClernand, who was present at the site where Custer and his men had been killed, observed before the bodies were buried that "a dead horse about 100 or 150 feet, more or less, from Custer Hill . . . was pointed out as the one ridden by Custer." However, he gave no information about criteria used for identification. Though "I do not say such was the case," McClernand noted, "it occurred to me at the time that the loss of his horse might have determined Custer to stand on the said knoll and mentioned ridge when he gained them, instead of trying to gain the still higher hills further" (1969:93). Colonel Homer Wheeler wrote that in examining the battlefield about a year after the Custer fight he and another officer "located the spot where Custer made his final stand," and "cut off the hoofs of the horse supposed to have been ridden by Custer (a sorrel with three white fetlocks)" (1925:184). Seventh Cavalry trumpeter, A. F. Mulford, on a scout to the Little Big Horn fourteen months after the battle, noted that "on top of the hill where Custer was killed, we saw the skeletons of four men and horses, among the latter being the skeleton of the horse that Custer rode" (n.d.:149).

It was natural for Custer's widow to assume that her husband's faithful horse died with him in battle. Horses were important in the Custers' lives, and it would take only a bit of empathy to understand that the thought of the General's war horse being in the hands of the enemy would have brought added sorrow to the already grief-stricken woman. In 1890, Mrs. Custer wrote that "General Custer rode a sorrel horse, a Kentucky Thoroughbred, on the day of the battle of the Little Big Horn, and 'Vic' was found dead beside his devoted master" (Donnelle 1889:17). And again in the same year she stated that Vic "was shot in the battle of the Little Big Horn" (1890:331).

Dandy was the other of Custer's personal mounts who was taken on the Little Big Horn campaign. He survived because he was left behind with the pack train under Benteen's command and thus did not participate in the Last Stand. This horse meant a great deal to both Elizabeth Custer and to the General. Custer had a close relationship with him and described his intelligence and loyalty in a letter to his wife, referring to him as "my own noble little steed" (Merington 1950:254) (see Chapter 14). In December of 1876, after Dandy had recovered from "a wound received near Reno Hill," the surviving officers of the Seventh Cavalry shipped the horse to Monroe, Michigan, to Custer's widow, following her request (Frost 1976:237–38). Dandy was then given to Custer's father, who, according to Mrs. Custer's observations, formed a "strongly welded" friendship with his son's mount, riding and driving him and appearing astride him in "public parades of the town" (Donnelle 1889:17).

As in the case of their human counterparts, stories of equine survivors turned up now and then, claimed by their sponsors to have lived through the Custer Battle. Such a horse was Billy, a light bay with four white feet who was said to have resided near Cheyenne, Wyoming, until his death in 1900. According to newspaper reports issued in that year, Billy, "the only survivor of the Custer massacre," had been discovered at the battle site moving among the dead, pawing at his master's body, displaying "that pathetic mysticism which dumb animals manifest in times of unusual happenings." The badly wounded horse was "taken in charge by an officer in Reno's command," and though at first it was thought he would have to be shot, "medicine and kind treatment" resulted in his recovery. In May of 1877, for fifty dollars, city and county Peace Officer Thomas F. Talbot reportedly purchased Billy from Quartermaster Sergeant Ross of Fort D. A. Russell. The mount proved to be ever faithful, a "true soldier," fearless, fleet, and possessed of great endurance—qualities which made him indispensable to his master's job of catching criminals. Unusual rapport existed between man and horse, and Billy alerted Talbot in times of danger, often saving his life. The horse was "Kentucky-bred," gentle, with "magnificent carriage" and "stately stride." When the thirty-seven-year-old animal died, Talbot reportedly placed an appropriately inscribed stone over his grave (An Old Timer Dead 1900; Wyoming Notes 1900; "Billy" Last Survivor 1900).

Despite diligent searches by interested people, Billy's gravestone has never been located. Nor have researchers who have tried to follow up on the story of Billy found any clues to validate his status as a Custer Battle survivor. Interviews with people who knew Talbot and with a number of his descendants have revealed that they never heard of the horse. A grandson who recalled that his grandfather "always had Sunday dinner with us" said he had been told nothing about the legendary mount. The same was true of his siblings and cousins. Perhaps the key to the mystery may lie

33

with one informant whose "granddad knew Talbot well." The man revealed, "Tom was a talker. He bellied up to the bar and told tales."

Even if the story of Billy is "just bar-talk," as most investigators who have attempted to trace it conclude, much can be learned from the story that has direct bearing upon Comanche. It shows the appeal of the sole equine survivor legend and the fact that many of its elements had become entrenched in the popular mind. The wounded horse's remarkable behavior when surrounded by the scenes of death at the Little Big Horn, his dramatic recovery, his sagacity, nobility, and unusual bonding to his master are all characteristics deeply embedded in Comanche's image.

Another alleged Custer Battle survivor is Nap, a gray cavalry horse, who, according to one writer, may be the animal pictured with Comanche in a photograph which he believes was taken at Fort Lincoln (Meketa 1984:2,7–8). (See fig. 3. Custer Battlefield records indicate this photo was taken at Fort Meade.) William G. Hardy, a trumpeter present at the Battle of the Little Big Horn who was interviewed by Walter M. Camp in the early 1900s, stated that "the gray horse found on the battlefield was taken to Fort Lincoln and children used to ride him. His name was 'Nap' " (Camp Manuscript, Lilly Library, Indiana University). Whether this could be the same horse seen by Lieutenant Edgerly, an officer in Captain Reno's Battalion, during the June 27 burial of Custer's men can never be determined. The Lieutenant, during an interview in the early 1900s, noted that "one of E Troop's gray horses was found wounded at the river near Custer battlefield, and appeared to be much frightened and very shy but followed the troops at a distance all [the] way to [the] crossing of the Yellowstone" (Hammer 1976:58).

Lieutenant Edward S. Godfrey, a surviving officer who commanded Company K at the Battle of the Little Big Horn, kept a diary during the campaign. Godfrey's entry for June 28 states that (while searching for bodies) "I found a gray horse with an Indian bridle, halter & lariat. The horse had a tuft of grass toed in his mouth to keep him from neighing. I took him in" (underlining by Godfrey). Though the editor of the diary states that "the use of the word horse rather than pony suggests that it was a Seventh Cavalry horse" (Stewart 1957:20, 67), according to Godfrey's own testimony it was an Indian mount. During an interview with Walter Camp in which it was suggested that the gray might have been a cavalry horse captured from General Crook by the Indians in the fight of June 17, 1876, Camp's notes reveal that Godfrey stated "No. It was a gray Indian pony." Godfrey revealed that he found a gray Indian horse beyond high ridge on which stage route to Busby now runs. He was in a coulee tied to a tree. Had a bunch of grass in his mouth tied to bit. On ground were marks in dust where a man had lain or floundered around, and there was a piece of a blue Indian leggins with fringe on it, as though had been torn up to dress a wound. Horse, evidently, had been tied there since 6/25. When Godfrey took horse to river he dived his head into water up to eyes, being nearly famished for want of water. When Godfrey first found this pony he (the pony) seemed very pleased to see him. This was unusual for an Indian horse, being usually afraid of a white man. When he cut the grass out of his mouth he seemed pleased. Godfrey kept this horse and this was the horse killed under Godfrey at Bear Paw. He was a good buffalo hunter. (Walter Mason Camp Notes, Harold B. Lee Library, Brigham Young University)

Forty-nine years after the famous battle, General Godfrey recalled his "white pony." At the time he found it, he told an interviewer, he "was looking for tracks of shod horses while on scouting duty." "I was on a ridge," he said, "scanning the countryside"

> when I saw a white horse not far away. I crawled up fairly close and kept calling the Indian word for friend. As I did not want my scalp taken I advanced slowly, for I could not see the rider. When I got up to the pony I found a bloody legging hanging to the stirrup. The rider had evidently been wounded but had made his escape. I took the pony.
>
> He rode it, got attached to it. The following year, when Captain Godfrey was riding that white horse at the Bear Paw Mountain fight against Chief Joseph of the Nez Perces, it was shot from under him. (Godfrey 1925)

The episode was obviously meaningful to Godfrey. In an article about the noted officer written by a relative soon after his death, there is again mention of Godfrey riding his white horse, "an Indian's [mount] captured by him soon after the Battle of the Little Big Horn" (Godfrey 1934:82).

Ours is an age of debunking heroes. In recent times, much has been made of the fact that Comanche, once celebrated as "the sole survivor of Custer's Last Stand," cannot with authenticity hold this title because of the other horses known to have survived this engagement. A source of confusion inherent in the "only survivor" title lies, too, in the fact that many men and horses of the troops which fought in the Battle of the Little Big Horn under Major Reno and Captain Benteen survived. And of course large numbers of Indians who fought in the battle lived on as well. But Comanche still holds his place as the only equine member of the federal cavalry forces in Custer's immediate command who was known to have left the battlefield in the hands of the military and whose life can be generally chronicled from that time until his death. His preservation as a mounted specimen (still on display in the Dyche Museum at the University of Kansas in Lawrence) has added greatly to his fame as a sole survivor.

The differences between the Indian and white forces locked in combat at the Little Big Horn, representing two opposing cultures, are staggering. Irreconcilable beliefs and ways of life, perceptions of the land, and views of the universe separated them, making the clash inevitable. Perhaps only on one point would they have been united—their dependence upon, and high valuation of, horses. The acquisition of the equine animal in the 18th century had utterly transformed Plains Indian society and culture, making former foot Indians into proud and powerful horsemen whom even their white enemies called the finest light cavalry in the world. The horse improved the quality of nomadic life in every possible way and became the natives' standard of value, their measure of wealth and prestige. For the whites, horses were the fundamental and necessary instrument for Anglo-European penetration into the frontiers of the New World, the absolutely essential element in making conquest and settlement possible. Thus two civilizations, one poised on the brink of destruction and the other about to be altered forever by the coming of the machine age, carried on their present way of life at that moment in time only through the use of horses.

Comanche, an equine survivor, stands as the perfect hero of the times, "a horse for all seasons." He existed not just physically beyond the tragic battle known as Custer's Last Stand, but he lived on in legend and lore, and his memory and spirit continue to give symbolic meaning to much that is universal in human experience. Whether Custer is ultimately perceived as hero or fool, whether his foes are viewed as noble or cruel, the war justified or needless, still the horse, joint ally of both sides, remains a hero. As for Comanche, seldom in history have people wished so fervently that an animal could possess the gift of speech, to reveal the firsthand knowledge that was forever locked within the dead of Custer's Last Stand. Nevertheless, Comanche's voiceless image has been used in many valid ways, transformed to express varied concepts, which will be evident in the chapters to follow. His metaphoric roles are innumerable, making him articulate even in his silence. He becomes at times a link between the dead and the living, a bridge between Indian and white, between humankind and animal, between the realm of speech and that of silence, between civilization and the untamed, between nature and the machine age, between the old order and the new. Having confronted the gravest of dangers and perils and having overcome them, Comanche stands as a classic survivor. The state of being a true survivor is described by Canetti: "He has proved himself for he is alive. He has proven himself among many others, for the fallen are not alive. . . . He is stronger. There is more life in him. He is the favored of the gods" (1973:228).

Chapter 2

Comanche the Horse

A choice lot of horses.
—Joel H. Elliott, Major 7th U.S. Cavalry, May 27, 1868
(Luce 1939:10)

Among a group of mounts purchased by the army quartermaster
on April 3, 1868, at St. Louis, Missouri, was the horse who was to
be known as Comanche (Luce 1939:6; Brown 1935:38). A short
time later, Comanche and 40 other horses were transported 'to
the army post at Fort Leavenworth, Kansas, to become cavalry recruits. Soon thereafter, this group of horses was sent to join the
Seventh Cavalry, then stationed in the field in Kansas. In charge
of escorting these cavalry mounts was First Lieutenant (Brevet
Captain) Thomas W. Custer, brother and fellow officer of George
Armstrong Custer, under whose command eight years hence he
would also meet an untimely death at the Little Big Horn. A letter
from Tom Custer to Lieutenant A. E. Smith, acting adjutant of
the Seventh Cavalry, dated May 27, 1868, states that the writer
left Leavenworth on May 16 with the 41 horses and arrived in
Hayes City, Kansas, on May 18. For some reason, Captain Custer
felt the need to explain that he "used every exertion possible at
Ellsworth City to be sent on to Hayes City without delay." On the
same day, May 27, Major Joel H. Elliott enclosed Tom Custer's
report in a letter to Major General Gibbs, commanding the Seventh U.S. Cavalry. Elliott, an officer who six months later was to
lose his life fighting in General Custer's second most famous engagement with hostile Indians, the Battle of the Washita, wrote
that "aside from the unnecessary detention I found no fault with
the treatment of the horses. The horses were in good condition.
Some of them had distemper but most of them were looking well
and I regard them as a choice lot of horses" (Luce 1939:6–10).

The cost to the government for Comanche was ninety dollars, and evidently the same price was paid to the army by Captain Myles W. Keogh, the officer who, according to Luce, selected the horse for his own personal mount (1939:11). Godfrey also specifically stated that in September 1868, Keogh "chose this horse for his field mount" (1921:37). In 1931, however, Godfrey inexplicably presented a more prosaic account of the acquisition of the horse. He wrote that in August 1867 [sic], Keogh was a member of a scouting force in General Sully's expedition. During a brief skirmish, Captain Keogh's horse was killed under him, and he called for another. Lieutenant Brewster, who was in command of Troop "I" at the time, ordered a sergeant to dismount. The horse turned over to Captain Keogh was Comanche (Brown 1935:40, 99–100). Such conflicting testimonies are commonly encountered in Comanche's history, even when the informants were close to the events and were believed to be giving "first-hand" data. Representing an extreme example of polarities in evidence is a 1910 letter from E. G. Mathey to Walter Camp. Lieutenant Mathey commanded the pack train at the Little Big Horn and was responding to questions posed by Camp, who interviewed and corresponded with battle participants. Referring to June 24 and 25, Mathey stated "At the time I was riding Comanche, the horse belonged to the Government and if Col. Keogh ever bought the horse I never heard of it and I believe the horse belonged to the U. S. at the time Col. Keogh was killed" (Hammer 1976:73). Another of Camp's informants, speaking of the Seventh's 1868 campaign, indicated that "Comanche had been bought just before this and was a troop horse but Keogh rode him on the expedition and Comanche was wounded in it" (Camp Manuscript, Lilly Library, Indiana University). One newspaper report attributed ownership to Tom Custer (Burt 1891:3).

According to most accounts, Comanche was Keogh's mount, and his ownership has been generally accepted. The horse was probably about six years old when acquired by Keogh (Luce 1939:85). Comanche was a gelding, but records do not reveal whether the castration surgery was performed before purchase or after he entered cavalry service. No source thus far discovered documents Comanche's breeding or reveals the details of his life prior to his purchase in 1868. Former cavalryman Edward S. Luce wrote that after Comanche entered the army, he would no longer "range the plains of Texas and Oklahoma" (1939:7); although this location may be likely, it cannot be established with accuracy as the horse's early home.

Comanche's genealogy is speculative. With regard to the

background of horses generally used during the Indian Wars, Luce argues that "at the close of the Civil War and for a few years afterwards interbreeding was tried, and it was found that a three-quarters American and one-quarter Spanish horse possessed remarkable endurance and stamina for western cavalry service. Such was the breed of Comanche" (Luce 1939:6). According to this assertion, Comanche's ancestry would be one-quarter western mustang, a type of feral animal descended from horses brought to the New World by the Spanish, and three-quarters from the progeny of European or English horses, which were first imported in colonial times to the New England and Southern states.

American settlers on the frontier, as J. Frank Dobie explains, "were riding and driving their horses west and ever west. These horses were patriotically called 'American.' They were not a breed; they were no more fixed in type than American dogs; they were bigger than the Spanish-Indian-Western horse. To the majority of American patriots, bigness long before this had become a synonym for superiority" (1952:61). American horses were originally a mixture of French, Spanish, Flemish, and English bloods, and were described in such terms as large, powerful, and heavy, in comparison to Western horses which were classed as rugged, sure-footed, and active (Albert 1941:12, 38). On the western frontier during the nineteenth century, mustangs were "free to any taker," while "an American horse of breeding, size and stamina brought a sum truly fabulous" (Dobie 1952:196). Despite this fact, mustangs were in many ways preferable. During frontier wars, citizens asked, "Why cannot our cavalry on picked, grain-fed horses overhaul Indians on their scrub ponies?" It had become evident that "Texas rangers on cow ponies of Spanish blood overtook them where grain-fed cavalry horses fell behind." Success was credited to the mustangs, for "these ponies, whether ridden by Indian, cowboy or ranger, would do to ride the river with. They would stay—stay till hell froze over and a little while on the ice"—a quality that "was the absolute for men who lived not only on but by their horses" (Dobie 1952:61–62).

Thus horse breeders reasoned that from the mustang blood would come the toughness and endurance necessary for a cavalry horse on the western plains, whereas from the American strain would come larger size, better conformation, and refinement. Luce notes that "horses of Comanche's breed were standing the tough campaigns better than their blue-blooded cousins from the blue grass fields of Kentucky, Virginia, and Tennessee" (1939:6). This comparison refers to the Thoroughbred, a spirited English breed of light horses that was specifically developed to produce animals possessing speed, generally to be used as race horses and sometimes as hunters and jumpers. This breed of horses had been imported first from England and later bred by colonists in eastern North America—racing was already established in the colonies before the end of the seventeenth century (Hope and Jackson 1973:314). In writing about the type of horses commonly used by the cavalry in the 1870s, Dr. Elwood L. Nye, an army veterinarian, praised the "Thoroughbred-bronco cross." Spanish-American "broomtail" horses, Nye explained, were "small, tough, ill-shaped," and had the disposition of Satan; hence they "saw little, if any, service with the Army." But the horse that resulted from the "Thoroughbred-bronco" combination "often became an excellent trooper's mount," because "to the bronco sagacity, cunning, and endurance was added the Thoroughbred speed and fire." The veterinarian concludes that "a troop of cavalry in 1876 had a varied collection of horses as to breed and type, with cold blood very evident" (1941:119).

Horsemen often refer to types of horses not possessing Thoroughbred ancestry as cold blooded (Self 1946:75). It is relevant to note that in his campaigns and marches General Custer "almost invariably rode far and wide in advance and on the flank, scouting ahead, or ranging beyond, simply because of his love of action. . . . To cover the extra miles, Custer could not, and did not, depend upon the usual cold-blooded public mount. He used Thoroughbreds and always had at least two available. . . . In his exultant physical perfection together with his superior mounts, Custer appears to have given little thought or consideration to the poor trooper on his cold-blooded mount" (Nye 1941:115).

Comanche, of course, was not Custer's horse, though after death he often has been mistakenly identified as such. Though he appears from photographs to have been a rather handsome horse in his heyday (see fig. 1), he was of a more coarse-bodied type in comparison to the grace and refinement associated with Custer's personal riding mounts. A farrier of Troop I called Comanche "neatly put up" and "quite noble looking" in a report in the *Bismarck Tribune*, May 10, 1878. He has often been depicted in terms such as "homely and scraggy" (The Globe 1939, e.g.), usually to emphasize his ruggedness in comparison to more beautiful steeds. E. A. Garlington (who in 1878, as first lieutenant and adjutant in the Seventh Cavalry, had signed Colonel Sturgis' famous General Orders No. 7) described Keogh's mount in a 1932 letter. He stated that "Comanche was a coarse hard horse—no exceptional style or good looks; but was a substantial, hardy animal, well adapted to the Cavalry service of that day: a good walker and

41

feeder; could live on what the prairie afforded when grain was no longer available" (UK Archives).

In form as well as temperament, Comanche exemplified the strength and endurance of the ideal cavalry mount—a match for the reputed toughness and bravery of his dashing soldier-of-fortune master, Captain Keogh. With this pair, though Keogh was Irish, one is reminded of Owen Wister's idea about the close interrelationship that existed between the temperament of the adventurous, courageous, and self-sufficient Anglo-Saxon New World settler and the horse, who has been "his foster-brother, his ally, his playfellow, from the tournament at Camelot to the round-up at Abilene" (1972:81). Seeing a likeness between the particular type of man and mount whom destiny brought together in America during the nineteenth century, Wister noted that "the hoofs of his horse were tough as iron, and the pony waged the joyous battle of self-preservation as stoutly as did his rider. When the man lay rolled in his blankets sleeping, warm and unconcerned beneath a driving storm of snow, the beast pawed through to the sagebrush and subsisted; so that it came to be said of such an animal 'a meal a day is enough for a man who gets to ride that horse' " (1972:85).

Circumstances had conspired to make the New World mustang an appropriately tough counterpart for his eventual "foster brother," the frontiersman. The ancestors of the modern horse had once evolved on the North American continent, spreading to other parts of the world before becoming extinct here just after the last Ice Age. It was the Spanish in the sixteenth century who returned the horse to its original territory when they imported to America the horses who were to leave progeny that would become feral (Chard 1940:98). The ancestry of these Spanish horses was mixed and included a type called Barb but according to Dobie, "beyond all question the best Barbs and the best Spanish horses—terms often not exclusive of each other—of the sixteenth century were strong in Arabian characteristics. . . . The steel, the spirit and the bottom of the best mustangs" can be traced to the Arabian, and "one quality out of the original that never withered was hardihood" (1952:7, 9, 14). Evidently, "Spanish horses found vast American ranges corresponding in climate and soil to the arid lands of Spain, northern Africa and Arabia in which they originated" (Dobie 1952:23). Thornton Chard emphasizes that the excellent traits of the mustang "are due to the hardiness acquired by four hundred years of natural selection, quite as much as to the inheritance of Arabian and Barb blood" (Dobie 1952:297). It is well established that several centuries of feral life following reintroduction to the North American continent produced changes in the original stock leading to more acute senses as well as increased hardiness in the mustang (Graham 1949:118–19; Dobie 1952:114–17).

Though his exact breeding can never be determined, Comanche exemplifies the best that heredity and environment working together produced in all his forebears. Because he embodies these traits, and most particularly because of the quality of endurance which enabled him to survive against all odds, it is understandable that proponents of certain horse breeds attempt to claim his ancestry for their breed. Advocates of the Morgan horse, for example—a distinctive breed of handsome, sturdy, relatively small horses, noted for intelligence, versatility, and endurance, that originated in New England—consider Comanche a Morgan. In 1966, a painting of Comanche was executed by Jeanne Mellin, author of a book on the Morgan breed (1961). The depiction is entitled "Comanche, Morgan Gelding and Sole Survivor of Custer's Last Stand" (see fig. 30), and copies were sold through advertisement in the *Morgan Horse* magazine. Mellin's book asserts that "Morgans were used in the Indian Wars as cavalry mounts" (1961:190), but provides no further explanation or references. When personally contacted, the artist/author disclaimed any knowledge of Comanche as a Morgan and referred me to the person who had commissioned the painting.

A brisk letter from this individual in response to my query concerning Comanche's alleged Morgan ancestry stated that the information that Comanche was a Morgan gelding "was mentioned in numerous books and I have no reason to doubt that fact." In a followup letter, answering my urgent plea to disclose the sources, he admitted that in going through all his books, he was unable to find reference to Comanche as a Morgan. Still, his reaction was to persist in claiming Morgan ancestry for the Little Big Horn survivor. "You will just have to attribute this to common knowledge like ancient repute which is admissible in a court of law," he wrote. "I suppose this is the only authority you will have for your statement." Another lifelong devotee of the Morgan horse told me she had read an article many years ago in an early issue of the breed magazine about Comanche's ancestry as a Morgan. After all attempts at locating the reference failed, however, she concluded that the information was a rumor evidencing the propensity of people to want their horses to be related to famous ancestors.

The caption under a picture of Comanche in a 1963 publication designated the horse "a Morgan by breed" (Children's Bookshelf 1963:45). In 1976, a feature about Morgan horses published in the *Smithsonian* contained the information that "Comanche, said to be the only cavalry horse to survive the Little Big Horn engagement was—that's right—a Morgan" (Chew 1976:47). My request for sources went unanswered, though the *Smithsonian* editor notified me that my letter had been duly forwarded to the author. In 1985, an article about Custer's "fabulous horses" still referred to "the Morgan cavalry horse, Comanche, the only survivor of the great battle of the Little Big Horn in Southern Montana" (Henderson 1985:35). Again, my inquiry to the author went unanswered. But the important issue here is obviously not documentation, but the concept in people's minds about Comanche and the strong desire to make him a Morgan. Comanche could be perceived of as a Morgan for many reasons. That breed is truly American, a native Yankee product, noted for adaptability to people as well as rugged conformation and stamina. The ideal of the Morgan horse, too, has a strong association with the frontier, and with pride in the conquest of the new land. Morgans are typically praised for the fact that they could work in harness all week for a pioneer who was chopping down forests to clear land, then act as plough horses in the fields, and still be ridden or driven to church in style on Sundays. This association complements the image of Comanche in the national mind as an authentic American product, the epitome of strength and endurance, and as both a real and symbolic instrument for the successful conquest of a continent.

On a more pragmatic level, Comanche's relatively small size, his weight, and his bay color fit the Morgan ideal type. Probably also influential in creating the legend is the fact that Rienzi, the Civil War mount of General Philip Sheridan, who made the celebrated ride from Winchester to Cedar Creek, as immortalized in poetry and song, actually was a Morgan with documented ancestry (Pittenger 1967:125). Showing some similarities to Comanche, Sheridan's famous cavalry charger, though wounded, lived through the war, and was ultimately mounted and displayed at the Smithsonian Institution (Pittenger 1967:137–38).

Almost as complex an issue as Comanche's breeding, and still the subject of argument even today, is the matter of the gelding's coat color. This is an important matter, not only for an accurate physical description of the horse but for what it reveals about unconscious factors that often become mingled with history. It provides a clear example of the way symbolic elements combine to create and maintain the Comanche legend. Today, as one looks at the old cavalry mount standing in the museum (after being preserved for nearly a hundred years) he would clearly be classified as a typical bay, the color that some believe, in comparison to chestnuts and blacks, to be "the most enduring" of horses (Walker 1953:24). Bay is a horseman's term for various shades of reddish-brown body coat ranging from tan to dark mahogany, distinguished by having "black points"—that is, black on the legs extending from just above the knees and hocks to the hoofs, which are also black—and black mane and tail (Green 1974:23–24; Self 1946:77).

The question is, then, why has Comanche, obviously a bay, generally been known as a buckskin or a claybank, especially in the important early sources and in first-hand testimonies by those who saw him. Describing the horse in 1934, W. J. Ghent wrote, "There has been some controversy as to his color, though usually he is termed 'claybank sorrel.' Godfrey, apparently following Nowlan's designation, calls him a 'buckskin,' which is pretty much the same thing. If the mounted horse is now a bay," he asserts, "he must have undergone some change in coloring since his death" (Ghent 1934:1). An official Seventh Cavalry document, executed at Fort Meade and dated July 25, 1887, lists Comanche's color as "Buckskin." Ralph Edwards, who states "Comanche was under my care, Nov. 1886 to July 1887 at Fort Meade, as assistant to Vet. Surg.," cited "Color—Buckskin" in a listing of the horse's characteristics for a 1934 Indian War Veterans publication. He must have thought better of this designation, however, for he adds the postscript, "In regard to color, I would say a dark dirty sorrel" (1934:3). An 1879 report called Comanche "clay-bank" (Comanche 1879), and an 1890 newspaper cited him as "dun-colored" (Progress of Fort Riley 1890). Captain Charles King, in an 1890 article, referred to him as "Myles Keogh's splendid sorrel horse" (1890:386). An editorial note to an article about Comanche in a 1936 issue of *Winners of the West* indicates he is "dark cream color, [with] black mane and tail" (Korn 1936:A3), a coloration also attributed to him in a 1909 magazine (Atkinson 1909). These designations reflect the general tendency to describe his color in terms of the more unusual and dramatic lighter shades. Luce calls him "buckskin" and also "light bay or buckskin" (1939:85, 7). Brown refers to Comanche as "chestnut but not quite a buckskin," a "claybank" (1935:34). Former Seventh Cavalryman E. A. Garlington wrote in 1932 that the horse was "a yellowish bay—or what we in the South called a 'clay-bank'—with a dark stripe down his back" (UK Archives). Edward S. Godfrey, a troop commander who survived the Battle of the Little Big Horn and must have seen Comanche, called him simply "a claybank gelding" (1921:37). Interestingly, though, Godfrey's description of Comanche appears as a later addition to his article on the Battle of the Little Big Horn, which, when first published in *Century* magazine, contained no mention of the horse (1892:358–84). Comanche lore, and the escalating sense of fascination with his legend, was undoubtedly already a powerful force by the time of the reprint version. "Claybank gelding" is also the designation used by Brininstool, who wrote about the Little Big Horn from first-hand narratives (1925:185).

Although Fairfax Downey called him a "bay gelding" (1941:48), many of the later writers kept the color of Comanche as claybank or buckskin. The author of a 1951 article in *Western Horseman* termed Comanche "a handsome claybank gelding" (Snyder 1951:13), and David Dallas in his 1954 work also called the horse claybank, although the term "yellow bay" was applied to him as well (1954:10). A popular article in *Coronet* for 1956 still referred to Comanche as "a claybank gelding" (Greenspan 1956:158). By 1961, though, the discrepancy regarding the cavalry charger's color began to be noticed, as evidenced by Anthony Amaral, who stated that despite his being alternately called mouse colored, claybank, buckskin, and sorrel, "general terminology in use today" would "most frequently classify him as a bay" (1961:78). Robert Mengel, a biologist who is admittedly not a horseman, in his article written for the University of Kansas Natural History Museum in 1968 combined two mutually exclusive terms in calling the famous horse "claybank bay" (1969:3). By the time of David Dary's 1976 pamphlet, Comanche has become simply "a bay colt" (1976a:1).

Connotations of horsemen's nomenclature, of course, vary over time, and reflect differences in regional lingo. As Tom Swearingen, who is in charge of the Comanche exhibit at the Dyche Museum, points out, clay from different areas can vary from dark brown to red as found in Oklahoma, to yellow as seen in the Dakotas. Thus if a horse were designated as claybank by a person from one geographical region, it could well be a different shade from that referred to by a native of another region. Additionally, it must be kept in mind that Comanche died during the cold season in November, when his winter coat would have been the heaviest and thus would appear darkest. A shorter coat, and perhaps bleaching in summer from the strong sunlight of the plains, might have made him appear lighter.

In 1868, Custer had issued an order "coloring the horses" of the Seventh Cavalry. Following a European cavalry tradition, this meant that horses were arranged within the regiment by color and by company, the men of each company riding horses of the same color (Utley 1977:204; Mills 1985:156). Keogh's Company I was one of those mounted on bay horses (Hunt 1947:56). But for all his life, and for much of the century of history that has followed that life with fascination, Comanche was most often known as a buckskin or a claybank. And so those terms, even today, in some other way than strict utility and surface meaning, seem to embody the best description of the timeless nature of what it is he represents. In an analysis of these color terms, much about the symbolic significance of Comanche is revealed.

Buckskin refers to a horse of a yellow-tan color with black points, including mane and tail, as described for bay. Such a horse frequently has a black stripe down the spine from the mane to the root of the tail (Green 1974:94–95). The dorsal stripe is especially significant, as this is a trait Comanche did possess, which is still visible in his mounted form. A claybank horse, in today's terminology, has a light copper-colored coat with a mane and tail of a darker copper-color, according to noted expert Ben Green (1974:118–19). Obviously, however, confusion in terminology accounts for the discrepancy between the description of this term and Comanche's coat color, for he definitely possessed the black legs, mane, and tail. J. Frank Dobie, whose extensive personal experience with Western horses is matched only by his scholarly knowledge of them, provides the answer: "Buckskin and claybank are other names for dun," he reveals, and "on the northern plains, buckskin was the usual term" (1952:300).

Many of the most meaningful elements of the Comanche story are embodied in this symbolic coloration. His coat relates him to the past of his species, imparting to him a sense of agelessness, of enduring from ancient times to the present. For in studying domestication, Charles Darwin noted what many horsemen know—that "the primitive colour of the horse" was dun, and describes it as including hues of "reddish brown which graduates into light-bay or chestnut" and "dark dun, between brown and black." Darwin remarks on the occurrence of the dark dorsal stripe among horses, and acknowledges the "probability of descent of all existing races of horses from a single, dun-coloured, more or less striped primitive stock to which our horses still occasionally revert" (1868,1:74, 79, 81). Selective breeding by man has resulted in fewer horses of a dun color occurring in domesticated breeds; however, for the mustang "centuries of wild and half-wild life in the Americas reverted the type toward the primordial." "Prolonged feral existence" had "accentuated the dorsal stripe" and favored the "primal tawniness," which is nature's "most protective shade" (Dobie 1952:297, 298). From study of prehistoric cave paintings, it is known that "the common pattern for wild horses was probably that which the western stockmen commonly call a line-back buckskin" (Haines 1971:13). In fact, the rare Przewalski's horse, the only equid surviving into modern times which may be an ancestor of the modern horse, is "light bay or yellow-reddish brown," with dark legs and a black stripe down the back (Hopf 1977:34). Interestingly, the variations in coat color said to be characteristic of Przewalski's horse (Mohr 1971:53–54) are the same as the word descriptions of Comanche's color.

And so, with his buckskin coat color, Comanche becomes even more the archetypal horse, a survivor with ancient roots, a vestige of the best that endures from old times into the new, with the strength of the past giving vital continuity to the present. Traditionally in the West, hardiness is associated with the buckskin, claybank, or dun horse. Established belief held that "primitive toughness and instincts had never been bred out of the dun's ancestors"; there was "hidden vigor" beneath the sand-colored coat of this true Spanish mustang. On the frontier, "the dun came to represent the best qualities of the breed," and people still say "he is of the race that dies before tiring" (Dobie 1952:296–97). "Dun mustangs, whose staying powers were already legendary, figured prominently in a number of endurance rides in the 1880s" (Worcester 1986:65). George Catlin's account of his travels on the frontier with a dragoon expedition in 1834 contains a depiction of the extraordinary hardiness of "Charley," his mount "of clay bank colour" who flourished while most of the horses of the regiment gave out (1876,2:89–90).

A buckskin cavalry horse, in addition to this aura of endurance, has an image as individual, distinct from his fellows, conspicuous. He stands out among the typical more ordinary darker colored coats of bay, black, or brown. Not only is he perceived as tougher, but also as wilder, with an unbridled strain of the primitive dominating his being. Buckskin has come to be strongly associated with the American West, with frontier life, and all that it implies of rawness and savagery. Fringed buckskin jackets, for example, symbolize the adventure and romance of the "wild West." It is interesting to note that General George Custer was fond of wearing a buckskin suit in preference to a cavalry uniform and is often depicted in this garb. The rider of Comanche, Captain Myles Keogh, was known to have dressed this way as well. Both may have been wearing buckskin when they died at the Little Big Horn.

There is more agreement on the matter of Comanche's markings than on his color. He had small white patches in the saddle area. Still visible today on his mounted form is a band of white encircling his left hind foot just above the hoof and extending about half-way up the pastern. In horse terminology, this is a "short sock." Comanche is also distinguished by a small white "star" on his forehead (see fig. 5). It is intriguing to find that according to ancient horse wisdom, a mount with white on the far (right) hind foot is "lookt upon to be unluckie in a day of Battle." But, "to have only the near [left] hind foot White, is a good mark, and if the Horse have also with it a Star in his Forehead, it is the best of all Marks, and is very rarely known to fail" (Howey 1958:222).

Luce's data indicate that the famous gelding stood about 15 hands high (a hand equals four inches), and that he weighed about 925–950 pounds (1939:7, 85). Edwards and Brown, however, cite Comanche as standing 15 and 1/2 hands in height. Edwards lists the horse's girth as 73 inches, while Brown gives a 70 inch barrel, and both claim his length as 86 inches. Brown states that the animal weighed about 940 pounds (Edwards 1934:3; Brown 1935:34).

Thus Comanche, in ancestry, breeding, color and markings, sex, size, weight, and general conformation, probably showed no unusual characteristics which would set him apart from other hardy and obedient cavalry mounts of his era. There was nothing to indicate that time and destiny would ultimately make of him a horse that history would never forget. Before the strange and tragic circumstances of a battle that left no human white survivors suddenly transformed him into a symbolic and near-sacred being of legendary fame, however, his existence undoubtedly involved the routine duties of any other Seventh Cavalry soldier's horse, and his travels were made accordingly.

Chapter 3

The Captain's Mount

You felt like you were somebody when you were on a good horse, with a carbine dangling from its small leather ring socket on your McClelland [sic] saddle, and a Colt army revolver strapped on your hip; and a hundred rounds of ammunition in your web belt and in your saddle pockets. You were a cavalryman of the Seventh Regiment. You were a part of a proud outfit that had a fighting reputation, and you were ready for a fight or a frolic. (Hunt 1947:53)

From its very inception, there was something special about the Seventh Regiment, United States Cavalry. The regiment was "organized at Fort Riley, Kansas [in] the autumn of 1866, pursuant to Section 3 of the Act of Congress, approved the 28th of July of that year. . . . It was designated the Seventh Cavalry by General Orders No. 92, War Department, November 23, 1866," with George Armstrong Custer assigned as Lieutenant-Colonel. At the time of his appointment, Custer was "26½ years of age. Young, vigorous, active, daring, and ambitious, he made an impress upon the Regiment that, notwithstanding the gallant old soldiers and distinguished generals that were its Colonels during his lifetime, the Regiment was soon known, and probably ever will be, as 'Custer's Regiment' " (Medley and Jensen 1910:49). Among the commissioned officers who joined the Seventh Cavalry during November 1866 were First Lieutenant T. W. Custer, detailed acting regimental quartermaster, and Captain M. W. Keogh, assigned to Troop I. Troop I spent the remainder of 1866 and the year 1867 at Fort Wallace, Kansas (Medley and Jensen 1910:49, 53).

By tracing the movements of the Seventh Cavalry, paying special attention to Troop I, it is possible to determine Comanche's probable whereabouts during his active military service and to learn what his life may have been like. He was acquired by the Seventh Cavalry in 1868, a year noteworthy for the November 27 Battle of the Washita, fought in what is now western Oklahoma. In this surprise attack against Southern Cheyenne Indians, the Seventh Cavalry surrounded and defeated Black Kettle's snow-covered winter encampment. The event brought the regiment accusations of inhumanity toward an unprepared and allegedly peaceful enemy, even as military leaders praised it as an overwhelming victory.

It is unlikely that Comanche was present at the Battle of the Washita, since his rider, Captain Myles Keogh, did not participate in that engagement. As described in Chapter 2, shortly after his purchase by the Seventh Cavalry in April of 1868, the new mount joined his command in camp near Ellis, Kansas. According to the Chronological Sketch of Troop I, that troop, which had been organized in 1866, was stationed in Kansas and Indian Territory from June 15, 1868, to November 1869 (Brown 1973:103–104).

The Battle of the Washita is relevant not only because it had an important bearing on the Little Big Horn, but also for what it reveals about human interaction with horses in the military at that time. Following the Washita, which is often called a massacre because of the large number of unarmed people killed, Custer ordered the shooting of about 800 captured ponies, the Indians' "most valued possessions." Among those shocked at this equine slaughter was Captain Frederick Benteen, who was later to fight at the Battle of the Little Big Horn (Hoig 1976:139). However, destruction of the ponies was considered a war measure, for, as F. M. Gibson, a Lieutenant who had participated in the engagement, noted, "the ponies were more or less unmanageable," and Custer "did not care to incur the risk of their recapture" (Medley and Jensen 1910:63). Interestingly, Indian women were pressed into service to round up the animals, for "Indian horses had an instinctive hostility to white men." The ponies shied away from the soldiers and struggled violently to escape when caught, while the Indian women could "walk up to the animals without causing the slightest disturbance" (Hoig 1976:138). In the same way, troopers' horses were known to be afraid of Indians (Sandoz 1966:129). The horses' remarkable ability to distinguish whites from Indians was largely due to their acute sense of smell. This phenomenon often drew attention on the frontier and became a recurring theme in Comanche lore and literature, as we will see.

Although some soldiers in that day may have looked upon horses as expendable objects, much as the tanks which replaced them are now, one Cheyenne woman who gave an eyewitness account of the soldiers' attack on her village saw the horses in a different light. She remembered that during the battle "the wounded ponies passed near our hiding place, and would moan loudly, just like human beings" (Ediger and Hoffman 1955:139). Of deeper concern to some Americans were reports about Indian women and children who were killed at the Washita in addition to the 103 warriors who lost their lives there.

After the battle, fifty-three of the survivors—Cheyenne women, children, and babies—were taken prisoner by Custer's troops (Hoig 1976:140). Among them was a young woman named Monahseetah (Monaseta, or Meotzi) who came to be romantically linked with Custer. Her alleged relationship with Custer has never been conclusively proven, though it has often been stated as fact (see Sandoz 1953:xvii; Brill 1938:46; Marquis 1933:1,8; Miller 1957:67–68). The legend of this Indian maiden as Custer's lover became almost as deeply embedded in the mystique of the Last Stand as the story of Comanche as its lone survivor. Because of the occurrence of Monahseetah in Comanche's legend, some associations between the Indian woman and the horse will be discussed in Chapter 12.

It may have been soon after Comanche became part of the Seventh Cavalry that he acquired both his owner and his name. According to Godfrey,

> When General Alfred Sully's expedition against the southern Indians was organized at Fort Dodge, Kansas, September, 1868, Captain Keogh was acting Inspector-General on General Sully's staff. He chose this horse for his field mount. During one of our engagements with the Comanche Indians on the Cimarron River or the Beaver Fork, the horse was wounded while Keogh was riding him. Thereupon, the horse was named "Comanche." Keogh became very much attached to him, and thereafter he was known as "the captain's mount," and Keogh rode him at the battle of the Little Big Horn. (1921:37)

Luce recorded that Comanche received his "first wound—by an Indian arrow—on September 13, 1868 in a skirmish with Comanches on Bluff Creek, Kansas. . . . Upon arriving back in camp, it was found that an arrow shaft had been broken off in his right hind quarter. With little display of pain he permitted the farrier to remove the flint head and in a few days was again ready to resume the duties of carrying his troop commander on many miles of scouting" (1939:27).

In an article published in 1926, Comanche's name is also described as having been "won on the field of battle" in an engagement with the Comanche tribe on the Cimarron River, but under slightly different circumstances. "While carrying Captain Keogh in [that] action, the horse was wounded by a rifle bullet, but continued to perform his duty. When I Troop returned to camp at the close of hostilities, it was nursed back to health, and the soldiers pointed with great pride to the wound. 'Comanche,' they would say, and gently massage the scar. In time the animal and not the scar came to be known as 'Comanche' " (Smith 1927:36).

Although details may differ, accounts of the wounding of Comanche always emphasize that Keogh did not discover the horse's injury until he returned to camp. Thus Barron Brown, like other writers, states that after being fired upon by Comanche Indians, "the Captain returned to camp and it was not till then that he discovered his horse had been wounded on the hip either by a bullet or an arrow, probably the latter. It was a long, raking, flesh wound which soon healed. The stoical behavior of the horse under fire while wounded, together with his other fine qualities already enumerated, greatly endeared him to the officer" (1935:41). Later accounts of the celebrated horse, such as Brereton's, virtually always reiterate the fact that after being hit Comanche "stoically carried his rider for the rest of the fight with the broken shaft still in the wound. Back in camp he patiently allowed the farrier to extract the steel head, and in recognition of his courage on that day, Keogh named him Comanche" (1976:112).

Margaret Leighton's fictionalized story of Comanche, which is based mostly upon data from Luce's book, describes Comanche's naming with the added imaginative detail that the horse's reaction to his wound, and also his color, were responsible for the choice.

> "I saw it hit him, Captain," McBane volunteered. "He sure squalled as loud as any of those Comanches when it struck, but he kept right on going. I never heard a horse let out just that kind of a holler. A sure enough Comanche yell."
> "Comanche! That's the name for him," Keogh exclaimed. "He's just the color of that big buck, old Ten Bear's son.* Comanche, yes, boy, that's your name." (1957:84)

Interestingly, this suggestion that the horse's naming stemmed from his yelling like a Comanche, though first written as part of a fictionalized narrative for young readers, found its way into subsequent historical accounts of the famous horse. For ex-

*An enemy Comanche warrior, Ten Bear's son, had just been described as "a gorgeous barbaric figure, lighter bronze than most Indians" (Leighton 1957:82).

ample, it appears in the informative monograph written to coincide with the centennial year of the Battle of the Little Big Horn which was published by the University of Kansas for distribution by the Natural History Museum in Lawrence, which houses the Comanche exhibit (Dary 1976a:2).

Leighton also recreated the scene of the treatment of Comanche's wound:

> Keogh held his buckskin's head, murmuring soothingly while the farrier carefully extracted the flint arrowhead, and cleansed the wound. The horse shuddered and flinched, but he did not fight against the men who were tending him. He seemed to know that they were doing their best to help him. (1957:84)

And similarly, the idea that "Keogh held his horse's head and talked quietly to the animal" while "the farrier removed the arrowhead and broken shaft and cleaned the wound" has been incorporated from the juvenile novel into Comanche's recent historiography (Dary 1975a:4, 1976a:2).

One writer ignored all tales and legends and took the horse's name at face value. "Comanche! What a becoming name for a cavalry mount whose record of faithfulness and stamina has done its share to glorify the old regular cavalry, and leaving a tradition that will never die. The trooper who christened this horse Comanche must have realized his true worth when he selected the name of an Indian tribe superior to all the Plains tribes in horsemanship, and were without a doubt the finest horsemen in the world. A name so appropriate to a horse who was destined to go down in the glowing accounts of subduing the mighty Sioux, along with Custer, Reno and Benteen" (Schultz 1939).

From the very first, Comanche became known as a horse with exceptional endurance. The winter of 1868–69, like most winters on the Kansas plains, brought harsh weather. Comanche's chronicler, Edward S. Luce, describes the horse's first winter with the cavalry as being very severe, quoting as evidence the difficult conditions for both men and horses (1939:43) which actually appear in the records of the Seventh Cavalry for the year 1867 (Medley and Jensen 1910:50). In contrast to Comanche, Luce reports that Captain Keogh's other horse, Paddy, "an eastern horse much larger and a dark bay in color," could not withstand the rigors of winter like his hardier stablemate; therefore, it was necessary to return him to Fort Riley with other horses who were being sent back for various ailments" (1939:43).

The subject of Paddy raises a question about how history is recorded. General Hugh L. Scott, who joined Company I of the

Seventh Cavalry the day after the Battle of the Little Big Horn, wrote in a 1931 letter that "Captain Keogh rode a horse called Paddy up to the fight and changed to old Comanche" (UK Archives; More of the Story 1932:10). Beyond this statement, it is not known where Luce got his description of Keogh's second horse. He may have heard it from someone who was familiar with the animal. A letter written to Myles when he was still a youth in Ireland mentions Paddy (author's collection), a horse whose name must have been given to this later mount (see Chapter 14). Robert Ege states as fact Keogh's ownership of "a long-winded, sturdy-legged charger affectionately named 'Paddy.' " This horse "was used for long marches, while 'Comanche' was held in reserve and kept fresh for use in close combat or in quartering with the enemy." The "trail-hardy 'Paddy' " was "left with the pack train when Custer divided the command" (1966:31, 35). The article provides no sources. Undoubtedly, it is based upon Scott's statement and upon Brown's assertion, also undocumented, that on the 1876 expedition "Comanche was led most of the way, Captain Keogh riding Paddy and less favored mounts and reserving Comanche for battle. We do know for a certainty that Keogh changed mounts and rode Comanche when the Indians were located." Comanche was Keogh's "favorite mount when making long, forced marches or when going into battle." Though other horses were handsomer and faster for short distances, Comanche was decidedly the captain's preferred mount (1935:46, 35, 42, 45). Brian Pohanka's more recent article indicates, on the contrary, that Comanche "was Keogh's second mount; his *favorite*, 'Paddy,' was with the pack train during the battle" (1986:24). Sources for this new data on Keogh's alleged preference for Paddy are not provided; nor, upon my inquiry, did the author reveal them. Yet he notes that Luce's book is "riddled with inaccuracies and is largely responsible for the mythology that surrounds Keogh." If simple facts published about a horse cannot be validated, are we justified in trusting data that pass for history in other areas? Exemplifying an attitude toward historiography that often surfaced during research is the advice I received from an informant involved in my inquiries about Paddy: "I think at this point you should use license and invent a little.'

But let us return to what the records reveal about Comanche's life. By consulting sources such as Medley and Jensen's 1910 history of the Seventh Cavalry (which was utilized for Chandler's 1960 book on this subject); the Chronological Sketch of Troop I, Seventh U.S. Cavalry, as published in the reprint edition of Brown's study of Comanche (1973:104–105); and the 1939 treatise by Edward S. Luce, who indicated that he had access to the "Regimental History Seventh Cavalry" once on file in Seventh Cavalry Headquarters, Fort Bliss, Texas (1939:41), we can obtain a general indication of Comanche's whereabouts during his military life. This sketch of the horse's history must be ascertained, of course, from an outline of the movements and operations of Captain Keogh's Troop I, from the time of Comanche's purchase to the day of Custer's Last Stand. Beyond this, we cannot know details of Comanche's life from 1868 to 1876 with any real accuracy. (Most of the material that was subsequently written concerning the famous horse's life during that period has relied directly upon Luce's book as a source.)

What little is known about the year 1868 in Comanche's life has already been described. During 1869 and 1870, Troop I remained in Kansas, performing scouting and escort duties to protect settlements along the Saline, Solomon, and Republican rivers and wagon trains traveling across the plains against hostile Indians. November and December of 1869 were spent at Fort Harker, engaging in escort, scout, and garrison duties. In 1870, Fort Leavenworth was the headquarters of the Seventh. Troop I remained there until May, when, as part of the command of Lieutenant-Colonel George A. Custer, it left for Fort Hays. Captain Keogh's troop scouted the country between Fort Hays and Fort Harker, to the Saline River and the Smoky Hill region of Kansas. In a skirmish with Indians on June 9, Comanche received his second recorded wound, this time in the right leg. Though he was lame for several weeks, "again Comanche came through like an old soldier and was [soon] ready for duty, as good as new" (Luce 1939:44). Winter quarters were at Fort Harker (Chandler says Fort Hays).

The Seventh Cavalry's tour of duty in the Department of the Missouri terminated early in the following year. By the end of March 1871, the headquarters of most troops had changed to assignments in the Department of the South. Troop I was stationed at Bagdad, Kentucky, from March to September, and at Shelbyville from September to December. The troop was employed to assist United States marshals in combatting problems in the South such as those caused by the Ku Klux Klan, northern "carpetbaggers," and illicit distillers, and in enforcing internal revenue laws. In 1872, the regiment continued on duty in the South for the purpose of protecting and assisting the civil officers of the government in the performance of their duties. At the end of the year, Troop I went to Lebanon, Kentucky, where it remained until March 1873. During this period, in an engagement with "moonshiners" on January 28, 1873, "Comanche was again wounded, receiving a slight flesh wound in the right shoulder, but as usual he quickly recovered" (Luce 1939:45).

In 1873, due to escalating problems with Plains tribes, the Seventh Cavalry was ordered to the Department of Dakota. Troop I proceeded to spend April through June at Fort Snelling, Minnesota. From there, under command of Major Marcus Reno, Troop I formed the escort for the International Boundary Survey Commission. Keogh's troop wintered at Fort Totten, Dakota Territory, remaining as part of the garrison there until May 1874, when, along with Troop D, it continued duty with the Northern Boundary Commission. Troop I marched by way of Forts Stevenson and Buford to Sweet Grass Hills, Montana Territory, where it furnished escorts to surveying parties during late July and early August. The duties of the Commission having been completed, the troop returned to Fort Totten for the winter.

Comanche's troop was garrisoned at Fort Totten until April of 1875, when it left for duty at Fort Abraham Lincoln, Dakota Territory, near present-day Bismarck, North Dakota, arriving there in May. Dary states that "in the summer of 1875, after covering nearly 1500 miles during their two years of escort duty, Comanche and Keogh were ordered south to help eject miners from the gold fields of the Black Hills" (1976a:71). The year 1876 found the Seventh Cavalry assembled at Fort Lincoln. The regiment was under orders to report to Lieutenant-Colonel Custer for duty with the expedition commanded by General Terry in movements against the hostile tribes of the Plains.

The ill-fated expedition which ultimately met disaster at the Little Big Horn left Fort Lincoln on May 17, 1876. Witnesses later described the pervasive feeling of dread with which the column went forward that morning. Before leaving, the regiment was ordered to march across the parade ground, presumably to allay the fears of those left behind by displaying the Seventh in all its splendor and fighting strength. "The number of men, citizens, employees, Indian scouts, and soldiers was about twelve hundred. There were nearly seventeen hundred animals in all," wrote Elizabeth Custer, widow of the man who that day had proudly led the Seventh westward. "The cavalry and infantry in the order named, the scouts, pack-mules, and artillery, and behind all the long lines of white-covered wagons, made a column altogether some two miles in length." She described a mirage which appeared as the sun penetrated a veil of mist which had enveloped the land just as the column departed. The men and horses were mirrored upward in the fog and "appeared equally plain to the sight on earth and in the sky." It seemed to be "a premonition in the supernatural translation as their forms were reflected from the opaque mist of early dawn" (1885:262–64).

On this march, the Seventh Cavalry was divided into a right and a left wing, each containing six companies divided into two battalions. Comanche would likely have been part of the right wing, which consisted of companies B, C, E, F, and L, as well as I, commanded by Major Reno, with battalion commanders being Captains Keogh and Yates. The left wing, composed of the remaining six companies, was commanded by Captain Benteen (Godfrey 1892:358–59; Stewart 1980:212).

Relying primarily on the first-hand account of Lieutenant Edward S. Godfrey, commanding Company K, Seventh Cavalry Regiment, during the Battle of the Little Big Horn, as well as documents by other participants and scholars of the campaign, we can obtain an idea of what the journey to battle was like for Comanche. According to Godfrey, the length of each day's march varied from ten to forty miles, depending upon conditions encountered. "To avoid dismounting any oftener than necessary" a procedure was followed in which "one troop marched until about half a mile in advance of the train, when it was dismounted, the horses unbitted and allowed to graze until the train had passed and was about half a mile in advance of it, when it took up the march again; each of the other two troops would conduct their march in the same manner, so that two troops would be alongside the train all the time. . . . Each troop horse carried, in addition to the rider, between eighty and ninety pounds," including "all equipments and about one hundred rounds of ammunition." When the wagon trains were delayed by difficult crossings, "the cavalry horses were unbitted and grazed, the men holding the reins" (1892:358–59).

Relatively few anecdotes of interactions between horse and man have survived in cavalry annals, but Lieutenant Godfrey has recorded one such scene on the Custer march. As he remembered it, "About noon the 'strikers,' who carried the haversacks, were called, and the different messes had their luncheon, sometimes separately, sometimes clubbing together. When the haversacks were opened, the horses usually stopped grazing and put their noses near their riders' faces and asked very plainly to share the hardtack; if their polite request did not receive attention they would paw the ground, or even strike their riders. The old soldier was generally willing to share with his beast" (1892:359). (See frontispiece.)

Each day's camp was made in the form of a parallelogram, with the cavalry wings on the long sides facing each other and the headquarters and guard located at one end nearest to the creek. . . . The wagon-train was parked to close the other end and was guarded by the infantry battalion. The troops, as they arrived at their places, were formed in line, facing inward, dismounted, unsaddled, and, if the weather was hot and the sun shining, the men rubbed the horses' backs until dry. After this the horses were sent to water and put out to graze, with side-lines and lariats, under charge of the stable guard. . . . The officer of the day, in addition to his ordinary duties in camp, had charge of the safety of the cavalry herds. Sometimes this latter duty was performed by an officer designated as "Officer of the Herd." To preserve the grazing in the immediate vicinity of the camp for evening and night grazing, all horses were required to be outside of the camp limits until retreat.

Stable call was sounded about an hour before sunset. The men of each troop were formed on the parade and marched to the horse herds by the first sergeant. Each man went to his own horse, took off the sidelines and fastened them around the horse's neck, then pulled the picket-pin, coiled the lariat, noosed the end fastened to the head halter around the horse's muzzle, mounted, and assembled in line at a place indicated by the first sergeant. The troop was then marched to the watering-place, which was usually selected with great care because of the boggy banks and miry beds of the prairie streams. After watering, the horses were lariated outside but in the immediate vicinity of the camp. . . . After lariating their horses, the men got their curry-combs, brushes, and nose-bags, and went to the troop wagon, where the quartermaster-sergeant and farrier measured, with tin cups, the forage to each man, each watching jealously that he got as much for his horse as those before him. He then went at once to feed and groom his horse. The officer whose duty it was to attend stables and the first sergeant superintended the grooming, examining each horse's back and feet carefully to see if they were all right. When a horse's back got sore through the carelessness of the rider, the man would generally be compelled to lead his horse until the sore was well. It was only after these tasks had been completed that the men ate their own supper. (Godfrey 1892:359–61)

"Retreat was sounded a little after sunset," at which time "the stable guards began their tours of duty." The troop commander then gave instructions for the night. These orders "usually designated whether the horses were to be tied to the picket-line or kept out to graze, and included special instructions for the care of sick or weak horses. At dusk all horses were brought within the limits of the camp" (Godfrey 1892:361).

Sometimes special circumstances changed the daily round of activities for the cavalry horses. On June 1, a snowstorm caused the expedition to remain in camp on the Powder River for two days, during which the animals suffered from exposure and the lack of grazing (Stewart 1980:220). On June 10, General Terry issued orders "for the right wing, six troops under Major Reno, to make a scout up the Powder, provided with twelve days' rations." Keogh would have participated in this expedition, and perhaps rode Comanche. On June 19, Reno reported that he had found a large Indian trail that led up the Rosebud River. The reunited command "reached the Rosebud about noon on June 21, and began preparations for the march and the battle of the Little Big Horn" (Godfrey 1892:362, 363).

At a June 21 conference held by Generals Terry, Gibbon, and Custer aboard the steamer *Far West* at the mouth of the Powder River, it was decided that "the 7th Cavalry, under General Custer, should follow the trail discovered by Reno." In addition to rations carried on the pack-mules, "each man was to be supplied with 100 rounds of carbine and 24 rounds of pistol ammunition, to be carried on his person and in his saddle bags. Each man was to carry on his horse twelve pounds of oats" (Godfrey 1892:363–64). At a meeting with his officers that evening, Custer announced that from that time on he would be responsible for "when to move out of and when to go into camp," but "all other details such as reveille, stables, watering, halting, grazing, etc. on the march would be left to the judgment and discretions of the troop commanders." Marches, he told them, "would be from twenty-five to thirty miles a day. Troop officers were cautioned to husband their rations and the strength of their mules and horses, as we might be out for a great deal longer time than that for which we were rationed," since Custer "intended to follow the trail until we could get the Indians, even if it took us to the Indian agencies on the Missouri River or in Nebraska." Godfrey, like other officers—certainly including Keogh—issued orders for the protection of the horses and mules in the event of a night attack (1892:364, 365).

Just before noon on June 25, the Seventh Cavalry under Custer crossed the divide between the Rosebud and Little Big Horn valleys. Shortly after that, the regiment was divided into three battalions. Troop I, led by Captain Keogh riding Comanche, was included in the five companies assigned to Custer's own immediate command. This command, after separating from the other two, was overwhelmed and annihilated by Indians in an engagement forever afterward referred to as "Custer's Last Stand." It was not until the morning of June 27 that General Terry and his staff and officers of General Gibbon's column arrived on the bluffs now known as the Reno-Benteen Battle site, relieving the beleaguered troops who had fought there and bringing them the tragic news of the death and defeat of Custer and all of his command.

Since no one who fought with Custer survived, details of the desperate struggle are not known. They have only been surmised from the positions of the bodies and from later Indian testimony given at varying intervals following the battle. Among the many causes that have been suggested as contributing to Custer's defeat is the condition of the cavalry horses as they went into battle. Although General James B. Fry wrote that "having marched leisurely from Fort Lincoln on the Missouri to the Rosebud on the Yellowstone," the men and horses of the expedition were "well seasoned but not worn," and "Reno has stated that when the regiment moved out on the 22nd of June . . . the horses were in best condition" (1892:387), others have disagreed. One trooper with Company A in Reno's command later wrote:

> Custer always had several good horses ready whereby he could change mounts every three hours if necessary, carrying nothing but man and saddle, while our poor horses carried man, saddle, blankets, carbine, revolver, haversack, canteen, 10 days' rations of oats and 150 rounds of 45-caliber ammunition, which of itself would weigh more than ten pounds—and we had no extra horses to change off. With the forced night march we made to get to the Little Big Horn, it is no secret why our horses played out before going into action. A number of these worn animals were brought in by the rear guard. A comrade friend of mine—a member of one of the companies with Custer, was fortunate in being detailed to go with the rear guard. His horse was played out and he could not go into action.

The same man noted that on June 25 "the grazing had been poor for several days, and as we were traveling in light marching order —that is, without wagons—there was little, if any, grain for our horses" (Brininstool 1925:26, 47).

Peter Thompson, of Troop C, would have been in Custer's charge against the Indians, but was left behind because his horse gave out, and finally reached the Reno command, with which he stayed for the remainder of the battle. In his account of the campaign, he noted that on June 24, "Getting up I strolled through the camp looking at the horses and noting how poor and gaunt they were becoming. This was not to be wondered at when we take into account the long marches they had made without any grain to sustain their strength; nothing but dead grass or perhaps a little green grass which was very short at this season of the year" (Brown and Willard 1924:148). In writing about the battle, Thompson revealed that "our horses had become quite jaded, for our grain had all been consumed and the grazing had been poor." As the editor of Thompson's narrative points out, grazing was poor because the huge Indian pony herd, estimated as high as 15,000 animals, had eaten most of the grass along the trail. The ideal amount of forage for cavalry mounts in garrison was fourteen pounds of hay and twelve pounds of grain per day. With only two pounds provided per day and grazing limited, it was no wonder that the horses were quite "jaded." The cavalry horses bore exceedingly heavy loads, and were excessively weary from the long six-week journey from Fort Lincoln (Magnussen 1974: 75–76, 109). Little Big Horn Battle participant Gustave Korn remembered that on June 25, about an hour before Custer's charge on the Indians, "when within about 4 miles of the village we came to a small stream called Goose Creek. There was very little water; one mouthful for each horse was the order" (1936:1). Benteen, too, noted the difficult conditions of the last few days' march and recalled his horses being badly in need of water in the June heat (Graham 1953:179, 180).

There has been much disagreement about the condition of the horses, as evidenced by conflicting testimonies given at the Court of Inquiry convened in Chicago in 1879 to investigate the conduct of Major Reno at the Battle of the Little Big Horn. Lieutenant George Wallace reported that the horses of the command were "worn out" and "exhausted." On the march from the Rosebud, he said, the horses had little grain and "there was hardly any grazing; the [Indian] ponies had clipped the grass almost like a lawn mower." Sergeant F. A. Culbertson stated that when Major Reno ordered Lt. Varnum to do something, "the lieutenant said his horse was worn out, but if he could get another horse he would go." Lieutenant Charles Varnum himself testified that the animals were "tired and panting and could hardly make it." John Martin admitted "my horse was tired" (Graham 1954:15, 32, 33, 48, 124, 130). Some witnesses disagreed. Interpreter Girard spoke of the horses being "on the bit," "comparatively fresh," and "not fatigued." Dr. H. R. Porter remembered "the horses generally were in good condition. High spirited—some wanted to run." Captain Godfrey felt "the general condition of the horses was good," though "the horses of General Custer's column were not in as good condition as those of other companies," and were "much ridden down." Sergeant Edward Davern, who had been with Reno, said "the horses of the command were in tolerable good condition," and a civilian packer, John Frett, reported that the animals had been "in average condition" (Graham 1954:43, 62, 113, 183, 186).

A surviving scout with Custer's column, George Herendeen, reported that "the horses were not tired . . . when we arrived at the battle field" (Graham 1953:264). In a 1953 letter, Fred Dustin, a discerning writer who had made intense long-term studies of the Battle of the Little Big Horn, shed light on the apparent discrepancies in testimony regarding the horses, pointing out that

> when one officer or man stated that both he and his horse were worn out, or that he fell asleep in the saddle, THERE MUST HAVE BEEN A CAUSE so that if another officer claimed that his horse was in good condition etc., or like Herendeen, stated that his mount was in very good order, BUT owing to the fact that he was not under the grazing restrictions that the soldiers were, HE PICKED GOOD FEEDING (grazing) PLACES FOR HIS HORSE! "Circumstances alter cases." (Custer Battlefield National Monument Files; hereafter designated CBNM Files)

In his book, *The Custer Tragedy*, Dustin concluded that despite "elaborate and ingenious efforts to prove the contrary, . . . the truth is that when men and horses went into the fight they were worn out" (1939:102). Another scholar who made exhaustive studies of the Little Big Horn, Dr. Charles Kuhlman, wrote that at the time of Custer's attack,

> Most of the horses of the regiment were exhausted almost to the point of unfitness, especially those of the six companies which had been on the scout with Reno about a week before. All five companies of the Custer battalion had been on this scout, and yet Custer crowded them unnecessarily on the attack theory, over several miles of the most difficult ground they had encountered since leaving the Yellowstone. Miles back he had left two men alone on the prairie, with horses completely exhausted—a sharp warning that before long many others would give out. (1940:3)

Interestingly, Gall, a noted Sioux chief who participated in the attack on Custer, returned to the battlefield in 1886 for the tenth anniversary proceedings. Standing near where Custer's command fell, the great warrior, who had a solid reputation for reliability, described the Last Stand, indicating that

> The soldiers were fighting on foot, so finally we rode over them with our ponies. Our ponies were well rested and fast runners, but the soldiers' horses were tired out before the battle began and would not have been any good if the soldiers had been mounted. These horses were so hungry that they were eating grass while the battle was going on and our braves had no difficulty in catching all of them. While making our way to Poplar River these horses were not much good and we left a lot of them on the Missouri River. (Burdick 1949:21)

One authority has argued persuasively that the general poor

condition of the horses on the 1876 Custer campaign contributed to the disastrous defeat of his command. Lieutenant Colonel Elwood L. Nye, who was a member of the Army Veterinary Corps for twenty-nine years, used his expertise to analyze and write about the condition of the horses and mules on Custer's expedition, a subject which he, with supreme understatement, said had previously been given "too little direct attention" (1941:114–40).

Indeed, the available literature's lack of attention to military horses is almost incredible. Many books and articles entirely devoted to cavalry contain few if any meaningful references to the soldiers' essential equine partners. Rare is the treatise that gives them a single paragraph in any depth. Yet it is obvious that, as Nye points out, "A paramount consideration with any cavalry leader is the condition, effectiveness, and well-being of his mounts." Nye asserts that "only the most urgent military necessity will cause a cavalry commander to push his mounts to the point where their efficiency is seriously impaired. The military situation must always govern, but even so, a good cavalry leader will conserve the strength of his animals to the greatest possible extent in order that they may reach the field of action in the most effective condition the situation will permit" (1941:114).

As a veterinarian, Nye declared unequivocally that "the whole story of his [Custer's] military life shows a brutal disregard of the well-being of his men and animals. There can be no doubt that this contributed, in part, to his tragic end beside the 'Greasy Grass' " (1941:114–15). In support of his views, Nye describes an 1867 march of 225 miles through central Kansas and into Nebraska which was performed under Custer's command. The leader's behavior and the pace of the expedition caused a trooper to say of Custer: "He thinks more of his dogs than he does of us." A small party of Custer's mounted escort "which fell behind because of the condition of the horses was attacked by Indians. One man was killed and another wounded. Custer made no halt to rescue his men, or attack the Indians, but pushed on to Fort Hays." Because Custer was not guided by military necessity, but indeed was violating orders for personal motives, it was all the more evident that the "condition of men or animals concerned him little" (1941:114–15, 120).

A participant in Custer's 1874 Black Hills expedition also reported an example of the controversial leader's inhumane treatment of a horse during that assignment. Recalling how several men decided to make the ascent to Harney's Peak, an 800-foot elevation, he wrote, "It was quite a climb, we took our horses as high as we could, then tethered them and went the rest of the way on foot. Custer went too, but he took his horse a great deal higher than we did." On the return trip "Custer's horse had a hard time getting down the steep peak—it was cruel, the horse's knees were bleeding, and he had a hard time to make the grade" (Wood 1927).

Analyzing the 1876 march of Custer's Seventh Cavalry from Dakota to the Little Big Horn, Nye asserts "it may be safely assumed that the condition of the animals was not too good" even as the unit left Fort Lincoln, for, possibly due to the uncertain and controversial conditions surrounding Custer's assuming command of the expedition, "the animals were not in the best condition for extended field service. . . . To add to the difficulties of the mounts, a large percentage of the enlisted men were recruits with little or no experience in the care of animals under field or any other conditions" (1941:120–21). Nye's daughter remembers her father emphasizing the problems during the Custer expedition that must have been caused by the fact that "there were many green remounts, as green as the men, and both horse and rider had to travel over unknown territory" (personal communication 1988).

Indeed, "the myth of the well-trained horses is part of the legend that the Seventh Cavalry was a 'superior' regiment. These cavalry horses were 'green' for the most part and were not used to gunfire. Many of the horses became unmanageable as they were not used to being pushed at a gallop for so long" (Magnussen 1974:130). Lieutenant Charles de Rudio specified at the Reno Court of Inquiry that some mounts "were rather unruly and men could not check their horses." The excited animals "had never seen such service, and horses generally get excited after galloping a mile or two" (Graham 1951, 1:268). These facts reveal that Captain Keogh was indeed fortunate to have a seasoned mount who was by this time almost certainly conditioned to gunfire and the harsh demands of being ridden on cavalry campaigns.

Undeniably, on the march many conditions adversely affected the horses. Much of the land traversed was rough country and badlands, often cut by steep ravines. Most of the terrain covered offered no roads or trails. Cold rain, hail, and snow made travel difficult and camps uncomfortable. Sometimes torrents had to be bridged, and winding rivers were crossed and re-crossed many times. Animals became mired in muddy stream beds, and mosquitoes were a torment. In some camps, water was in short supply or so alkaline it could not be used by men or horses. Due to the lateness of spring in 1876, grass was scant and grazing poor in many places. Animals which became nutritionally depleted and exhausted during the expedition were given little opportunity for rest and recuperation (Nye 1941:126). There is no evidence that professional veterinary care was provided for horses during the final weeks of this campaign.

Details such as distances covered and time spent on the move during each day's march are documented and can be analyzed in light of the horses' capacities and endurance. The Seventh Cavalry horses of Custer's command, according to Nye, were pushed especially hard after separating from the rest of the expedition during the rough march up the Rosebud. Though Custer had been cautioned at a conference with Terry just before this departure to take special care of his men and animals, being "impatient of restraint and control," he gave little regard to these instructions. If one accepts Custer's alleged disobedience of orders and his consequent unreasonably fast forward advance and premature attack upon the Indians, it is easy to understand that, as Nye points out, the "animals could not be spared." On June 24, the horses were under saddle, on the alert, or marching for fourteen hours and forty-five minutes. According to studies by Fred Dustin, an eminent investigator of the Little Big Horn campaign, "Custer's and Reno's battalions marched over sixty miles from five o'clock in the morning of the 24th to approximately 2 o'clock in the afternoon of the 25th" in a "period of 33 hours, including halts, with very little sleep or food, hardly any water, almost no grass, and but few oats for the animals" (1939:102). Since Custer arrived at the Little Big Horn 24 hours prior to the pre-arranged date of the 26th, when he was to meet Gibbon's force, "military necessity cannot be used as the motive for this abuse of men and animals." Nye believed that "had this additional time been allotted the marches, men and animals would not have reached the scene of action in the exhausted state which was theirs" (1941:128, 130, 133, 134).

If Reno's horses were tired and worn out, those under Custer's immediate command must have been even more jaded, his troops having covered about seven miles of "very rough going" after separating from Reno. This rapid march "must have involved much extended trot and gallop, not considering the wild dashes to charge or escape which must have marked the end of that fatal conflict." During Custer's march "at least four troopers dropped out of the column because their mounts were so exhausted they could not be goaded forward" (Nye 1941:135, 138).

As his 1940 letter to the editor of the *Cavalry Journal* reveals, Dr. Nye, in his article, "avoided the battle and its controversies," focusing rather on "the use and abuse of animals and its effect on the final result," and had "covered it [Custer's 1876 march] as might have been done by a veterinarian, had one been with Custer" (CBNM Files). The Veterinary Corps colonel had studied Custer's last campaign for many years, reading extensively and corresponding frequently with the most prominent scholars and authors on the subject. Captain E. S. Luce, Fred Dustin, Colonel W. A. Graham, Dr. Charles Kuhlman, and R. G. Cartwright were among the authorities who consulted him about many matters regarding the battle having to do with horses, and who respected his knowledge. Nye was personally acquainted with Charles Varnum and Charles Windolph, two Little Big Horn survivors, and had conversed with them extensively about the battle. According to an officer who had served with him during the 1920s and 1930s, Nye had interviewed Little Big Horn participants E. S. Godfrey and W. S. Edgerly, as well as some enlisted men (Zacherle 1976:23). Most importantly, the veterinarian and cavalry officer had been over the battleground himself numerous times, studying it in detail with special expertise regarding an army mount's endurance and capacities.

In 1938, just before the U. S. Cavalry became mechanized, Colonel Nye organized and participated in a final mounted cavalry maneuver. During this expedition, which became known as "the last great cavalry march," his Fourth Cavalry regiment covered the distance between Fort Meade, South Dakota, and the Pole Mountain area of Wyoming—said to be the longest cavalry march in contemporary times. Nye's experience as the veterinarian in charge of the horses on that expedition gave him first-hand knowledge of the capabilities of a cavalry horse regarding gaits, speed, and distance covered over rough terrain as well as providing data about the water and forage requirements of a cavalry mount on the march. This personal experience in the field contributed greatly to his understanding of what it must have been like for the animals during the Seventh Cavalry's journey to the Little Big Horn in 1876 (Sibrava and Ober n.d.:2–3; Nye n.d.(b):1–2,4–5).

On a trip over the battleground, Colonel Nye and R. G. Cartwright were responsible for finding empty cartridge casings on the ridge east of Medicine Tail Coulee, a discovery which was a valuable addition to knowledge concerning Custer's (and Comanche's) route to the Last Stand. The area was named for Nye by Dustin, who in a 1946 letter to the veterinarian referred to "the ridge where you found the shells, . . . which I have called Nye's ridge" (CBNM Files). (This is presently referred to as Nye-Cartwright Ridge.)

Regarding Nye's views about the animals on Custer's expedition, Dustin wrote to the veterinarian in a 1940 letter "Your point as to the overuse of horses and mules seems well taken." Dustin noted that the Ree scouts had indicated "their ponies were worn out, and in spite of their lashing, their fatigued mounts fell far behind." And "as for the cavalry horses, the condition of many of them was pitiful. Varnum, with all his reticence, said in a letter to me, 'I was worn out: I did not even attend the last officers' call,' and later on, states that his horse was in like condition, but even at that, was better than Hare's, who borrowed Varnum's when Reno sent him post-haste for the ammunition packs." Dustin confirmed "It seems to be a well-established fact that Custer used little judgment in his marches, but that at times he would relentlessly push his command, large or small." Just before the Little Big Horn Battle, "as far as the cavalry was concerned, the forcing [of] the march for the last 48 hours was probably the strongest factor of the worn-out condition, but of course previous use or misuse would certainly have a direct bearing" (CBNM Files).

At about the same date, Little Big Horn scholar Charles Kuhlman, whose forthcoming book owed much to Nye's contribution of knowledge, wrote to the Colonel "I am greatly interested in the article you are preparing on the abuse and condition of the horses and mules." He revealed "I have been of the opinion for some time that when Custer reached the field his horses were not in condition for a charge on the village. Last summer I learned that Brigadier General Hamilton S. Hawkins is also of that opinion." Kuhlman indicated "the subject is clearly worth a special study," which "will be especially valuable to a civilian like me who cannot speak with any degree of assurance on such a subject. I have not yet told my story of the battle and need the information" (CBNM Files).

Colonel W. A. Graham, whose books are cornerstones of Custer literature, wrote to Nye just after the publication of *The Custer Myth*, stating that he especially appreciated the veterinarian's praise of his work "for the reason that you, as a retired Regular, can and do speak 'as one having authority.' " Regarding his new book, Graham told his correspondent

> You, as a retired member of the Veterinary Corps will be especially interested, I am sure, in Benteen's narrative, which emphasizes the physical strain on both men and horses of the forced marches the regiment made after leaving the Yellowstone. The horses, in particular, must have been jaded and exhausted, and the men in almost as bad condition, and this condition probably had a considerable bearing on their fighting capacity.

In the same letter, Graham confides to Nye

> Ever since "The Story of the Little Big Horn" was first published in 1926, Custerophiles have accused me of being Pro-Reno; while Custerophobes, on the other hand, have insisted with equal vigor that I am Pro-Custer, when as a matter of fact, I am not Pro or Anti anybody. What I did, to the best of my ability, was to marshal the demonstrated facts impartially and let them speak for themselves. I have tried to be equally objective in "The Custer Myth," and I hope I have succeeded. (CBNM Files)

Like Graham, Nye strove for impartiality to validate his work. In the introduction to the 1964 reprint edition of Colonel Nye's *Marching with Custer*, Carroll Friswold, a well-known scholar in the field, points out that Nye's study "adds a valuable facet to our attempts to unravel the happenings of that Sunday afternoon on the Little Big Horn." Identifying objective criteria for use in considering the evidence Nye brings forth, Friswold notes that the reader should "keep in mind that Colonel Nye is not only a trained professional in the care, use, and treatment of animals, but he is a specialist in the use of animals from the military viewpoint." Nye, as a veterinarian and cavalryman, "makes a careful analysis of the marches, day by day, noting all conditions and happenings which might affect the animals, even reminding us of Custer's personality and its effect on men and horses." Evidence certainly leads to agreement with the assertion of Friswold that Nye's "conclusion is entirely sound and accurate: the great exhaustion of both men and animals certainly had its effect on the conduct and outcome of the battle" (1964:9).

In spite of the plausibility of Nye's analysis, however, the condition of the cavalry horses at the Little Big Horn has become one more pawn used in the ongoing dispute between people who regard Custer as a villain and those who view him as a hero. Nye's legitimate advocacy for horses and their welfare, for example, has caused the veterinarian to be discredited by at least one Custer defender. Asserting that Nye's article "almost reached the zenith of misstatement," Dr. Lawrence Frost, a podiatrist, states "Nye obviously disliked Custer, that feeling coloring his conclusions" (1986:223, 226). This assertion is clearly a tautological trap, for if Nye did hold negative feelings toward Custer, these feelings were the *result* of the General's treatment of horses, not the other way around. One's like or dislike for a person does not influence one's view of how that person interacts with animals or affect the knowledge that horses are sentient beings, deserving of humane consideration. Indignation at abuse of horses is a necessity for any veterinarian worthy of his or her profession, and all the more so for Dr. Nye as a cavalryman. During my extensive conversations with his daughter, Kathleen Nye Smith, I have learned of this man's "tenderhearted fondness for horses." She remembers her father as being "a tough disciplinarian, but when he talked about horses, his eyes would mist over. His stern exterior concealed sympathy and tenderness for horses. He was always concerned about them, and couldn't stand to see them abused." To the end of his life, Mrs. Smith told me, Nye had an intense interest in Comanche, and always wanted the horse's mounted remains to be displayed at the Custer Battlefield Museum. He wrote an article entitled "What of Comanche" recounting the animal's life (see Chapter 14). Her father's opinions on General Custer, she says, were "the middle of the road."

In writing about the horse that Custer rode into the fatal battle, Frost states that "had Vic survived even though captured by the Indians, he would have received top billing. Comanche would have been unimportant." No one would disagree that the flamboyant general's Thoroughbred horse would have eclipsed the mount belonging to a subordinate, had they both lived. The idea is taken further by Frost, however, when his own pro-Custer advocacy determines that words are extracted "from the horse's mouth": "[If] only Vic had survived; if he could have left a message, it might have read 'General Custer's exploit (on Custer Hill) is unequaled' " (1986:230–31, 241).

Though it is fascinating to find that horses can be used as vehicles of expression for such opinions, my purpose in writing this chapter is not to expand the controversy about Custer's character. Rather, I seek to use available data to describe, as far as possible, what life was like for the cavalry horses of the campaign, and to illuminate the compelling significance of Comanche's survival. The point is often made that other cavalry leaders of the day may have been just as hard on horses as Custer. Reporter John F. Finerty, who accompanied General Crook's column during the 1876 campaign, for example, repeatedly documented the deplorable condition of the horses (1970:especially 236, 255, 257, 260, 277, 304, 306). And the claim is made that "None of his [Custer's] marches compared to that of Terry's June 25th march across the arid badlands" (Frost 1986:226). What should receive emphasis, however, is not a meaningless game of who is the cruelest cavalryman, but rather the overwhelming debt of gratitude which is due to the horses themselves for the terrible suffering they have endured, not only in the 1876 campaign to "win the West," but throughout most of human history. As one writer observed

Of all the animals, the horse is probably the shyest, most highly strung and least aggressive. Yet for four thousand years he has been our most faithful ally in war. He has thundered unquestioningly into the mouth of the cannon. He has carried the military leaders and their vast armies to the far corners of the earth, allowing them to carve out their great empires. Yet despite the millions of words written to glorify the soldier's courage in war, little praise has been given to the horse that bore him. To single out a horse for praise seems to be as alien to most military commanders and historians as to suggest a tank or a helicopter fought with particular gallantry or stoicism. (Cooper 1983:12)

Custer's rough usage of horses has received attention because of his flamboyant character and the great appeal his exploits and his dramatic death have commanded from his own day to contemporary times. This attention is also due, however, to the fact that throughout his life, as reflected in his own writings and those of his wife, he was depicted as an admirer of horses and a person to whom the animals were of special importance. When not fighting on horseback, his deepest joy was the strenuous outdoor life associated with horses—riding, hunting, and racing. Those who have spoken and written about Custer from his own times through the present have made much of his prowess as a horseman. Thus, assumptions of an extra measure of concern for the animals not expected from other cavalry officers have undoubtedly existed.

Dustin, in his commentary about Nye's article on cavalry horses at the Little Big Horn, showed remarkable insight when he drew attention to the vast difference between true solicitude for animals and the "craze" for horses or other animals that often accompanies vanity, egotism, and immaturity—qualities often attributed to Custer. A man who is "brutal, callous, and unfeeling in his treatment of men and beasts," Dustin wrote, is lacking mature mentality. He believed Custer demonstrated arrested development, acting in many ways like a child in his interactions with animals, as well as in such traits as an abnormal delight in posing for photographers in bizarre costumes (1941:1). Recognizing this distinction between a juvenile "craze" and mature feelings of genuine affection and respect is essential to understanding human relationships to animals. A recent biographer expressed Custer's inherent paradox: "He loved animals, including those he killed and stuffed" (Connell 1984:205). Just as many well-documented instances show Custer was exceedingly cruel in dealing with his men, there are also indications that he was kind to people he cared about. The same type of discrepancy existed in his treatment of horses.

71

Using knowledge of horses and terrain as well as the most reliable sources available about the Little Big Horn campaign, it cannot be argued with validity that the Seventh Cavalry mounts were generally in good condition for the battle. Nor can it be anything but debatable to claim that Custer was unique among his contemporaries in what appears today to have been his reckless exploitation of horses. Veterinary military historians Merillat and Campbell stated that "the great cavalrymen of American history without exception neglected their animals to their own sorrow" (1935,I:82).

Frost has asserted that the events of Custer's Last Stand could not have been affected by the horses' condition, since that engagement was ultimately "a dismounted action" (1986:226). But it is short-sighted to assume that the events preceding Custer's final hour did not affect its disastrous outcome. Because they march and fight as a unit, the fates of cavalryman and horse are inseparably linked. Prior to the engagement on the hilltop, worn-out horses who could not respond to their riders must have contributed greatly to the demoralization of the soldiers and detracted from, or even destroyed, the organization of the battalions. It is hard to imagine anything more devastating to a cavalryman who is totally dependent upon his equine partner than the loss of that partner's ability to cooperate. As Merillat and Campbell have pointed out, the most effective and successful cavalry leaders knew that "Dilapidated animals are an emblem of dilapidated morale. The one sinks [to] the other's level" (1935,I:85). It is important to recognize that the condition of Reno's and Benteen's mounts on June 25 could well have contributed to motivation and actions that determined whether these officers could or would go to Custer's support, with the possibility, many allege, of saving him from annihilation—a subject that forms the very core and heart of the ongoing controversy surrounding the Battle of the Little Big Horn and its principal figures.

During the Custer Battle, a great number of mounts, of course, were killed. Some animals undoubtedly broke away from the horse holders (in a dismounted battle, one out of every four cavalrymen held the mounts of himself and three comrades, leaving the other three free to engage in combat), and were captured by the Indians. Some of these were recognized as they were ridden by the warriors attacking Reno's men on the bluffs, after the destruction of Custer's command. A few were identified in subsequent Indian battles, as mentioned previously, or seen later in Indian camps. It is also clear from studies of the battlefield immediately following the fight that some of the besieged cavalrymen had shot their mounts to form breastworks to shield them from the enemy onslaught. It was perhaps their final expression of desperation in knowing they would never ride out of this valley of the Little Big Horn.

The impact of the hopelessness and tragedy of Custer's Last Stand upon the shocked men who discovered its grisly evidence two days later had only one recorded moment of relief—the finding of Captain Keogh's horse, Comanche, alive upon a field of death.

Chapter 4

Keep Him to the End

If you have a horse with four white feet,
    Keep him not a day;
If you have a horse with three white feet,
    Send him far away;
If you have a horse with two white feet,
    Sell him to a friend;
If you have a horse with one white foot,
    Keep him to the end.
—Old horseman's adage (Walker 1953:24)

Although from the beginning special significance was ascribed to the discovery and recognition of the surviving Seventh Cavalry mount known as Comanche, uncertainty surrounds the facts concerning the actual event. Because of conflicting testimonies, it is not definitely known who was responsible for finding the horse, the location where he was found, or the number and severity of his wounds.

General Terry's command arrived at the Valley of the Little Big Horn on June 27, discovering only then the evidence of Custer's disastrous defeat. It was on that date (or possibly it was a day later) that Myles Keogh's mount was found and recognized. According to one of Comanche's earliest biographers, Barron Brown, "an old Sioux, still living, who took part in the battle and who was one of the last to leave the scene, told the writer that he saw a light bay horse standing in the river too badly wounded to be of any use, which was left there as the Indians moved away. This horse may well have been Comanche" (1935:56). Certainly, it would be natural for the wounded horse, suffering from heat and thirst, to make his way to the river.

E. S. Luce, former cavalryman and generally acknowledged

authority on Comanche's history, who had access to Seventh Cavalry records, stated unequivocally that "while the last rites were being performed on June 27, a lone horse was observed by First Lieutenant Henry J. Nowlan, Seventh Cavalry" (1939:64,77). Godfrey's account, dated 1908 but published in 1921 to coincide with the 45th anniversary of the battle, also stated it was Nowlan who "recognized 'Comanche' [and] took him in charge" (1921:37). In a book published in 1909, Joseph Mills Hanson likewise wrote that it was Nowlan who discovered and recognized the horse (1909:296). Logic dictates that Nowlan, as Keogh's close friend, would be the one to recognize Comanche and would be strongly motivated to save the wounded animal.

Even when others are credited with first finding Comanche, Nowlan is generally named as identifier of the horse and organizer of his rescue. Brown, for example, cites a letter to General Hugh L. Scott in which Godfrey mentions that a cavalryman named McClernand on June 27 at the site of the Indian village "saw some scouts assembled around a horse some distance from him, and as the horse was a good looking one he rode over intending to take him for his own use; but when he saw the condition of the horse he abandoned the idea. Captain Nowlan, who was with General Terry, was curious about this horse and rode over to him and recognized him as *Comanche* and took charge of him" (1935:53–54). As McClernand himself described the incident, "I sighted a large American horse grazing about 1/4 mile away in the valley, and as my horse was thin and weak I galloped over to the free animal intending to transfer my saddle to him, but found he had been wounded and was unserviceable. He was branded U.S. This was probably Comanche" (1969:59). Thus the difference between finding the horse and recognizing him as Keogh's mount is made clear in some accounts.

Though most sources credit Nowlan with both, as well as for initiating the animal's rescue, there are other claimants for the honor of discovery. According to an article published in *Winners of the West* in 1936, a Seventh Cavalry farrier of Troop I who later cared for Comanche, Gustave Korn, was a contender for the distinction. On May 21, 1888, while at Fort Meade, Dakota Territory, Korn wrote on the back of a large photograph of the famous horse an account in which he asserted that he had found the animal. As he described it on the "morning of June 26th," when "we went down into the ravine to look for Custer," there "standing alone on the battlefield, bleeding, dying from six bullet wounds in his side, was the horse COMANCHE." He explained that "One trooper by the name of Brown wanted to cut COMANCHE'S throat to end his misery but a trooper named Ramsey and myself remonstrated and got COMANCHE down to the river, bathed his wounds and finally got him in condition to get on the boat. He was then taken to Fort Lincoln, tenderly cared for, and finally recovered." His statement, he declares, is "the truest and most accurate ever published of the famous battle" (1936:1, 4–5). More will be said of Korn later, for he took care of Comanche following his rescue from the battlefield and was in close association with the famous mount for many years.

John C. Lockwood, at one time adjutant of the National Indian War Veterans, "volunteered an authentic history of [Comanche's] life" in 1923. In an account in the *Kansan*, Lockwood stated

> After the Custer massacre Comanche was the only living thing found among the dead. A private of M troop, James Severs, better known as "Crazy Jim," and myself found Comanche, too weak to walk, but with only flesh wounds. We took water in our hats and gave him a drink. He soon showed signs of regaining strength, and by constant care and nursing, he was gotten to the steamboat "Key [sic] West." (1923)

Lockwood's account, which stated again that he had been "one of the two men who found Comanche on the battlefield after the Custer massacre," was published in *Winners of the West* in January of 1934. Immediate reactions to this article from readers reveal the prominence of the horse in Custer Battle lore and the importance that had become attached to his history. For the journal's editor wrote in the very next issue of *Winners of the West* that "nothing we have published in a long time has stirred up so much comment as our article and picture of the horse, Comanche, the only survivor of the Custer fight." A letter from W. J. Ghent was included, not only denying that Lockwood was a finder of Comanche, but also identifying other errors in Lockwood's facts regarding the horse's origin and history which serve to discredit his claim (1934:1). In a 1938 letter to the museum curator at the University of Kansas, Luce, too, casts doubt upon Lockwood's statements about his military record and about his connection with Comanche (UK Archives). Amaral has pointed out that Lockwood did not enlist in the Seventh Cavalry until more than two months after the Custer Battle and that he was later accused by the Indian Veterans Association of "unsubstantiated pretensions" (1961: 33–34).

But that was not the end of Lockwood's claims. In 1966, his nephew published a book, *Custer Fell First: The Adventures of John*

C. Lockwood, written from "Uncle Jack's" story as dictated to the author in 1922. Lockwood's participation in the Battle of the Little Big Horn is described, and his finding of Comanche is repeated, this time with the addition of the detail that the horse was found "lying in a bunch of dead men and horses, unable to get up until he was lifted" by Severs and Lockwood (Ryan 1966:51–52, 109–16). In 1923, Lockwood wanted to have his picture taken standing beside Comanche. An official of The Kansas Authors' Club wrote to Kansas University Chancellor E. H. Lindley requesting that Lockwood, as the one of the two men who rescued Comanche who was still living, be photographed with the horse. Permission was promptly given by the chancellor, who promised to make the necessary arrangements (UK Archives). If such a photograph was made, however, it has not been located.

Confusion exists not only as to who found the horse, but where. There is "testimony that the horse was found, not on Custer Field but in the [Indian] village, and that the discoverer was Capt. Thomas McDougall, of Company B. In a letter to Godfrey, May 18, 1909, McDougall wrote: 'I took my troop B (on June 28) to the Indian Village to look for implements to use in burying the dead. Upon crossing the river I found Keogh's horse in the small bushes, and detailed one of the men to look after him until I reported the same to Reno, which I did immediately upon my return'" (Ghent 1934:1; Graham 1953:377). McDougall also indicated he found Comanche "on the Village side [of the river] opposite mouth of deep gully" (Hammer 1976:73). General Godfrey wrote to General Scott that Comanche "was found on the flat" at the Indian village (Brown 1935:53–54). From one of his interviews with survivors conducted in the early 1900s, Walter Camp noted, "Hammon said Horse Comanche lay on top of ridge where monument now stands. Keogh must have been shot off him down in hollow and the horse followed on after the rest." Camp also recorded that "Roy says Ramsey of I troop recovered Comanche from [the] village" (Field Notes Folder #18, Brigham Young University). In 1908, Dennis Lynch of Company F told Camp "Comanche stood on Custer Hill near where monument is with head drooped. Shot five times. He recognized his friends. When men came up and called him by name he nickered." A year later, Lynch changed his mind about the location, saying "Comanche was found down near mouth of deep gully a little way back from river. Dave Heaton, who was with Lieut. Bradley, says Comanche was the first signs of Custer fight they saw" (Hammer 1976:139–40). One early newspaper report indicated the surviving horse was "found about a day's journey from the scene of the battle" (Sullivan n.d.).

"To add a bit more to the history of 'Comanche,'" Nita Baldwin wrote in 1934 of her visit with Henry Brinkerhoff, "an old trooper" who "was with Reno that 26th of June '76": "He told me that he discovered Comanche in a patch of trees, pretty well done up. He reported the news to some officer of Reno's command who told him to 'shoot the horse if he was done for' for of course all badly wounded animals were thus handled. On his return from taking a note to Terry he came across the good charger again, but this time Comanche whinnied and came to him—his many wounds were none of them deep and he was rested and beloved of the 7th Cav. until he died years later" (1934:1).

As early as 1878, the Bismarck *Tribune* reported that Comanche had been "found by Sergeant Milton J. DeLacey of Company I in a ravine where he had crawled, there to die and feed the Crows." In 1890, Charles King wrote that Comanche "came straggling into the lines some days after the fight" (1890:386); however, an 1891 newspaper reported that "Captain Charles King, who was coming to the scene of the massacre, . . . met Comanche dragging his weary limbs over the trail on which he had traveled a few days before bearing his brave master" (He's Joined 1891). In a 1910 interview, Jacob Adams, who in 1876 had been a private in Company H, told Camp, "When we found Old Comanche he was sitting on his haunches, braced back on his forefeet. We lifted him up in his feeble condition" (Hammer 1976: 121–22). In Adams' personal account of the battle, first published in 1909, he recalled that Comanche had whinnied when approached by the men, and he referred to the wounded mount as "this splendid old horse, which was later to attract so much public attention" (Ellis 1909:232). The cavalryman's recollections were subsequently published as *A Story of the Custer Massacre* "Written by Jacob Adams, A Man Who Was There." He related

> I have read many articles about this horse Commanche on the way up to where General Custer and his men were killed. About a mile before we came to any dead men this horse was off to the left of us in a sitting position with his front quarters up. I rode over to him and said to them: Let's us help this fellow up and see if he can walk. We helped him up and he stood up alright and went to eating grass. We got on our horses and rode off and left him there. We went to camp that night at the same place General Terry was camped and sometime through the night Commanche came to camp. I read where some writers said the soldiers carried Commanche four or five miles before he was able to walk. Now if you believe what this writer said about the soldiers carrying Commanche just stand on your head. (1965:12)

The existence of multiple claimants for the honor of finding Comanche is easy to understand, considering the special significance that accrued to the surviving animal immediately after the battle and that escalated during the years of interest in and controversy about that event which followed. Private Theodore W. Goldin, who was assigned to the Little Big Horn burial detail, perhaps best described the circumstances of identification by more than one person when he wrote in a letter in 1921 that "many of us went over and recognized Comanche, the favorite mount of Major Keogh." He recalled that "as we were moving over the field with the burial party on the 28th, one of our men discovered something moving on the hillside some little distance from where we were working, and hurrying over soon returned with word that a horse, apparently severely wounded, but alive was over there. . . . The poor fellow was too weak to stand, and many of the men mounted, galloped to the river and returned with water carried in their hats which was given to the poor famished horse. Later, he was able to get to his feet and in time was brought into camp where his wounds were washed and the soreness relieved as much as possible" (UK Archives).

Although it can never be determined for certain who first found and identified Comanche, the important result was that the surviving horse became the object of so much interest and emotion that having discovered him was regarded as an honor and brought considerable distinction to those who claimed it. Perhaps there has never been another mount whose fame could confer such status upon those associated with him for even such brief moments in time.

Sometimes, as much is learned from those who do not comprehend a phenomenon as from those who do. Something about Comanche, for example, rankles Daniel O. Magnussen, editor of a battle participant's narrative. He comments "One of the worst fallacies to come out of the Battle of the Little Big Horn was the famous tale that Captain Keogh's horse, Comanche, was the only surviving thing found on the battlefield." Magnussen points out that there were other wounded horses discovered, and that "with the exception of Comanche, all were mercifully shot by the cavalrymen." Therefore, "with the Indians taking all useable mounts and the cavalrymen shooting the remainder, Comanche was hardly the only survivor." Rather petulantly, the editor complains, "Considerable argumentation even continued over who found the horse, as though this was a highly important point concerning the battle" (1974:275).

Magnussen's rejection of the dimension of human reaction

to finding Comanche is a classic example of denial of an emotional element that is not well understood or with which a person feels uncomfortable. Identifying the finder of the wounded war horse is not, of course, significant to battle chronology; however, the number of men who claimed the distinction and the interest the event has engendered throughout the years make it worthy of consideration. The Comanche phenomenon takes its fundamental meaning from the Custer Battle, an event which is fraught with psychological and sociocultural, as well as historical, significance. In fact, the human-reaction component is undoubtedly more influential than the purely historical in giving the event importance, since historians frequently point out that the battle was actually a relatively minor episode. The gigantic proportions which the battle has assumed (measured by popular interest) are claimed to be due primarily to the appeal to the human psyche. When history is interpreted by means of inclusion of broader psychological and anthropological perspectives—rather than just through the recounting of events according to the traditional approach—new dimensions of understanding are realized.

Although the importance attached to Comanche's personal rescuer means nothing to the battle strategist, it says something about life and people (to say nothing about its revelation of the uncertainties of historiography as well!). Comanche's power to confer honor speaks first to the deep significance of the horse himself, a being who had shared the horror and suffering of those killed, yet represented the living. The finder of the horse must have felt empathy for a living creature miraculously located among the dead and a genuine appreciation for the vital significance of a cavalryman's horse, viewed at the moment of discovery as the only living tie to many friends now lying among the corpses and the carnage. Animals, as will be discussed in the final chapter, can often have calming and healing effects upon people under certain circumstances, especially in stressful situations. An animal may act as a bridge between human consciousness and the unknown or the feared, linking reality with what is only conjectured. To be the first to come upon such a survivor, being perhaps for an indeterminate time the only holder of privileged knowledge about the survivor's existence, and then to share this extraordinary news with others who would surely react with strong feeling is not a minor consideration when placed within the context of the particular time and place. Who can deny the honor that, from the first sighting, was accorded to Comanche? What cavalryman of that day would not have wanted to share the honor of discovery or of reconstructive reflection of an event whose meaning only grew deeper with the passage of time?

Taking into account all that is known about the cavalry horses' experiences in the 1876 Little Big Horn expedition brings into focus the unusual impact and importance of Comanche's survival. That unscathed horses were taken by the victorious enemy and that some badly injured mounts found after the battle were mercifully killed by troopers to prevent further suffering does not detract from Comanche's unique status. The deep significance that the horse quickly assumed for his rescuers and the cavalrymen of the campaign, which grew to such great proportions over time and was transformed into "sole survivor" status, is understandable in the light of special circumstances.

Comanche's wounds were severe enough to make him a true comrade-in-arms of the many troopers who had died of similar wounds and of those who suffered from the same type of injuries. This commonality of experience made him different from the horses who had escaped without arrow or bullet wounds. Rendering him too weak to go any further from the scene of destruction than to the river for a drink, Comanche's wounds had inextricably bound him to the place of battle. Presumably he was too badly hurt to be of use to the enemy, yet not injured severely enough to warrant mercy killing by his own troopers. Thus, through the strange and unlikely circumstances that saved his life, the horse could become a link between the dead and the living, in a way no other being could. His endurance, his invincibility, became profound symbols for survival in the face of overwhelming odds. The story of Comanche, understandably, contained the raw material of legends which were immediately crystallized into the "sole survivor" concept and which have never ceased to hold fascination. It was as if he were an embodiment of the old horseman's adage which associates "one white foot" with the quality of stamina that enables a rider to "keep him to the end."

Chapter 5

Comanche's Rider

He was as handsome a young man as I ever saw. . . . He rode a horse like a Centaur. (Allen 1898:227)

Most of the celebrated horses in history have achieved hero status primarily through the fame of their owner-riders. Although mounts such as Alexander the Great's Bucephalus and General Robert E. Lee's Traveller possessed marvelous and admired qualities in their own right and contributed immeasurably to their masters' accomplishments, they would not be remembered as they are without the secure place accorded to their riders in history. Comanche is different in this regard, because the intense interest centered around his rider, Captain Myles W. Keogh, results mainly from his being the man who rode Comanche. A handsome and dashing military figure, Keogh would be noted, even without his mount, as one of the bravest and most honored officers who fought with Custer and would have achieved immortal fame in dying with his comrades at the Last Stand. But it cannot be denied that Keogh is known and recollected *primarily* as the proud rider of the remarkable cavalry horse who lived through the Custer Battle. As Evan Connell recently wrote in concluding his remarks about the officer, "Keogh is remembered these days not because of a musical contribution [Garryowen], not for his gallantry, not for his sex appeal, but because of his horse Comanche, reputed to be the only survivor of the Little Bighorn" (1984:294).

E. S. Luce, whose book undoubtedly has been the most influential of sources concerning the surviving horse, associated the three names in his title, *Keogh, Comanche and Custer*, giving them an aura of romantic heroism and glory (1939). Military reporter John F. Finerty in his 1890 account described Keogh as "a noble-hearted gentleman, the beau ideal of a cavalry commander, and the very soul of valor" (1970:212). Although this is the way he was generally portrayed in subsequent writings, there are exceptions. Certain authors who held a negative view of Custer have cast aspersions on Keogh as well. Frederic Van de Water, for example, who depicted Custer as a *Glory-Hunter*, claimed Keogh was "a devil-may-care Irishman with mustache and imperial and an unholy thirst which he could curb only by placing all his cash in the hands of Finnegan, his striker and actual guardian." He viewed the captain as a "swaggering, bibulous soldier of fortune," and noted that drinking liquor and gambling caused him to be "red-eyed and impoverished" as he "stumbled down the Far West's gangplank" a few days before the Battle of the Little Big Horn (1934:152, 297, 319). Some of this material about Keogh's character was taken from Elizabeth Custer's description of an "Irish Officer," though in her book the man referred to was not named (1890:150–51).

Fred Dustin, whose researches on the Little Big Horn led him to see both Custer and Keogh in an unfavorable light, revealed that nine or ten years after the battle he interviewed two former Seventh Cavalrymen who had served with Keogh in Company I. These informants described Keogh as "continually under the influence of liquor." They also stated that "when not under arms, he habitually carried a cane . . . and he was not at all hesitant in using it on the heads of enlisted men who incurred his displeasure." He was a "brutal" captain, they said, and his troop, "Wild I," "reflected the character of its commander" (1939:236).

Probably Custer and Keogh were together only infrequently between 1866 and 1876 (Hayes-McCoy 1965:51). Their relationship may have been somewhat strained by embarrassment, judging from Custer's 1871 letter to his wife in which reference was made to Keogh's asking him for certain favors, prompting Custer to say, "He must think I am made of money." Custer mentions Keogh's "suspicious nature"; yet, the rift does not seem to have been serious, for Custer reveals that "I bear not the slightest animosity toward him, tho I think he treated me unfairly. I do think him rather absurd, but would rather have him stationed near us than many others" (Merington 1950:236).

No doubt Custer knew of Keogh's fine reputation as a fighting man and was willing to tolerate small faults in an officer he could depend upon in battle. At any rate, Keogh's image as a superb soldier has triumphed, and the captain is generally regarded as a hero, often drawing admiration from Little Big Horn scholars that is second only to Custer for valor and skill as a cavalryman.

Setting the tone for what follows in his study of the dashing soldier's active and romantic life, Luce's initial words about Keogh describe him as the "kindly master and rider" of Comanche, a horse that "was indeed fortunate in having such an owner as this gallant Irishman." The life of this man, according to Luce, "was as interesting as it was exciting," and "reads almost like that of a fictional character" (1939:11–12).

It is fascinating to find that etymological analysis reveals that the family name of Keogh foreshadows the destiny of the man who would achieve fame because of his horse. According to the *Sketch of the Family History of the Keoghs or Kehoes*, the name of Keogh is derived from the word for "a steed, and signifies a bold horseman or knight" (Sketch n.d.:1). Myles Walter Keogh who, according to his baptismal record, was officially named "Myles T[h]omas," was born at Orchard, Leighlinbridge, County Carlow, Ireland, on March 25, 1840. It is now known from genealogical studies that Myles was one of twelve children born to John and Margaret Blanchfield Keogh (personal communication: Gary Keogh). Orchard, the spacious family estate where he was born and spent his early years, has not changed much since those times. On a recent visit to this lovely, tranquil country manor, it was easy to picture Myles and his brothers and sisters growing up surrounded by a sparsely populated, pastoral landscape of infinite brilliant green grasslands. The terrain of the area provides perfect pasture for horses, which the family must have possessed in abundance. One can imagine a spirited young boy finding close companionship with his mounts and speculate that riding them was the main diversion providing an outlet for the dynamic energy he was known to possess. The present owner and resident, Myles Keogh, who still farms on the estate, is a great-grandnephew of Comanche's rider.

Orchard seems an idyllic place to grow up. It provides the kind of environment, devoid of distractions, that tends to foster introspective thinking in certain individuals. Myles, as revealed by his letters, was an intelligent and sensitive person, and it is likely that he learned early in childhood to look inward and consider himself in relation to the wider world beyond Carlow. As an ambitious youth, he must have felt the need for more stimulation than was provided by his isolated and provincial setting. If in such a situation a boy did not wish to become a farmer, it was natural to feel the lure of the excitement and adventure of soldiering in faraway places.

Myles was restless or at least eager to be independent, despite his pleasant environment, and he left home when he was twenty. He went to Italy and served with distinction, first in the Pope's army and then in the Papal Guards and Zouaves from 1860 to 1862. According to his biographer, Myles brought with him from Italy "a medal and Cross, a photograph, and a taste for soldiering that was to remain with him to the end of his life" (Hayes-McCoy 1965:6). The medal and cross were rewards from his papal service. These were replaced after the originals were lost in a fire, and Keogh "kept them carefully for the remainder of his life" (Hayes-McCoy 1965:6). The photograph, taken in Rome, shows Keogh proudly wearing these awards on his papal Zouave uniform. It was this photograph that was reportedly taken from his pocket by an Indian following the Custer fight and recovered from a Sioux about a year later by his friend, Captain Nowlan (Hayes-McCoy 1965:6,47n15; Luce 1939:opp.16, 63). A prevalent belief is that Keogh wore the papal medal during the battle and that the Indians refrained from mutilating his body because of respect for this charm (Luce 1939:62–63; Miller 1957:173). According to Hayes-McCoy, however, "It seems more likely that the object which Keogh wore around his neck was a scapular" (1965:47–48).

Service in the Papal War must have developed Keogh's fighting skills and his self-image as a soldier. In 1862, he came to the United States to fight for the Union as a cavalryman in the Civil War. Early in his American military career he was one of three men praised by his superiors for "the prompt, efficient, and officer-like manner in which they discharged their duties assigned them" (Luce 1939:19), and was referred to as "the gallant Myles Keogh" (Johnson and Buel 1956,2:313). Soon afterwards, General G. B. McClellan said that Keogh's record "had been remarkable for the short time he had been in the army. He appeared to me a most gentlemanlike man, of soldierly appearance, and I was exceedingly glad to have him as an aide" (Hayes-McCoy 1965:13). A few months later Brigadier-General Buford wrote of Keogh and another aide that "their duties had been 'very arduous' and that they had 'proven themselves to be dashing, gallant and daring soldiers, ready and anxious for service at all hours and under trying circumstances' " (Hayes-McCoy 1965:15).

The son of General James Shields, for whom Keogh served as aide-de-camp in the campaign against Stonewall Jackson around Winchester, Virginia, in 1862, later recalled that "my father thought him the finest and best natural soldier and officer he had ever met." Fifty-four years after the Custer Battle "the veil of years was pierced by Dr. Daniel F. Shields," who saw the Comanche display in the Kansas natural history museum and recognized

the name of Myles Keogh, the horse's rider, as the gallant cavalryman praised by his father. Following his visit, Shields presented to
the museum a photograph of Keogh that had been inscribed to
his father. Until that time, "the historic horse had stood alone in a
glass case in the Dyche Museum at the University of Kansas with
only a small card in a corner to announce the name of his rider.
But now Capt. Myles W. Keogh is known to have been a brave,
romantic personality, and his picture occupies a place in the case
with his horse." Thus Comanche's rider "emerged out of the
misty past to become something more than a name." The General's son explained, "I am glad to give Comanche back his rider,
because Capt. Keogh was a brave man and a fine soldier" (UK Archives; The Owner of Comanche 1930).

Keogh and Custer may have met during 1862, since both
cavalrymen fought in battles at Aldie and Gettysburg. Keogh received praise from Brigadier-General John Buford for his actions
and was later brevetted Major for "gallant and meritorious services at the battle of Gettysburg" (Hayes-McCoy 1965:18). In
1864, Keogh was commended by Major-General George Stoneman for "his long and varied experience, his well-known coolness,
gallantry and dash, his strict integrity, his devotion to his profession . . . his universal popularity with all officers and men [and] his
soldierly bearing." A member of General Sheridan's staff wrote
to Myles' brother in 1864 that "everyone admired his reckless
bravery in rallying the men." Praising Keogh to General Grant,
Major General Abram C. Gilleum indicated that "he is unsur-
passed in dash, has admirable judgement—is peculiarly fitted for
a cavalry officer—is highly educated and accomplished." Some
who observed him during the war described him as a "born soldier," and in 1866, Stoneman called Keogh "as brave a soldier
and as patriotic an officer as has drawn a sabre during the past
war of the rebellion." He was brevetted Lieutenant-Colonel of
Volunteers for uniform gallantry and good conduct during the
war (Hayes-McCoy 1965:18, 26–27; letters in Keogh family
collection).

A fellow cavalryman in the Civil War wrote that when
Keogh, "as handsome a young man as I ever saw," first joined his
division as aide-de-camp to General Stoneman, "We did not care
much for Captain Keogh, and particularly did not like his style."
The men, he remembered, poked fun at the Irishman and gave
him the "cold shoulder." But Keogh's boldness created a success
story. When, with remarkable courage and decisiveness, he led a
victorious charge against the enemy, "Keogh ever afterwards was
a most welcome guest at every campfire, and every canteen in

the regiment was freely proffered to him." Years later, when they learned of the disaster at the Little Big Horn, his former comrades-in-arms "sincerely mourned" his death (Allen 1898: 227–28).

Keogh's strong desire to remain in the military following the close of the Civil War was fulfilled when he was commissioned 2nd Lieutenant in the 4th regular Cavalry on May 4, 1866. When on July 28, 1866, the first commissions for the newly organized Seventh Cavalry were issued, Myles Keogh was designated Captain. He was "overjoyed" with his appointment. At 26, he was the 4th senior captain in his regiment, which was "almost unprecedented in the regular army with probably the exception of General Custer and one or two others." Keogh joined the regiment on November 16 and was assigned to the command of Troop I, which was stationed at Fort Wallace, Kansas. There he spent his first year on the plains, and he "took to the rough frontier life from the start" (Hayes-McCoy 1965:28, 29, 30).

Keogh may have been responsible for introducing to the regiment the tune "Garryowen" that became the Seventh's official marching song (Luce 1939:123). Although his role in the adoption of this rollicking Irish quickstep (whose rhythm sounds to me like hoofbeats) cannot be proven, Keogh did take an interest in music. In an 1870 letter to his brother from Fort Leavenworth he wrote about a song he had brought to the post. The band played it "at Mrs. Custer's and everyone was enchanted with it and the ladies besieged me for a copy for their pianos. It is [a] splendid tune" (author's collection).

An 1867 letter written from Fort Wallace revealed the pleasure Keogh felt in his newly found friendship with fellow Irishman and Catholic, Lieutenant Henry J. Nowlan, who was six years older than himself and had fought in the Crimea before joining the Seventh Cavalry in 1866. Describing Nowlan as "quite handsome and exceedingly passionate," Keogh wrote his brother, "He will come to Ireland with me next year" (National Library of Ireland; hereafter designated NLI). Their comradeship lasted until Myles' death. If Keogh had earlier been the victim of depression, as Francis Taunton has suggested (1967:70), he had overcome it, at least temporarily, by March of 1870, for he wrote Tom, "[I] have not felt so well for years both in spirit and health and every way. . . . I feel like a new man." He indicates his continuing relationship with his friend: "I am living with Nowlan and I find he is engaged to be married . . . to a sweet girl," adding, "He seems to like being in love." The importance of Keogh's association with horses is evident when he mentions "I provide him [Nowlan] all the time with a ladies riding mount out of my Troop." In the same letter there is another tie with the future involving Comanche. Keogh writes: "Mrs. Sturgis the wife of the Colonel of my Regiment is perfectly charming & I find myself going there every day" (author's collection). Thus Keogh was well-acquainted with Colonel Sturgis, the officer who would later write the famous orders establishing the honored status of Keogh's surviving mount following the tragedy of the Little Big Horn (see Chapter 6).

Keogh's attitude toward Indians is indicated in his letters. They were "nobler game" than the black-tailed deer and the antelope that he delighted in hunting. Writing in 1867, he told his brother about shooting ducks with Nowlan, but mentioned, "We have to take an escort with us when we go more than a mile from the post as the Indians are on the lookout for stray scalps" (NLI). In the same year, he "promised his brother to be cautious in his dealings with the Indians, not because he feared death at their hands, but because he owed 'the rascals' a grudge and was determined to 'have some of their hair' before they got his" (Hayes-McCoy 1965:30–31). In an 1869 letter from "Camp near Fort Hays," Keogh reported, "We have knocked the Indians with a cocked hat. But they are still on the war path. We have about ninety squaws spared from our last fight—some of them are very pretty—I have one that is quite intelligent—It is usual for officers to have two or three lounging around" (NLI).

Evidently Keogh was quite anxious to begin fighting Indians because in March of 1868 he hoped that General Sheridan, Commander of the Military Division of the Missouri, would "rush things" (Hayes-McCoy 1965:34). In August of the same year, from Fort Harker, he wrote Tom, "I am sorry to say that the Indians have again broken out. They yesterday attacked a settlement within forty miles of here & having plundered the place brutally ravaged the women & got away. We are preparing for an Indian War during the ensuing fall" (NLI). Action came soon, for in September 1868, as previously described, Keogh took part in General Sully's campaign against the hostile Arapahoes, Cheyennes, and Kiowas in the Cimarron and Canadian River districts, south of Fort Wallace. He was mounted on Comanche, the horse he had bought during the summer (Luce 1939:11, 27, 86). As far as they are known, Keogh's and Comanche's movements during the next eight years, culminating in the Little Big Horn, have been traced in Chapter 3.

There is some evidence for the idea that Keogh may have had the traditional Irishman's "eye for a horse," and that he had a special interest in horses and probably formed a close relationship with certain of his mounts, which supports his legendary regard for Comanche. In an 1864 letter to his sister Ellen, from Atlanta, he wrote

> Our expedition was very successful until our return when we met a very superior force and after a sharp engagement had to surrender about a 3rd of our force the remainder getting away. I of course remained with the General, he had his horse shot and I lost my old charger that had carried me through so many charges since the battle of Port Republic when Keily was wounded. I felt his loss severely. I wish you could have seen the poor fellow how he could leap and on the 4th of July he saved my life, whilst riding on a bye road carrying an order. I suddenly rode into a heavy outlying thicket of the enemy. "Tom" saw them as they rose up to deliver their fire and I jumped sideways over a rail fence into the wood skirting the road. He carried me safely out of range. I shall never have a horse like him again. (NLI)

It is tempting to think that he did feel later that he obtained such a horse when he acquired Comanche.

Writing to his brother in October 1867, Keogh was concerned enough about his mounts to mention "my horses are in excellent condition. I have had some hay cutting machines sent me & I mix the oats & hay—it is very fattening. We had eight-hundred tons of hay put up this fall" (NLI). Again, in a letter written the same year, Keogh informed his brother "I bought a fine horse last week out of my Troop—for fifty dollars. He is very fast & I expect to make a large addition to my travelling expenses by his sale by and by." In March 1868, he mentioned sending a photograph of his horse, as "it will give you an idea what Mark looks like now." In an 1869 letter from Fort Hays, he related, "we have now been in camp here some time & although worked pretty hard drilling and training young horses, we are on the whole pretty comfortable." In the same letter, Keogh wrote the prophetic words, "We shall have a stirring summer up & away after Indians, the most worrying service in the world" (NLI).

Years later, while en route to the Little Big Horn, Keogh evidently had the same premonition of disaster that was experienced by other Seventh Cavalrymen. Before marching with his regiment on June 22, 1876, he gave his will in a sealed envelope to Lieutenant Nowlan, with instructions to send it to his sister if he were to die (Hayes-McCoy 1965:42). In his will, Keogh stated that he had already disposed of his property in Ireland. He indicated that he had a life insurance policy "in the N. Y. Life Co. amounting to $10,000," and specified that $1,000 of that money would go to Nowlan "for his own use." The remainder, after his debts were paid, was to be sent to his sister, Margaret. Nowlan was designated to send Keogh's personal effects to her, except for a leather valise that was bequeathed to another individual. Keogh also stated, "I desire my papers to be burned except as Lt. Nowlan may select to send to my sister" (Keogh family records). It is tantalizing to think what information about Keogh, or possibly Comanche, may have been destroyed by the loyal Nowlan in following his friend's final instruction.

The last thing definitely known about Keogh is that he and Lieutenant W. W. Cooke, the adjutant, rode forward with Reno's battalion as far as the river and remained there while Reno watered his horses, crossed, and began to form on the other side. Then, they rode back to meet their deaths with Custer (Graham 1926:35, 126). Keogh's remains were found on June 27 by Lieutenant Bradley of Gibbon's force on the ridge stretching southeastward from the part of the battlefield where the Last Stand was made. The body had been stripped of its buckskin suit but not mutilated. Brown points out that "since [Keogh's] horse's wounds were mostly on one side, it is possible that the officer fired from the side of the animal in a standing position" as the battle drew to a close (1935:48). Keogh's left leg and knee had been shattered by a gunshot wound. From the location of a wound on Comanche's side, it is surmised that the same bullet which caused Keogh's injury passed through his leg into the horse. Two days after the battle, the Captain's body, like those of his comrades, was hastily buried where it fell and a marker placed over it. Exhumed in 1877, his remains were reinterred with full military honors in the Throop Martin lot, Fort Hill Cemetery, Auburn, New York, in October of that year. A magnificent monument bears Keogh's monogram and depicts cavalry accoutrements hanging on a hook as though their owner sleeps (see fig. 9). A verse from a poem is inscribed, and the details of his military career appear on the back. In Montana, Fort Keogh was named in his honor.

Traces of the gallant cavalryman can also be found in his native country. I recently traveled to the chapel of St. Joseph at Tinryland in County Carlow to see a stained glass window of the Holy Family, a memorial to "Thomas Keogh of Park, his wife Alice Keogh, and his brother, Brevet Lieutenant Colonel Myles W. Keogh, Capt. 7th U. S. Cavalry, killed in action, June 25, 1876." The church is not far from the country estate known as Park House, once the home of Myles's brother, Thomas. Another site associated with Myles and his family is Clifden, an imposing home and farm located on the border of Kilkenny and Carlow in Rathgarvin township, still owned and inhabited by Keogh descendants.

It is this estate which, according to the records, was owned by Miss Mary Blanchfield and, upon her death in 1874, was inherited by Myles W. Keogh (Sketch n.d.:13).

Myles' Irish relatives believe that he planned to come back to Ireland after the battle and settle at Clifden, the homestead he had inherited (though his will indicates he no longer owned it). They say that he sent some of his effects there in anticipation of his return. Perhaps with all his adventures behind him, he could have found contentment living on this grand estate whose location, at least today, seems somewhat less isolated than Orchard. Looking at the green countryside of Clifden, with its lush pastures, I could not help musing about what might have been. Aloud I said "I wonder if Myles, assuming he was attached to his mount, would have ever found a way to bring Comanche here." But the question was no sooner verbalized than it echoed emptily, like the proverbial fall of a tree in the forest where there is no ear to hear the sound. The difficulty of horse transportation, of course, was not the issue. Rather, if Keogh had lived, neither he nor his horse would be famous, and no one from across the sea or anywhere else would be asking about his life or visiting this Irish manor house!

Because of his fate and his surviving horse, however, people in his native country, as well as elsewhere, do know about him and his fame as an American cavalryman. From time to time, Irish newspapers include an article about him. In the little towns where there is a trace of him, however dim, residents smile good-naturedly and give information to the best of their ability. One woman who helped me with directions remembered, "Oh, yes, he fought in the 'Battle of Little Rock,' " and seemed proud of his association with her locale.

Myles Keogh was issued United States citizenship papers on August 25, 1869, when he was described as having blue eyes, brown hair, a small chin, and standing six feet one-quarter inches tall. American citizenship, of course, did not necessarily mean he would not return to Ireland, and, in any case, the status was established five years before he inherited his estate. His interest in American land was evident in an 1867 letter when he wrote, "I have made a claim of 160 acres of good land here & if the Railroad comes out it may turn out something good. Army officers are entitled to this amount of land in every state and territory where there is land unclaimed. I have only to place a stake of wood on one corner of it with my name on it." His plan, however, was not to settle but to realize a profit, for he admitted "This is my first land speculation but I do not think it will make me any money!" (NLI).

For a large majority of those who have studied and written about the Battle of the Little Big Horn, Keogh has emerged a hero. Custer Battle scholars Edward Luce and Charles Kuhlman both believed that Keogh was the man referred to in 1881 by Red Horse (who was an Indian battle participant) as a soldier of extraordinary valor (Luce 1939:49–63; Kuhlman 1951:203-204, 240). As Red Horse described him, "The Sioux have for a long time fought many brave men of different people, but the Sioux say this officer was the bravest man they ever fought." Warriors observed that "this officer saved the lives of many soldiers by turning his horse and covering the retreat." The man in question wore a "large-brimmed hat and deerskin coat," and was reportedly "killed by a Santee Indian, who took his horse." Red Horse, however, indicated that this man was "an officer who rode a horse with four white feet" (Mallery 1893:564–65). It is difficult to say with any degree of certainty that this soldier was in fact Keogh, though belief in the possibility persists.

In his 1876 biography of Custer, Frederick Whittaker describes the Captain by virtue of military experience as "an older soldier than any there" and writes of Keogh's men rising to the "pitch of sublime heroism" (1876:597–98). David H. Miller, the author who gathered extensive first-hand testimonies from the Indians concerning the Battle of the Little Big Horn, believes that Keogh may have been the last man of Custer's detachment to be killed (1957:154). Miller, like many of the present-day Crow Indians whose ancestors served as scouts with Custer, holds that Custer was killed early in the battle at the ford leading to the village and was carried by his men to the site of the Last Stand. If this were true, then Keogh would probably have taken command.

Members of the family in Ireland were grief-stricken at the news of their relative's tragic death with Custer and took pride in his fine record as a soldier. Tom Keogh, who had been his brother's correspondent and confidant during his absence from home, kept in touch with Myles' former comrades and friends in America. In 1879, he wrote to Captain Nowlan, "I got the Army and Navy Journal, things look black for Reno. I would rather be one of those who fell in that unfortunate and disastrous affair than Reno. I always thought he acted shamefully" (author's collection). Myles Keogh is never far removed from the aura of chivalry when remembered in his own times or in ours. Even his handwriting, analyzed by an expert in 1966, is said to reveal "a brave, courageous nature," with "independence in decision," and "great depth of emotion." He was "of noble stature and greatly loved" (Friswold 1968:12).

In July 1986, the annual Little Big Horn Associates Convention was held in Auburn, New York, in order to especially honor Captain Keogh. A memorial service was held in the Fort Hill Cemetery Chapel, with eulogies to Keogh, as well as to General Emory Upton and General Andrew J. Alexander, who are also buried there. A procession marched to the Keogh burial site, where a service was held in which a wreath made from sagebrush from the Custer Battlefield was placed on the grave. A color guard, a firing squad, and members of reactivated 19th-century military units participated. Many guests were dressed in 1876 cavalry outfits with appropriate accoutrements. Volleys were fired "Over the Honored Graves," and taps was played. Featured throughout the entire proceedings was "Bobby," a bay "riderless horse" chosen to represent Comanche. He was fitted out as a military horse draped in traditional mourning, with the cavalry officer's boots facing backwards, as the real Comanche often appeared on ceremonial occasions of the Seventh Cavalry following Sturgis' famous orders (see fig. 20).

Of all those involved in the Battle of the Little Big Horn, the romantic figure of Myles Keogh today still captures the imagination to a degree exceeded only by Custer himself. The fact that "there seem to have been more relics of Captain Keogh recovered than of any other officer who fell with Custer" (Hanson 1909:379) is because of his special appeal and the unusual amount of interest he has inspired. As previously mentioned, in 1876, at Slim Buttes, Keogh's gauntlets were recovered from the Indians along with the guidon belonging to his Troop I which had been taken at the Little Big Horn. In 1877, "on the field Sergeant Caddle picked up a shoe which he recognized as having belonged to Captain Keogh" (Hanson 1909:379). But of all the "relics" ever found upon a battlefield later to become a cherished symbol of all that was lost in a tragic military engagement, the most unique must be Keogh's horse, Comanche. For the cavalry mount who survived Custer's Last Stand would miraculously live out not only his own natural lifetime, but he would ultimately exist long into the future, to take on undreamed of new images and fresh meanings as the history of the young nation evolved.

Chapter 6

The Second Commanding Officer

> There is many a war horse who is more entitled to immortality than the man who rides him.
> —Robert E. Lee (Peterson and Smith 1961:160)

From the hour when the dead of Custer's command were first discovered and it was realized that no man lived to describe the details of his disastrous defeat and from the moment when Comanche was found alive, legend and history regarding the horse and his rider have been inextricably mingled. Since no known whites survived the Custer Battle, information about Keogh's actions, as well as those of the other cavalrymen, must rest upon conjecture. It is possible, as some have suggested, that Captain Keogh could have abandoned Comanche when the horse was badly injured and obtained another mount. But there is reason to believe that when Keogh received his mortal wound, he was still riding Comanche. Those who arrived at the scene following the battle observed that "Keogh's left leg and knee were badly shattered by a gunshot wound, and Comanche had suffered a severe bone-hit, the bullet entering the right shoulder and emerging from the left—exactly where Keogh's knee would have been. This would indicate that Keogh rode Comanche to the last, and both went down together" (Luce 1939:59–60).

There is disagreement about how Comanche appeared when he was found. A 1921 newspaper article indicated that the saddle and bridle were still on the horse at the time of his discovery, for "the saddle and bridle which form 'Old Comanche's' trappings [in the museum] are those that he wore when he was ridden into the Custer massacre by Captain Keogh" (Old Comanche 1921). In response to that statement, Theodore W. Goldin, who claimed he was present when Comanche was found, wrote to the curator of the museum to say that "the article is in error stating that Comanche was saddled and bridled. Every saddle and bridle was taken by the Indians when they left the field" (UK Archives). Although Brown also states that victorious Indians had stripped Comanche of his bridle and saddle (1935:50), the generally accepted description of the horse when discovered indicates that the headstall of his bridle was still in place. Major Peter Wey, one of Comanche's caretakers in the final year of the horse's life, wrote to Luce that "he was found with one of the cheek straps of the bridle broken which permitted him to slip the bit out of his mouth but the throat latch kept the bridle on him. The saddle had turned under his belly but the blanket and pad were missing" (Luce 1939:65). These details appear throughout Comanche literature and in numerous artistic depictions of the wounded survivor. Luce acknowledged his debt to Wey's recollections of the horse when he wrote to Nye in 1939 that without Major Wey, who had looked after Comanche, his "book would have been a fizzle" (CBNM Files). In 1926, Major Wey gave a slightly different version: "Comanche was found grazing some distance from the battlefield without a bridle." Wey attributed the turning of the saddle to the horse's rolling, and also noted, "He had several gunshot wounds, around which the blood had spread and dried, presenting a rather deplorable sight" (Comanche 1926:433).

As Canetti has pointed out, the quality of invulnerability is important in the making of a hero (1973:229). Comanche is no exception to this, and many related factors have been proposed as responsible for the horse's miraculous escape from death. Both nature and nurture, of course, have been called to account for his unlikely survival—nature as his own genetic strength and fitness, nurture in the sense of the way he had been trained by Keogh. It is logical that his bond to his rider would be credited for making him invulnerable to death and cited as a reason for his escape. The Indians felt that it was Keogh's medals, acting as "powerful charms," that made the Captain, whom the Indian participants told Miller was the "last man killed on Battle Ridge" (1957:173), invulnerable to final mutilation by the enemy. One account of Irish soldiers who fought in foreign countries reveals little about Keogh except an undocumented anecdote concerning his papal award: "When Chief Sitting Bull died, the *Pro petri sede* medal was found on his body. The Sioux chief had taken it from around the neck of the fallen Keogh after the battle of the Little Big Horn and had worn it as a tribute to the paleface warrior" (Hennessy 1973:140).

Accounts of Comanche's rescue generally mention that the first thought of the men was to end the suffering mount's life humanely. Yet something held them back, either the qualities of the horse himself—that he "clung to life tenaciously with his ever-present stoicism" (Luce 1939:65)—or the urging of a comrade-in-arms that the animal be preserved in recognition that he was Captain Keogh's mount. Also, motivating them must have been deeper insights into the meaning assumed by a survivor amidst the horrors of a desolate battlefield strewn with mutilated human corpses and bloated bodies of the obedient horses who had followed the will of their riders when going into battle, only to be put into service as final but useless bulwarks to protect dismounted cavalrymen from the fatal Indian onslaught.

There is disparity between sources as to the number and extent of Comanche's wounds. They are variously numbered at two, three, four, six, seven (the most popular number), ten, twelve, or twenty, and there is no agreement as to whether they were caused by arrows or bullets. Since details describing bullet wounds and protruding arrows from different Indian tribes do not rely on any known first-hand records, such accounts must be viewed as speculative. The official "descriptive list of Comanche," compiled at Fort Meade and dated 1887, simply documents "12 scars caused by wounds" (Luce 1939:85–86), but some of these, of course, resulted from injuries sustained prior to the Little Big Horn.

One newspaper reported that after his discovery, the soldiers managed to get Comanche to his feet and administer first aid to stop the profuse bleeding. Only then were they able to get the suffering animal a few miles away to the steamboat, "where his wounds were carefully dressed, after which he was taken down the river" (Progress of Fort Riley 1890). Virtually all accounts indicate that Comanche was severely wounded and weak when discovered. Some people report that the horse was immediately given water. Theodore Goldin, who said he was present at the time, wrote in a 1921 letter that in addition to the water the men brought to the horse in their hats, "Dr. Paulding of Terry's medical staff sacrificed the larger part of a bottle of Hennessy brandy in concocting a mash for the wounded horse" (UK Archives). Goldin noted that in 1877 Paulding told him that he (Doctor Paulding) "personally emptied brandy into the hats of some of the men from the emergency canteen that he carried, and that this with water was given to the horse, Comanche" (Carroll 1974:45). A few sources indicate that Comanche's wounds were immediately washed and treated to the extent possible under the circumstances.

In discussing the phenomenon of Comanche's survival, people invariably express interest in knowing what medical care the horse might have received. Since no specific records of that treatment exist, it is necessary to resort to "educated guesses." During a recent conversation with a fellow veterinarian who had practiced equine medicine for the preceding fifty years and was familiar with the treatments of the era just before his own, he indicated that bichloride of mercury solution or carbolic acid were the favored medicines for treating wounds. Veterinary medical texts which reflect the treatments administered in Comanche's times indicate that once any embedded arrowheads were surgically removed, the wounds were often washed with a carbolic acid solution (whiskey and water in equal parts were an acceptable substitute). This was followed by the application of a poultice, perhaps made of flaxseed (Dadd 1854:367; Miller and Tellor 1885:225). The army reports of human arrow wound treatment from 1865 to 1871 shed little light on any details applicable to horse medicine beyond describing surgical excision, the use of rest, nursing care, "simple dressings," "cold applications," "nitrate of silver locally," drainage of exudate, and "saline cathartics" (Billings 1974: 143–63). Bullets were generally removed from gunshot wounds only if they were superficially lodged. In the case of either type wound, the horse's flesh would not be sutured to risk sealing in an infection but was left open in order to allow drainage. If "wound fever" did develop, the horse would have been dosed internally with a mixture of sulfur and sassafras or something similar which the farrier or veterinarian had found from experience to be helpful (Dadd 1854:367–68).

It is difficult to know how much first-aid treatment Comanche received when initially taken into custody or what administrations followed during the trip to Fort Lincoln and after his arrival there. Dennis Lynch, who was on board the *Far West*, years later told Walter Camp that after Comanche was found, he "dressed his wounds the first time by orders of Nolan. Dressed with zinc wash on 28th. That night started for boat. Comanche limped down to boat with the men carrying wounded men." A subsequent interview indicated that "Lynch dressed Comanche's wounds first down at steamer. Lynch demonstrated that wound in breast and on side were made by same bullet by blowing in one with quill and discharge came out of wound in side" (Hammer 1976:39–40).

Following discovery of Comanche and the making of the decision to preserve his life, history records that the horse was led the fifteen or sixteen miles to board the steamer *Far West*. This vessel, which was then anchored at the confluence of the Little Horn and Big Horn rivers, is generally believed to have carried Comanche along with the wounded men from Reno's and Benteen's command to Bismarck, Dakota Territory, in the record-breaking time of fifty-four hours (Hanson 1909:306; Luce 1939:66). According to his biographer, Grant Marsh, Captain of the *Far West*, turned away from his grief over the death of a special friend who was a scout with Custer and from the calling of "a hundred duties" associated with the transportation of wounded soldiers, "to look after the accommodation of another passenger brought down with the wounded, whose housing, in the now crowded condition of the boat, was no easy problem. The passenger in question was a horse, but with such tender interest and affection was he already regarded by every man on board that they would almost rather have been left behind themselves than to have had him deserted. He had been the sole living thing found on the Custer field, two days after the battle." It is recorded that "Captain Marsh at length found a place for Comanche at the extreme stern of the *Far West*, between the rudders. Here a stall softly bedded with grass was made for him and his care and welfare became the special duty of the whole boat's company" (Hanson 1909:295–96).

It seems remarkable that such great importance was placed upon a lone cavalry horse in the face of so much individual and collective grief and shock following the men's personal losses of comrades, at the realization of the national disaster which had occurred, and in the presence of so many wounded soldiers to be tended. If Hanson's account can be relied upon for accuracy, overwhelming interest in and concern for Comanche existed right from the moment of his rescue. It is possible, however, that the events described above were later recollections formed in the retrospective light of more tranquil times after Comanche's unique significance had brought him remarkable fame.

Regarding Comanche's medical treatment, Marsh's narrative records that "a civilian contract veterinary surgeon" came "with the main column, which arrived at the river bank not long after the wounded." This veterinarian was described by the captain as "the worst scared man I ever saw." Purportedly, "the terror of the Indians had entered his soul, but the captain induced him by forcible persuasion to control his fears sufficiently to extract the bullets and arrow-heads from Comanche's body and to dress his wounds thoroughly" (Hanson 1909:296–97). The ludicrous and denigrating picture of the veterinarian which emerges may be taken as typical of Marsh's times—a persistent image of

the befuddled and unstable "horse doctor." This depiction undoubtedly represents a sociological view of the veterinarian in mi-
crocosm that was more than a little influenced by the jaundiced
views held by contemporary physicians. This concept becomes
clearer by contrast when in the same narrative the Seventh Cavalry physician, Dr. Porter, is described as having "worked over
the wounded and dying with unremitting heroism and total disregard of his own safety. After Terry's relief had come he still continued his devoted services, which did not cease even after his
charges were safely on the boat" (Hanson 1909:294). The scenario of the frightened veterinarian is strongly suggestive of an
old T.V. western, and undoubtedly reflects a corresponding mentality.

Once more relying upon Luce's account, which is generally
accepted, following Comanche's journey to Bismarck via steamer
"the badly wounded animal was tenderly conveyed by wagon to
Fort Lincoln, the same garrison which he had left only eight
weeks before" (1939:66). A slightly different version maintains
that after the burial of the dead "Comanche was taken with the
wounded soldiers to Bismarck by boat. There he was placed in a
livery stable where he remained until fall when he rejoined the
Seventh Cavalry at Fort Lincoln" (Pride 1926:206). John Gray recently found evidence indicating that the famous horse was not in
fact a passenger on the *Far West* with the wounded men. Instead,
he spent a month recuperating at the mouth of the Little Big
Horn River and then moved with the Seventh Cavalry to the
mouth of the Rosebud at the end of July. It was here, as Gray re-
constructs the story, that Comanche was first cared for by veterinarian A. C. Stein, who would have treated the horse for only two
days because he left the area on August 2. Comanche then sailed
as recorded in the Chicago *Times* of August 8, 1876, on the next
boat, the *E. H. Durfee*, which left the Rosebud depot on August 5,
and reached Bismarck on August 10 (1977:261–62). (This new
facet of Comanche's history has been adopted by at least one historian, whose 1966 account of the Little Big Horn campaign has
Comanche on the *Far West*, but whose 1980 revised version
changed the conveyance to the *Durfee* [Hammer 1966:6;
1980:14].)

Regarding veterinary care, Gray, in rather sarcastic terms,
discredits Marsh's story of the "hysterical dutchman" working
"his healing magic on the exsanguinated Comanche," by pointing
out that the Seventh Cavalry veterinarian, Dr. Stein, was not present on the *Far West* that night, having not yet left the Powder
River depot, and logically noting that when the treatment was

said to have been carried out, "Comanche had just made a night march of 15 miles over rough terrain." The pejorative horse doctor image, however, is still pervasive. Dr. Gray, a physiologist, said in his article that Dr. Elwood Nye (already referred to in Chapter 3), with whose views about horses in the Custer Battle he disagrees, is "the only competent veterinarian to study the Custer campaign" (1977:256, 258, 261–62). This is an incomprehensible statement in view of the fact that, as Dr. Gray himself wrote in answer to my puzzled inquiry, "so far as I know, Dr. Nye was the *only* veterinarian to publish anything on the Custer campaign." How the judgment implied by "competent" crept in, or what it signifies, must be again attributed to the power of the "horse doctor" image, for it really makes no sense in context, as Dr. Gray admits. Attitudes have not changed too much. Seventh Cavalry physician Dr. James DeWolf wrote in 1876 of a "visit from the Veterinary Surgeon" C. A. Stein, who is "not so very nice but tolerable," and who "imagines he knows something about medicine" (Luce 1958b:66).

As far as history reveals, no veterinarian accompanied Custer's command en route to the Little Big Horn in 1876. Veterinarian C. A. Stein was "attached for duty with the 7th Cavalry" at the time. He "participated in the Sioux expedition and accompanied the column from Fort Lincoln on May 17, arriving on the Powder River on June 7. He remained at Yellowstone Depot when the 7th Cavalry departed on the campaign to the Little Bighorn River" (Hammer 1972:11; Stewart 1957:29). Army veterinary service in the United States was very poorly organized at the time. Educated veterinarians were scarce in America and as a result, not only farm animals and urban driving horses but also the mounts of the cavalry were often "denied the benefits of the simplest prophylaxis and medical ministrations." Under these conditions, "self-made animal doctors cropped up in every corner of the country and the army found it expedient to make doctors out of its horseshoers and blacksmiths. Almost a century of veterinary education in Europe had not registered on the consciousness of the American people" (Merillat and Campbell 1935,1:66).

It was lamentable that "the army of a nation carved out of the wilderness with horses . . . overlooked contemporary veterinary medicine as long as did our active military forces." The advice of people like General Philip H. Sheridan, who realized the need for the inclusion of scientific veterinary medicine in the cavalry, was overruled for a long time. Sheridan, "after making a personal investigation of horse management in European armies, advocated that an army veterinary school be established. He visited the School of Veterinary Medicine, University of Pennsylvania, for additional information and [in 1877–78] prepared a bill to be introduced into the Congress, providing for a much improved veterinary service within the army. The General died before his measure reached Congress. . . . Loss of the leader meant loss of the cause." The proponent who took over the effort to secure the measure's passage failed to get it passed in 1889. Throughout his career, Sheridan

> was noted for his thoughtful attention to horses. He would postpone an operation to allow his animals to rest and graze, instead of forcing them on to a state of exhaustion. His fame among the great cavalrymen of history may well be attributed to that foresight. Though many a military operation has been checked and stalled owing to the exhaustion of its animals, it is strange how few army commanders mention that fact as the cause of their failures. In this respect General Sheridan's writings are the exception. He refers often to the condition of his men and animals and the importance of caring for both in order to obtain the maximum result. (Merillat and Campbell 1935,1:80, 84, 89, 161, 222)

It is noteworthy that in an 1868 letter to Custer detailing preparations for the forthcoming winter campaign against the Indians, Sheridan's first order to Custer was "Get your horses in as good condition as you can" (author's collection).

"In 1876, or ten years later, there were only nine veterinarians in the whole army." This is not surprising, since army veterinarians received poor pay, little or no respect, and few benefits (Merillat and Campbell 1935,1:154, 155, 166–67). Though no veterinarian was with Custer at the Little Big Horn, the facts regarding a former Seventh Cavalry veterinarian, John Honsinger (sometimes spelled Holzinger, Huttinger, or Hallsinger), are relevant to the present story for what they reveal about interaction with horses in the regiment and for their bearing on the Custer Battle. In the summer of 1873, ten troops of the Seventh Cavalry under Custer accompanied the Stanley expedition in support of the Northern Pacific's surveying parties that explored westward along the north bank of the Yellowstone River. The veterinarian, Honsinger, accompanied the expedition. He was a native of Germany who lived in Michigan and had been appointed senior veterinary surgeon of the Seventh Cavalry on May 14, 1869. At that time, army veterinarians often came from Germany and England, some "doubtless for adventure in the constant Indian warfare on the western frontier" (Merillat and Campbell 1935,1:202; 2:979).

In my efforts to find out more about Honsinger, I wrote to every veterinary school that was in existence when he would have studied for his profession. Graciously, they examined their records of attendees and graduates but replied that his name was absent from their files. This failure to establish his enrollment is understandable, since it was not until 1897 that, by an act of Congress, graduation from a recognized veterinary college was made a prerequisite to military veterinary service in the United States. Army veterinarians in Honsinger's day, then, were generally men without formal schooling. It was not until "toward the close of the period ending in 1879 [that] a few graduates of British veterinary colleges and one a graduate from a German veterinary school took positions in this uninviting field" (Merillat and Campbell 1935, 1:13, 66, 166–67).

Little is known about Honsinger's life except for his unfortunate participation in the Yellowstone expedition. It was natural that the Indians would resent and oppose the army's invasion of their territory. On August 4, 1873, Dr. Honsinger, along with the sutler (both men were said to be unarmed) became separated from the main column and were killed by a party of Sioux believed to have included the warrior Rain-in-the-Face. The veterinarian has been described as "a great favorite with his regiment, being a kind, genial old man, but with no interest in the profession beyond a personal one." He was "a corpulent old man of the quietest and most inoffensive habits," who was in the habit of "straying off from the main body of the command, picking up natural curiosities" (Holcombe 1881:346; Whittaker 1876: 496–97). According to one writer, "The two noncombatants were both men of scientific tastes and interests, and often left the column in search of the fossils which abounded along the Yellowstone," in spite of having been warned about the dangers of doing so (Stewart 1980:59). Jacob Adams recalled that the two civilians became "separated from the command in their zeal to study the flora of that new region" (Ellis 1909:227). Other accounts, however, relate the veterinarian's death to a search for water for his horse. A newspaper reporter who encountered Honsinger just before his untimely death described him as

> a fine-looking portly man, about fifty-five years of age, dressed in a blue coat and buckskin pantaloons, mounted on his fine blooded horse, leisurely trotting along the cavalry trail. No man in the regiment took more care of his horse than he. It was an extra professional care—a love of the horse for its own sake, much less a veterinary surgeon. He had taken the horse at Yankton, in the Spring, from one of the cavalry troops—a gaunt-looking steed then, but under his fostering care he had grown fat and sleek. Poor man! he was soon to make a last long camp on the lonely banks of the Yel-

lowstone. Without dirge or funeral note, he was slowly marching to his own grave. When I saw him again, a few hours later, he was a corpse. He died a victim to his devotion to that noble horse. (Hunt 1947:20; see *New York Tribune* September 8, 1873)

Sergeant Charles Windolph, a survivor of the Battle of the Little Big Horn, described Honsinger as one who would ordinarily never straggle from the column as some others did, "to hunt game or moss agate." The doctor's actions on that particular day, which "was one of intense heat," he remembered, were easily explained by the fact that his horse had had no water since morning. So the kind-hearted doctor headed for the river, and by so doing "he took the chances, risking his life to give his horse a drink of water." The veterinarian "had been a long time connected with the Seventh Cavalry, and was greatly esteemed by officers and men for his personal and professional qualities" (Hunt 1947: 27–28).

Seventh Cavalryman John Ryan, a participant in the expedition, also stated that the veterinarian and the sutler "left the bluffs and went down to the river to get water." Shots were heard, and "some time later the bodies of both men were found down there. Mr. Hallsinger was a very heavy man and he rode a very fine bay horse." As a poignant finale to the story of a man who evidently cared so much about his horse, Ryan related that later, after a fight with the Indians, "We found Mr. Hallsinger's horse about 40 miles from where his rider was killed. It appears that the Indians after getting that horse rode him until he probably could not go any farther. Then they shot him and cut steaks out of his hind quarter to eat" (Ryan 1980:55).

Although some doubt exists that Rain-in-the-Face was actually the murderer of the veterinarian and the sutler (Stewart 1980:60), virtually all sources assert that the noted Sioux warrior was overheard by a Custer scout boasting of having perpetrated the killing of the two unarmed men. Subsequently, Tom Custer brought about the capture and arrest of Rain-in-the-Face, who confessed to the murders of the horse medicine man and sutler, and the warrior was imprisoned. Escaping from the guard-house, Rain-in-the-Face fled to Sitting Bull's camp, and, according to the deeply entrenched legend which was made famous by Longfellow's poem, swore vengeance on his captor and later made good his vow by cutting out the heart of Tom Custer following that officer's death at the Last Stand (Custer 1885:203–15; Brady 1904:283–84; Brady 1916:18–19).

Had Honsinger lived to accompany the 1876 Indian campaign and not been detailed under Custer's immediate command, he would no doubt have provided the best possible care to the regimental horses on the march and would certainly have treated the wounded survivor. But, as fate would have it, other men took his place and gained their own degree of fame through association with the celebrated horse.

The recorded history of Comanche states that he was suspended in a sling for nearly a year as an invalid (Luce 1939:66). Employment of this measure on such a long-term basis seems unlikely because the horse was able to walk the distance between the battlefield and the *Far West;* therefore, presumably he would have been able to use his legs well enough at least to bear his own weight. Further, veterinary practitioners know that it is difficult, if not impossible, to maintain a horse for extended periods in a sling. According to an army manual on medical treatment of horses (which, though published thirty-three years later, still reflected therapy used in Comanche's era), a blister might have been applied to help close a wound and relieve the pain. Advice follows to "use the slings if the wound is very painful" (Plummer and Power 1909:52). An 1872 equine medical text sheds light on the contemporary rationale behind the therapeutic use of the sling for wounded horses. The author explains why "wounds in veterinary surgery rank among the most formidable cases with which the practitioner has to contend." The flesh of the horse is not slower to heal, he points out, but the equine animal is by nature "impatient of restraint," and "delights in motion." The difficulty of imposing quietude to allow healing of wounds "favors the gravitation of pus between the muscles, and thus generates sinuses." Therefore through the horse's movement its wounds become extensive and malignant. "These are the torments of veterinary surgery" (Mayhew 1872:432–33).

Unfortunately, most of the details of Comanche's medical history were not recorded or have not been preserved. In 1878, a Minnesota newspaper writer reported that Dr. Stein "was among the first that reached the battleground where Custer and his comrades were slaughtered." There, he said, Stein extracted thirteen of the twenty bullets lodged in the horse. In the next day's paper, however, a "slight inaccuracy" was corrected. "The thirteen bullets were not extracted by Dr. Stein on the battlefield, but at Fort Lincoln, to which place the noble animal had been transferred." After visiting the famous horse, a reporter for the Bismarck *Tribune* learned from Comanche's "official keeper" that "he carries seven scars from as many bullet wounds. There are four back of the foreshoulder, one through the hoof, and one on either hind leg. On the Custer battlefield three of the balls were extracted from his body and the last one was not taken out until April '77" (Gray 1977:262–63).

Records indicate that "with the daily care of Veterinarian Stein, and of Blacksmith Gustave Korn and John Burkman, (nicknamed "Old Nutriment") who were detailed on special duty as his personal attendants, Comanche was able by the spring of 1878 to move around without assistance." As the "second commanding officer" of the regiment, Comanche was then "shown every consideration," and was "turned loose to graze and frolic as he wished" (Luce 1939:66; Brown 1935:71–72).

On April 10, 1878, Colonel Samuel D. Sturgis, commanding officer of the Seventh U. S. Cavalry, whose son had been killed with Custer at the Little Big Horn, issued special orders regarding Comanche that are unique in military annals. "General Orders No. 7" express the extraordinary importance and powerful symbolic meaning that the surviving mount had taken on in a little less than two years since Custer's defeat. They specified that:

> 1. The horse known as "Comanche" being the only living representative of the bloody tragedy of the Little Big Horn, Montana, June 25, 1876, his kind treatment and comfort should be a matter of special pride and solicitude on the part of the 7th Cavalry, to the end that his life may be prolonged to the utmost limit. Though wounded and scarred, his very silence speaks more eloquently than words of the desperate struggle against overwhelming odds, of the hopeless conflict, and heroic manner in which all went down that day.

> 2. The commanding officer of "I" troop will see that a special and comfortable stall is fitted up for Comanche. He will not be ridden by any person whatever under any circumstances, nor will he be put to any kind of work.

> 3. Hereafter upon all occasions of ceremony (of mounted regimental formation), Comanche, saddled, bridled, and led by a mounted trooper of Troop "I," will be paraded with the regiment.

> By Command of Colonel Sturgis:
> (Signed) E. A. Garlington,
> 1st Lieutenant and Adjutant,
> 7th U. S. Cavalry. (Luce 1939:67)

The tie between Comanche and personal as well as national grief is evident through the measure taken by Colonel Sturgis to create the horse's honored status. No Little Big Horn loss seems more poignant than that of Jack Sturgis, described as "a young boy, hardly in his twenties, who only graduated last year from West Point, a good student, a thorough gentleman, and brave and conscientious." An editorial writer expresses both the family's and the nation's feelings: "I cannot endure to think your bright, fine young life has been extinguished by the murderous knife of a painted savage. Is this the result of a West Point education? To be reared and carefully tended in order to sacrifice life on an Indian battlefield! The gods forbid." His parents must "weep over the untimely death of their oldest born, whose remains have not been found, and whose bullet-pierced clothing, discovered inside the Indian village, suggests the fearful thought that the poor lad was captured and then put to death by slow torture" (Custer and Jack Sturgis 1876). Parental sorrow and guilt must have been compounded by evidence of Jack's premonition. Two weeks before his death, the young man had written a letter to a young lady which closed "with the portentous words 'Good-by. Perhaps I am bidding you my last farewell, as I am ordered out a couple of days hence to be scalped by the red-men'" (Custer and Jack Sturgis 1876). Given the circumstances, it is understandable that Colonel Sturgis' special recognition of Comanche would help to assuage his grief. Years later his daughter noted that "my dear father, mourning the loss of his son in that fatal battle must have written this order with deep emotion" (Dousman 1926:7).

As Goldin described Sturgis' unusual action regarding Comanche, "By a regimental order he was allowed the freedom of the Post, the only living thing that wandered at will over the parade grounds at Lincoln without a reprimand from a commanding officer and the old fellow was a great pet of the soldiers." He could "never be molested in his wanderings about the reservation, even if he were found grazing on the parade ground." According to subsequent tales, Comanche enjoyed many adventures made possible by his unique privileges. "He would on many occasions take his former position at the head of his old troop and go through the different drill formations, as though his old rider was leading him." Goldin related that "several times when the band would be out, or the bugles sound for squadron formation, I have seen the old fellow come trotting across the parade, head up, and trot to his old place in front of the line of his master's old troop. . . . No matter where he happened to be on the reservation when stable call was sounded in the evening, he never failed to make his appearance at the stable of Troop 'I' to receive his daily grooming and feed." Major Wey reported that the required deference afforded to Comanche was taken seriously. Once when Wey was on stable guard at Fort Meade, the famous horse was roaming loose and annoying the mounts on the picket line. When attempting to chase Comanche away by throwing a small pebble at him, the major was warned by the corporal of the guard not to molest him and was reminded that "it was a court-martial offense to either strike or ride him" (UK Archives; Brown 1935:71; Luce 1939: 67–68; Comanche 1926:433).

The order that no one could ride Comanche is often traced to rivalry between the "ladies of the post," who vied with each other for the privilege (Brown 1935:69). A retired army officer, who likely learned of this rivalry through his friend, Captain Nowlan, wrote that previous to 1877, the daughter of the colonel of the regiment habitually requested and was granted permission to use the famous horse "to take a lope on the beautiful prairies surrounding the fort" on "every pleasant afternoon." When the major's daughter was given the same privilege, the colonel's daughter reacted with evident "disappointment and discomfiture" leading to "extreme bitterness. . . . That was the last time that 'Comanche' ever appeared with a saddle on. The next day the colonel issued the 'General Order' forbidding anyone from ever riding him again" (Inman 1891; Godfrey 1921:37–38).

Stories are told about the development of Comanche's taste for alcohol, beginning with his year of convalescence during which he was given a whiskey bran mash about every other day. When he wandered over to the enlisted men's canteen, he was treated to "buckets of beer." His food tastes were likewise indulged, and he begged for lumps of sugar and overturned garbage cans to "select whatever articles of food he craved." Wey noted that "after completing one of his tours of the garbage cans, [Comanche] would present a comical appearance, in that his entire head would be covered with dried coffee grounds and similar matter." Front lawns and flower gardens were not forbidden areas, and "sun flowers were a special diet to him." He was free to roll in a wallow, and often was covered with mud when he returned at evening stable call. Since the gate on his stall was never closed, his freedom allowed him to manifest his appreciation of music by attending regimental concerts where he would "calmly nibble grass around the band stand" (Luce 1939:68–69; Comanche 1926:433).

Comanche became very fond of blacksmith Korn, reportedly following him around like a faithful dog. When unable to find his comrade at the garrison, it is said that the horse, with perhaps "a little jealousy" in his nature, would go to the home of Korn's lady friend and neigh until the man would come out and lead him back to the post. On June 25 of each year, Comanche took on the more serious and somber role of leading I troop in the ceremonial parade. For that occasion, Comanche was "draped in a black mourning net, with saddle reversed and a pair of riding boots also reversed in the stirrups, in memory of the fallen troopers and his gallant master" (Luce 1939:67–70).

Luce states that following his recovery, although relieved from further duty, Comanche accompanied his old regiment "on its many scouts and skirmishes in the Dakota and Wyoming Territories and Nebraska. During the last five months of 1878, more than twelve hundred miles were covered, but old Comanche showed his stamina and fortitude by remaining with the troop in all its expeditions." During the years 1879 to 1887 Comanche may have stayed with the regiment at Fort Lincoln and vicinity. In 1887 Comanche accompanied his troop to Fort Totten and to Fort Meade. According to Wey, though the horse had been previously stabled with the band mounts, Comanche was turned over to Troop I for care and stabling at Fort Meade, in deference to his dead rider's position in that troop. In 1888, he went to Fort Riley, Kansas (Luce 1939:72). There is no exact knowledge of the horse's whereabouts at all times during the fourteen years he lived after the battle, and various accounts of his movements differ. Edwards stated that Comanche was at Fort Meade from November 1886 to July 1887 (1934:3). Brown and Willard indicate that Comanche was at Fort Meade from 1879 to 1888, when he was taken to Kansas (1924:222). Today, visiting the forts where Comanche once lived, one has to imagine the presence of the illustrious horse. There are no markers, plaques, or physical reminders of him, and little or no special recognition of his remarkable story by personnel. In 1971, I went to see the last remaining horse stall at Fort Riley and discussed with officials the importance of its preservation. The stables have now been converted to a warehouse, but the curator still hopes to restore one stall for a future exhibit.

During the Battle of Wounded Knee in December 1890, Comanche was present, although he took no part in the action but was kept at a distance with the lead horses of I troop (Luce 1939:72, 75). Through participation in this engagement against the Sioux many Seventh Cavalrymen felt they were avenging the deaths of their comrades who died with Custer; thus, it was particularly appropriate that the horse who survived the Last Stand and symbolized its tragedy was there. Keogh's close friend and the probable discoverer of Comanche, Captain Henry J. Nowlan, was commanding Troop I.

Blacksmith Gustave Korn, also of Troop I, Comanche's "personal attendant and friend for over fourteen years," was killed at Wounded Knee, and it appeared that afterward Comanche "mourned continuously for him." After the horse's return to Fort Riley in January of 1891, he "seemed to have but little interest in life." Despite the solicitous care of Peter Wey, Comanche became "morose," and his scavenging for garbage and his sprees at the canteen "became more frequent" (Luce 1939:77). By June of 1891, Comanche's failing health was revealed in a letter written by Nowlan stating "I fear the famous horse will not last much longer" (Inman 1891). On November 6, 1891, at the age of about twenty-nine years, he died of colic. Farrier Samuel J. Winchester was with Comanche to the last. He documented the experience:

> Fort Riley, Kansas, Nov. 7, 1891—in memory of the old veteran horse who died at 1:30 o'clock with the colic in his stall while I had my hand on his pulse and looking him in the eye—this night long to be remembered. (UK Archives)

Thus the special care and attention that Comanche had received since he was rescued from the battlefield at the Little Big Horn had continued to the end of his long life. The one thing that everyone had vainly longed for since the first moment of his discovery, of course, had not come true. Comanche could never speak and reveal the answers to the many burning questions concerning the ever-controversial Custer Battle. Probably the ancient language barrier between man and beast was never more deeply lamented than among those who brooded so intensely over that event and continue to do so even today. Almost all chroniclers of Comanche's life have shown empathy with what the horse must have experienced on the day of the battle as well as after his rider's death and wished that the animal could express himself in human speech. But in a sense, Comanche did and still does communicate by means of the most articulate language of all—the symbolic. As Sturgis wisely noted in his famous orders concerning the horse, "his very silence speaks in terms more eloquent than words." In the years since Comanche's death, those terms have become only clearer, more eloquent, and more heavily laden with meaning, as will become evident in the chapters to follow.

Chapter 7

Comanche Still Lives

A World's Fair can be seen as one of a series of mammoth rituals in which all sorts of power relations, both existing and wished for, are being expressed. (Benedict 1983:6)

Comanche's death in 1891 marked the end of an era. The Indians' victory at Custer's Last Stand represented a high point of almost four centuries of native resistance to white encroachment. The Battle of Wounded Knee had been won by the Seventh Cavalry in 1890, and for all practical purposes, the tribes which fought against Custer had been conquered. The "glorious Seventh" would never again be the fighting force it had been under its flamboyant leader in 1876. For the past fifteen and a half years, Keogh's horse had been looked upon by many as the last direct living tie to Custer and his martyred men—beloved American heroes who had died courageously. As a "sole survivor," Comanche's fame and glory had steadily grown over the years since the Little Big Horn. By transcending the national defeat of the Custer tragedy, which was felt so keenly by the young country, the horse had come to symbolize not only the grief and bitterness of loss but also the destined victory of "civilization over savagery," the final Euro-American conquest of a once wild continent.

The United States was a newly emerging nation, fast becoming industrialized. In the face of the swiftness with which revolutionary changes were taking place on many fronts, few people probably took time to reflect about the fact that horses would not occupy the same role in the new order soon to be ushered in. Yet somehow there was unspoken knowledge of the finality that Comanche embodied. His death was not accepted in the traditional sense but rather evoked an unwillingness to part with not only his memory but even his actuality.

Cavalryman W. F. Pride wrote that Comanche's "body was buried at Fort Riley with military honors" (1926:207) but regrettably provided no details. I was recently told by the curator at the U.S. Cavalry Museum at Fort Riley that the records from that particular period had been destroyed. The loss of such data is irreparable because much valuable information about the times and people's perceptions (as well as the horse) might have been revealed. It is possible that the burial rite or memorial ceremony for Comanche resembled the service that was held in 1968 following the death of Chief, the last cavalry horse at Fort Riley. That event included troop maneuvers under an honor guard, remarks by the commanding general, the playing of "Garryowen," and taps. A plaque describing the horse was unveiled, and the service concluded with band music (Chief 1968). At Fort Riley there is a cavalry monument "to commemorate the part the horse and the cavalry played in winning the West," and the move to create that memorial "was inspired in part" by Comanche (Frazer 1960).

Even if Comanche's ceremony was much simpler, one can imagine that the dead animal was honored at least with a few moments of respectful silence by the sorrowful cavalrymen who had been his comrades-in-arms and faithful care-givers. But it is possible, too, that all the feelings and energies of the bereaved men were soon channeled into other, more pragmatic considerations after it was decided that Comanche was not to be disposed of following his death. Though some parts of his body may have been buried or cremated, Comanche's major bones and skin were preserved.

For many reasons, people found it was impossible to bid the traditional good-bye to Comanche. Tenaciously the men of the Seventh clung to their symbol and refused to let his death be a final parting. Preparations were immediately made to have him mounted. As was succinctly (and erroneously with regard to ownership) stated in the Topeka *Daily Capital* of November 11, "Prof. Dyche has been summoned to Ft. Riley to take charge of the remains [of] General Custer's famous war horse" (State University 1891:8). As early as November 13, 1891, the Bismarck *Daily Tribune* carried the straightforward story of the death at Fort Riley of "the most celebrated horse in the United States cavalry service," who was well remembered by Bismarck residents because he was once stationed at nearby Fort Abraham Lincoln and was often seen in public parades. The article went on to note that "his skin will be stuffed and mounted and kept in the Kansas State university until the World's Fair at Chicago, where it will be taken for exhibition" (Sole Survivor 1891:3; Old Comanche 1891a:1).

Responding to a telegram, Professor Lewis Lindsay Dyche reached Fort Riley "a little after midnight, Sunday morning. It took the rest of the night and most of the day to properly measure the animal and care for his skin. He was mounted in the taxidermic laboratory at the University, with the understanding that he might be shown with the exhibit at the World's Fair" (Report of the Kansas Board 1894:36). According to Godfrey, Dyche "made a proposition to the officers of the 7th Cavalry to mount 'Comanche' for $400, and the officers retain him, or he would mount him for the University and put him in the University museum. Captain Nowlan called the officers together and they decided to let the University have him, principally because they had no way of transporting him when changing stations" (1921:38). Luce's account of Comanche articulates the situation in further detail. Empathizing with the Seventh's attachment to the horse, Luce denies the truth of an "undercurrent of feeling" that the regiment had "not done right" by Comanche by leaving him in "hock" with the university. It was originally intended, Luce points out, that Comanche remain with the regiment, but, since the troops would be constantly moving about, the decision was made to place the mounted horse temporarily in the museum at the University of Kansas "until a suitable place was found" (1939:77–78).

Subscriptions were to be taken from members of the Seventh in order to meet Dr. Dyche's fee of $400, but evidently this debt was never paid. Luce states that the regiment made an agreement with Dyche that if he were permitted to exhibit Comanche with the university collection at the 1893 Chicago World's Fair, the debt would be cancelled (1939:78). Luce, however, was deluded in believing that the famous mount's stay in Lawrence was temporary. As a former cavalryman and eminent Little Big Horn historian, Luce was instrumental in bringing about the establishment of a museum at the site of the Custer Battle. He felt very strongly that Comanche should be placed in that museum upon its completion and made every effort toward this end. Although his dream of becoming superintendent of the Custer Battlefield National Monument did finally materialize, his hopes to have Keogh's horse enshrined there did not.

In a letter to Colonel Charles H. Bates in December of 1940, Luce describes his efforts in "lobbying" for the museum, and refers to "my last book, *Keogh, Comanche & Custer*," explaining that "this last literary effort you could very well term 'propaganda' for the new Custer Memorial Museum soon to be erected on the site of the Custer Battlefield, Montana." Later in the same letter,

Luce wrote, "I might also add that one of my motives in writing the book, *Keogh, Comanche and Custer*, was to stir up interest in the idea of getting the horse Comanche back on the Custer Battlefield where he so rightly belongs" (author's collection).

The arguments and events involving Comanche's ownership and location will be described in the next chapter, but it is significant to note here that the roots of these proprietary controversies sprang up early in Comanche's history as a mounted specimen. A July 12, 1893, Chicago newspaper article, reporting about his appearance at the World's Fair, erroneously stated that the horse "was stuffed by the order of the government," and added that "the horse remains the property of the United States. But as Kansas was to make a great exhibit of the animals of the plains mounted by Professor Dyche, it was thought a graceful act to loan Comanche to that State" (Escaped the Massacre 1893:supp.7). Even the *Cavalry Journal* mistakenly reported later that Comanche was "mounted by the orders of the War Department" (Ultimus 1928:258).

The interaction between Dyche and the Seventh Cavalry has been given interpretations which differ from Luce's idea that Dyche's unpaid fee was waived in return for exhibiting Comanche at the Fair. Quoting General Scott, Brown states that following the horse's death, "Captain Nowlan called a meeting at Fort Riley of the officers of the regiment to determine what disposition should be made of the remains." It was decided that because of the Seventh's constant movement and lack of facilities to care for the dead horse, "the remains were consequently presented to Professor Lewis Lindsay Dyche," who "set him up in life-like shape" in the museum (1935:72–73).

Written records of Dyche's transaction with the Seventh have never come to light; according to a 1932 newspaper report, however, General W. H. Sears had been told by the professor that he "sent a bill to the officers of the 7th Cavalry for $400 for his services; but told them if they would leave Comanche at the Dyche Museum at the University, there would be no charge for the mounting" (More of the Story 1932:10). Whatever the bargain, Kansas obtained Comanche, and Dyche succeeded in mounting his skin and bones into a museum specimen. Dyche's own description of his taxidermy methods and the photographs taken during the mounting of Comanche show that it was an arduous process. The horse's skull, pelvis, and leg bones were used, and a wooden frame or body board bolted with iron extended from the base of the neck to the pelvis. Heavy string and excelsior were wound around the form to create realistic musculature. According to Dyche, "with a year's practice men in my laboratory usually become very good mechanical winders." The manikin was then covered with clay to mold the final contours "after the fashion that a sculptor finishes a statue." The cleanly scraped skin, which had been preserved in brine and "kept in tan liquor for at least six months" to make it flexible, was then put on and sewed up (see fig. 11). As the stitching progressed, additional clay was filled in to insure accuracy of outline. Great anatomical knowledge and skill were required, and Dyche pointed out that "the feet, joints, flanks, shoulders, ears, muzzle and eyes take days and sometimes weeks of painstaking labor to give them that delicate touch of ease and grace seen in the living, breathing animal." The minute anatomy of the nose and eyes could take months or even a year to be worked out in detail (1893:234–35).

Brown attributes to Godfrey the detail that "Adjutant J. T. Bell of the Seventh Cavalry at Fort Riley sent a saddle, bridle and complete outfit for use on the horse at the Fair" (also mentioned by Scott [More of the Story 1932:10]), and, in a footnote, points out that the Whitman saddle then appearing on Comanche "was not introduced until long after the Custer Battle," and that it was the McClellan saddle which was used by the troopers in 1876. Brown had obtained this information in a 1934 letter from the Chief of Ordnance of the War Department, who stated that although "the McClellan saddle was the standard government type at the time" of Custer's campaign, "many of the soldiers were equipped with their individual saddles of various commercial types" (UK Archives). The issue is further clouded by General Scott's purported statement that "the saddle now on Comanche's body had belonged to Captain Nowlan" (Brown 1935:74). As with other incidences involving Comanche, controversy surrounds each detail. Interestingly, the pattern of associating Nowlan with all Comanche-related events is constantly repeated. In the saga of the post–Little Big Horn years, Nowlan seems to represent a living contact with the dead Keogh in the same psychological way that Comanche represented a tie to Custer and the Seventh. The friendship between Keogh and Nowlan, as previously mentioned, is well documented. Strangely, though, Nowlan did not attend the funeral which was held in connection with the reinterment of Keogh's remains in Auburn, New York, in October of 1877 (Manion 1986:22).

Whatever confusion about the provenance and former ownership of the saddle that arose, no doubt about legal custody of the stuffed horse existed. Keogh's mount in death belonged to the University of Kansas. Throughout the 1960s, the museum official who answered frequent letters about why the stuffed horse was at the university explained,

> Comanche became the property of the University of Kansas and the State of Kansas by default of the soldiers at Fort Riley not keeping their terms in the mounting payment agreed to between themselves and Professor L. L. Dyche. Professor Dyche agreed to mount the skin of Comanche for a certain fee in return for being able to exhibit Comanche at the World's Fair in Chicago. When the fair was over 4 years later and Comanche was brought back to Lawrence, the soldier personnel at Ft. Riley had changed and the new men were not interested in paying for preserving Comanche and so the mounting fee was never paid and the State of Kansas became the owner. (UK Archives)

As later events proved, that institution's claims on the horse were binding and could withstand all other future demands for possession, which would vary from polite requests to verbal onslaughts. Comanche's life after death was to prove almost as eventful as his days with the Seventh Cavalry.

According to plan, Professor Dyche exhibited the famous horse at the World's Columbian Exposition in 1893, along with his other faunal specimens. As one historian of the Fair reported, "The exhibit of mounted animals in the Kansas State building is considered by thousands of people to be the most interesting show on the grounds. It has, from the very first day of the Fair, attracted large crowds of enthusiastic admirers" (Campbell 1894:380). An annex especially arranged and designed in a semicircle shape for the exhibit of North American mammals formed the north wing of the building (Johnson 1897,2:453). It must have seemed strange for visitors unaware of the mount's dramatic story to find an ordinary domesticated horse among the many wild species in the natural history displays housed in the Kansas State Building.

Among many diverse Kansas attractions ranging from a liberty bell made of grains and grasses to Indian relics and graphic representations of the growth of the state from the beginning of its settlement, "the point of greatest interest was the exhibit of natural-history specimens contributed by the State University." Prepared by Dyche, "by whom nearly all the animals were killed and mounted, and who undertook the work without remuneration," the "collection, which represented the labor of a great many years, and the encountering of a great many dangers, comprised one hundred and twenty-one specimens of North American mammals, ranging in size from prairie dogs to elks, moose, and buffalo." The animals were arranged in lifelike poses with realistic backdrops (Johnson 1897,2:454–55). One wonders if the labors of a cavalry horse on the plains or the hardships and dangers Comanche encountered were emphasized in any way for the education of the hordes of visitors who viewed him.

Data on how Comanche was spatially related to these displays, and description of the background against which he stood, were not recorded, although photos of some of Dyche's collections at the Fair were made (see Campbell 1894:380–81; Johnson 1897,2:454). One photograph of Comanche (see fig. 12) which may have been taken at the Fair includes only the horse's form. However, a line drawing of Comanche at the Exposition appeared with a contemporary newspaper article which showed "General Custer's Horse Commander" standing on a simple wooden base with a large circle containing wavy lines as a backdrop (Escaped the Massacre 1893). In this article, the mistakes concerning the horse's name and his former master, the erroneous location of Fort Lincoln in Nebraska, and the statement that he was "stuffed by the order of the government," give some idea of the confusion of facts and the tangled roots of the many legends that grew up about the celebrated equine survivor, both in life and during his postdeath existence.

Some first-hand sources provide insight into Comanche's significance in the context of the World's Columbian Exposition and reflect the tenor of the times in that transitional period when the frontier years passed into nationhood, seventeen years after Custer's defeat. In one report by an eloquent observer, the horse was described as standing "with his mild, intelligent face fronting the throng of visitors, surrounded by all sorts of beasts that in life would have frightened him out of his senses. Still, Comanche was a battle horse of high degree, so perhaps the mountain lions and prairie wolves would not have greatly worried him after all" (Escaped the Massacre 1893:supp.7).

The Kansas building was said to reflect that state's strong emphasis on instruction. "Probably no state in the whole exposition devoted so much attention and space to educational matters." Kansas seemed to be ahead of its time in the techniques of museum display because "the Kansas exhibit of natural history was outstanding, and the exhibits of stuffed animals or replicas, were placed in settings realistically produced, in a manner not to be attempted by the New York museums for decades later. Nor did the Kansans see any incongruity that the scientific exhibit included the stuffed horse, the only surviving steed of the Custer massacre at Little Big Horn, in 1876." It was noted that "thousands of people came to the Kansas building for the special purpose of seeing what is still in existence of this memorable and historic horse. One woman wept as she read the general orders of the seventh cavalry that Comanche, as long as he lived, was to be paraded in all regimentals 'saddled and bridled, draped in mourning.' The period saw no harm in mixing the scientific with the purely sentimental and historic" (More of the Story 1932:10; Beals 1942:18–20).

In describing the mounted fauna of Dyche's display, the *Report of the Kansas Board of World's Fair Managers* reflects the mixing of science, anthropomorphism, and racism in terms far from objective. Two wolverines were said to be "meditating upon some kind of meanness," and thus were referred to as "Indian devils. . . . The old war horse 'Comanche' was also part of the University exhibit." Keogh's horse was billed as "the only surviving horse of the Custer massacre" (1894:36). A massacre, of course, was the term generally used when the Indians won a victory. Its real meaning, designating the wanton slaughter of unarmed people, was ignored. Custer's engagement at the Little Big Horn was in fact a military battle between Indian warriors and U.S. cavalrymen. In contrast, when whites defeated Indians, the engagement was called a battle, even when it was more like a massacre, as at Wounded Knee. For many decades, even into the 1960s and 1970s, the misleading designation "Custer massacre" typically found its way into print—and even sometimes does so today (see Lawrence's Year 1987:C1). In 1893, there would have been few to question the pejorative use of the term in this context.

To understand Comanche's place in history, it is relevant to briefly examine the purpose of the Exposition in which he was exhibited so soon after his death. The symbolic significance which he had already acquired was closely related to American attitudes about Indians and about the growth of their nation which were expressed at the Chicago event. The magnificent Fair, commemorating the 400th anniversary of the landing of Columbus, was held to celebrate progress—white American progress. Yankee ingenuity and hard work had carved a nation out of wilderness, and 1893 was a time for comparing the past to the present and taking pride in the accomplishments of expansion and conquest—of taming the wild and "civilizing the savage." Concluding their official report, Kansans were pleased with "the place that Kansas occupied in the great Columbian Exposition," where "all nations assembled . . . to do homage to the great republic—the child of the discoveries of the great Columbus." In citing the wonders of their contribution to the Fair and relating these to the virtues of their state and country, the exploitative ethos of the vigorous, young country was clearly expressed. "The capitalist and the miner" who "bring forth and utilize their millions of hidden treasure" as well as the farmer, husbandman, and educator, contributed to "placing Kansas in the front rank of the states and nations of the earth." Significantly, "in the forestry building, among other things, was exhibited the trunk of a walnut tree grown on Kansas soil that was 40 years old when Columbus discovered America. Four hundred years of that time that monarch of the forest had no associates but solitude and the Indian; but in the last 40 years of its life it looked on the triumph of American genius, and the skill and intelligence of the Kansas pioneer" (Report of the Kansas Board 1894:94). Such was the spirit and ambience of Comanche's new environment in Chicago.

Ironically, at the World's Fair the tough and hardy former Indian-fighting cavalry mount had more than Dyche's mountain lions and prairie dogs to symbolize the realm of his old enemies. One wonders whether the living human representatives of his plains war days ever made their way to the Kansas building to join the throngs who viewed him. It is unlikely that Chief Rain-in-the-Face, alleged killer of the Seventh Cavalry veterinarian and sutler and one of the most prominent of Custer Battle participants, ventured far from the "Plaisance," the term (meaning "pleasure" in French) used for the midway area of the World's Columbian Exposition (now part of the University of Chicago campus). It was there, amid the displays of cultures from all over the world, that a reconstituted Sioux encampment had been set up with the celebrated warrior, Rain-in-the-Face (fabled in Custer lore as the sworn enemy of the General's brother, Tom), as one of the occupants. An imposing photograph of that Sioux chief wearing war bonnet and full regalia appeared in a publication about the Fair midway, bearing the caption "A Professional Scalper." The accompanying article provides insights into contemporary views of Indians when it relates that "foreigners must have been surprised when informed that among this band were men who had waged a bitter war against the United States, and who, unpunished, tented upon the most famous arena of peace the world had ever seen. History is not so old, nor memory so weak, as to permit the Custer Massacre in 1876 to be forgotten; yet Chief Rain-in-the-Face, whose picture is above, was a prominent actor in that massacre. His presence secured him an admiring audience, the recollection of his atrocities being no bar to that sentiment of adulation that transforms murderers into heroes" (Midway Types 1894:130).

Rain-in-the-Face, whose fame had been enhanced by Longfellow's celebrated poem about Custer's Last Stand in which the vengeful warrior cut out Tom Custer's heart and who was "reputed by some to have killed General Custer," appeared as one of nine "genuine Sioux" Indians in a show held in the Plaisance during the Fair. Described by an observer as the "piece de resistance" of the side show, the chief was featured as the principal "fiend incarnate." Reporting on this show and on the nearby American Indian Village of sixty Indians, the Commissioner of Indian Affairs wrote that the performers exhibited the "degradation of the tribes," that "the explanations and historical information" given by the person in charge were "of the most meager character," and the Commissioner concluded the show was "a failure and a disgrace" (Smith 1949:244; Russell 1970:65).

Another of the "copper-colored wards of the nation to put in a few months visiting at the Exposition" was Lone Dog, a Sioux whose picture in the gallery of midway attractions is sarcastically captioned "A Gentleman of Leisure." This warrior, a "valiant and veteran scalper," the article reveals, is "not the most insignificant" of those Indians "who have been thorns in the sides of Uncle Sam." Scantily attired, but "clothed in his own vanity," he "took an infinite delight in checking off his record of atrocities in peace and war." The writer heaps the final degradation upon this native American by dehumanizing him when he states, "With all credit to Herr Hagenback [Hagenback's circus at the Fair was "an exhibit of the triumphs of German lion tamers and trainers of animals" (Johnson 1898,3:444–45)] for his skill in taming the most ferocious of animals, he failed nevertheless to try his ability on the Indians of the West, and has not, therefore, satisfactorily demonstrated the completeness of his powers. Lone Dog has returned to his agency to be a 'good' Indian until he thinks it will pay him to be a bad one and so enhance the historic value of his portrait" (Midway Types 1894:173). The name Lone Dog may have been confused with Low Dog, a Custer Battle participant whose photograph is indeed valuable in today's market for historical memorabilia.

As a reminder of Comanche's heyday with the cavalry, a poignant symbol of the Seventh's old nemesis, Sitting Bull, was also displayed on the Exposition grounds. Although the celebrated Sioux leader had been killed in 1890, the log cabin in which he had spent the last years of his life and in front of which he had been shot still existed, and it was hauled from Standing Rock Agency in North Dakota to the Plaisance in Chicago. One observer pointed out that the principal interest evoked by the cabin was "a purely morbid one," for a few bullet holes were still visible in the logs (Smith 1949:244). The venomous writer of captions for the midway displays compares this example of "squalid huts" to the "magnificent structures on the Exposition grounds proper." The exhibition of Sitting Bull's cabin is attributed to a "craze for the fantastic humbleness in dwellings" and to "a judicious catering to the popular craving for oddities." Once belonging to "the man who defied the great United States, who fought, defeated and slaughtered its troops, who caused the government more trouble than any other savage has ever caused it," the noted warrior's house was "as imposing as a castle to his admirers; but to his enemies was the rudest kind of cattle shelter. The difference between it and the frontiersman's dwelling was in the color and the diffused variety of the dirt of its occupants." The contained "scalps, war clubs, rifles and papoose cradles" were the only objects needed to satisfy "the cunningest Indian politician of the century" (Midway Types 1894:212). Another account provides more details of objects on display with the cabin, listing "the arms used in the arrest and killing of that chief, an oil portrait of him, and his buckskin shirt, trimmed with porcupine quills and human scalps." Additionally, "there was a collection of arms and guns found on the battle ground where General Custer fell; also a large variety of Indian work and curios." Sitting Bull's niece, Pretty Face, "the best bead worker in the Sioux nation, exhibited her handiwork" there (Johnson 1898,3:444).

Beneath the photograph of Pretty Face, a serene-looking woman who appeared to live up to her name, and her equally attractive and well-dressed female companion, the following information was provided for those who would learn about the midway attractions. "Any superfluity of sentiment is wasted on the Indian. He prefers scalps to taffy, and fire-water to tracts. He is monotonously hungry to kill somebody, a white man, if possible. . . . The Indian woman, or squaw, is a shade worse in human deviltry than the male. In the picture above mildness, docility, kindness, loveableness, seem impersonated. Yet the records of massacres, for centuries, show that the squaw is the apotheosis of incarnate fiendishness." As "savages, pure and cunning, they gave to the Midway the shadows of characters that cannot be civilized, and the solemnity of appearances as deceptive as the veiled claws of the tiger" (Midway Types 1894:183).

There was at least one notable cavalryman from Comanche's side of the battle in attendance at the exposition—Lieutenant Charles Varnum, who had commanded a detachment of Arikara scouts at the Little Big Horn. The account of his death reveals that "by refusing to obey orders, he won the Congressional Medal of Honor [for heroism at Wounded Knee]—his men were ambushed in a ravine, and ordered to remain and wait for relief.

Braving a hail of tomahawks, arrows and bullets, he led them to safety. For that, they sent him to the Chicago World's Fair, to be idolized by effete easterners" (Last of Custer's Officers 1936).

Thus Keogh's mount, after death, had been thrust into a remarkable situation in which there were many reminders of his past life and of the ethos and struggles of the people he had served. Everywhere about him were expressions of the ideology of the young nation, including belief in the Manifest Destiny for which his master and the other men of Custer's cavalry had died. He himself was the perfect symbol of the historic period his life had spanned, a time of conquest when all wild things were to be cleared from the new continent to make way for civilization and settlement. Indians had often been considered merely as part of that savage wild realm, no different from the hunted animals and other elements of nature which had to be destroyed in the winning of the West. It seemed that by perceiving the natives as savage creatures who in general were not capable of being tamed, Americans were better equipped to erase the guilt which might otherwise have been experienced if the natives were viewed as human beings possessing the intrinsic rights attributed to that status.

As wild, free Indian life on the plains came to an end, so did the horse age draw to a close. In 1893, a horse race heralded as "the greatest one ever seen" took place between Chadron, Nebraska, and the Nebraska Pavilion at the Fair. Cowboys riding their "cow ponies" competed over the thousand-mile course, and the event was said to demonstrate that "western bronchos are possessed of remarkable endurance." Some cyclists, however, challenged the horsemen, and a world champion cyclist trained specifically to make this race "one that would, once and for all, usher in the machine age in transportation" (Fredriksson 1985:143–44, 174).

A very popular building at the Exposition was devoted to the entire history of transportation and was advertised to contain everything "from a toy tin wagon to a mogul locomotive, and from a two-log raft to the model of an Atlantic liner." Inside, a bas-relief entitled "Apotheosis of Transportation" featured horses, but the emphasis was on America's leadership in the invention and improvement of all forms of mechanical transportation. Although it had been only approximately thirty years since the pony express and overland mail—"those opening wedges into western civilization"—were instituted, they already seemed "far away." They were of interest as "relics" of the days when "their speed was accelerated by the sound of an Indian war-whoop or the whistle of an Indian bullet" (Davis 1893:263–99). In another section of the grounds was the Zoopraxographical Hall; this building housed a display of Eadweard Muybridge's revolutionary animal locomotion studies, resulting from electro-photographic investigation (Davis 1893:574–75). Thus for the first time, just as the horse era was ending, equine gaits became accurately understood and concepts about them previously held by scientists and artists alike were proven false. Painters and sculptors could now more realistically portray the "western" art featuring horses which would nostalgically recreate and glorify scenes from the disappearing frontier.

Comanche, like other horses used by the cavalry, the stage coach, the pony express, and other agents of westward expansion, would soon become incongruous with the future operations of the newly industrialized nation that celebrated its 400th anniversary in 1893. But as the quintessential representation of the American frontier, the mount who had served with Custer's regiment caught and held for a moment in time the spirit of a fast-disappearing era. It was as if a skillfully constructed classic tragedy were being enacted at the World's Columbian Exposition, and all the diverse threads woven together spelled the end of the old order in the third act. A world more predictable, staid and sophisticated, civilized, and tamer would soon replace the individual challenge, the drama, excitement, and uncertainty of the raw frontier.

Not far from the mounted horse that was the last remnant of Custer's cavalry—one of the most memorable and dramatic instruments of Manifest Destiny—members of the American Historical Association gathered for their 1893 meeting held in Chicago in conjunction with the Fair. That year the historian Frederick Jackson Turner, first scholar to give serious theoretical consideration to the American frontier, was the speaker, and it was there that he presented his now famous thesis, *The Significance of the Frontier in American History*. Turner's thesis asserted that the frontier had been the most important factor in shaping American character and history. From the wild and rugged land itself, Turner argued, had come the main stimulus for the development of the strength, self-reliance, and individualism that characterize Americans and formed the basis for the growth of American democracy (Turner 1894). Ironically, a few years before, the United States Census Report of 1890 had declared that the "frontier of settlement" in this country no longer existed.

Even as Turner spoke amidst the dazzling enchantments of the Exposition, which included the Kansas building housing Comanche, another very different celebration of nostalgia for the

122

lost frontier was taking place only a few miles away. Buffalo Bill's Wild West, having been refused space inside the exhibition "on the plea of incongruity," was nevertheless a "phenomenal success." Located outside the Fair enclosure, "Colonel Cody [Buffalo Bill] broke all records by giving 318 performances to an average of 12,000 spectators" (Cameron 1893:851). The Indian Wars were over by 1893, and the real West that Buffalo Bill's Wild West was commemorating had passed into history. Since the rugged and adventurous frontier life epitomized by the dramatic episodes of Cody's spectacle had all but vanished, it was being valued and perpetuated in memory by scholars and showmen alike. During this peak year for his show, sell-out crowds testified to the Chicago Exposition visitors' fascination with the events portrayed in the Wild West.

Far from being incongruous with the Fair, Buffalo Bill's portrayal of American Indians was similar to that within the Exposition. Wild West shows containing such reenactments as an Indian attack on the overland mail and the surrounding and burning of a wagon train—scenes of rapine, murder, and robbery—served to perpetuate the stereotypic image of the "blood thirsty savage," while "glorifying the deeds of the well-loved frontier hero." They promoted the Turnerian notion that frontiersmen symbolized America's greatness and they justified white acts of vengeance against Indians, who were viewed as barbaric, inferior, and incapable of being civilized. American culture, in contrast, was portrayed as progressive, uplifting, and superior. Some felt that "the prime objective of wild west shows was to make money by a display of savage and repulsive features of Indian life" (Braun 1975:26–29, 70).

The famed Sitting Bull had traveled with Cody's show for a season, and quite a number of other Indians, including some Sioux prisoners of war, had been hired to participate at different times. Other Wild West companies, too, had boasted of Indian warriors taking part in their shows. Significantly, "Custer's Last Stand" was a popular and frequently reenacted scenario in Buffalo Bill's Wild West, and it often constituted the rousing grand finale. The Battle of the Little Big Horn was indeed the subject for an action-packed "climactic spectacle" on the 1893 program, "showing with historical accuracy the scene of Custer's Last Charge." It is noteworthy that General Custer's widow, Elizabeth, once attended a performance of Cody's Wild West, and was among those who "had words of praise for the show" (Russell 1970:25, 47, 65). Mrs. Custer's staunch loyalty and unceasing defense of her dead husband during her lifetime were legendary,

and her feelings and sentiments were shared by Buffalo Bill. Elizabeth Custer corresponded with the showman, and she inscribed a
photo of the General: "For my husband's unwavering friend,
Colonel Cody" (author's collection).

It is reasonable to expect that a riderless bay horse might
have been included as part of the authentic Wild West extrava-
ganza—the fabled "lone survivor" of the Custer "massacre." At
any rate, Comanche's posthumous appearance as an exhibit at the
World's Fair was as fitting as Buffalo Bill's. If the Indians were
treated more as specimens than people in the scientific areas of
the Fair and degraded and dehumanized by their appearance at
the Midway Plaisance, the honky-tonk sector of the Fair, Comanche was, in contrast, humanized by many who viewed him in the
area designated for scientific objects. It is safe to assume that the
one wish shared by his many admiring observers was that the
horse could break what Sturgis had termed "his very silence," and
answer some burning questions about Custer's Last Stand. For already the mysteries and controversies surrounding that battle had
made it one of the most appealing and famous of all national
events. Although he never spoke, the dead horse eloquently communicated sentiments of the times: the bravery of his master as
one of Custer's heroic men, the hopelessness of the doomed cavalrymen's plight, the tragedy of their defeat, the pride of ultimate
conquest, and the glory of an epic struggle that was part of the
heritage of a nation wrested from the wilderness.

Such symbolism fit well into the overall scheme of the Fair,
where small things progressed into larger elements and all totaled
up to a grandiose whole. The World's Columbian Exposition was
ostensibly a "celebration of Chicago, the United States of America, the achievement of Christopher Columbus, and the progress
of civilization." As "the greatest international fair of its time," it
expressed "the continuity of progressive American civilization,"
and it opened "a new epoch in man's comprehension and control
of nature." As with other great world's fairs, "industrialism, nationalism, urbanization, and the rise of science" were the "forces
and factors" producing it. In complex societies, world's fairs provide a "focus for cultural self-examination and self-expression,"
and represent "the attempt to both acknowledge the reality of
rapid change and to understand and control its direction"
(Badger 1979:xi, xiii, xv, xvi). In short, the central message of the
Fair emphasized "American progress through time and space
since 1492" (Rydell 1984:46–47).

"Progress" meant not just material benefits but the alleged
advancement of the human race through various stages and hier-

archies of evolutionary process. Many of the Fair's displays were a bulwark for racism—upholding beliefs that one group of people is hereditarily above another in moral, cultural, and intellectual qualities. The prestige of "science" was drawn upon in demonstrating that whites were superior, and progress, which was "synonymous with America's material growth and economic expansion," was "predicated on the subordination of nonwhite people" (Rydell 1984:4–5).

The Chicago Fair was regarded as "a tremendous opportunity to introduce the science of anthropology to the American public" and to exhibit "the steps of progress of civilization," particularly the stages of the evolutionary development of man on the American continent. In the anthropology building, life-size statues of Indian people wearing characteristic clothing were displayed in their natural environments. Yet, even this new exhibition technique fit into a prevailing view of native Americans as "lower races" who were "living an outmoded life." Their portrayal as racially inferior was made clearer by the sharp contrast between their culture and the technological wonders of the great "White City" (Rydell 1984:45, 57–58).

The living ethnological displays corroborated what visitors learned from the museum. Despite its carnival atmosphere, the Midway Plaisance or "caravansary of nations" was officially classified under the auspices of the Exposition's Department of Ethnology. It purportedly allowed visitors to "study all phases of the daily life of people from all over the world." Although "hailed as 'a great object lesson in anthropology,' " the Midway in actuality promulgated evolutionary ideas about race, as it "provided visitors with ethnological, scientific sanction for the American view of the nonwhite world as barbaric and childlike." The Midway was said to be organized along evolutionary lines, "tracing humanity in its highest phases down almost to its animalistic origins," and "afforded the American people an unequaled opportunity to compare themselves scientifically with others." Though the cultural exhibitions were supposed to educate, they had turned into "a side show" where "evolution, ethnology, and popular amusements interlocked as active agents and bulwarks of hegemonic assertion of ruling-class authority." Significantly, the Rand-McNally Guidebook to the Fair advised the visitor to visit the Midway "only after having seen the edifices of modern civilization in the White City." There was a lesson to be learned from the apparent contrast, "as the 'primitiveness of nonwhite cultures' was compared to 'civilized' America" (Rydell 1984:40–41, 61–62, 65; Benedict 1983:49; Badger 1979:105; Johnson 1898,3:433).

Ideally, the gathering together of "different natives of this continent" was supposed to be beneficial by providing them the opportunity to see "the material advantages which civilization brings to mankind." In actuality, the native Americans in the Midway exhibits received no advantage from their participation and "they were the victims of a torrent of abuse and ridicule. With Wounded Knee only three years removed, the Indians were regarded as apocalyptic threats to the values embodied in the White City who had to be tamed." The Indian people were seen as specimens and objects of curiosity "in special enclosures with the trappings of their culture or performing indigenous tasks or ceremonies," who must be taught by their superiorly endowed "masters." This view is closely allied to the idea of conquered peoples as trophies and was displayed by other imperialistic nations from all over the world who exhibited along the Plaisance. Through demonstrations of native "barbarism," the idea of social Darwinism, a prominent theme at the time, was used as a justification "for the expansion of American civilization at the expense of the Indians." By invoking evolutionary theory, Anglo-Saxons, as superiors, were destined to conquer the land. "America's belief in nationalism, expansion," and "racial superiority" which "dominated the thinking of the late 19th century," made conquest of the natives seem to be "the great destiny and duty of America" (Rydell 1984:63; Benedict 1983:45, 50; Braun 1975:17, 20, 23, 25).

Bias was created by the fact that Indians from the more acculturated groups and "self-civilized tribes" were not chosen for participation at the Fair. By exhibiting only natives who illustrated "savagery in its most repulsive form," and choosing those "noted for bloodthirsty deeds," it was alleged that Americans were misled "to work up sentiment against the Indian." Such displays served to "show the need of Government officials to civilize them, and furnish argument to those who wish to drive them from their homes or plot to handle their money." In planning the artifact displays at the Exposition, museum officials had emphasized the collection of materials representing Indian life prior to white contact, which would "illustrate the Indian in his primitive condition." Thus natives were selectively chosen to be seen as nonprogressive, an anachronism in the modern world. The "average interested spectator" learned little of positive value concerning Indians and their way of life and merely had existing stereotypes reinforced (Braun 1975:65–68, 89–91).

The subject of museum displays—the question of how they are to be exhibited and interpreted—is closely related to the story of Comanche, who, of course, for the rest of his existence was to be, and still is, featured in a museum. In planning the Chicago Exposition, it was felt that the displays should "give adults the opportunity to continue the learning process." As "the people's museum," it "should be much more than a house full of specimens in glass cases." The "exhibition of the future will be an exhibition of ideas rather than of objects, and nothing will be deemed worthy of admission to its halls which has not some living, inspiring thought behind it, and which is not capable of teaching some valuable lesson" (Rydell 1984:45). Thus the ideal for museums would be to get away from dry and dusty collections of artifacts which were not interpreted in a meaningful way as part of a total picture. This is a theme which would often arise in the future in connection with Keogh's famous war horse and his proper museum context and interpretive significance, especially in regard to Indians (see Chapters 10 and 11).

The World's Columbian Exposition was a turning point in developing better exhibition techniques through the introduction to America of life-size groups and the sorting of artifacts by culture area. For the first time in 1893 human "life groups" of "costumed figures were arranged in dramatic scenes from daily life and ritual." It was hoped that cultural integration would be accomplished for viewers through the visual association between figures and artifacts (Braun 1975:97; Stocking 1985:81). Ironically the human "life groups" were organized by the same principles as Dyche's ecologically oriented and realistic action-displaying animal groups. But the mounted Comanche was a true outsider, a domesticated species unsuited to his context and lacking an appropriate backdrop. As one Dyche Museum visitor later noted upon observing Comanche and failing to read the accompanying text, "The sight of a domestic creature in one of the halls always comes as an unwelcome shock." After learning the story of the famous survivor from museum official Robert Mengel, however, the writer, who was "always fascinated by Custer's Last Stand," admitted that "in this instance I found a domestic animal a most fascinating subject in a natural history museum" (Maslowski 1978). Some viewers, though, do see the horse as an inappropriate display. A biologist who once worked at the Kansas University Natural History Museum speaks of the overwhelming sense of incongruity he always felt at seeing Comanche displayed there, a creature entirely "out of context." In reference to the symbolism of the horse and its relationship to views of nonwhite Americans, he remembers that "a museum official at that time [of his employment] was a racist who believed in subspecies of the human

127

race. He classified Indians and Blacks in Harlem as different sub-species. This man thought Comanche was important in drawing visitors to the museum. But for him a stuffed Indian would have served the same purpose."

Although the display of living Indians at the Chicago Mid-way was an innovation in American exhibit techniques and was theoretically an improvement over previous arrays of mere cata-logued objects, its effects upon fairgoers still left much to be de-sired. For reportedly the Indian people on the Plaisance, some of whom had themselves petitioned for the chance to participate and see the "greatness of America," were viewed in much the same way as specimens or animals in a zoo. "Animals as well as the Indi-ans at the live display could be seen in their 'natural habitations.' They were given the status of 'picturesque species of wildlife,' or 'interesting curiosities.' " Unfortunately, there had been little change in general perceptions of native Americans since the 1876 American centennial celebration, during which the shocking news of Custer's defeat had been announced. At that time, the outcome of the Battle of the Little Big Horn had greatly reinforced public intolerance of Indians. By the date of the World's Columbian Ex-position, attitudes were still basically the same, though the subse-quent confinement to reservations of many tribes and the army's 1890 victory at Wounded Knee had undoubtedly lessened the threat by making Americans feel stronger and superior (Braun 1975:64, 98, 101, 103, 108, 111). Thus, in spite of improved dis-play techniques, the Chicago World's Fair had little or no effect in changing American attitudes toward Indians, attitudes which still resembled those of the government which had sent men like Keogh riding Comanche into battle with Custer's cavalry against the Plains tribes.

At the time of the American centennial celebration in 1876, when the Custer Battle was fought, predictions were made that "Indians 'would cease to present any distinctive characters, and will be merged into the general population' by the time of the 200th anniversary of the American Republic." Yet the natives, proving otherwise, "have survived and although many have been assimilated into the dominant society others have chosen to live on reservations and maintain their cultures and traditions" (Braun 1975:109). If evidence is needed of the continuing strength of Indian ethnic and tribal identity, as well as the value still placed upon preserving native culture, one had only to be present at the centennial ceremonies held at the Custer Battlefield National Monument in 1976 to commemorate the 100th anniver-sary of the Battle of the Little Big Horn. Although there were messages extolling peace, the Indian contingency, by actions and by speeches, left no doubt that modern-day tribespeople represent discrete social and cultural entities and that their native heritage would continue to be respected and preserved at all cost.

On June 25, 1976, within sight of the slope where a century before Custer made his Last Stand against the onslaught of their Sioux and Cheyenne ancestors fighting desperately for their way of life (just over the ridge from where death at the hands of the Indians parted Keogh forever from his wounded but still-living mount), a formidable, somber, but peaceful parade of contemporary native American men, women, and children marched slowly from the entrance of Custer Battlefield National Monument to the museum. Those in the front bore the United States flag held upside down to indicate their dire distress at injustices they felt were still perpetrated upon them by the government. Thus, some Indians continue to resist, in whatever way they can, both integration and total white domination. There continue to be repercussions of the unsolved problems inherent in the clash of cultures that made Custer ride into battle and incidentally transformed a surviving cavalry horse into a national celebrity in life and a notable World's Fair display in death.

Chapter 8

Life on Mount Oread

Comanche seemed to be quite unconcerned and calm about the hullabaloo which had been blowing about his ears. He seems to want to stay right where he is.
—Deane W. Malott, University of Kansas Chancellor, 1947

The set of circumstances which determined that Comanche would not be allowed to "die" in the sense of being buried or cremated were the same motivating factors that made him a prime attraction at the World's Fair. They were indeed the very issues that would keep him often in the public eye, a center of curiosity and fascination throughout the years to come. Still today a unique and extremely popular museum attraction, the object of intense interest and controversy almost one hundred years after his death, the old Seventh Cavalry mount remains an extraordinarily complex and powerful symbol whose meanings have often shifted with passing years, adapting to suit the needs of changing eras.

During his long and eventful career as a museum display Comanche, except for the time spent in Chicago, has been housed at Lawrence, Kansas, where the University of Kansas is located on a slope known as Mount Oread. One writer claims that the horse was exhibited at the Louisiana Purchase Exposition in St. Louis in 1904 (Swergal 1949,1:1) but this is not confirmed. Little information has come to light regarding the horse during his first few decades as a museum specimen which presumably began in 1902 when he was placed in the newly constructed Dyche Hall. A 1907 article describes Comanche "standing saddled and bridled in an obscure part of the basement of the natural history building of the University of Kansas" (Bronson 1907:345–46). Sometime after that date he was protected by glass and moved to a more favorable location. UK News Bureau releases indicate that he "stood in the most prominent part of the building, just inside the door, until the building was condemned in 1932."

Before the museum was closed, an especially meaningful and probably unique visit to view Comanche took place in April of 1931. During this encounter "Years fell away from Major General Hugh L. Scott, U.S.A., retired, at Dyche museum. . . . Peering through a glass case at the stuffed skin of Comanche, . . . the 77-year old general, who long ago put aside thoughts of fighting, went back in memory to the days of his dashing and adventurous youth . . . when he took up on the plains of the West the career that was to lead him to fame and high position." Throughout Comanche's "thirty-eight years in the museum," it was reported, he had been "gazed upon by thousands," but not until that day "had eyes peered through the glass at him that had known him in the days of his fame and strength." Calling Comanche "a fine horse" who "went many a mile with the old 7th cavalry," Scott reviewed his own part in the care given to the wounded animal at Fort Abraham Lincoln, where he had been restored to health following the tragic battle. The officer had arrived at Fort Lincoln just at that time "as a young lieutenant newly out of West Point." He explained, "Blacksmith Korn and myself doctored and watched over Comanche all that summer and winter and I remember personally washing his wounds many a time. He was a great animal and his endurance shook off the effect of eight wounds and he recovered." General Scott still had a clear memory of Comanche "even after 55 years" and was able to discuss details of the horse's wounds with onlookers in the museum (An Old Friend 1931).

In 1934, the old war horse was moved from the building that had been labeled a firetrap. On January 12 of that year, a Lawrence, Kansas, newspaper report indicated "Comanche moved today," and stated that the horse had

> taken up a temporary abode under the floor of the auditorium until Dyche museum can be rebuilt.
>
> For 20 years or more, Comanche in his glass case, has greeted every visitor as he entered the main floor of the museum. This morning workmen took him from his cage, placed him on a truck, and drove carefully across the campus to the temporary resting place.
>
> Few of the students arriving for their eight thirties even turned to look. It was just a stuffed horse on a truck. They could not know the history and the sentiment that cluster about that animal which nearly 60 years ago bore Captain Myles W. Keogh to the Wyoming [sic] battlefield. (Comanche into Storage 1934:1)

Publicity for Comanche, of course, was closely related to the remarkable and widespread fascination with the Battle of the Little Big Horn and the special curiosity about all its aspects and controversies which were rapidly developing in the American mind. Indications of early interest in Comanche are exemplified by the public's concern with details about the mounted horse. Controversies arose, including charges that the horse on display was not authentic, since the real Comanche was gray (see Chapter 1). But "a check of U.S. Army records, and interviews and letters from people who had seen Comanche proved that it was indeed Comanche (a red) who stood in the Dyche Museum" (Jones 1964:6). As previously discussed, Comanche's color has been a perennial subject of fascination. A letter written to General Godfrey in 1930 by S. W. Fountain of Gloucester, Massachusetts, for example, typified that concern. The brief query begins:

> Dear Godfrey
>   Please tell me the color of Comanche? Captain Keogh's horse? I thought he was a "Claybank" or as we used to call it, a "Buckskin." Now I am told that he was a "Grey" and still later that he was a "Chestnut."

The letter ends with a question about another debatable issue— the area in which the equine survivor was found (author's collection).

Even with his identity authenticated, the mounted horse has seldom stood for long without exciting some form of controversy. In 1938, E. S. Luce wrote to the assistant curator of the Natural History Museum at the University of Kansas to ask about the possibility of returning "poor old Comanche" to Custer Battlefield in Montana. "What a wonderful thing it would be if Comanche could be escorted back there by his old regiment to take up his watch again over the graves of his fallen riders and brother horses" (UK Archives). In a letter written about a year later to his friend and fellow Custer Battle enthusiast, veterinarian Elwood Nye, Luce revealed

> here is a subject that I trust you will keep in confidence and on the q. t. There is a move on hand to get Comanche back to the battlefield and rightly installed in the new Museum when completed. Are you familiar with taxidermy? Would you be interested in this movement along with Brininstool, Hart, Osten, Kuhlman, Ellison and many others? Here are the details of the story.
>   A year ago last August when I started to write this book *[Keogh, Comanche and Custer]*, I went up to the University of Kansas to see Comanche. They were rather reticent to show him to me. He

wasn't on display in the Dyche museum. He was in a damp cellar of a warehouse, where he had been for five years. Poor old hoss, he was sway-back and hay-belly. He had elephantitis, and acute laminitis. When he was prepared and mounted in 1891 they had used clay and excelsior. The Curator told me that the hips, leg-bones, shoulders and skull were there. Only the vertebra was missing, and that it would cost about $500.00 to remodel him and place the skin over a form, papier-mache I believe he said.

When I saw Comanche in such a pitiful condition and what he stood for in the regiment and the mounted service, the thought, "he belongs back at the battlefield" flashed through my mind.

Last November (1938) I met Senator Wheeler while he was in Boston, and the result was, that Senate Bill 28 was approved and at the present minute the Director of the Budget has an item of $25,000.00 in his budget for the erection of the Custer Museum.

In some way or other, the news got out that there was an attempt to "get Comanche away from the U of K." That started an investigation, and the Kansas City Star wrote up an article that was anything but complimentary to the care that the U of K had shown. It will take subtle propaganda, but William Allen White of Emporia has told me, quote: "Let me know when to fire, and I'll let go with both barrels." That practically assures us of getting Comanche back.

Luce had formulated rather detailed and colorful plans for the proposed transfer of the mounted horse. He wrote

I have taken the matter of transportation up with General Herr and Colonel West. At Fort Bliss we have a 4½ ton truck on which Comanche can be very nicely transported, and when the dedication of the Museum is ready, it is the plan to have the W. D. issued a "tactical problem" order to cover the cost of gasoline, oil, etc., and the 7th Cavalry Band with about 150 men, will proceed by motor from Fort Bliss, to Lawrence, Kansas, and accept from the U of K (with proper presentation ceremonies) the carcass of one Comanche. The column will then move to Fort Leavenworth, where Comanche entered upon his military service; then to Fort Riley, where he died; thence to Fort Meade, and then to the battlefield where he will again take up his watch over the battlefield where he was found on the 27th of June, 1876.

All of us interested in Custer and 7th Cavalry history are getting behind this dedication of the Museum, and we want to form a Committee to further the movement. Would you be willing to be a member? . . . We would indeed value your suggestions as to the proper taxidermy of Comanche.

Luce closes by "saying that I would appreciate anything you might be able to do to promote the sales of this book, as I entered into this book with the idea that if there were any profits, it would go toward the expenses of returning Comanche back to the battlefield and the Museum and toward the incidental expenses of the dedicatory exercises of our Committee" (CBNM Files).

Nye's prompt reply dated three days later is gracious as well as warmly receptive to Luce's ideas and reflects the gentility of that slower-paced era. Before turning to the serious matter at hand, the veterinarian responds to Luce's reminiscences about Fort Meade, where, it turns out, both the cavalrymen had once been stationed. In connection with the history of that fort, Nye reveals "a recent happening which you will find amusing," in which "certainly not earlier than 1930, a civilian tourist came into the Post and wanted to see Comanche. One wonders what this man's idea of history, or the maximum age of the horse might have been." Neither Nye nor Luce seems to have considered that the person might have been referring to the stuffed horse or to have thought that indeed by mounting the horse, the animal had achieved a certain kind of "immortality" that had blurred the distinction between the actual mount and the specimen. Luce's comment in his next letter to Nye was that the anecdote "reminds me of the man who was walking along on Riverside Drive, and asked: 'What building is that?' 'Why that's Grant's tomb.' 'Yeah! who is buried in there?' " Common interests and jokes served as bonds between these two men who were both so sincerely devoted to the cavalry.

Approaching Comanche in the light of his present plight, Nye assures his correspondent

> I was very glad to learn of the project to move Comanche back to the battlefield where he belongs. I think it is an excellent idea and should be carried out as soon as possible. I will be very glad to do anything I can to assist.
>
> I will write Brininstool, with whom I've had some correspondence, concerning the matter. I do hope the old horse can be properly rejuvenated. I had no idea he was kept in such an unsuitable place.

Of Luce's *Keogh, Comanche and Custer*, Lieutenant Colonel Nye, then stationed at West Point, wrote "I learned of your book through the book department here and as soon as I receive a copy, will see that it receives notice. I hope it may have a wide sale. If you would care for it, I will be glad to give you my opinion and reaction, after reading the book" (CBNM Files).

In a letter to Nye written in March of 1940, Luce confides "I would not only be thoroughly happy, but supremely as well if I could get that position [of superintendent] at Custer Battlefield." The mounted horse was still a prime concern. Referring to enclosed pictures of the horse in life and after death, Luce asked the veterinarian

What do you think could be done about Comanche's present condition? You can see from comparing the two photographs that they hardly look alike. Especially about the head. Could the skin be removed and a paper matrix made more along the lines of Comanche as he appears in his living picture? Around the mouth there seems to be a certain rotting or erosion but I suppose a good taxidermist could repair that. His skeleton except his entire vertebra was mounted, that is, the skull, ribs, shoulders and legs are in the mounting.

Dr. Nye's response is supportive of Luce's efforts to become Custer Battlefield superintendent, and he hopes his friend will "hear something very favorable soon on this appointment." He uses his expertise in reference to possible taxidermic improvements in Comanche's form.

As you state there is considerable difference between Comanche alive and mounted. It is practicable to replace the actual bones with a composite skeleton. It is done regularly. I believe that if competent people from a reputable museum, or perhaps an anatomist from a veterinary college did the work a composition skull could be made from the picture that would closely approximate the original. It is my opinion that the hide would have been reduced in size somewhat in tanning and mounting, and that anything we could get now would be smaller in general than the original horse. However I believe that the right man in charge could reproduce the lines shown in the picture very closely.

It is interesting to note that in a letter to Nye dated about two months later, Luce wrote that the Karl May Museum in Dresden, Germany, possessed "at least one-third of the total Little Big Horn and Custer Collection in the World." Luce describes plans to obtain government funding to buy items from this collection for the new battlefield museum. No mention, however, is made of whether the present owners would be willing to part with their exhibits (CBNM Files).

In a letter to Colonel Charles H. Bates in December of that same year, 1940, Luce documents plans to establish a Custer Memorial Museum at the battle site and announces his official appointment as superintendent of the Custer Battlefield National Cemetery (as the area was then called). Here he again shows concern about the state of the equine survivor and indicates his strong desire for Comanche to be relocated at Custer Battlefield, "a national shrine of Western Americana." He wrote:

During the summer of 1938, I visited Comanche at the University of Kansas, Lawrence, Kansas, and was very much chagrined to see the lack of interest that the University had for that noble animal in

135

storing him in the basement of a damp warehouse where he has been for almost the past ten years. The poor horse has had no attention and the hide and mounting is sadly in need of immediate attention, and William Allen White has promised me his assistance in "propagandizing" the University of Kansas to give Comanche back to Custer Field when we can show that a proper place has been made for him.

Describing his credentials as a former Seventh Cavalryman and "unofficial regimental historian," Luce explains that "one of my motives in writing the book, Keogh, Comanche and Custer, was to stir up interest in the idea of getting the horse Comanche back on the Custer Battlefield where he so rightfully belongs" (author's collection).

Luce, for whom the stuffed remains of the Seventh Cavalry survivor were charged with such special meaning, had good reason for concern. In the early 1930s the Natural History Museum had been closed and until its reopening in 1941, Comanche was placed "in a corner of Hoch Auditorium's basement" (Jones 1964:6). That is the location where the neglected specimen was seen by the man who was almost fanatic in his devotion to the horse and all that the animal symbolized.

A 1939 release from the University of Kansas News Bureau reveals that "for many years Comanche stood in a great glass case just inside the main door of the Dyche Museum, an object of admiration and comment." As indicated in a Kansas newspaper article of the same year, thousands of students recalled the horse in its former location, since they had passed the doorway of the Natural History Museum daily on the way to their classes. But, as the university spokesmen admitted, "Five years in storage such as could be found when Dyche museum was closed as unsafe, have brought wrinkles and cracks in Comanche's coat that make him an unlovely sight." According to museum curator Dr. H. H. Lane, "The damage to Comanche while in storage is typical of what is happening to many of the fine specimens we had in Dyche Museum before it closed. . . . A hot summer following a damp spring started the specimens under the auditorium mildewing and we had a hard time preserving them." He felt that "at least $100, and perhaps more would be required to restore the horse to exhibit condition. . . . Funds and time" necessary for the project, Lane said, "were not available at the present" (Dill 1939; Survives Massacre 1939; Comanche Not in Trim 1939).

Reportedly, Comanche's removal from "the most prominent part of the building" to the storeroom prompted many queries concerning his whereabouts on the part of "visitors from all parts of the country" who formerly stopped at the museum to see the horse. At that time many people who drove out of their way to see Comanche were disappointed at finding the museum closed and the horse stored where he could not be viewed (Tyler 1939).

A crisis arose in 1939 when early in the year the citizens of Hardin, Montana, the nearest town to the Custer Battlefield, started a movement for the return of Comanche to that area as part of the upcoming celebration of the 63rd anniversary of the battle. "Hardin people had proposed to make the return of the mounted body, accompanied by a guard of Legionnaires, as a highlight" of the observance. But "Comanche is going to make his last stand at the University of Kansas, objected Marvin Goebel, student publisher of the campus *Daily Kansan*. 'Custer made his last stand in Montana but Comanche is going to make his in Dyche Museum and any attempt to remove him for a frontier celebration will be vigorously protested.' . . . Goebel said he intended to start a movement to 'keep Comanche at K. U.' " The decision as to "whether to take Comanche out of moth balls and send him to Montana" created considerable stir at the University. Student opinion was "against letting the horse leave K. U." The president of the men's student council said "the students 'want the horse kept here. Kansas has figured heavily in the development of the West and Custer spent some time in the state' " (Kansas "U" Editor Says "No" 1939; Hardin Wants Comanche 1939). One newspaper reporter agreed that permanent possession of the horse should not be given to the people of Hardin, but wrote that "it might be an appropriate and friendly gesture to lend Comanche for the purposes of the celebration. If horses have a Valhalla, Comanche has won a place therein, and it would add a thrill to the observance of the historic occasion if the old warhorse once again could be seen at the bloody battlefield which he alone of all the participants under the United States flag, lived to remember" (Comanche and the Custer Fight 1939).

University authorities and Kansas legislators who made a trip to view the famous horse at the time of the Montana request agreed with Dyche Museum curator Professor Lane that the "frail" specimen was in no condition to be moved or placed on exhibit anywhere (Comanche Not in Trim 1939; See a Frail Comanche 1939). As later demands for the horse would bear out, the university would have been unwilling under any conditions to part with Comanche, who was, according to contemporary newspaper accounts, "one of the most cherished objects in the Dyche Museum Collection." Certainly no one could seriously challenge a negative decision based on risks related to the mounted horse's degenerating state. Thus, from the Kansans' point of view, the poor condition of Comanche, though disastrous, may have had some fortuitous results in justifying his retention at Lawrence. Additionally, the episode of the Hardin request for the horse may have served to draw the attention of Kansas lawmakers to the need for completing reconstruction of the museum before sustaining further irreparable loss of valuable specimens. Although a subheading for a contemporary newspaper article stated "K. U. Fears It May Lose Its Famous Horse," the Montana threat to what was "long Mt. Oread's Most Cherished Museum Piece" did not materialize (Stir over Comanche 1939). Comanche stayed in Kansas.

Vituperative reaction from Montana quickly followed the decision. Comanche's treatment "at the hands of Kansas" was viewed by at least one newspaper source as "desecration." The Butte, Montana, *Standard* claimed that "none of the students at the University of Kansas knew of Comanche's valiant past," and voiced the opinion that "he should not be allowed to stay where his memory is not appreciated." Kansas defenders answered that, while due to storage in a basement the stuffed skin was "a little worse for the wear of all these years," nevertheless "it should be remembered that it was Kansas that first offered him a home and cared for him through the decades" (Kansas and Kansas History 1939).

In 1941, "the sole survivor of 'Custer's Last Stand' was back once more in a position of honor in Dyche Museum of Natural History." As described in the Kansas University *Graduate Magazine*, "Since the time of the Fair, until the closing of Dyche Museum eight years ago, Comanche stood in the most prominent part of the museum, just inside the door. He stands there again, but in a setting greatly changed. Dyche Museum has been entirely remodeled and modernized. The museum will be reopened with appropriate dedicatory service at 4 p.m., Friday, June 6, with Dr. Alexander Wetmore, '12, director of National Museums, Washington, D. C., as the main speaker" (Comanche Back in Dyche Museum 1941). Thus, following restoration of the Dyche Museum, Comanche, in the words of the University of Kansas News Bureau, "resumed his place as a prize exhibit." Early in the year, Klaus Abegg, taxidermist of the Dyche Museum, undertook "a complete renovation of Comanche" (Comanche Returns 1941).

If Luce knew about the mounted horse's upgraded status in Lawrence, it still did not deter him from continuing to endorse the move to Montana. Responding to a letter he received concerning the horse, the Custer Battlefield Superintendent wrote in

May of 1945, "I, too, hope that we can get Comanche back again, but I lost an ardent 'backer-up,' in fact, I lost two backers within the last two years. William Allen White who was on the Board of Regents of the Kansas University, and Ralph T. O'Neill who was president of the Board. Both died within six months of each other."

Neither did the indomitable Luce give up on the issue of aggressive acquisition of the Little Big Horn artifacts located in Germany, for he disclosed to his correspondent

> I wrote General Patton (I knew him when he was a 2nd Lieut. in the 7th Cavalry) about a month ago if he went through Dresden to grab off all the Custer material in the Karl May Museum and send it back here, but I learned over the radio today that Dresden is in Russian Territory and that the Russkys captured Dresden yesterday. So, there goes my Custer material.

Colonel Nye was for a long time unaware of the improvements which had been brought about in the Dyche Museum's prized mounted cavalry horse. In 1947, he wrote to Dr. Robert Taft, a University of Kansas professor and author of *Artists and Illustrators of the Old West*, which included a chapter on Custer's Last Stand, and *The Years on Mount Oread*, a history of the university which included material on Comanche. "Can you tell me about the condition of Comanche?" he asked. "I have heard, very indirectly, that the mount is disintegrating. Of course there is a limit to the time he can be preserved" (CBNM Files).

A well-publicized furor over the horse occurred in 1947 when General Jonathan Wainwright, who had first proposed the idea a year earlier, spearheaded a movement to relocate the remains of the mount at the U. S. Cavalry Museum at Fort Riley, Kansas. The former cavalryman and contemporary military hero had proposed that Comanche's transfer be discussed with Major General I. D. White, commandant at Fort Riley, Governor Frank Carlson, and the board of regents at the university. Wainwright wrote, "Fort Riley long has been the cavalry center of the United States, and while we now have no more cavalry, as such, there are now and undoubtedly will continue to be many former cavalry officers stationed there, and all who knew the history of this fine old horse, I am sure, would be pleased to have his mounted remains find their eternal resting place at Fort Riley, Kansas." White was enthusiastic, asserting that it was appropriate to have Comanche at Fort Riley, "since the 7th cavalry was organized and trained on this post." He gave assurance that "if this relic is offered to Fort Riley, we will accept and agree to provide a suitable place for its permanent display" (Files of the U. S. Cavalry Museum, Fort Riley, Kansas; hereafter designated FR Files). The Governor tried to remain neutral, pointing out that Comanche was the property of the university and that any change in his status would be the decision of university officials (McCoy 1947).

One proponent of the transfer wrote to Kansas University Chancellor Deane W. Malott that he hoped the university would "comply with the sentimental request of General Wainwright and others," claiming that "Comanche in the Natural History Museum there on Mount Oread is just another museum piece of no great moment to curiosity seekers who look upon his mortal remains so well preserved by your school. But to soldiers at Fort Riley Comanche is a stirring symbol of heroic traditions of their calling." A former cavalryman, referring to Wainwright's recent retirement from military service, wrote Malott that "it would have been a fitting tribute to the hero of Bataan if your magnanimity had," on that occasion, "provided for the presentation of Commanche to the Cavalry museum at Ft. Riley in honor of General Wainwright." For himself and his fellow cavalrymen, he explained, "Commanche epitomizes many things associated with our glorious branch of the military service. While the circumstances may justify your keeping the mounted animal as property of the University the patriotic thing to do would be to place Commanche where he rightfully belongs: Ft. Riley." He goes on to say "you can appreciate the immeasurable sentiment felt by every man who has ever ridden under a cavalry pennant. For us of the mounted service there is something profound in the horse; something that can never be fully transmitted to those who have never passed the reviewing stand at a gallop." The letter ends "On behalf of the hundreds of troopers who served with me, I humbly petition that you place the beloved Commanche, veteran of the Little Big Horn, under the permanent jurisdiction of the men who revere his memory." Malott's brief reply included the explanation, "You realize, I am sure, that it is more than a question of personal magnanimity on my part which is involved in any transfer of University property" (UK Archives).

Indeed, there was a great deal more. The University of Kansas rallied to the defense of the museum display which had become a source of such great pride. Letters exchanged during this controversy reveal the depth of meaning the horse had acquired and the strong proprietary feelings these meanings aroused. What at first must have seemed to army personnel a reasonable suggestion was soon a battle which one source described in humorous terms: "Stuffed with some permanent oats and stabled in a glass stall in K. U.'s Dyche Museum, Comanche stands quietly while the Army and the University Administration feud and fuss over the possession of his historic hide" (Feudin' and Fussin' 1947:16). Many people, however, took the controversy quite seriously.

There was concern on the part of alumni who felt that Comanche belonged at the university and must always remain there. The chancellor was importuned to "Hold That Line" in not letting Comanche leave the campus. Reasons for retaining the war horse varied from the removal being seen as an insult to Professor Dyche to the fact that Comanche was the only thing remembered from the museum. One alumna, in response to the army's bid for the horse, wrote "Such a request, I sincerely hope, will be vigorously denied. Comanche belongs to KU. Frankly, I remember nothing else but Comanche. . . . He is a KU tradition like low students whistling on Green steps—Please keep him at home." Alumnus A. Wetmore, Secretary of the Smithsonian Institution, wrote Malott to "assure you of my full backing in retaining him by force if necessary for the Dyche Museum," adding "he is as much a landmark to those who frequent the museum as Fraser Hall is on the campus." Referring to the horse as "the old boy," he noted that "we had many arguments about him during my years at the University." The chancellor's reply is particularly revealing: "I should almost as soon think of giving away part of the library as to part with Comanche. He's almost an alumnus of the institution! I have no idea why General Wainwright allowed himself to get out on a limb by entering a plea for the removal of Comanche, a subject which he obviously knew very little about. I have had a perfect deluge of correspondence from all kinds of people being tremendously affronted by the idea." As in other replies, Malott pointed out that "Comanche is quite safe as a matter of law. I have no right whatever to give away property of the University!" As he phrased it to one alumna, "I have no authority or power to 'preside over the disintegration' of the University of Kansas and I have no disposition whatever to do so" (UK Archives).

The wider community of the University of Kansas joined the battle to keep Comanche, a now famous display which had become increasingly meaningful over the years. Officials countered the army's claims of "prior possession" of the "tough, many-times wounded warhorse" with their present physical possession of the mount. Though the army, "represented by high ranking officers, graciously but firmly" demanded his return, Malott, "equally firmly" said "Never!" It was true that the army had a "well-documented case" in wanting the horse to return to the former cavalry school at Fort Riley. "To a cavalryman, Comanche, typify-

141

ing everything a trooper wanted in a horse, is an almost sacred symbol. The fact he was the sole living survivor of the massacre of General George A. Custer's troops in the Battle of the Little Big Horn, June 25, 1876, and was wounded seven times, adds to his glory." (Thus in 1947, the "sole survivor" status and the "massacre" concept were still strong.)

"Thousands upon thousands of students see Comanche in the museum," Malott told the press. "No one would see him at Fort Riley. Civilians have difficulty getting into the place. It doesn't seem to me the atmosphere is right." Amplifying his argument to stress the importance of the horse to the university, the beleaguered chancellor explained,

> Tens of thousands of students and alumni of the University of Kansas have more than a passing acquaintance with Comanche. Virtually every student has seen him. For many, Comanche was one of the first historic relics to make a deep impression on freshmen students on Mt. Oread. His weathered and scarred hide illustrated both the vicissitudes of Indian fighting and life in a museum. I am sure that every student and alumnus of this institution will look aghast upon any suggestion of Comanche's removal. The university administration does not expect to dispose of Comanche or any other exhibits in its museum of natural history. (McCoy 1947; Feudin' and Fussin' 1947)

A reporter for *Newsweek*, commenting that "nowadays everyone seems to want an old Indian fighter's hide," referred to Custer's Last Stand as "a prime example of American fortitude" and used cavalry idiom to describe the army-versus-university battle which it entitled "Comanche's Last Stand." When "Fort Riley Army officers charged at a full gallop upon the university museum" to retrieve the horse, the writer indicated, Chancellor Malott "gave a brass-rattling reply" to the army's "saber swing" (Comanche's Last Stand 1947:25). A week after the appearance of this issue, an editor of the *Elkhart Daily Truth* in Indiana wrote to Luce that the magazine "carries a picture and short story on Comanche. There seems to be a controversy on, as to whether he should stay at the University of Kansas or be taken to Fort Riley. You may want to add this item to your bibliography." The superintendent's vehement reply ignored the Fort Riley claim and implied that if Comanche were to lose his "last stand," he would be surrendered not to the old cavalry post but to the Custer Battlefield site: "Yes, I saw the article in Newsweek. The president of the U of K left himself wide open when he said that thousands of students saw Comanche. When we get the museum here, I can say that tens of thousands if not hundreds of thousands can see him at

Custer Battlefield." Six months later, when writing to Little Big Horn scholar Colonel W. A. Graham, Luce expressed his thanks for the *Newsweek* clipping, reiterated his claim that "hundreds of thousands" would see Comanche in Montana, and again lamented the loss of his two "backers" for the project. Still optimistic, especially in view of the progress of the Custer Battlefield Museum, he concluded, "But, we'll get him at the proper time" (CBNM Files).

Letters to the university expressed many points of view. One Kansan felt Comanche should stay at Dyche Museum, but if he was moved at all, it should be to a Deadwood, South Dakota, museum. If the army can "lift the remains of Comanche," another asked, "what is to prevent a certain Indian tribe from returning to the Governor of N.Y. beads valued at $20 and claim Manhattan Island?" (UK Archives).

Ultimately, Malott wrote to Kansas Governor Carlson outlining eight reasons why he "should actively resist any attempt by the Army to take over this historic exhibit." Stated briefly, his reasons were that the Board of Regents had vested in him the responsibility for building the university, not for its disintegration; Comanche became the property of the university by agreement between Dyche and the cavalry; but for the university, the horse would not have been preserved at all; he was a traditional part of the university especially for returning alumni; he was valuable in the university public relations program, viewed annually by thousands of visitors; as a historical exhibit, Comanche served as a greater incentive to a knowledge of history than would be true at Fort Riley; the statutes of Kansas make no provision for giving away state property; even assuming a vested interest by the army in Comanche (which the university did not), a dangerous precedent would be set in returning a gift at the behest of the donor, complicating future relations with donors who might change their minds (UK Archives; Clark 1947:14).

Publicity about the Fort Riley assault on Comanche was communicated far and wide, with the result that the mount was again stormed from an unexpectedly exotic front. Malott received a letter from an army colonel, postmarked Tokyo, reading, in part:

> It seemed appropriate for me to write to you about [Comanche] because I find myself commanding the famous 7th Cavalry Regiment, the same one once commanded by General Custer, and now doing duty in the occupation of Japan as part of the 1st Cavalry Division. I am not taking sides in the controversy other than to say that if ever the time comes for Comanche to leave his hallowed place in Dyche Museum, please consider sending him back to the 7th Cavalry, the regiment from which he came.

143

No wonder that the following month Malott was quoted as saying, "Everyone wants Comanche. . . . The Army isn't the first," he explained. "I was in Yellowstone Park a few years ago hunting for a black bear for the museum. The Superintendent said he wanted Comanche. There's a Custer national monument there" (UK Archives; Feudin' and Fussin' 1947:16).

In the correspondence that has surfaced regarding the controversy between the army and the university, there is revealed a strong and unmistakable inclination to view Comanche as a live specimen and to make him the subject of anthropomorphic speculation. One alumna, for example, who signed her letter to Malott "Loyally," stated:

> I am writing you in behalf of Comanche, that battle-scarred old "Faithful" who, through the years, has kindly looked down upon tens of thousands of students and alumni, never once having been offered a piece of sugar or nosebag.
> Many of us as students would drop into the museum on occasions to "look around" or perhaps, to discuss some perplexing "campus problem." There was Comanche! No eaves dropper was he! Yet always out of the corner of his eye would he express his approval—or disapproval. He deserved a place on both the Men's Student Council and the W. S. G. A. . . . He was our "silent partner" and in our hearts became a real part of the University. All power to you, then, when you say *"Never"* to the Brass Hats! Comanche belongs to the University and the University belongs to him!
> Yours for a blanket of the "Crimson and the Blue" for his noble frame and the same place he has always honored at Dyche Museum. (UK Archives)

A retired United States Army captain wrote to the chancellor

> Have word of the efforts being made to remove "Comanche" from the Museum at K. U., and I hope all such efforts fail. Had it not been for the interest of a few cavalry officers, M. Dyche and others, Comanche would long since have mingled with the dust of his ancestors.
> Comanche was, and is, a stout hearted hero, and I am sure he would prefer to remain [in] his present "Happy Hunting Grounds." (UK Archives)

Expressing himself in the same mode regarding Comanche, Malott replied to some of these letters as follows:

> I went in to see him the other morning and he seems to be quite calm and self-confident about the outcome of the whole affair, so I suppose he will continue to greet the students and returning alumni and visitors to the University for many a year in the future.
> [He is] quite unconcerned and calm about the hullabaloo which

has been blowing about his ears. He seems to want to stay right where he is very much indeed and I am very confident that he will remain there.

[He] seemed to be taking the tempest beating about his head in quite a calm manner and gave me the impression of definite assurance that his future would not be disturbed.

I have dug my heels in and am hanging onto the bushes and I suspect we will continue to find Comanche in his usual place. I was over at the Museum a few days ago and he didn't seem at all concerned about it.

I looked in on Comanche and he seems to be taking the whole thing very calmly. (UK Archives)

When notified of the university's stand, one supporter of the move to Fort Riley, in a letter to the Commandant of Fort Riley, wrote "It seems to me Chancellor Malott is unnecessarily disturbed over this and to my mind his real thought is directed to the publicity he can get out of it more than anything else which is absolutely contrary to our wishes. I am sorry there is so much unnecessary publicity on this" (FR Files). Certainly the "hullabaloo" drew attention to the famous war horse and must have served to unify the opinion of everyone connected with Kansas University regarding the far-reaching value of their mounted horse and its connection with the most famous of Indian battles. In September of 1947, according to a university news release, the Dyche Museum, "proud possessor of Comanche, sole survivor of 'Custer's Last Stand,' " was the site of a display of relics from the Little Big Horn Battlefield. The anthropologist who had gathered them, "hearing of the thus far unsuccessful efforts of army cavalry officers to regain possession of Comanche," brought the artifacts to the university museum. The items of "old army paraphernalia" were arranged near the glass showcase in which Comanche was mounted, forming a "frame" for Comanche (KU Museum Has Display 1947).

The skirmish with the army proved to be far from Comanche's "Last Stand." In 1948, the people of Miles City, Montana, made a strong case that Comanche should be displayed at their Range Riders Museum, which they explained had been built on the site of the "first cantonment . . . erected by the then Col. Nelson A. Miles" who "followed Gen. George A. Custer . . . to complete the task" of defeating the Sioux and Cheyenne and returning them to their reservations. Cited as a further reason why Comanche should be transferred there was the fact that Miles City was the location of Fort Keogh, named after the famous horse's rider. In a letter written by a Miles City newspaper editor, the University of Kansas museum authorities were asked to consider "relinquishing possession of the horse Comanche—upon the condition that the taxidermist's bill of around $400, unpaid, . . . was not liquidated and stands as a lien against the animal." The writer suggested that if "we up here in Miles City . . . paid the bill and guaranteed transportation charges, your institution would, or might consider the offer." The Kansas museum's response indicated that Comanche was one of its most popular exhibits and they could not "look with favor upon transferring him elsewhere" (UK Archives).

About two years later a request for Comanche was made by a person from Billings, Montana, who wanted to buy the stuffed horse to display among the many Custer Battle items (later to be known as "Treasures of the West") at a museum in that city located "50 miles from the Custer Battlefield." This time the acting director of the University of Kansas museum cited "public opinion" against disposing of the horse and a statute "prohibiting the sale of state property without condemnation proceedings" as reasons for his refusal to sell Comanche (UK Archives).

The next battle over Comanche involved a site at which he had once been stationed—Fort Meade. In 1950, R. G. Cartwright of Lead, South Dakota, a Little Big Horn scholar, wrote to Colonel Nye

> There is a movement at Sturgis [South Dakota] to have Comanche shipped back. I do not believe it will be successful. One of the statements made was that he should be among his old comrades of which it was stated there are fifty buried at Fort Meade. In order to check up on the statement I visited the cemetery which as you perhaps remember is located on the heights behind the hospital. I found twenty four Seventh Cavalry markers but only four had participated in the Battle of the Little Big Horn.
> Only one man now survives who was in the regiment on its most fateful day. Jake Horner of Bismarck.

Revealing the importance some historians and buffs attach to Custer relics, Cartwright incidentally added, "I have not been up to the Battlefield for two years but did visit Old Fort Abraham Lincoln last summer. Managed to grab some half bricks from the central fireplace of the Custer home."

In his brief reply, Nye fails entirely to mention the movement to ship Comanche to South Dakota and, as usual, focuses on his hoped-for relocation of the horse in Montana. He informs Cartwright, "I had a letter from Luce a few days ago. He said he had $106,000 for the museum and that it was supposed to be started in May. Comanche should be there, of course" (CBNM Files).

The 1949–50 campaign to secure Comanche for South Dakota, however, was carried out with enthusiasm. The fact that Comanche had once resided at Fort Meade, where local people had come to know the horse, was used as a strong argument for returning him to his "old stamping grounds." In support of the move, a woman wrote of her childhood experience: "I remember when the Seventh Cavalry moved from Kansas to Fort Meade in 1889. The company camped one night on the prairie near Tilford not far from our home. We children went out to see Comanche and were allowed to stroke him, which was an event we would never forget." Another person who had seen Comanche alive remembered, "I laid my hands on him when I was a kid." An eighty-year-old man recalled often seeing Comanche led up Main Street in Sturgis, where the soldiers exercised him. Several other citizens of Sturgis reported seeing Comanche many times during their youth (and even at the New York World's Fair and at the Smithsonian!). The name Comanche was proposed for a Sturgis theater, and a bucking horse named Comanche was scheduled to perform in the local rodeo. A marker was suggested "to recall Comanche" at Fort Meade. Proponents of Comanche's transfer emphasized that the town itself had been named for Colonel Sturgis' son, who was killed with Custer (Hunn 1950; The Backlog 1950; Waldman 1964:83, 84).

Sturgis residents asserted that Comanche's "whole life and history is wrapped up in this area." The fact that "First Sergeant Charles Windolph who is [the] lone living survivor of the 7th Cavalry, who fought with General Custer," lived near Sturgis was cited as a strong point in favor of the horse being relocated there. A local newspaper editor reasoned, "Picture the horse 'Comanche' standing alone amid the dead at the battle of Little Big Horn. He stands amid desolation and death. Today he should stand along with Sgt. Windolph and others who knew him when he was alive. The people of Kansas should be more than willing that he should return to his beloved land." It was said that "Comanche should never have been taken away from here . . . because here is where his comrades were, several still living, many buried in heroes graves. A bunch of tenderfoots took Comanche along with them when the 7th went to Fort Riley. . . . They were an entirely new outfit, with none of the old timers who fought with Custer, Reno, and Benteen. . . . They were the ones who knew of the battles, and especially the Battle of the Little Big Horn, from which Comanche alone emerged." Comanche seemed alive to those who felt that "he should be shipped back here, once more to parade up and down the streets and pastures he knew so well. . . . When he is

returned he can again take part in military funerals, . . . and gaze
again out over the countryside he knew so well in days gone by"
(Waldman 1964:84).

Correspondence between the proponents of the transfer of
the famous mount to Sturgis "where he belongs" and officials at
the University of Kansas reveals that the South Dakotans' accusations that Comanche was "not appreciated" and was "gathering
dust" in the museum were firmly denied by the university. In response, a Sturgis businessman wrote to the University of Kansas
Museum: "Here in Sturgis we feel that even tho' Comanche is NOT
gathering dust at the University of Kansas, we would like to have
him back at Sturgis where, if he were alive, he could stand and
look where Custer camped at the foot of Bear Butte, and see the
place . . . where Chief Sweet Medicine received the sacred arrows
from the Great Spirit." The horse could also "see Reno Drive,
named for Major Reno, and Custer Drive, named for General
George Custer." Not only would he find many places named for
Seventh Cavalrymen, but he could see "Comanche Court where
over forty houses are built in one unit named for him." Then
Comanche could visit the cemetery at Fort Meade, "where about
fifty members of the 7th Cavalry Unit are buried—men that he
knew." (This is the statement that had prompted Cartwright to go
to the cemetery and investigate). The writer concludes that
"there are many people living in Sturgis and vicinity who have
seen Comanche when he was alive. However, I will drop the
whole matter if there are more people at the University of Kansas
who have seen Comanche alive than there are here who have seen
him alive" (Morrell 1949; Hunn 1950; The Backlog 1950; UK
Archives).

In 1951, the University of Kansas received two requests to
borrow the famous mount. Malott must have been relieved that in
these cases only temporary custody was sought. In February, the
sales promotion manager of The World Publishing Company
wrote the chancellor that "On May 21 of this year, exactly three
quarters of a century after Custer's Last Stand, the World Publishing Company is proudly publishing COMANCHE, a book for children on the life of the heroic U. S. Army horse who alone survived that massacre. The author is David Appel, Book Editor of
the *Philadelphia Inquirer*." He went on to explain

> In order to present this book to the American people in as excit-
> ing a manner as possible, we wish to hold an autograph party on
> publication date at one of the large Chicago Department stores.
> This party will receive nationwide publicity. Many mementoes from

the Custer battlefield will be lent to us for display at the party, but there is one crowning touch which would really complete this auspicious occasion.

That is, Comanche himself.

The letter concludes with the assurance that the company would "take care of every arrangement, ship him with utmost care, and return him to you immediately following the party in the same perfect state he was lent to us." The page from the company's spring catalogue described in glowing terms the forthcoming book about "the most famous military horse in American history" who "emerges from this unusual story as a sensitive, living, lovable creature" (UK Archives).

This time Comanche probably came about as close to leaving Lawrence as he ever would, for Dyche Museum Director E. R. Hall wrote to Malott that after consulting museum personnel, "initially, our reaction was favorable to loaning Comanche," contingent upon credit being given to the University Museum, provision of proper insurance, and adequate funding for his transport. But, Hall explained, "Since we are contemplating providing a humidifier for Comanche's quarters so as to retard the cracking and splitting of the skin that inevitably takes place, it seems to us upon reflection inconsistent to hasten his deterioration by sending him on a trip as long as the one to Chicago." The director pointed out that "the mount is now 60 years old; it is fragile and brittle and with the best of care would suffer some damage in being transported to and from Chicago." The decision not to loan Comanche was transmitted to the publishing company by the chancellor, who wrote that "it would be unwise to make any change in our present policy of keeping Comanche on the campus of the University," and explained "we are convinced that the preservation of Comanche can best be assured by keeping him in his display case on our campus" (UK Archives).

How many more books about the noted Seventh Cavalry horse would have been sold if his mounted remains had been on the site cannot be determined. What is certain is that the mount's fame was spreading. Within a few months another urgent plea for borrowing Comanche reached the chancellor, this time for display in connection with the 75th anniversary celebration of the state of South Dakota. Giving only very short notice, the governors of both Kansas and Montana were involved in the request, with the latter official urging in a telegram that Comanche be displayed during the Wild Bill Hickok festivities at Deadwood, South Dakota, on June 21 and at Custer Battlefield in Montana on June

24. The senator from Kansas wrote to Malott on behalf of the senator from South Dakota asking if arrangements could be made to "secure the mounted horse, Comanche" for display in South Dakota. In his letter the senator noted that "if I remember correctly, the mounted specie is not too strong but Senator Case assures me that the specie would be returned to the University of Kansas in equally as good condition as it was received."

Malott's reply assured the senator that "you are quite right in your recollections that Comanche is in no condition to travel. As a matter of fact, the scientists on our staff advise me that in their judgment, Comanche could not possibly survive a trip. His deterioration has been quite marked in recent years, and we are in the process of installing a humidifier in his display case in the hopes of prolonging his days." Malott went on to clarify why he must "reluctantly say 'no' to the South Dakota request. . . . We feel that Comanche will be of greater value to the young people not only of this community but of the entire country if, by keeping him on permanent location in the Museum, his 'life' can be extended."

Following his telegram with a letter, the acting director of the Dyche Museum expressed regret to the governor of Montana that the mounted horse could not be loaned to the Black Hills and Badlands Association for the forthcoming ceremonies. He explained, "Comanche was mounted over 50 years ago. The antiquated methods used by the taxidermist included building the body of the horse largely out of clay. This clay is now extremely brittle, fracturing very readily when the horse is moved. We have installed Comanche in a permanent exhibit, and we are now installing a humidifier in the case to preserve the horse for as long as possible." Expressing the ever-growing value of the mounted horse to the university museum, he informed the senator that "Comanche is the most popular single exhibit in our museum, especially among the school children. We feel that our obligation to the many thousands of children who visit this museum each year prohibits our exposing Comanche to the hazards of a long trip. The condition of the horse makes it probable that Comanche would be destroyed by a long trip—even if given elaborate care" (UK Archives).

Admirers everywhere were evidently becoming more concerned with Comanche's condition. One citizen of South Dakota was reconciled to celebrating his state's anniversary without the mounted horse. He wrote to the museum's acting director, "We have tried hard to have Comanche returned to this territory, but realizing now his state of condition we do not think it advisable."

150

Advice and aid were offered: "We do think that it would be possible to have him covered with plastic such as used on the noses of airplanes which would preserve him indefinitely. . . . We will advise you if we can be of any help to you on such a project" (UK Archives).

A South Dakota newspaper editor reasoned that "Montana has no claim to Comanche. While the Battle of the Little Big Horn was fought in Montana, the fighting was over possession of the Black Hills. That gives South Dakota prior rights." South Dakota's bid for Comanche caused some sentiment in North Dakota that the famous horse should be removed to that state. This claim might have been expected, since Comanche had close ties to Fort Abraham Lincoln. Many years previously, author P. E. Byrne had written to the Kansas museum curator from Bismarck (near Fort Lincoln), "Comanche has a special interest to the people hereabouts, for many people resident here knew personally General Custer and Captain Keogh and the rest, and also they remember Comanche after his return from the Little Big Horn." As one North Dakotan expressed it in 1953, Comanche "belongs to Kansas no more than Montana or Missouri and we say not as much as North Dakota. . . . If it hadn't been for the TLC he got in North Dakota, Comanche would have died! That gives North Dakota a very valid claim on him today. Obviously if the liverymen in Bismarck, N. D., had not given Comanche excellent care he would have died there or been cashiered out of the service. Let Kansas ship Comanche to North Dakota forthwith." Commenting on the North Dakota claim, a South Dakota editor remembered the University of Kansas museum curator saying that in moving Comanche, "the old warhorse would turn to dust. And since we and North Dakota have enough dust as it is, it—sad to say—is better that Comanche remain where he is" (Summer Reading 1953; UK Archives).

A great deal of interest centered on Comanche in 1951. On November 6 of that same year in which Chicago and South Dakota both lost their bids to borrow the horse, E. S. Luce, Superintendent of the Custer Battlefield National Monument, wrote to the regional director, Region Two, of the National Park Service, U. S. Department of the Interior. His attempt to move the horse to the battlefield reflected the intense interest Comanche always held for this former cavalryman, Custer Battle historian, staunch admirer of Custer and Keogh, and biographer of the famous mount and his rider. "Inspection of the horse, Comanche, with regard to a possible museum exhibit" was the subject of Luce's memorandum. "I have always felt that he would be a most desirable exhibit," the superintendent admitted. "There has been a universal demand and interest by our visitors that this horse be brought back to Custer Battlefield and installed as a permanent exhibit." Luce explained that during the previous month, without anyone at the museum knowing who he was or why he was visiting there, he had made a trip to Lawrence for the purpose of examining "the condition and presentability of the horse." His visit, he wrote, was prompted by "certain information which came to me as hearsay regarding the State of Montana's intent to make an effort to obtain this horse for the new Custer Battlefield Museum."

Luce reported, "I found the horse was in very good condition. The University of Kansas has placed him in a specially constructed glass case, about 20 feet long and 4½ feet wide, so that he can be viewed from both sides and ends. The tips of the ears are a bit ragged but not very noticeable, nor are they objectionable. My personal opinion is that he makes a very fine exhibit as a standard cavalry horse as he now stands." Admitting that "we have no space in our museum at the present time to exhibit this horse were it possible to obtain him," Luce noted that although the chief of the museum branch has not always agreed with the desirability of Comanche being exhibited at the battlefield, this official did remark last month that "if the State of Montana had plans in this regard, they would need to provide a wing on the present museum building for such display." Aware that "in the past, the University of Kansas has been rather indignant at efforts of other organizations or museums to obtain the horse," the superintendent suggests that they cause no "anxiety on the part of the university until such time that we are in agreement in the National Park Service that the horse would be a desirable exhibit and that we have a proper place for his exhibition."

Following Luce's missive, memoranda on the subjects he had raised were exchanged between various National Park Service officials, who agreed that there should be no move to return Comanche's remains to the Custer Battle site. As the regional director explained to the regional historian

> the horse is not essential to the proper interpretation of the battlefield. It seems to me that if we retrieved the horse, it would be entirely on sentimental grounds, that is, with a sense of appropriateness in returning to the battlefield all authentic relics thereof. I am not opposed to acquisition of the horse on sentimental grounds alone, but I fear that the practical obstacles, coupled with the "unessential" character of the horse as an interpretive exhibit, militate against officially starting any movement to acquire the animal.

Additionally, he pointed out that the high cost of Comanche's "stable-ization" in Montana with the consequent "disruption of the present architectural design" of the battlefield museum to house the proposed exhibit were factors which made the move inadvisable.

The historian expanded upon his views:

> I appreciate the fact that Custer Battlefield looms large in the field of American military traditions and everything associated with the battle necessarily has rather special antiquarian value. I can understand the potent spell which the horse would hold, not only upon students of the battle but on the average American visitor. However, this horse as an exhibit would add little to the visitor's comprehension of the important forces involved in the battle nor would it enlighten him on the historical background, the tactics and maneuvers which make the story so fascinating. Its only value would be to give the visitor a more intense feeling of immediacy with that fatal encounter of June 25–26, 1876. To me this appeal would put Comanche in the same class as most exhibits to be found in any ordinary museum which is filled with "relics" and curiosities intended to make the visitor goggle and exclaim rather than to make him understand. From the standpoint of the 7th Cavalry, the sentimental regard for Comanche is understandable; but its intrinsic historical value is debatable. My considered view is that the horse is not sufficiently vital for interpretive purposes to justify the very substantial investment of time and funds which the proposed exhibit would entail.

The regional director confirmed his agreement with the historian in a memorandum to the National Park Service director and recommended that "the Service make no effort to secure the horse for exhibit purposes at Custer Battlefield," since it "would prove to be a costly yet unessential exhibit." Receiving copies of these memoranda, Luce may have been surprised by the completely negative response of the National Park officials to his suggestion of returning Comanche to the site of the Custer tragedy. As one who understood the link between Comanche and the popular appeal of Custer's Last Stand, Luce must have been shocked by the obviously false idea that it was "the tactics and maneuvers which make the story so fascinating." Luce definitely seems to have been made uncomfortable by the correspondence he initiated, for he changed his stance somewhat, writing again to the regional director, Region Two, stating that the purpose of his original memorandum had been "merely to inform your office of the results of my inspection so that you would be prepared in case the question was brought up at some later date. I am not requesting action on the horse nor do I think it advisable at this time. . . . It was to protect myself if outside pressure were brought to bear upon the National Park Service to bring the horse Comanche to Custer Battlefield Museum for display."

The regional director responded to Luce, informing him that "we felt a policy decision was in order since the evidence indicated that there might be a request for such a decision in the not too distant future. If the subject was of sufficient importance to warrant your travel to Lawrence, Kansas, to inspect the horse, then the matter cannot be purely academic, and we cannot see any advantage in postponing its consideration." The subject was then summarily closed, at least for the time being, in a January 1952 memorandum from the assistant director of the National Park Service to the regional director, Region Two, stating "We are in agreement that the stuffed horse 'Comanche' would not be a desirable addition to the Custer Battlefield. . . . We hope no attempt will be made in any way to stimulate interest in this proposed transfer from the University of Kansas which would be highly reluctant to agree to such action" (CBNM Files).

Although this particular National Park Service correspondence was probably not revealed to the University of Kansas Museum authorities, the undercurrent of feeling that Comanche belonged at the Custer Battle site and the various overt movements to relocate the horse either temporarily or permanently must have contributed to the impetus to improve conditions for the celebrated mount's display. Preservation of Comanche's remains received strong assurance in January 1952, when a special humidifier was finally placed within the glass enclosure which surrounded them. In *Newsweek*, a brief description of the famous mount who had "earned an honorable old age" as the recipient of Sturgis's "General Order #7," was followed by the latest news report about the horse presented in a typical tongue-in-cheek tone: "Last week, the prize exhibit of the Kansas museum was honored some more. Like da Vinci's 'Last Supper,' which is now air-conditioned in a church in Milan, Italy, the animal received a special humidifier to preserve him from possible deterioration." The article, entitled "Warhorse and Weasels," refers additionally to E. Raymond Hall's "completion of a less historical but far more scientific project," a "25-year study of the American weasel," and notes that the Kansas Natural History Museum, of which he was Director, "ranks among the top university museums in the country." Under Comanche's photograph is the caption "A soothing mist enshrouds a legend of the West" (Warhorse and Weasels 1952:50). In 1953, the New Hampshire company that had built and installed Comanche's humidifier proudly declared in its advertisements that Comanche's "safe keeping" was guaranteed, that he was now "properly cared for," and that Mount Oread's " 'humidified air' agrees with him" (He Is Properly Cared For! 1953).

The special equipment installed for Comanche served to make him more firmly entrenched in his glass stall on Mount Oread, but it did not prevent the development of further onslaughts to remove him. The 1953 request for Comanche seemed to produce more bitter reactions than the preceding "attacks." Perhaps university officials were becoming more annoyed with the requests; certainly they were more sure of the university's position as rightful possessor of the remains and could "hold that line" more firmly.

In September 1953, the university made "a gallant stand to rescue Comanche" when the Kiwanis Club of Lewistown, Montana, initiated a movement to bring the mounted horse to the Custer Battlefield Museum. Petitioning the governor of Kansas, club members "passed rousing resolutions demanding that Comanche be moved to Montana." Malott was no longer chancellor, but Dr. E. Raymond Hall took over as the horse's defender. A heated verbal battle ensued, often expressed by the news media in equine metaphor. "Pawing and snorting members of the Kiwanis Club," which is "working itself into a lather," are "seeking to gain title to the famous stuffed horse which is nothing short of Dr. Hall's pride and joy. . . . Possession is nine points of the law. We're going to keep Comanche," responded the "indignant" Dr. E. R. Hall, curator of the Dyche Museum, "and therefore keeper of the stuffed horse. . . . Never, never will Kansas surrender possession of Comanche, sole survivor of Custer's massacre" (K. U. in Gallant Stand 1953:22; Shultz 1953; More Shots at Old Comanche 1953).

Dr. Hall was "particularly irked" at the statement of the Lewistown Kiwanis Club president that "We understand the gallant gelding has been allowed to get dusty and moth-eaten in the K. U. Museum" and the officer's "arrogantly" spoken assertion that "the famous horse is little appreciated by students and members of the K. U. faculty." Even worse was the club president's declaration that although Hall admittedly has "a personal respect and reverence" for the stuffed horse, "most people in Kansas have never heard of Comanche." Calling the Kiwanians' charges "ridiculous," Hall pointed out that "the horse has been treated with insecticide and sealed in an air-tight case to protect him from dust. A machine has been installed to keep a constant humidity in the case." The beleaguered curator retorted further that "thou-

sands of people come to see Comanche every year—from all over
Kansas, from every state in the nation, folks from abroad. They
bring friends and relatives." As one writer phrased Hall's explo-
sive reactions, "The mere thought that Comanche is neglected or
unappreciated stirred his soul" (K. U. in Gallant Stand 1953;
More Shots at Old Comanche 1953; Shultz 1953).

The civic club's allegations "kindled fires of defiance at the
statehouse and on Mount Oread." The illogic reflected in the in-
vocation of Colonel Sturgis' 1878 order regarding the equine
Custer Battle survivor who was at that time a living animal was not
a deterrent to use of the unique order as a weapon of defense. For
Dr. Hall "clinched all claims regarding title to Comanche" by asserting that the horse is the legal property of the state by virtue of
Sturgis' famous Order No. 7. "That order recites the kind care
and treatment accorded Comanche and stated that responsibility
for his care and keeping rests with the Seventh cavalry, stationed
at Fort Riley, where Comanche died. That was the only order
ever given in behalf of a horse by [a] commanding officer of the
United States Army." The governor of Kansas stood "firmly behind Dr. Hall's claim to Kansas rights for perpetual possession of
the famous stuffed horse. . . . My recollections are that Gen. Samuel D. Sturgis ordered the remains to be kept in Kansas where the
horse can be given the best of care. I know of no better jurisdiction in the case. . . . That order by General Sturgis seems conclu-
sive," he declared. "I can't imagine any clearer title than the general's directive" (Shultz 1953; K. U. in Gallant Stand 1953).

As the fight for Comanche escalated, territorial loyalties between the two states gave emphasis to the clash. In response to a
Kansas editorial assertion that the stuffed horse was receiving the
best care at the university, the Lewistown Kiwanis president alleged in an interview that the editor and "99.8 per cent of all the
KU students never took the trouble to go see Comanche until we
Montanans put in our rightful claim for the horse." "This is further proof of the lack of homage shown by Kansans for this gallant gelding which is famous only because it came to the Treasure
state," he added (Shannon 1953a:8).

The intensity of the 1953 Montana versus Kansas controversy stimulated partisans to do for the old war horse what it had
always been hoped he could do for himself—speak. Claiming empathy with Comanche, the Kiwanis chief officer wrote to the governor of Kansas asking him to act "in fairness to the horse. . . . A
stuffed horse can't speak for itself. . . . If Comanche could, the
Kiwanis Club of Lewistown, Montana, is sure the gallant gelding
would want to get out of Kansas and return to Montana where it

helped General Custer ride to death and fame. . . . Horse heaven to Comanche," the club president claimed, "is on the banks of Montana's Little Big Horn River." A letter from "The Spirit of Comanche" expressing the mount's own desire to remain in Kansas appeared in the *Daily Kansan* (1953). Having "fought gallantly for my country," the horse pleads to have his story heard. "I loved it in Kansas," where "the grass was lush and green rather than scorched and dry as it had been in Montana. . . . I reside today one of the best known, loved, and respected citizens of Kansas. Yearly thousands of Kansans and people from all over the world come and visit me. . . . [I only fear] that I will be sent back to Montana." In response to this missive, Old Stud, a Montana horse, wrote to the news editor from "the lush green grass" of his "home range" to say that "the supposed letter from Comanche" is "so obviously a fake and a fraud that I must answer it. No horse that had ever been to Montana—and particularly a smart horse like Comanche—would ever write such a letter, though a jackass might." Old Stud reveals that any horse would know that native Montana bunch grass is "the world's finest," and that Man of War, "when he was winning all those races back in those eastern cities, ate nothing but native Montana hay, which was shipped to him from the Little Big Horn country in Montana, where Comanche rode to fame." It was obvious that some Kansans had "taken advantage of a defenseless dead horse, trying to put words into its mouth by faking a letter from Comanche's spirit to that college paper down in hot, humid Kansas. As a horse, who knows best the thoughts and desires of other horses, I deplore this crude forgery, and appeal to Kansans to send Comanche back to the museum on the Custer battlefield in the high, cool, glorious, and lush Montana plains" (Shultz 1953; More Shots at Old Comanche 1953; Shannon 1953a:8).

Since, as the Lewistown Kiwanians agreed, the mounted horse "can't speak for itself," numerous self-appointed spokespersons put words into the mouth of Comanche—"a nag stone-cold dead and stuffed." Montanans pointed out that the horse "did not have anything to say about its final resting place [in Kansas] and should come back to Montana where it would be the happiest." One Kansan empathized with the horse, saying he "probably wouldn't like the [Montana] climate anyway, and where could he be admired by more pretty coeds than right here on top of Mount Oread?" The "horseplay" continued, as a museum visitor pointed out that Comanche still stood, "life-like," and "with all the composure of a five-star general. Contrary to the Montana charges, Comanche's fluffy locks look as if he has always enjoyed the privilege of a toprate barber shop." A sour note was struck when someone commented on the tug-of-war: "It'll be a close race to see whether Montana Kiwanians or the moths get Comanche first" (Comanche, Weary 1953; Montana In Bid 1953; Montana Sets 1953; Comanche Faces 1953).

In a more serious vein, the editor of the Kansas alumni magazine noted that "official records will show Comanche was a remount bought in Kansas in 1866, and spent most of his life here. Let the Kiwanians go whistle for the horse. We'll keep him in our museum where he won't be exploited, and give him a little of the peace and quiet he justly deserves." A university alumnus ("now absent from Kansas only long enough to get Seminary training in the East") said, "I was first taken to see Comanche when I was only five years old and have been going back often ever since. . . . While a student I was always interested in Comanche and the museum as were a great number of other students." He confessed to being the author of the "Spirit of Comanche" letter, and explained that a recent trip through Montana proved to him that "there is little of either lushness or greenness about the state," and that "irrigation is all that keeps it from being completely barren. The tourist trade is the principal industry of Montana and this, of course, is why Comanche is wanted there" (Regnary 1953; Smith 1953).

It was later reported that "a group from the University of Montana" had "offered to steal" the mounted horse from Kansas in 1953, but the effort "fizzled out" (Comanche: Diary 1966:13; Jones 1964:6). According to the *University Daily Kansan*, an offer to help Montanans kidnap Comanche was made in an anonymous letter by a University of Kansas student. The student said he had never heard of Comanche before Montana claimed him and felt the horse "would like it better in Montana." The same article reported that the governor of Kansas wrote the Montana Kiwanis Club president "I regret that you are considering taking your Comanche claim to the War Department." He also pointed out that when Comanche died he had "been in Montana Territory only about a month, so rather than being a bona fide resident of your state—when it wasn't even a state—he was in fact a tourist in a military sense." Allegedly, the club president had proposed a compromise for Comanche: "Kansas can have him in the winter and Montana in the summer (when the students are gone)" (Shannon 1953b).

Montana's well-publicized fight for Comanche caused at least one other state to put in a contemporaneous bid for the mounted horse. A Missouri newspaper writer speculated, "I am not sure that Livingston, Montana, should have any more claim to the mounted specimen of Comanche than Missouri. In 1864, the Missourian pointed out, Keogh served as troop commander of the Tenth Missouri Cavalry, and in that year the Captain "purchased Comanche from a government remount herd in Sedalia, Mo." when the horse was "4 years old. . . . Missourians should be acquainted with the fact that this was a Missouri horse." Despite the states that claim him, the article gives assurance that Comanche "sits out the battle" in his glass case at the university (Grisham 1953).

The Lewistown battle for Comanche died hard. Two years later, in November 1955, a bitter flare-up occurred. At that time, the Kansas University Natural History Museum received as a gift a pair of General Custer's fringed buckskin riding pants "to go with Comanche." Lewistown news reporters took advantage of this new presentation to restate Montana's claim to the war horse's remains. In an article headed "Kansas can keep Custer's pants, but Lewistown's Kiwanians still want the General's horse, Comanche, back in Montana," the service club's vice president stated that "so far as I'm concerned, Kansas stole Comanche and should return the General's horse. If they do, I won't begrudge them one pair of Custer's pants. After all the General was a dandy and had plenty of pants, but only one horse." According to the museum director, the pants would be "exhibited for a time in the museum's 'Case of the Month' display." But "Dr. Hall hasn't decided whether they will be shown with the horse, which occupies an air-conditioned, glassed-in cubicle on the second floor" (Kansas Can Keep 1955).

Old arguments about the horse's location during which, it was recalled, "even the Governors of the two states were embroiled in the brawl" were revived. The 1953 Kiwanis Club president's arguments that "no one would have ever heard of Comanche had the horse not come to Montana territory with Custer" and that "Comanche should be returned to Montana where it rode to fame, and would be happier" were once again emphasized (Kansas Can Keep 1955; General Custer's Pants Given 1955). Perhaps University of Kansas officials were becoming sensitive to criticism of their institution holding Little Big Horn associated historical relics, for a subsequent newspaper article describing the gift of the pants indicated that "the trousers may be ultimately transferred, if the University of Kansas deems it best to do so, to the Kansas State Historical Society, which also has some of General Custer's personal effects, or to the Custer Battlefield museum which is on the actual site of the battle in which Custer lost his life" (Custer's Pants Given 1955).

Although the Lewistown battle had been one of the most intense in Comanche's existence as a mounted specimen, "after the dust had cleared, Comanche was still in his same old 'pasture' in the glass case in Dyche Museum" (Jones 1964:6). Proponents of relocating the horse at the Montana battle site were still making efforts, however, to have their wishes realized. In 1958, a national park staff historian wrote to the superintendent of Custer Battlefield advocating active efforts to acquire Comanche from the University of Kansas. The reply which the acting chief, Museum Branch, sent to the chief historian in response to this matter of "Comanche and the Custer Battlefield National Monument" is very revealing of the mindset of those who disapproved of the move for reasons other than the unwillingness of University of Kansas authorities to part with their specimen. The memorandum reads, in part,

> The Museum Branch has consistently advised against the display of Comanche at Custer Battlefield. We believe the horse is too big to be exhibited effectively in the Visitor Center. This horse is the focal point display standing alone in a case in the center of the main museum rotunda about 400 feet in circumference, and at least two stories [sic] high. This setting alone would account for some of the attention which it has doubtless attracted. No comparable setting can be given at the Custer Battlefield.
>
> Even if the building at Custer were enlarged, the size of this specimen would make it the most prominent feature in the museum and it would therefore tend to overemphasize a secondary part of the story.
>
> In its present form, Comanche is an interesting example of the techniques of taxidermy in a period of transition. In a natural history museum this aspect of the specimen is quite significant. If Comanche were to be used solely as an historic specimen, it probably would be desirable to have it remounted in accordance with modern standards which would be an expensive and difficult undertaking.
>
> While we realize the paramount importance of genuine historical objects interpreting the Custer Battlefield story, we do not think that the specimen in question would function well as part of the Custer Museum. (CBNM Files)

Talk about a downplay! Surely "the setting alone," which in that day actually did little to enhance or enrich the significance of the famous mount, could not account for Comanche's profound and widespread appeal. As for Comanche being a "secondary part of the story," one could ask what was more primary in the Indian campaigns than the role of the cavalry horse, which Comanche represented. As for being "an interesting example of the techniques of taxidermy," nothing could be farther from explaining the specimen's unique importance. If Comanche was not a "genuine historical object," what could fit that requirement?

In spite of the banality of such uninspired responses, the conviction continued to be strong among interested individuals that Comanche should stand at the battlefield where he achieved immortality. From time to time, petitions to this effect were drafted. In 1960, for example, George Osten, long-time Custer Battle buff and benefactor to the National Monument, and J. K. Ralston, noted Montana artist whose works include depictions of Comanche and of the Battle of the Little Big Horn, "expressed keen interest in persuading the University of Kansas to part with the stuffed horse, Comanche, in the Dyche Museum at Lawrence for permanent display at Custer Battlefield." Briefly, the regional director responded to the superintendent that "the reasons previously given to decline this proposal are still valid." Point one is the unwillingness of the University of Kansas "to part with their prize trophy." Point two is that the Museum Branch "has always been strongly opposed to this move," since "it is felt that a stuffed animal in a historical museum strikes a jarring note. Also, proper placement of the specimen would require space out of proportion to its importance in the history of the battle itself." Though "familiar with the excellent unselfish contributions by Mssrs. Osten and Ralston and others to the furtherance of the purposes of the National Monument" and appreciative of "the sincerity of their proposal," the conclusion is that "in all honesty we cannot give any encouragement to its renewal" (CBNM Files).

Meanwhile, University of Kansas officials were more convinced than ever of the value and popularity of their mounted horse. From time to time, especially on the anniversary of the Little Big Horn Battle, articles about Comanche's history were republished. Accounts of some of the many unsuccessful attempts to remove him from Mount Oread were included. In 1964, one such article emphasized Comanche's significance to the institution's graduates, indicating that "thousands of K. U. Alumni pay visits to Comanche when they return for class reunions. He has been part of the university scene longer than many of the buildings." Readers were assured that Comanche was still in a "place of honor" on campus and that he was well cared for. He was shown in his air-conditioned glass case in order to refute any doubts about his condition, and a caption noted that "he could give a horse laugh to his living kin, toiling in the summer sun" (Rutter 1964:40).

Although it was clear that the university planned to keep Comanche, requests for the famous horse continued to arrive. In 1967, the curator of the Amon Carter Museum of Western Art in

Fort Worth, Texas, wrote to the director of the University of Kansas museum to ask whether Comanche could be borrowed for an exhibit of works of art depicting the Custer Battle. The request was politely refused because of the inadvisability of removing the mount from his humidified case. The director expressed the hope that "those visitors who are really interested in seeing Comanche will want to travel to Lawrence, Kansas, to see the famous horse. Many visitors who have been to the scene of Custer's Last Stand tell us they have traveled 500 to 1,000 miles out of their way just to stop by the Museum of Natural History to view the remains of this famous horse" (UK Archives).

Many of what Chancellor Malott would have called "hullaba-loos" continued to revolve around the horse. One Kansan who "visited the Custer National Monument twice" wrote to the Secretary of the Interior in 1970 to state that "both times I've felt Custer's horse Commanche should be on display there. At the present time there is agitation on the KU campus for his removal. This would seem a most advantageous time for the Department of Interior to benefit from a controversy. I would appreciate anything you can do to acquire Commanche for the Monument." The letter was referred to the National Park's midwest region director, who had jurisdiction over Custer Battlefield, to the chief historian, to the assistant director for cooperative programs, and then back to the Custer Battlefield superintendent, who had already received a letter identical to that sent to the interior secretary. A memorandum to the midwest regional director from the superintendent indicated that they "goofed" in their response to the Kansas woman

> by not indicating that we would follow through on her suggestion. Actually, we purposely did not follow through because of a local situation. A good friend of Custer Battlefield and a member of the Board of Directors of the area's cooperating association, Mr. George Osten, has been working for years to acquire Comanche for the battlefield. It was our understanding that he was going to contact Kansas University again this year with the view of having Comanche donated or loaned to the battlefield by 1976, the centennial year. We have neither encouraged nor discouraged his efforts. The Service's position on the subject is not entirely clear to us. We know that Superintendent Luce was interested in securing Comanche, but there has not been a lot of official enthusiasm for the project since his retirement.

The superintendent then indicates that "the problem hinges on two questions"—whether Kansas would transfer the mount and whether the horse would add anything to the interpretive program. The answer to the first question, he indicates, is undoubtedly no. Probably the simplest answer to the Kansas woman's letter, then, would be to ask the university if their attitude about transferring the mount had changed.

The answer to the second question, he says, "is not so simple." Display space according to the superintendent was not adequate at present but might be available in the future. As to what the horse would "add to our program," it "would not be inappropriate to have the exhibit here, but its presence might overshadow our other interpretive efforts. Instead of developing the pros and cons of the subject at this time, we would prefer to think about it a while longer. A new Master Plan and Interpretive Prospectus is scheduled for the battlefield in FY 1972 so logically the subject should be deferred until that time."

Enclosed with this memorandum was "Historian Soubier's report on the subject." The superintendent indicated that "while his [Soubier's] tongue-in-cheek approach would not be appropriate for a public inquiry, most of his observations on the subject are valid and are seriously presented." This report, entitled "L'Affaire Comanche, or Flogging a Dead Horse," which will be referred to again later, was a review of the cavalry mount's history that contained more than its share of inaccuracies. Soubier's argument against the relocation to Montana takes an unexpected twist when he points out that though the horse's

> skin is preserved and draped over a form at the University of Kansas, the rest was buried ceremoniously at Fort Riley. In terms of bulk, the latter certainly represents the greater, if not the most presentable, part of Comanche. Presumably the fleshy parts have returned to dust, leaving the bones, traditionally the most significant earthly remains. If this is not the case, then the repository of bones at Custer Battlefield becomes a mockery. It is our official opinion that consistent with the nature and purpose of National Cemeteries, Comanche is actually at Fort Riley.

As to the desirability of displaying the horse at Custer Battlefield, Soubier explains that Comanche's connection with the Battle of the Little Big Horn "is no greater than any other single relic of the battle. The horse played no strategic role in the battle. Historical significance rests entirely on sentiment and the mythological aura surrounding the Custer disaster." Additionally, "the presence of so large an object" would "command excessive attention. It would represent an object of curiosity out of proportion to its significance. It would be a pity if a visitor left Custer Battlefield with his strongest impression that of a stuffed horse, but this would no doubt occur in many cases." As an almost anticlimactic conclusion to this particular episode, the Kansas petitioner received a letter from the acting director, midwest region, stating that the Kansas University administration "has taken the position that the horse was more accessible to view at the University museum," that he "was unequivocally the property of the University," and that "we do not have, at the present time, display space for the mount at Custer Battlefield" (CBNM Files).

The next year, in the fall of 1971, an Iowa resident who visited the Custer Battlefield while on vacation managed to stir up quite a fuss when she found that the famous mount was not there. Writing to her congressman about "a problem which is occurring in Montana but affecting many persons," and admitting "it is nothing earth shattering," she protested that, although the famous battlefield "was indeed preserved for posterity," there was a matter which troubled her, for

> it seems the monument is missing one thing—an item that should be at the monument and its being anywhere else is really very absurd. The missing item is the statue of Comanche—the only survivor of the battle—which I'm told is in a University of Kansas.
> First of all, what is the university doing with the stuffed horse which so obviously belongs in the Custer Monument? That's like putting the San Francisco trolley cars in Cedar Rapids, Iowa.
> Secondly, I don't see how a state completely removed from the area of the battle of this historic value could lay claim to one of the major artifacts of the battle.
> Can you advise me of persons I might contact about this gross injustice to the Custer Memorial.
> I can even see the soldiers being buried elsewhere at families request but the lone survivor would hardly have a "speaking" family.

On behalf of his constituent, the Iowa congressman immediately sent an inquiry about the appropriateness of Comanche's location to the director of the National Park Service. After exchanging some interdepartmental correspondence about the details on just how such constituents' letters were to be handled, the Custer Battlefield superintendent replied to the Iowa congressman

> We are pleased to acknowledge your inquiry . . . concerning the display of Comanche at Custer Battlefield National Monument. The University of Kansas has been approached a number of times regarding the transfer of Comanche to Custer Battlefield National Monument. Each time the University has stated that the mount was not available for transfer. The University is obviously very pleased to have Comanche in their collection and have no desire to see the mount moved to another location.
> We are enclosing a copy of an article on Comanche from the

Winter 1970 edition of the "Research Review" of the Little Big Horn Associates. The article gives the history of Comanche and information on how the Dyche Museum at the University of Kansas acquired the horse. (CBNM Files)

The next request for Comanche's transfer came in the following year when the newly appointed curator of the U. S. Cavalry Museum at Fort Riley, Kansas, petitioned the director of the Museum of Natural History at Lawrence in May of 1972. Calling his inquiry "a stab in the dark," the curator asked for the horse "on either an outright or a loan basis." He explained that "Custer's Quarters are about 150 yards from me, in sight, as I write. Many of those men are buried here, and the legends of the American Horse Cavalry are thick. It would be most appropriate here, if it were possible to arrange this." The next event in this saga was that Laurence Chalmers, current chancellor at the university, received a letter from Edward M. Flanagan, commanding general at Fort Riley, stating that

> My museum curator . . . has coordinated with Dr. Phillip S. Humphrey regarding the possible transfer of COMANCHE to the US Cavalry Museum here at Fort Riley.
> The permanent display of this exhibit would be the focal point in our museum since Comanche was the sole military survivor of the US Cavalry at the Battle of the Little Big Horn.

The curator, he assured the chancellor, "would handle all details of the transfer and personally accompany the exhibit during shipment." The vice-chancellor wrote to Museum Director Philip Humphrey, "I shall appreciate your comments on General Flanagan's request and your recommendations for an appropriate reply." Meanwhile, Dr. Humphrey had already written directly to the Fort Riley curator

> As you probably know, Comanche has had a long history here in the Dyche Museum, and while I can appreciate the appropriateness of having Keogh's horse at the U. S. Cavalry Museum, I am also mindful of the long history of association Comanche has had with the Museum of Natural History here at U. K. History and traditions are difficult things to break. Perhaps at some time in the future this matter can be rethought, but for now, I cannot envision giving Comanche permanently to the U. S. Cavalry Museum. Nevertheless, during the coming academic year, I will discuss this matter with the curators of the Museum of Natural History and the Chancellor of the University so that at least the question will have an opportunity of being aired once again by the appropriate authorities here at the University.

165

Humphrey adds that "during the last several years, I have refused the loan of Comanche to various organizations because the horse, as presently exhibited, is extremely fragile and could be seriously, if not irreparably, damaged by being moved." The vice-chancellor wrote to Dr. Humphrey asking for his recommendations about the Fort Riley request, but the answer had been predetermined by the statement, "In view of the long history of these discussions and the tradition of Comanche at this institution, I should expect that only the most compelling arguments could justify Comanche's transfer to another museum." The vice-chancellor, after discussing the request at length with Professor Humphrey, wrote a polite refusal resting mainly on the fact that "the exhibit has become a traditional part of the Museum and indeed of the University and is viewed annually by scores of thousands of viewers," and upon the "large public and University sentiment" concerning the long association of the Comanche exhibit with the University of Kansas Museum. In 1973, Chancellor Emeritus Raymond Nichols evidently wanted to be reassured about the university's arguments for retaining the famous horse. A letter from Stephen R. Edwards, Assistant at the Museum of Natural History, with a copy to Dr. Humphrey, briefly reviewed the circumstances surrounding Dyche's mounting of the horse and the army's failure to make payment. The conclusion was definite: "From everything that I have read it seems clear that Comanche is the property of the University of Kansas (or the Dyche Estate) as a result of default of payment" (UK Archives). In 1975, soon after Archie Dykes became chancellor, he turned down a similar request for Comanche's removal to the former Kansas cavalry post. Undaunted, the curator of the Fort Riley museum said "we'll keep trying" to get Comanche (Dary 1976a).

Comanche's popularity continues. In 1986, for example, the museum denied a Californian's request to have the horse "moved from your locale to the beautiful confines of Santa Anita Race Track, where he would be viewed by millions." The optimistic petitioner believed "the US Gov't would pay for the transportation." The writer explained that his father-in-law had been a stable boy with Custer and had worked with Comanche, the "strange yet intelligent horse." The remains of the horse "belong in the beautiful country where thousands of horses run the paths at Santa Anita every year," he asserted, for "an institution of learning is too confining for ultimate exposure" (UK Archives).

Although it is clear that Comanche will stay in Kansas, Little Big Horn enthusiasts still discuss and argue about the issue of Comanche's location. The majority of Custer buffs who make their opinions known would like to see the mounted horse relocated at the Montana battlefield. A typical expression of this view is, "It has been a very long time since I last saw Comanche. He didn't look like much and I'm certain his appearance has not improved. I do expect with proper treatment his appearance could be restored. He is a symbol of the Little Big Horn Battle and should be preserved. I would like to see him on display at the battlefield if they would find a place for him." Another devotee explains, "I have often wondered if it would be possible to house Comanche at the Custer Battlefield. It has always seemed to me that he is far removed from the scene of Comanche's greatest glory, and that many people don't know of his existence. I'm sure children across the nation would contribute to his moving. The money could be used for an addition to the battlefield museum and for the movement." As a less hopeful buff articulated his ideas,

> Comanche should remain in a museum—that at the Battlefield, of course. My rationale is that everything pertaining to the Custer fight should be at Custer Battle National Monument and not scattered all over and in private collections as it is today. Since Comanche was the most famous of living things, all animals, i.e., one dog, one grey horse that followed the Seventh down to the Yellowstone (or maybe only to the Yellowstone River) and several other wounded 7th Cavalry horses that were mercifully shot, it should be given more and better exposure as the "last survivor." The Kansans, naturally, will have a different opinion and outside of outright kidnapping the stuffed animal, I personally don't think there's anything that any person or group can do to change what is already a *fait accompli.*

Concerning the present location of the horse, another Custer Battle enthusiast points out,

> Most people visiting the museum at Lawrence, Kansas view Comanche's remains as a curio. I dare say that very few people know Comanche's remains are there until they arrive and are either told about it or stumble on to it. He should, in my judgment, stand where he would be most appreciated by the greatest number of Americans. I would put him in the Smithsonian in Washington, D. C. in an appropriate setting. His presence at the Custer Battlefield National Monument in summer time would also be most appreciated and meaningful.

A long-time student of the battle said,

> I have been fortunate enough to visit the Dyche Museum at Lawrence, so I am a little familiar with the topic. I think it is a fine dis-

play in its own case right where it is. I know the story behind WHY it's located in an out of the way place on a small college campus, and that of itself has historical meaning to me. However, many people probably never see it who should see it. As such, it probably would be of more benefit on display at the Battlefield, National Cowboy Hall of Fame, or the Buffalo Bill Museum at Cody, etc. For dramatic reasons, I would like to see Comanche in a diorama setting, say with Gustave holding his reins or some such. The glass enclosure is somewhat sterile. Space and money are probably the limiting factors.

As "one of the really great ties we have with the wonderful Custer story," another believes, "Comanche should be kept the way he is in the museum. I have high hopes of seeing him, myself, someday. If he can't, for some reason, be kept there, what about the historical museum in Monroe, Michigan [Custer's hometown]? I've been there and the rooms are big. What a nice addition he would be to the existing Custer display!" And one person who devotes full time to Custer studies feels, "I don't believe the horse should be removed under any circumstances. The horse is protected behind glass, and once removed it may just fall into disregard in a basement full of rats and other infestations. It would be the ruination of this wonderful symbol" (letters to and interviews with the author).

Nothing seems to change. In 1980, officials at Fort Riley told me, "We still want Comanche here. But the only way to get this accomplished would be by gubernatorial intervention." Custer Battlefield personnel indicate that visitors to the museum continue to inquire about Comanche quite frequently and express disappointment that the mounted horse is not there. In 1987, the historian of the National Monument revealed that each year a considerable number of individuals ask him, "Why isn't Comanche on display here?" He answers, "We don't want him here. The horse would become more important than the battle. . . . Many people," he pointed out, "believe Comanche was Custer's horse." It is also noteworthy that "about a half a dozen times a year" the National Park historian said, "I am approached by an older visitor who asserts 'Comanche was here 30 years ago,' and demands 'Where is he?' " When it is explained that the horse has always been in Kansas, not at the Montana battle site, the youthful historian is then asked "Were you here 30 years ago?" To the obvious negative reply the visitor indignantly retorts "Well *I* was, and I saw the horse here!"

Many people continue to feel that Comanche belongs at the site of the Little Big Horn Battle. Kathleen Nye Smith, whose father, Colonel Nye, urged Comanche's "return to the field of his greatness" (n.d.(a):3), recently communicated this idea to the superintendent of the Custer Battlefield. "One of the finest things that could happen to the C. B. N. M.," she claimed, "is to get Comanche back where he rightly belongs. The sentimental and historical value of the presence of this national treasure within the museum is immeasurable, and think what a drawing card he would be. In all probability, the museum is going to have to be enlarged someday anyway," to display the "ever-growing collection of Custeriana" and to accommodate increasing numbers of visitors. "The resurgence of interest in this chapter of American history is heart-warming." She realized that it would take time to convince authorities at the University of Kansas to return the "old fellow" to the Custer Battlefield. But she also knew "there are many Custerphiles with whom I keep in contact who feel passionately about this and plead for his return. I refuse to believe it can't be done." In a 1988 conversation, Mrs. Smith told me she "would bend all efforts to get Comanche back, if the superintendent would take him." But whenever she has approached Custer Battlefield officials in person, she has been disappointed by being told "we don't want Comanche here," and "there's no room for him."

The number of requests to borrow or possess Comanche, the widespread public interest in the resultant "battles," and the sentiments and vehement opinions expressed by both sides attest to the remarkable significance attributed to the mount who survived Custer's Last Stand. His endurance as a museum specimen after death matches the fortitude he showed in life.

In spite of all the controversies regarding his whereabouts, Comanche has remained on Mount Oread, much to the satisfaction of Kansans and particularly the university community. Undoubtedly more deeply appreciated as a result of the skirmishes involving contested ownership and of the often expressed opinions of those who would like the display to be moved elsewhere, Comanche's remains appear to have entered a new era of careful preservation after the various claims were defeated. Expressing their concern, "When officials at Dyche Museum of Natural History talk about 'watering the horse' they don't mean they are tending a live animal. Instead, they are making sure there is enough moisture in the glass cabinet which holds the mounted remains of Comanche, the only survivor of the Battle of the Little Big Horn" (Jones 1964:6).

Chapter 9

The Tail of Comanche

For those who feel compelled to worship at the hoofs of a horse, all is not lost. One has only to travel to the Great Plains of our own Midwest to Lawrence, Kansas. (Ballantine 1964:268)

The physical remains of Comanche—hoofs, hair coat, mane, and tail—have been objects of intense, and sometimes humorous, fascination. Exemplifying the remarkable appeal of even trivial traces of his being is the reported 1963 event in which a piece of Comanche's hoof (evidently once treasured by someone at Fort Riley) was transmitted to the University of Kansas archives from the University of California at Los Angeles. The artifact was accompanied by a document from the post quartermaster's office at Fort Riley, dated September 29, 1891, authenticating its provenance. In a long and humorous letter stressing inter-university cooperation, the California university official informed the University of Kansas chancellor, "I have the great honor to transmit officially to you for the KU collections the enclosed remarkable museum specimen, a fully attested fragment from the hoof of the sole survivor of the Little Big Horn, General Custer's great horse, Comanche." This "inter-institutional gift" was made, he explained, because "KU is distinguished the world over as the public resting place of Comanche, a shrine to which countless worshippers of the American heritage have always turned." The University of Kansas chancellor responded to his colleague that his institution was "tremendously pleased" to accept the gift, adding "this is the first instance in my recollection that I have had the opportunity to correspond relative to this portion of a horse" (UK Archives).

Hair from Comanche was embued with special meaning, both in life and after his death. It was reported that "Comanche —in his declining days, had his troubles—whenever there was a crowd of sightseers visiting Fort Riley, it was necessary to keep him closely guarded in order to prevent the souvenir and curio collectors from plucking all the hair from his tail and mane" (Schultz 1939). When he became a mounted specimen, his hairs, particularly strands from his tail, were taken by acquisitive museum visitors. At just which point in his existence the greatest loss of those black tail hairs was sustained is uncertain, but undoubtedly it occurred during times when the mount was accessible to admirers, unprotected by the glass case. A 1936 newspaper article describing the "Latest Tail" of Comanche reported that "between the Pacific and Atlantic oceans there are several persons who treasure among their many souvenirs of their several travels, little whisps of horse hair. Each of the souvenir collectors and relic seekers fondly believe that they have some of the hair from the tail of Comanche." But the secret that has been guarded by the "mysterious grin" of the stuffed horse's museum caretaker has now "leaked out":

> Since his death Comanche has had seven tails. Mayhap before many more years pass, that historic horse will have even more and all because of the souvenir hunters, each of whom in visiting the state university museum, have secretly and with much caution stolen a few hairs from the tail of the stuffed remains of Custer's horse.
> Whenever Comanche's tail becomes so thin as to appear positively shabby the attendants at the museum deftly remove it and some unknown and defunct horse donates another supply of caudal appendage to the cause of history and the religious faith of the relic hunters. (Famous Comanche 1936)

The magic number of tails for the Seventh Cavalry horse who was so often said to have sustained seven battle wounds is cited in a brief undated newspaper report stating that "General Custer's war horse Commanche, which stands stuffed in the museum of the University of Kansas, 'has had seven tails since its death, because souvenir hunters have robbed it, a hair at a time, all thinking that they were getting a strand of the original tail'" (CBNM Files). Visitors did this, according to one report, "believing that because Comanche survived Indian ambush a hair from his tail would bring good luck" (Snyder 1951:36). E. S. Luce, who, because of his former membership in the Seventh Regiment, U. S. Cavalry, would be expected to especially honor that number, wrote to Colonel W. A. Graham in 1948 that "students have perpetrated vandalism on Comanche's tail to such an extent that he has been re-tailed six times. They would pull the hair out of his tail as a good omen to pass their final examinations" (CBNM Files).

A University of Kansas News Bureau release describes the 1939 Hardin attempt to relocate the horse in Montana and reveals the damage sustained by the mounted specimen while in storage. As evidence of the popularity of the exhibit in the Dyche Museum, it was noted that "The University was often asked for pictures of Comanche, and on one occasion a letter came from an Irish lad asking for 'just one hair' from Comanche's tail" (1939). In 1950 an Illinois resident wrote to ask for "a lock of hair from Comanche's mane." As the museum director explained his refusal, "a positive response to this request and others like it would shortly result in nothing being left of the hide of the mounted Comanche" whose hair has already been depleted by souvenir hunters (Museum Gets 1950).

Information released by the U. K. News Bureau after General Wainwright's 1947 unsuccessful effort to obtain Comanche for the museum at Fort Riley, Kansas, "the Mecca of all horse cavalrymen," indicates that "he is now kept under a glass case—too many visitors had wanted a hunk of hair for a souvenir. In fact, in the first three decades of the century, so much hair had to be replaced that there is now some argument about Comanche's original color" (UK Archives). A 1951 article revealed, "The moths have found provender in his hide and his once sleek hair now is scant and spotty" (Snyder 1951:36). A strong reason later cited for not moving him to the cavalry post was that if the stuffed horse were taken from his special humidifier to a museum where there is no air-conditioning, "he'd be balder than an egg in no time" (Redskins Attack 1970).

Hair from Comanche's body coat may have been taken by souvenir hunters. In 1931, when viewing the old horse whose wounds he had once helped to treat during the animal's convalescence, General Hugh Scott had reportedly been "asked by an onlooker whether a scarred place on Comanche's neck was also a wound." In answer, "the general immediately replied that he did not remember any wound being on the animal in that spot. And he was right, for a museum caretaker explained that the marks on the neck were caused by souvenir hunters cutting off hair some years ago before the animal was put in a protective glass case" (An Old Friend 1931).

A writer who viewed Comanche's form in the 1960s stated, "For years it stood without a protective case; visitors, students, and faculty plucked many a tail-hair talisman from the stuffed hero. In time, Comanche's rump and nose became rather ratty-looking from too much affectionate patting. An aura of folkloric superstition hung over the great horse. It was decreed that any undergrad who could, with eyes closed, on one try touch Comanche's jock was considered a shoo-in for final exam passing'' (Ballantine 1964:271).

Thomas H. Swearingen, Director of Exhibits at the Dyche Museum, has been chief caretaker of the remains of the famous mount since 1956. He believes that most of the pulling out of Comanche's tail occurred in the 1940s and '50s, years during which the horse was moved to different areas of the museum and was out in the open. "Many people picked out hair for souvenirs," he says, "and a few of these hairs were even sent back to the museum, where they are now in the files."

Swearingen points out that he was told by the exhibits specialist who preceded him and with whom he worked when he was first hired by the Dyche Museum that Comanche still had his own tail. "None of Comanche's tail hairs have been supplied by other horses," Comanche's loyal modern-day caretaker states. Rather, he was told by his predecessor that over the years Comanche's tail had been rearranged. "Hairs were removed from the underneath parts where they remained more abundant," Swearingen explains. "Holes were made, and these tail hairs were inserted in the outer, more conspicuous places where the tail was getting thin because of the strands that had been removed." Although some hairs had been taken from the mane as relics, the exhibits director points out, the mane has never shown the effects of the loss. He believes that body hairs were never clipped out from the horse's coat, and sometimes has to defend this assertion.

One of Comanche's most devoted admirers kept a close watch on the horse's hair. In a 1969 letter to museum officials, he claimed that the "coat appears to have been sheared to summer style, as different from the winter coat in which he died." The man also felt that "the holes from which the arrows were pulled out" now "appear to have been combed over" thus "hiding the holes and fully destroying a great part of his history and record." The writer believed "this feature should be restored by the artist with a pair of scissors so that the holes would show." Criticism also focussed on the allegation that "strips of faded hair [that] were caused by the slings used to hold [the wounded horse] upright during the long time it took to restore him to health" had been obliterated with dye. Hiding the arrow holes and dyeing the faded strips "destroyed entirely the Historic and Battle value of Comanche," and thus he is no more than, and could be replaced by, any other horse "with no wonder record such as Comanche has."

In his reply, Swearingen explained, "I could no more bring myself to take a pair of scissors and mutilate that horse than I would try to fly off the Empire State Building." He also made it clear that the horse's "coat has never been touched with dye and is the same as when he was alive." Any marks from a sling would have soon vanished since the horse "shed out and grew new hair many times between his recovery and his death. From his own experience with horses, Swearingen related that "scars heal over and are, in many cases, impossible to see any signs of after a year's time." As to the "scars on the horse's hips where the arrows were lodged," mentioned by the correspondent, the exhibits director pointed out that "these are places that dried out and cracked before Comanche had his own humidifier. These cracks were so bad that skin had to be cut away from under his saddle to fill in these bad cracks" (UK Archives).

Swearingen, who is an expert horseman as well as an artist skilled in depicting equine subjects, remembers the taxidermy performed on Comanche around 1950 in which skin was removed from under the saddle area of his back and used to patch areas between the horse's front legs and over his hips, where the skin had dried and cracked open. At that time, he points out, techniques were not developed, as they are at present, to enable workers to relax the skin of specimens and give it the elasticity necessary to make repairs by stretching it smoothly.

All the taxidermic skills of this genial and talented man were recently called into play. On March 6, 1986, the famous "Army horse that escaped the guns and arrows of the Battle of the Little Big Horn more than a century ago" fell "prey to an attack by a frozen bird." The mishap occurred when a rhea, a large South American bird, was being thawed out in preparation for a museum exhibit. The bird's carcass, encased within a plastic bag, slid into the nearby sink, turning on a faucet as it fell. The plastic bag clogged the drain, causing water to run over and seep through five floors and onto Comanche, who "happened to be in the direct line of fire" of this flood (Survivor of Little Big Horn 1986:B5; Swearingen personal communication 1986).

The result of this unfortunate sequence of events was that the old horse was drenched by water which, Swearingen told me, ran from 8:30 P.M. until 6:30 the next morning. When the disaster was discovered, the horse's entire body was wrapped in gauze to prevent the skin from splitting as it dried out and to insure that the skin and the stuffing would dry at the same time. At that point

"Comanche looked just like a mummy" the exhibits director noted. When the gauze was removed, a great deal of painstaking repair work had to be done. Swearingen worked at the reconstruction of the horse for four months, not two weeks as one Lawrence newspaper reported. "The horse swelled when it dried," he said. "There was a four inch gap in the neck and the leg seams opened because the stitches had rotted away." In the restoration process, the old seams in the hide were opened, the old stuffing was scraped out, the insides were repacked, and then the horse was sewed up. This time, a special longer-lasting non-acidic taxidermic clay replaced the previous material used for stuffing. "We now have newer materials and techniques to relax the hide so we can stretch it out and sew it together again, without causing it to split," the exhibits expert explained.

Working about six hours a day on this tedious job gave him a sore back, he said. But Comanche needed taxidermic reconditioning even before this accident, and Swearingen declared proudly that "Comanche is in better condition now than he has ever been since I've seen him. It was time to re-do him. I fixed the tip of his right ear that had been missing for years, and spent a lot of time on the details of his eyes, lips, nose, and sheath. He looks like a new mount now, better than ever. I worked on one leg at a time, then the body, and re-painted everything; then I re-did the case."

"There is a silver lining," Museum Director Philip Humphrey said of the water damage. "Comanche is fit as a fiddle." Now, according to Swearingen, "with proper care," the horse "could last for several hundred years." The flood brought a renewed surge of publicity for Comanche, billed once again as "a star attraction" of the Dyche Museum, and as the lone survivor of the Custer Battle for whom this incident was "not the first time in the line of fire" (Twardy 1986; KU Gets Comanche 1986; Bird Douses 1986; Wilmsen 1986).

Now that the horse is restored, the exhibits director noted, "the lighting in his case will be improved. The museum plans to put in plexiglass to shield the mounted specimen from ultraviolet light. A lighting expert from the Smithsonian Institution has been called in as a consultant. . . . I don't want anything like this to happen again," Swearingen said. "The horse might make it, but I don't think I will. . . . So that there won't be another flood to damage the horse again," he explained, "a plastic tent has been placed over him so water can't reach him. If it happens again, the water will run down the walls instead and won't run over him. . . . He's getting too old to re-do again. And I'm under too much pressure. Everyone stands around watching and asking if you can do it. . . . There was a lot of publicity, the TV people were there. In Lawrence, it won the news story of the year award for 1986. Newspapers all over the country carried the story. It was even on the news in New York. People have sent me clippings about it from all over. Old friends see my picture in the paper and say 'Tom, only you would drown a dead horse to get publicity!' Here at the museum people stopped me in the hall and said 'I saw your picture in San Francisco. You saved the horse, didn't You?'"

Several times previous to the March 1986 flooding at Dyche Museum, Swearingen had discussed with me the subject of the famous horse's brand. There never had been an established certainty that Comanche had, in fact, been branded. While it was expected that as a cavalry mount this would have been routine, perhaps as Keogh's personal property he might have been exempted. Even Luce did not know whether Comanche had been branded. In 1938, following a visit to the horse, the former cavalryman wrote to the curator asking him to "take a close examination of Comanche" to see if there was a brand mark on his left shoulder, under his mane, or on either of his front hoofs (UK Archives). In 1985, the exhibits director told me that he felt Comanche had been "branded lightly when he was a young horse, even though it doesn't show now." He believes that certain photos of the famous war horse have been retouched to make conspicuous a brand on his shoulder. The taxidermist who preceded Swearingen at the museum, he said, did not think there was a brand but would sometimes "put a spit brand on Comanche," moistening the hair with his fingers along the lines of letters to form the brand.

The freakish flooding accident in 1986, it turned out, cleared up the mystery of Comanche's brand. Swearingen told me that when the horse was soaked he not only found a lot of scars on the hide, but he also could see, for the first time, the faint marks of Comanche's brand. Whereas he had never before been able to make it out, when the skin was wet, there was a unique opportunity, and the brand "U S" on the left shoulder became visible. "With the hide soaked," he explained, "I could see faint scars of the brand. It was not heavy, Comanche is lightly branded. If he were not wet down, you couldn't see it. But there it was, only a faint tinge. It's there and I saw the impression. It was never seen before but now I know for sure it's there." "You can see a brand well on a horse's summer coat," he reflected, "but you don't see it as well on the winter coat. Comanche died in the winter, when it was not as visible."

The present-day caretaker of the old cavalry horse undeniably harbors a special feeling for the unique exhibit. As only a person with an "eye for a horse" can, Swearingen appreciates this mount's unusual qualities. Interacting with his own horses on a daily basis gives him a constant frame of reference for Comanche, not merely as a museum specimen, but as a once-living animal. "He was quite a horse. Nothing spooked him," the exhibits expert says. "He took life as it came. He was strong and lived to an old age that was unusual for those days, on the kind of rations they had then. Of course, he got good care, but he didn't have the feed chopped up that we have now. Today, a horse's life can be prolonged five to eight years with the modern feeds. A horse can go to thirty-five with that kind of care plus vitamins and special diets that are available. Comanche liked to drink beer, too, just like one horse I knew that loved Mountain Dew. Animals do have a taste for those things."

The University of Kansas Natural History Museum and the numerous people who cherish Comanche's remains with deep appreciation of their symbolic significance have been fortunate in having Thomas Swearingen and his staff on duty throughout the past three decades. The Dyche Museum is "the most popular tourist attraction in Kansas" according to recent statistics based on a study of eighty-one tourist attractions which was carried out by a Wichita consultant for the Kansas Department of Economic Development. Dyche Hall, which "beat out the State Capitol at Topeka, Boot Hill at Dodge City and all the state's federal reservoirs in tourist attraction appeal," was built in 1901 and is on the National Register of Historic Places. Calling the good news "fantastic" when told of the top rating, Museum Director Humphrey said the institution draws "visitors not just from the KU student population, but also from all 50 states" (KU Museum Given 1978; Peterson 1981; KU's Dyche Museum 1978:1).

Few people who were acquainted with Comanche's position in the museum were surprised at the statistics. In 1950, a writer for the university newspaper had declared that "the most popular exhibit at the University Museum of Natural History is Comanche, sole survivor of Custer's famous 'Last Stand'" and that "visitors' first question usually is: 'Where's Comanche?'" (Last Stand 1950:2). The conclusion of a chronicle of the events in Comanche's life published in 1966 had also indicated that

> With the many dioramas and the panorama at the Museum, with the animals in natural poses in real-life settings, Comanche, in a special humidified case on the second floor, still commands the most attention. "I doubt if there is a child who enters the Museum who doesn't make sure to see Comanche," notes Dr. Hall, adding that sixty percent of the requests for pictures of the lonely survivor come from girls.

Comanche may have died physically 75 years ago, but his courageous fighting spirit lives on, stronger than ever, particularly in the
minds of the young in heart. (Comanche: Diary 1966:13)

And after describing some of the finest Dyche Museum attractions, Robert Mengel, who had been on its staff for twenty years,
stated, "but none of these commands the most visitor interest or
draws the most requests for information." Rather, it is Comanche
"which for decades has led the Museum's displays in popularity"
(1969:5).

Although some people deny that Comanche is the most popular exhibit in the museum, there is a very good chance that it is
indeed true. Certain museum personnel express mild annoyance
grading to real indignation when people indicate that the first
priority of their visit is to see Comanche. The gift-shop manager
once told me, "I don't appreciate Comanche; he's too romanticized. I like the fossils better, and the panorama." She admitted,
however, that "many people come and ask first for Comanche.
They're respectful. Most people really love that horse. All comments about him are positive." Another museum employee also
thinks the stuffed cavalry horse is "too much romanticized," and
would prefer visitors to appreciate the scientific exhibits more.
"The big problem," she indicates, "is people coming to see Custer's horse. Even if you tell them it's not Custer's horse, they say
'be quiet.' They don't want to believe it, and they don't listen."
Mengel complains "everyone who sees the display believes it was
General Custer's horse. Telling them doesn't do any good. It's
like any cherished myth, they don't want to give it up. I always tell
visitors it is not General Custer's horse."

Tom Swearingen, referring to the results of the survey indicating the top ranking of the Dyche Museum, emphasizes that
"Comanche is a big part of this popularity." He designates the
mount as "one of the most well-known displays in the museum,"
and also indicates that "the first thing visitors say is that they want
to see Custer's horse. They're upset when they find it's not really
Custer's horse, and this takes away a little bit of the inflated idea
of the thing."

Whether people know that Captain Myles W. Keogh, who
went to his death with General Custer and the men of the Seventh
Cavalry under that flamboyant leader's immediate command on
June 25, 1876, rode Comanche, or whether they initially believe,
inferring from the General's higher rank and greater fame, that
the horse belonged to Custer, there is no doubt that Comanche
draws large numbers of people to the Dyche Museum for the spe-

cific purpose of viewing him. Virtually all active Little Big Horn Battle enthusiasts and Custer buffs (and there are many such devotees) plan a trip to the Lawrence museum to see the equine battle survivor's remains at some time in their lives. During my own first visit to the Custer Battlefield National Monument in 1958, I was instantaneously captivated by the whole dramatic clash of cultures which had occurred in the hauntingly lovely Montana valley that still retains a special ambience, an unmistakable spirit of place. Completely under the spell of its pervasive intrigue, and so taken with Comanche's story that I could think of little else, I remember driving almost nonstop to the Lawrence, Kansas, museum to glimpse the horse. Others, I suspect, have done the same.

One knowledgeable Custer Battle devotee who is now a bookseller specializing in Custeriana relates the following experience regarding his visit to see the famous mount. When asked by a co-worker in his Michigan office how he had spent his recent vacation time, he confided that he had driven to Kansas to see the stuffed horse that had survived the Custer Battle. "You drove all that way to see a dead horse?" the incredulous man asked. Calling a nearby fellow worker into the conversation, he related the astounding tale of the dead horse seeker for whose sanity he feared. "What's so unusual about that?" questioned the second man, very seriously. "A couple of months ago I made the same trip to Kansas myself to see Comanche."

Threads of humor are interwoven through Comanche's story. Sometimes the horse is simply the object of good-natured ridicule to belittle the idea that the animal has assumed so much importance. Accordingly, one newspaper reported that "Comanche, Custer's favorite horse, graces the museum at Fort Riley," and he "has been the recipient of more wreaths than most generals. Whenever any of the boys went out on a party they usually wound up by decorating Comanche with a few wreaths" (Sheridan's Horse n.d.). Comanche's reported taste for alcohol draws attention through humor in articles such as the one entitled "Cavalrymen Fed Beer to Wounded Horse" (1965). And Goldin's description of the stricken mount receiving brandy after he was found on the battlefield provoked the jibe that "the dark inside story" of Comanche is "just coming to light. It has just been learned from good authority that this respectable appearing old fellow at the door of Dyche Museum used to hit the bottle; that those mild, placid eyes have looked upon the wine when it was red" (Old Timer 1921).

A nonsensical "True Tail of Comanche" by an anonymous "Professor of Socioequestrianology" (n.d.) relates, for example, that the horse joined the army "wearing the fashionable halter tops so popular among his kind." When his mount was wounded, Keogh exclaimed "Now ain't that the horse's ass!" Following the battle, Comanche answered "neigh" when "asked if others had survived." And despite the fact that the man who mounted him has been dead for many years, "Comanche to this day refuses to leave the building where the tryst took place, always awaiting Dyche's return." The horse is also used to insult Custer, as in the description of the General as "Top Jockey in Seventh Cavalry. Led the field in most events until June 1876 when entered in Little Big Horn Handicap against Sitting Bull and Crazy Horse. Went down at odds of 20–1. Last seen entering the losers circle minus his hair. He was survived by his horse 'Commanche' which lived a further 17 years. The animal was then mounted and stuffed. Custer should have been similarly treated, preferably at an early age" (Alderdice n.d.:15).

A Kansas newspaper, tongue-in-cheek, carried the story of a man who claimed he stole Comanche from an Indian camp and sold him to Custer. Two months later the same newspaper published Luce's overly serious rebuttal of the tale, and his proposal of the man for the "Liar's club." This article, like all writings that use the horse to evoke laughter, stresses the incongruity of a stuffed museum specimen, relating that Comanche's "mangy old hide is now in the archives of Kansas University, if horse hides are kept in archives" (The Globe 1939).

The ultimate sarcastic humor appears in Soubier's *L'Affaire Comanche*, in which the animal is embued with religious symbolism. "Considering the God-like quality of Custer and the unofficial canonization of him that has occurred since his ascension, it is likely that Comanche has assumed the role of a more earthly intermediary for supplicants unprepared to approach the throne of the Most High." Keogh, according to the author's reasoning, has legendary supernatural associations through his papal medal that conferred bravery and his spirit that clutched his horse's reins after death. "Thus, for the worshipful student, the hierarchy stands with Custer as the God-head, Keogh his only-begotten son, and Comanche as the Virgin Mary, more or less" (1970:3). Juxtaposition of the sacred and the profane is a common ingredient of humor. Moreover, dead bodies and especially preserved remains stimulate a morbid element in people that may be expressed in the guise of humor. Clowning, for instance, is frequently observed in dissecting labs, whether the cadavers studied are human or animal. Some of this macabre aura clings to the stuffed horse in the Kansas museum.

People travel to the museum in Lawrence not only to see Comanche, but to obtain information for use in writing term papers, college theses, newspaper articles, magazine features, books, and lectures. Comanche's popularity, however, extends far beyond his visitors. Letters arrive at the museum from all parts of the nation and even from foreign countries. These contain queries about the famous horse's color, pedigree, and wound marks. Many ask about Comanche's condition and seek to be reassured that he has not been "destroyed by moths or natural deterioration" and that he has not been moved elsewhere in response to the numerous well-publicized requests. Special interest is shown in whether or not he once belonged to Indians. People want to know how, as a mounted specimen, he came to be in the Dyche Museum.

Some correspondents, after reading about Comanche, just want to exclaim about his remarkable story and say how impressed they are. Others write of experiences like winning second prize in a parade by dressing as a Sioux and decorating a bicycle to resemble Comanche. Often, people associate Comanche with patriotism and delight in a tangible remnant of the past by referring to the Comanche display as "one of the greatest pieces of military history to be found in the entire country." Most commonly people write to ask for photos of Comanche, order postcards with his picture, and request materials about him for teaching school or groups like the 4H. One person sent Comanche a Christmas card signed "your friend." The common theme of the enthusiastic correspondence is admiration for the equine survivor. One man who noted that the horse's story "intrigues the imagination" wrote to share his plans for a commemorative stamp to honor Comanche. A ninety-one-year-old man sent a copy of a letter he wrote to Walt Disney describing a boyhood visit to Fort Meade. "I met the Top Sergeant who had charge of the horse COMANCHE. He took me to the stable where the scarred pony was kept, and put me up on his back. I remember seeing a lot of scars all over the body of the animal." Some letters, sent to the museum after individuals had made the trip to see Comanche, express appreciation for the experience (UK Archives).

Though many people in search of Comanche go to Lawrence to view him and learn about him, I have not yet found anyone else who became so fascinated with probing all aspects of the horse's mystique as to visit the town of Comanche, Montana, as I did. Learning of my trip to that mere dot on the map, a Custer Battle buff and ardent collector of battle artifacts who had ranched all of his life near the Little Big Horn battlefield declared, "But there is nothing there! Imagine driving all that way to see a town named after a dead horse!" In the true cowboy tradition, he and his fellows had a good laugh poking fun at the eastern dude who traveled many miles to get to a deserted place that is merely a name on a map (and it has to be a specially detailed map, at that) only to be in a town named for a long-dead horse. All that could be accomplished in such a place that has no tangible trace of the animal for whom it was named was to look around at deserted buildings and a grain elevator by the railroad tracks, and take a photograph of a sign that states, simply, COMANCHE (see fig. 19).

That town which, history records, was actually named after *the* Comanche, was, despite its desolation, worth the trip. Being there, I reflected upon how one person's, or perhaps a committee's, remembrance of the horse might have resulted in the naming, and I wondered about the circumstances of that decision and the thoughts and feelings that may have underlain it. That kind of information, I found after inquiries to many different likely sources, had evidently not been recorded, and hence is unavailable. The existing data about the town, according to the authority on Montana place names, indicates that Comanche, in Yellowstone County, "was a station on the Great Northern Railroad. It was named for the famous horse that was the only living thing found on the battlefield after the Battle of the Little Big Horn. The post office was opened in 1909 with Lola Dell Helm as postmaster; it was discontinued in 1942. Only the station, a few houses and some deserted buildings remain" (Cheney 1984:59). Other reliable sources on American place names are in agreement that the Montana town was not named for the Comanche Indians, as might be assumed, but for "the historical horse" named from that tribe "which was the sole survivor of Custer's command at the Battle of the Little Big Horn" (Rydjord 1968:323; Stewart 1985:108).

My inquiry to the historical division of the railroad company elicted only the response that "Comanche was named for a stream with that appellation in the area. The stream was named after a horse, the sole survivor of the battle of the Little Big Horn in 1876." No source for that data could be located. A contemporary newspaper report about the new town, indicating that "lots will immediately be put on sale by the Billings & Northern townsite company," reveals the high hopes with which it was founded. "It is safe to say that Comanche will not remain merely a dot on the map, for it is most favorably situated and has as good prospects for developing into a lively little community as had Broadview or any of the other towns on the Billings & Northern." The town was expected to "draw its trade from two sources"—dry farming and the sheep industry (New Town 1909:1).

An official of the Montana Historical Society points out that the naming of the town for the horse was "done by the Northern Pacific Railroad—often in search of names to enliven its station stops, after commemorating all of the Company officials" (personal communication 1981). According to Roberta Cheney, at the time the surviving cavalry horse's name was chosen, "the Great Northern went through a phase of using historic and romantic-sounding names for its stations" (personal communication 1987). It is appropriate that Comanche was commemorated by such a frontier town, just as his closest rival in equine fame, Bucephalus, was honored with an Old World city. When that celebrated mount died of battle wounds, Alexander the Great was "no less concerned at his death than if he had lost an old companion or intimate friend." Grieving over the loss of the faithful war horse, who for seventeen years had played such an important role in his victories, Alexander founded in the animal's memory the city of Bucephala (or Bucephalia) on the banks of the Jhelum River (in what is now northeastern Pakistan), where the horse was buried (Plutarch n.d.:845; Lamb 1979:309). J. M. Brereton reports that the city's name has now "vanished from history," for "nothing like it has survived in the neighborhood" (1976:19). If so, Comanche, whose town is still identified, has fared slightly better than his counterpart.

Comanche's fallen rider was honored in August of 1876 by having an army post, Fort Keogh, named for him. Located on the right bank of the Yellowstone River, just west of present-day Miles City, Montana, the fort was first used as a base for troops engaged in subjugating rebellious Indians. It was there that a band of Northern Cheyennes under Two Moon, who had been an important leader in the Battle of the Little Big Horn, surrendered to General Miles, commander of the fort until 1880. Fort Keogh, an army post until 1900, later fittingly became a remount station where horses were trained for the army. Following this, the military reservation was converted to a livestock experimental station. Postal records were kept under the name of Fort Keogh from 1878 to 1908, when the office was discontinued (Cheney 1984:97; Frazer 1972:82).

A watercolor painting of Fort Keogh was owned by Thomas Keogh, Myles' brother, and was evidently prized because it was specifically mentioned in his will of 1897. This item is now in the possession of a great-grandnephew of Captain Keogh, Gary Keogh of Dublin, who takes an interest in the life of his famous forebear who was a native of Southern Ireland. "Myles would be only a number if it hadn't been for his horse surviving the Custer Battle," Gary says. "Without that horse, he would be just another 'wild goose,' which is the name given to people from Carlow who left home to fight in wars. He wouldn't be a bit more famous than his Irish friend, Nowlan."

The Montana landscape commemorates other related historic areas. A few miles south of the Custer Battlefield the small town of Garryowen perpetuates the name of the stirring regimental marching song of the Seventh Cavalry, which Comanche's rider may have brought from Ireland (Cheney 1984:112–13; Luce 1939:123). In addition to Fort Custer, located on the bluff above the confluence of the Big Horn and Little Big Horn rivers, both a town and a county in Montana, as might be expected, bear the name of the dashing Seventh Cavalry leader. But for a state whose history is interwoven with horses and that counts Horse Creek, Horse Plains, Horse Prairie, and Hungry Horse among its towns, it is not surprising that someone involved in the naming process remembered not only the human hero but also the horse who won undying fame in that state's Little Big Horn Valley—Comanche.

Fig. 1. Comanche, saddled and bridled, stands at attention with Gustave Korn and appears to have been a rather handsome mount. (Courtesy of Custer Battlefield National Monument.)

Fig. 2. Comanche with attendant, photo probably taken by D. F. Barry about 1878. (Courtesy of Custer Battlefield National Monument.)

Fig. 3. Comanche with an unidentified gray horse, probably at Fort Meade about 1887. Captain Charles S. Ilsley stands to the right. (Courtesy of Custer Battlefield National Monument.)

Fig. 4. Comanche with unidentified attendant, photographed by J. C. H. Grabill of Sturgis, Dakota Territory, in 1887. The brand "U S" is faintly visible on the horse's left shoulder. (Courtesy of Custer Battlefield National Monument.)

Fig. 5. The only known photograph of Comanche without an attendant, taken by W. R. Cross of Hot Springs, South Dakota, probably during the late 1880s while Comanche was at Fort Meade. (Courtesy of Custer Battlefield National Monument.)

Fig. 6. Comanche in 1891 at Fort Riley, Kansas, with farrier Samuel J. Winchester. (Courtesy of the Kansas State Historical Society, Topeka.)

Fig. 7. The man who rode Comanche—Captain Myles W. Keogh— probably in the early 1870s. In spite of his colorful and romantic life as a soldier-of-fortune, the bold and gallant cavalryman owes much of his fame to Comanche, the horse he rode into battle at the Little Big Horn. (Author's collection.)

Fig. 8. Floral tribute at the marker indicating the spot where Comanche's rider fell, Custer Battlefield National Monument. (Photo by author.)

Fig. 9. Monument at the grave of Myles W. Keogh, Fort Hill Cemetery, Auburn, New York, bearing cavalry accoutrements hung up as though the owner were asleep. (Photo by author.)

Fig. 10. Testament to the sacrifice of the Seventh Cavalry mounts, this pile of horse bones on the crest of the hill where the Custer Battle monument now stands was photographed by Morrow in June of 1877. (Author's collection.)

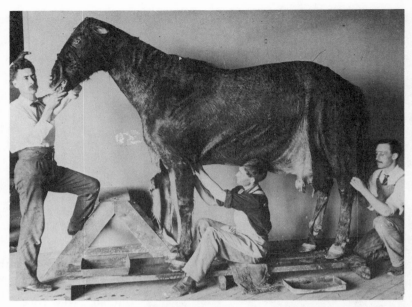

Fig. 11. L. L. Dyche and his helpers pulling the skin over Comanche's form during one of the final stages in mounting the horse for display. (Courtesy of the University of Kansas Archives.)

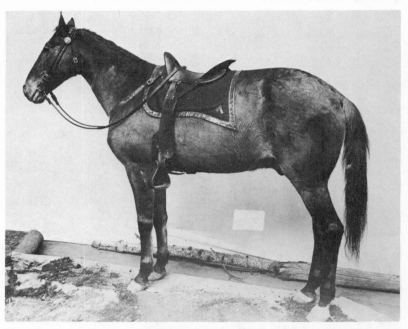

Fig. 12. An early photograph of the mounted Comanche, possibly taken at the World's Columbian Exposition in 1893. (Courtesy of the Kansas State Historical Society, Topeka.)

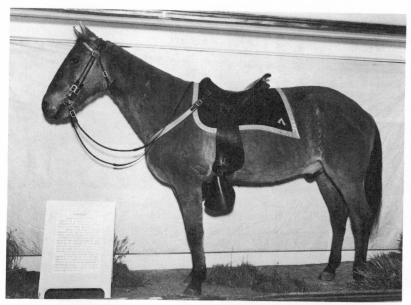

Fig. 13. Comanche on display in the Natural History Museum of the University of Kansas, showing the original exhibit label, which was removed as a result of the 1971 Indian protest. (Courtesy of the Museum of Natural History, the University of Kansas.)

Fig. 14. Often the first question museum visitors ask is "Where's Comanche?" To countless numbers of children who come to see him, the horse who survived Custer's Last Stand is a true hero. This 1975 photo shows the placard placed in Comanche's display case after the Indian protest. (Courtesy of Kansas Alumni Magazine, University of Kansas Archives.)

Fig. 15. Sioux Indian patterns painted over the mounted Comanche symbolize aspects of the Battle of the Little Big Horn. From left to right the designs signify "Dead man's body showing wounds and spears," "Horse-killed-in-battle," and "Shooting-of-arrows from between the hills." Centered directly over Comanche, one motif of "Horse-killed-in-battle" is missing—the empty space denoting that the famous horse did not die, but rather was a survivor of Custer's Last Stand. (Photo by author.)

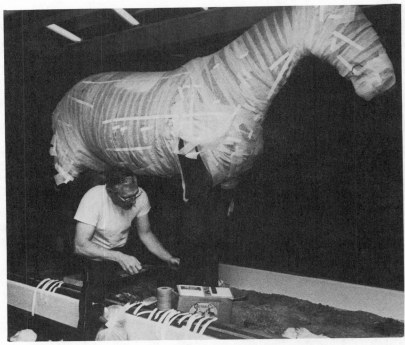

Fig. 16. University of Kansas Natural History Museum Exhibits Director Tom Swearingen engrossed in the arduous task of repairing damage to Comanche resulting from a flood in 1986. (Photo by Michael L. Horton.)

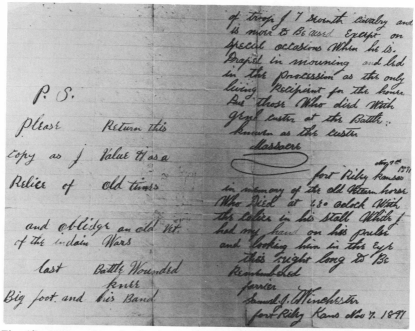

Fig. 17. Note written by farrier Samuel J. Winchester to document Comanche's death on November 7, 1891. (Courtesy of the University of Kansas Archives.)

Fig. 18. The wounded Comanche as a "silent messenger of disaster" returns alone to Fort Lincoln in this dramatic scene from Thomas H. Ince's 1912 film, "Custer's Last Fight." (Courtesy of Custer Battlefield National Monument.)

Fig. 19. The town named for the horse who survived Custer's Last Stand—Comanche, Montana. At the time of its naming in 1908 the Northern Pacific Railroad chose historic and romantic sounding names to enliven the station stops along its route and provide appeal to travelers and prospective settlers. (Photo by author.)

Fig. 20. Contemporary representative of Comanche, draped in mourning, participating in a memorial ceremony held by the Little Big Horn Associates at the grave site of Captain Myles Walter Keogh in Auburn, New York, July 19, 1986. (Photo by author.)

Fig. 21. "Outrage" shows the severely wounded horse, Sefton, the British Household Cavalry mount who, like Comanche, became a national symbol of suffering, courage, and survival. (Painting by Terence Cuneo, O.B.E., owned by Mr. Raphael Djanogly, F.R.S.A., J.P.)

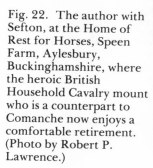

Fig. 22. The author with Sefton, at the Home of Rest for Horses, Speen Farm, Aylesbury, Buckinghamshire, where the heroic British Household Cavalry mount who is a counterpart to Comanche now enjoys a comfortable retirement. (Photo by Robert P. Lawrence.)

Fig. 23. "He Screamed Like a Comanche." This oil painting by Thomas
H. Swearingen illustrates one version of the naming of Keogh's mount.
When hit in the rump with an arrow during a skirmish with Indians, it
was said that the horse made a sound "like a Comanche yell." (Courtesy
of Thomas H. Swearingen.)

Fig. 24. Starkly realistic, this drawing focuses on the pain and suffering of the battle participants—both horse and man. (Drawing by Ernest Lisle Reedstrom, author's collection.)

Fig. 25. "Bringing Water from the River." This pencil sketch by Thomas H. Swearingen depicts the scene described by a participant who stated that when Comanche was found two days after the battle, he was too weak to stand, and men rode to the river to bring water for him in their hats. In the background, cavalrymen who fell at the Last Stand are being buried near the foot of "Custer Hill." (Courtesy of Thomas H. Swearingen.)

Fig. 26. In this rendition of Comanche after the battle, the horse stands alone and dejected, but still appears strong enough to transcend the carnage which surrounds him. (Painting by Charles O. Kemper, author's collection.)

Fig. 27. The bond between horse and man is the focus of this work showing Comanche keeping watch over his dead master. (Painting by Pat Hammack, author's collection.)

Fig. 28. "Silent Horse on a Silent Field." The artist has shown
Comanche just as the tragic battle ended. Here the surviving horse
clearly triumphs over death and defeat at the Little Big Horn. (Oil
painting by Thomas H. Swearingen, courtesy of the Museum of Natural
History, University of Kansas.)

Fig. 29. "The Empty Saddle" shows Comanche in his ceremonial role as the symbolic riderless horse during a Seventh Cavalry regimental parade. (India ink drawing by Mrs. P. A. Haynes, owned by John M. Carroll.)

Fig. 30. Although there is no evidence that Comanche was a Morgan, the artist has depicted him with some traits of that breed in this dramatic scene in which the famous survivor is proudly led on review. (Painting by Jeanne Mellin, owned by W. Robert Morgan.)

Fig. 31. "Get Comanche!" depicts the fierce struggle of Indian warriors at the Little Big Horn to capture the hardy cavalry horse who eludes them. (Painting by James E. Connell, owned by John M. Carroll.)

Fig. 32. Myles Keogh riding Comanche in the thick of the fight at the Little Big Horn. (Bronze by Rogers Aston.)

Fig. 33. Molded figure of Comanche as a dun-colored mount. (Creator unknown, author's collection.)

Fig. 34. "The Spotted Horse Returns Alone." An Indian counterpart to Comanche, the spotted horse was ridden by one of Custer's Arikara scouts who was killed at the Little Big Horn. After the battle, the wounded mount returned alone to his rider's village. The reins were up as though the rider had just been shot off his horse. (Tempera painting by Brummet Echohawk, created especially for this book, author's collection.)

Chapter 10

Comanche and the Indians

If we're going to start educating people, Comanche is a good place to start.
—Member of UK Committee on Indian Affairs, 1971

The Comanche affair was one of the greatest learning experiences of my life.
—Dr. Philip Humphrey, Director, Dyche Museum of Natural History, 1980

Throughout most of Comanche's museum existence, good humor and sometimes wry wit have often been intermingled with the respectfulness with which the survivor has been regarded and the genuine awe toward him that has been felt ever since the time of the Custer tragedy in 1876. But one important phase of his career seems to have been marked mainly by somberness. For the first time in the early 1970s Comanche and all he stood for came under suspicion, and the people who drew attention to him were totally serious. As the one-hundredth anniversary of Custer's Last Stand approached, Comanche was attacked, this time by a once-familiar foe—Indians.

It is not surprising that native Americans became involved with Comanche. He was, after all, named for an Indian tribe and drew his fame from surviving the most celebrated Indian-white clash in New World history—which is generally considered the greatest victory for the indigenous people. Indians were nothing new to Comanche; he had encountered them both in active cavalry life and in the legend and lore which, after death, has enveloped him as a mounted specimen.

As recently as 1964, the story of Comanche as published in the University of Kansas newspaper included data that "born about 1860, Comanche was once a member of a wild herd in the Dakotas. It is believed he was captured by the Dakota Indians and through traders found his way to Fort Riley, Kansas" (Jones 1964:6). In 1967, a man who believed that Comanche was "bred and trained in Ireland" wrote to the museum to verify his information. The official of the Natural History Museum who for a number of years answered such inquiries about the famous mount responded that Comanche was not an Irish horse, but rather was a wild horse that the cavalry had obtained from Indians (UK Archives). The idea that the famous Seventh Cavalry survivor had once been an Indian mount, though never substantiated by factual data, appeared quite early in the development of his legend. In 1923, John C. Lockwood, previously referred to in Chapter 4 as one of the many claimants to the honor of finding the wounded animal, wrote a letter to C. D. Bunker of the Dyche Museum, enclosing

> a brief but true history of the horse, Comanche, that you have in the University of Kansas.
> The first part of the history I got directly from Captain M. W. Keogh who rode the horse all the time it was in service after the horse was captured on the Staked Plains in Texas in 1867. Captain Keogh's horse, the one he was riding, got killed in the fight with the band of Comanche Indians that General Custer had followed for some time, and captured them at the edge of the Staked Plains. The Indians had a goodly number of horses, and the horses that had been put out of service in the running fight with the Indians were replaced by horses captured from the Indians. Captain Keogh selected the one you now have at the K. U. Museum. The horse was six years of age when captured, and that was the way the horse got the name of *Comanche*. (UK Archives)

Although "no aspersion of the veracity of Mr. Lockwood is intended," Brown explains, "the preponderance of evidence is that *Comanche* was purchased by the Army supply depot in St. Louis, Mo. [and] that he joined the regiment (Seventh Cavalry) at camp near Ellis, Kansas, that he was then about five years old and that he was assigned to Company 'I' " (1935:36–38).

A slightly briefer version of Lockwood's 1923 letter was published in *Winners of the West* (the Indian War veterans' periodical) eleven years later (One Horse Survivor 1934:6). Again, it elicited a rebuttal, this time in the form of a response which appeared in the next issue of the same periodical. W. J. Ghent pointed out several errors in Lockwood's history of Comanche, including the fact that he "was not captured from the Indians by Gen. Custer or by anyone else, but was purchased in St. Louis in August, 1867, and sent to the regiment at Ellis, Kansas" (1934:1). Later, in a book written from his reminiscences, Lockwood's story of the acquisition of the horse from captured Comanche Indians was repeated. It was explained that "the Comanche Indians were noted for their good horses and Comanche's equal was not to be found in the regiment" (Ryan 1966:51–52).

Although Lockwood's assertion was not accepted as authoritative, nevertheless, it appears that the seeds of the legend of dual ownership by Indians and whites had been sown in fertile soil. The drama and symbolic irony of capture from Indians enhanced the appeal of an almost incredible but otherwise authentic horse story. In 1951, David Appel's fictionalized story of Comanche for young readers was released by the World Publishing Company— without, it will be remembered, the presence of the stuffed horse at the autograph party for its author. According to this autobiographical narrative written in the first person, which will be discussed more fully in Chapter 12, Comanche was captured as a young horse by a Sioux boy. Eventually escaping from the Indians, Comanche was retaken by a white youth and then sold to the Seventh Cavalry, whereby Captain Keogh soon obtained him. Appel's creation was the story upon which Walt Disney's 1958 film *Tonka* was based. In this popular movie version, the versatile horse was beloved by two masters—a Sioux boy, White Bull, who first caught him and named him Tonka Wakan, and Seventh Cavalryman Myles Keogh, who rode him to war under the name of Comanche. After the wounded horse's rescue following the Battle of the Little Big Horn and his subsequent recuperation at Fort Lincoln, the horse, in a sense, became an Indian horse again because the Sioux youth was designated as the sole rider of his former mount. Day after day, the pair raced over the rolling prairie —"two wild spirits with the wind in their faces" (Beecher 1959).

Disney's film brought added publicity to the celebrated mount. "Comanche To Gallop Again In Disney Movie" was the headline of the *Daily Kansan*'s announcement that Disney Productions would make a full-length movie about the famous horse, concerning whom "each year museum officials receive more than 100 inquiries" (1956). As reported in a Topeka newspaper (in an article inexplicably labeled "TV Spurs Interest in K.U.'s Comanche"),

> There is a resurgence of interest in the sole survivor of the Custer massacre, Comanche, a clay-baked [sic] gelding whose mounted body stands in the Dyche Museum at the University of Kansas in Lawrence.

Periodically interest in the valiant old horse is revived as a new motion picture or book appears on the modern scene depicting the Custer mystery. . . .

The current story which is sending more visitors than usual to the Dyche Museum to view the remains of Comanche is "Tonka," a new Walt Disney movie. (TV Spurs Interest 1959)

Despite its appeal, however, the film in which he was "brought to life again" did little to disturb the calm that pervaded Comanche's regal stance on Mount Oread. Nor did it change his firmly entrenched image as a U. S. cavalry horse and lone survivor at the Little Big Horn. Although the Indians had been victorious in the battle that gave him fame, their descendants found nothing in the museum display to which they could relate.

Accompanying the stuffed horse prior to November 1971 was an explanatory sign in the form of an "A frame" placed on the floor just anterior to Comanche's front legs bearing a label which was intended to interpret the exhibit for visitors. According to Tom Swearingen, the sign was placed there sometime between 1944 and 1951. It read, simply

Comanche was the sole survivor of the Custer Massacre at the Battle of the Little Big Horn on June 25, 1876. He was ridden by Captain Myles W. Keogh of Troop I, 7th Cavalry.

In May of 1876, the 7th Cavalry under the command of George Armstrong Custer left Fort Abraham Lincoln in North Dakota to round up a large number of Sioux and Cheyenne Indians who had not yet been placed on reservations. In Montana, on June 25, a detachment of the 7th Cavalry under Custer was surrounded and annihilated by Sioux and Cheyenne warriors led by Chiefs Gall, Two Moons, Crazy Horse, and Rain-in-the-Face.

Two days later, troops arrived, and found Comanche so severely wounded that it was proposed he be put to death. Instead, he was transported by boat to Fort Abraham Lincoln where he was nursed back to health. His later years were spent at Fort Riley, Kansas, where he died on November 7, 1891, at the age of 31.

Over the years, few visitors appear to have questioned this wording. If they did, their objections were not recorded or made public. But the idea of Comanche as the "sole survivor" and the pejorative inaccuracy of the word "massacre" (for what was in reality a battle) took on new significance in 1970. Times were favorable in that year not only for the questioning of time-honored assumptions and stereotypes but for action. A spirit that had been building up for a decade or more gave fresh strength to many people's pride in their ethnic identity and provided the impetus for outspoken expression of the values in the native heritage.

American Indian students at Kansas University took up the challenge that, for them, had come to be embodied by the display and interpretation of the cavalry horse in the museum. As a result of this different kind of onslaught, the old order was destined to fall, and Comanche's image would be transformed to accommodate new symbolic meanings for the modern age.

In September 1970, reports were issued indicating that Comanche had "come under attack" by present-day Indians. Some unidentified native American graduate students in the Kansas University School of Social Welfare, according to newspaper accounts, had drafted a petition to Chancellor E. Laurence Chalmers that he "overlook the default of payment" (to Dyche by the Seventh Cavalry officers) and that the stuffed horse be removed from the university museum and sent to Fort Riley. Calling Comanche "a racist symbol," the students asserted that "the horse doesn't deal properly with history," and went on to explain that

> The museum visitor gets a stereotyped image of Indians from viewing the horse, and images of massacres and such things, that makes them forget the problems of today's Indians—poverty and unemployment, for instance.
> The mezzanine (where the horse stands in a carefully humidified glass case) contains exhibits of Indian, Eskimo, black and white cultures, yet in the center of all that is a horse that gives the whole thing a carnival atmosphere.
> Visitors tend to think only of Custer and not of the wounded Indians.
> Indians are distressed at the sign attached to Comanche's side, which calls the horse "the only survivor of the Battle of the Little Big Horn river."
> Plenty of Indians survived the battle, too. (Comanche's Last Stand 1970; Redskins Attack 1970; Comanche Now 1970)

When museum officials heard about the petition for transfer of Comanche to Fort Riley, they said they had not been contacted about the horse. It was reported that "they laughingly speculate that the protest may be an Army plot—another attempt to get possession of the horse." This time, however, the president of the Fort Riley Historical Association said that "much as we'd love to have the old horse back," Fort Riley could not "in the foreseeable future" accept it because of the potential damage which would result from removal of the specimen from the humidity-controlled glass case at Dyche. "But thanks to those young people who may not appreciate what Comanche means to this old cavalry post maybe some new interest will be stimulated and we can get something done about getting him back where he belongs" (Redskins Attack 1970).

Evidently Natural History Museum personnel were not directly informed about the petition because according to one museum spokesperson, "an aura of mystery" surrounded the dissatisfied students' efforts to relocate Comanche. "They didn't contact anyone at the museum," she said. "If the group—whoever it may be—is serious in its efforts to have Comanche moved, it should contact the museum administration to discuss the issue" (KU Museum in Dark 1970). Chancellor Chalmers' reaction to the petition was direct. He immediately telephoned Attorney Don L. Dyche, grandson of the famous taxidermist, who confirmed their conversation with a brief but emphatic and revealing note:

> My grandfather was an outspoken defender of the Indian cause long before it became a popular issue and I am of the same persuasion. Since Comanche is still technically a property of the Dyche family, I would welcome the chance to talk with those who believe that he is a "racist" symbol. I believe that they would find me agreeable to almost anything except returning him to the soldiers as they request. That to me would be opening the horse to an open campaign of "Massacre" propaganda. (UK Archives)

Surely Dyche's descendant was correct that "returning him to the soldiers" would make Comanche more than ever a symbol of the white side of the battle. But the primary aim of the student group, whose members must have known about prior requests from Fort Riley for possession of the horse, was the specimen's removal, and probably little thought was given to the meaning it would take on after leaving the university. The chancellor's reply to Dyche assured him that "the parties who were interested in moving Comanche from the museum have become disinterested and that Comanche will continue to rest in peace at the museum." The students, however, did not abandon their cause. Rather, it gained momentum, and ultimately an active demonstration concerning Comanche was carried out. In September 1970 (some recall it as 1971), a group of students protested that the explanation accompanying the stuffed horse designating him "The Sole Survivor of All the Forces in Custer's Last Stand" was misleading, for "there actually were many other survivors. According to Eva Hudson, hostess at the museum, the protestors posted signs outside the museum and asked that the display be removed. No formal petitions were presented and no action was taken" (Riley 1971; UK Archives).

As the museum director explained the incident:

190

It all began in the Spring of 1971 when I was informed that a group of Indians with posters, placards, and the like were "picketing" in front of the Museum of Natural History. They weren't keeping visitors from entering the Museum; rather they were putting on a demonstration and drawing attention to the fact that they objected strongly to our exhibit of "Comanche" billed as the "sole survivor" of the so-called Custer Massacre.

Some members of the Museum staff were deeply upset and indeed frightened by the Indian demonstration; they felt that the next step probably would be an invasion of the Museum by the Indians and possible destruction of some of the exhibits. However, nothing of the kind happened and in fact there were very few Indians involved, perhaps no more than a dozen or fifteen.

My first reaction to the demonstration was very negative. I felt if there was something wrong with one or more of our exhibits why didn't the Indians come and talk to me about it instead of putting on a demonstration. I concluded that the Indians were simply trying to get a little attention and were not the least interested in seeking a constructive solution to the problem.

Subsequently, I talked to the Dean of the School of Social Welfare (and others) about the demonstration and what it meant. I learned to my fascination that my "reasonable" approach to problems was not in fact "reasonable" from the standpoint of the American Indians. I was told by Dean Katz and others that it was unreasonable for me to expect the Indians to consult me about the problem exhibit since the Indians themselves have not had a history of successful experiences in dealings of that kind with white men in authority. Nevertheless, I let it be known that I would be willing to talk about the matter. There were no further demonstrations and the summer passed without incident.

I think it was in September 1971 that five or six members of the Committee on Indian Affairs came to the Museum and told me that they wanted the Comanche exhibit removed unless the label were changed so that it more accurately reflected the true situation. Moreover, they wished the Comanche exhibit to be closed to the public until the label was changed. Actually, these points were made in several meetings rather than in just one and other things were going on at the same time. Unfortunately, the student newspaper unwittingly (and with no knowledge of what was going on in the Museum in relation to the Committee on Indian Affairs) published an article about Comanche that emphasized precisely the points about which the Committee on Indian Affairs was strongly objecting. This, of course, fanned the flames and it was as a result of that article that the Indians insisted that the Comanche exhibit be closed to the public. (Humphrey 1974:1–2)

The university *Daily Kansan* article referred to, purporting to clarify what has always been a major source of controversy, reiterated what had been many times stated—that is, "the notion that Comanche was the sole survivor of the Little Big Horn stems from the fact that there were numerous battles incorporated in the Battle of the Little Big Horn. Although historians disagree widely on the events of the battle in 1876, many claim that Comanche was the sole survivor of the battle of Custer's field" (Riley 1971). Once again, as so often in the past, the words *the federal side* or *the white side* were omitted as modifiers of "the sole survivor." Previously, the shared assumptions underlying such omissions went largely unchallenged. But times were changing now, and the Indians had advocates. One of these was Murray L. Wax, Professor of Sociology, whose eloquent letter to the editor in response to Riley's article was published in the *Daily Kansan* a week later. He wrote

> If the horse Comanche was "The sole survivor of all the forces in Custer's Last Stand, the Battle of the Little Big Horn" what does that make of the Indians who won the battle—sticks? rocks? vegetables? non-persons? The children of those Indians are today's American citizens, and the Battle of the Little Big Horn is part of their history and ours. They see that battle with more clarity than did your staff writer (Peg Riley, Oct. 7, page one) or the museum personnel who are responsible for the exhibit. For Custer was one of the greedy and vicious types who inhabited the armed services of the 19th century; he wanted to make his reputation by slaughtering Indians.
>
> The Sioux that he pursued were acting lawfully and peaceably, but he was intent on a battle and he got one. History does not offer many such simple stories in which evil receives its just deserts, but the Battle of the Little Big Horn was such an instance, and if the Museum of Natural History is to display an exhibit about that battle, then the history should be full and accurate.
>
> As a cavalry mount, Comanche was not responsible for Custer's morals; and, as a symbol of a great battle, he merits the popular attention that he receives. But a university museum should exhibit truth rather than comfortable prejudice. (1971)

As the author of this article, which he wrote, he explained, "in order to censure the reporter," it is clear that Professor Wax was the right person to act as faculty sponsor for the University of Kansas student organization known as the Committee on Indian Affairs, an office which Wax himself described to Robert Mengel as "interesting, educational, and a mite difficult at times" (UK Archives).

In September 1971, committee members began meeting with museum director, Dr. Philip Humphrey, and the museum administrative assistant. Members of the native American committee expressed their concerns that the "sole survivor" notion concerning Comanche discredited the fact that a large number of Indians lived through the Battle of the Little Big Horn. "We're

dissatisfied with the explanation under the display of Comanche
—highly offended, really," one committee member said. "Lots of
Indians survived the Little Big Horn," another member pointed
out. "But American history teaches that nobody survived. Nobody white is what that means" (Hall 1971; Fisher 1971). Speaking for the committee, one Indian student revealed, "When we
first met with Steve (Steve Edwards, administrative assistant to the
director of the museum) there was some feeling that the horse was
so offensive to the memory of the Indians who had suffered at
Custer's hands that we wanted it removed. We're dealing with a
mystique—call it a stuffed horse," she said. "For years it has been
the 'sole survivor' because in those days Indians didn't count. Custer's last stand became a massacre when in reality it was a battle
between two military forces and the Indians beat the white man at
his own game and beat him bad." "The whites called the Washita
a 'battle,' " another Indian student pointed out. "And the Little
Big Horn was [termed] a 'massacre' " (Fisher 1971). With such
misinterpretations rankling in their minds, it was clear that the
first undertaking for the committee was to change the sign accompanying the display of the stuffed horse. Dr. Humphrey asked the
committee to draft a new text for the label on the Comanche exhibit which would then be reviewed and agreed upon by the cura-
tors of the museum (Humphrey 1974:2).

Meanwhile, as a result of committee action, on or about November 9, 1971, the celebrated exhibit was closed to the public.
In addition to preventing access to the horse until the label was
replaced by a more accurate explanation, the committee "demanded that all postcards and museum brochures that mentioned
Comanche as the 'sole survivor' of the Custer Massacre be made
unavailable for sale or other distribution by the museum" (Humphrey 1974:2). Humphrey agreed to these actions, and the Comanche display was then covered by a black shroud.

The other Indian exhibits remained open during the period
when what Edwards called "the highlight of a tour of the museum
for many visitors, the display that busloads of children rush to see
first when they arrive at Dyche," was draped in black. Even while
the exhibit was closed, the administrative assistant described an
incident in which "a college-age man, showing his parents
through the museum, lifted the curtain so the parents could see
the famed horse. He told his parents: 'It was the only living thing
that survived.' " Edwards noted "That's exactly what we're fighting." The committee began the task of creating a sign for Comanche that would tell both sides of the story of the famous battle, using "documented histories" that would "explain why the general

was there, why the Sioux were there in the first place, where Comanche was found, and how he got here," making clear that "in effect, they [the whites] declared open season on the Indian" (Hall 1971).

As it turned out, the change in the cavalry horse's label was to be only the beginning of many innovations for the Dyche Museum. Comanche's influence, as always, extended way beyond his status as a mere stuffed mount. The museum director related the way in which a whole series of changes was initiated through the horse:

> The Committee on Indian Affairs returned in a couple of weeks or so with a long proposed new text for the label on the Comanche exhibit. While a considerable amount of history was woven into the text, there was an overwhelming emphasis on genocide, slaughter of helpless Indian women and children, and so on. My reaction was that all the new label would do would be to make any non-Indian American reader angry. I said as much to the Committee on Indian Affairs and asked what in the long run the Committee wished to accomplish with respect to the Comanche exhibit. After a long discussion, we agreed that the Comanche exhibit could be used best along with other exhibits to educate visitors about American Indians, their culture, their relationships with the natural environment, and the history of their interactions with white people down to, and including, today. During the course of the conversation leading to this agreement the Committee on Indian Affairs made a number of observations about our exhibits that had never occurred to me or my colleagues in the museum before:
>
> 1) They were offended by the fact that exhibits about American Indians were cheek by jowl with exhibits about prehistoric or "primitive" man; this implied something that the Committee on Indian Affairs didn't like at all.
>
> 2) They objected very much to the fact that our exhibits had on display a number of religious objects that were labelled totally inadequately and probably shouldn't even be on display.
>
> 3) They felt that a sense of "Indianness" could not be gotten into the exhibits by non-Indians who don't know how Indians really feel.
>
> 4) Some of the Indians felt that having Comanche on exhibit in an "Indian Hall" would be sort of like having a statue of Hitler in a hall devoted to Jewish history and culture.
>
> The Committee on Indian Affairs and the curators of the museum finally were able to agree on a mutually acceptable text for the label on Comanche; it was also agreed that the Committee on Indian Affairs in consultation with me and some of my colleagues in the museum would begin work on development of plans for an Indian Hall in the museum. (Humphrey 1974:2–3)

And so, although he had first been the center of controversy, there now seemed to be agreement that the old Seventh Cavalry mount was well adapted to his new role. "Comanche is the most obvious example of the preconceived notions that people have about Indians," said a committee member. "If we're going to start educating people, Comanche is a good place to start" (Carlson and Gustin 1971a). Indian students were now convinced that Comanche could "be used to teach non-Indians the truth of what happened during the Indian wars, in opposition to the romanticism which has characterized much of the information about this period." "We know the results [of the Custer Battle]," said a committee member. "All of us do. But how do you fight films, novels, histories, slides, exhibits and everything else which has made the Custer Battle so romantic? Indians know. They know. But how do you start to teach non-Indians?" The committee has decided, members revealed, "to take Comanche for what he is worth—a stuffed horse. . . . Comanche is a drawing card to the museum. Thousands of children arrive every year and the first thing they ask is to see Comanche, 'the horse that Custer rode.' " "We can teach non-Indians through Comanche," one committee member went on. "We can teach the kids that the Indians survived the Little Big Horn. That they were fighting for their lives, for their land, for their game. That's why we have a new sign in Comanche's case and that's why we'll have new signs in the other Indian cases" (Fisher 1971). Once the Committee on Indian Affairs and the Museum of Natural History became "very deeply involved together in the development of plans for an Indian Hall," the museum director wrote, "all of us in the museum [became] vastly more sensitive to American Indians as human beings" (Humphrey 1974:3).

When the exhibit was reopened, the new label on the Comanche display read

> Comanche stands here as a symbol of the conflict between the United States Army and the Indian tribes of the Great Plains that resulted from the government's policy of confinement of Indians on reservations and extermination of those Indians who refused to be confined. In 1851 the government decided that boundaries were to be established for the tribes of the plains, and that these lands were to be guaranteed to the Indians "as long as the grass shall grow."
> But the lands lay in the path of westward migration of the Caucasian-European peoples bent on subjugation of the continent. In the 1830's and 1840's the mountain men, as free and capable as the Indians in the wilderness, had trapped and lived in peace with their American predecessors; then came the Oregon trail and the wagon

trains of the '50's and early '60's and troubles began. These were followed by a flood of cowmen, prospectors, and people of all sorts intent upon conquest of the Indian's land, people either unable or unwilling or both to care about treaties, rights, and promises. Incident followed incident; the treaties were broken and more and more of the territory promised to Indian tribes was taken. The United States Army, under the determined and merciless direction of General Philip Sheridan, was charged with "punishment" of Indians who rebelled either against the confinement of reservation life or the outrages of settlers and others. The Seventh U. S. Cavalry, under Lt. Colonel George A. Custer, was one of Sheridan's principal forces in these activities, and achieved considerable reputation, largely as a result of sudden attacks on unwarned and defenseless villages (for instance, an attack on Black Kettle's Cheyenne Village on the Washita River in Oklahoma, in which one hundred and three Cheyennes, including numerous women and children were killed).

In 1874, gold was discovered in the Black Hills of the great Sioux Reservation, on a "scientific" expedition led by Custer. He was followed by hundreds of thousands of eager, heedless prospectors. When the Indians protested this invasion of their reservation, and especially of their sacred grounds in the Black Hills, the government turned a deaf ear.

Forces under Generals Terry and Gibbon, including Custer and his Seventh Cavalry, were sent to round up and "discipline" those Sioux, Cheyenne, and other Indians who had left the reservations in protest. When the Seventh Cavalry finally engaged a very large band of Sioux and Cheyenne in the Battle of the Little Big Horn on June 25, 1876, Custer and five companies separated from the remaining six companies of his force. When night fell on the day of the battle there was no further sign of Custer and the remaining six companies were besieged. When relief came on the following day, it was found that Custer and over 250 troops lay dead. The victorious Indians had withdrawn, leaving Comanche the sole living creature to be led away from the battlefield.

The Indians' struggle to preserve their freedom was not successful, despite the outcome of the Battle. By 1890, the last element of resistance to the reservation policy of the government was crushed at the Massacre of Wounded Knee Creek in South Dakota, where over 300 unarmed Sioux were killed. The Indians were confined to their reservations. Comanche remains as a reminder of the outcome of their tragic attempt to keep the land and the way of life that had been theirs, and the tragedy of the U. S. government's Indian policy.

Museum Director Humphrey indicated he was "terribly pleased" with the new sign and admitted that "in working with the committee on the Comanche exhibit he had learned to appreciate more fully the problems of the 20th century American Indians." One committee member expressed satisfaction in the victory that had come about through negotiations, calling the label a "successful beginning point" that "proved to the Indian committee that the non-Indian community was willing to acknowledge the fact that history had been depicted wrongly" (Carlson and Gustin 1971b). The amicable outcome was reflected in the fact that both Indians and whites shared in a gala celebration which was held when the Comanche display bearing the new label was reopened.

Comanche was formally uncovered during an invitation-only open house and Christmas bazaar sponsored by the Natural History Museum and the Committee on Indian Affairs held in the museum at 7 P.M. on December 2, 1971. A newspaper announcement of the event showed that the concept of the "only survivor" persisted, although the issue of qualifying the horse's survivor status had been taken seriously (even though the confusion about white survivors of the Custer portion of the battle in distinction to the total Little Big Horn Battle remained): "Comanche, the controversial stuffed horse which in life was the only survivor among the federal force participating in the Battle of the Little Big Horn, will be back on display at the Kansas Museum of Natural History early in December." Approximately nine hundred of the twelve hundred invited guests attended the open house, the first such affair ever sponsored by the museum. A sale of American Indian arts and crafts from Kansas, Oklahoma, and the Southwest was held at the gift shop during the evening, with profits being designated to finance long-range changes and developments in the museum's Indian displays. An ecology film was shown during the festivities, and in the Dyche diorama containing a simulated background of the Kansas plains containing buffaloes and prairie dogs, members of the Indian Club at Haskell Junior College performed various native dances accompanied by authentic music (KU Museum to Improve 1971; Carlson and Gustin 1971b; Fisher 1971). Swearingen remembers the affair as "the most exciting event we ever had. Everybody likes Indian dances. It was like a pow-wow, with tom-toms, whistles, and bells, and the place was full of people." Humphrey recalls that "the grand opening celebration," which had press and TV coverage, and in which Haskell participated, was "a wild success."

Following his three weeks under a black shroud, nothing was physically different about the unveiled bay gelding who had been the center of controversy and now was once again being made available to the public as the focus for a unique celebration. Guests, as well as newspaper reporters and television crewmen, had to concentrate on the new sign accompanying the familiar display if they were to interpret the real significance of the event. Replacing the old placard because, native American students had pointed out, "it didn't tell both sides" (Carlson and Gustin 1971b), this new label, far longer than the original, revealed the "Indian perspective on the Battle," tracing the white conquest of Indian lands. Through the new text, major changes ultimately had been wrought by the small group of Indian students who had initially begun a protest over a "racist symbol" whose label excluded fair and proper consideration of their ancestors' role in the events of the Little Big Horn, inaccurately termed a "massacre." Members of the Committee on Indian Affairs had felt that the famous exhibit, in its former state, actually honored the U.S. government's action against Indians. The group's success in making its views understood and the willingness of museum personnel to bring about changes in the exhibit to reflect these views were indeed optimistic signs that times were ripe for a more far-reaching program of improvement.

Swearingen refers to the protest over Comanche as "a sign of the times," pointing out

> there were problems throughout the country, not just here—like Martin Luther King and the Blacks marching. The Indians were looking for their own identity, and wanted to be called native Americans, not Indians. That was a bad label, anyway. It was slanted toward the army's viewpoint and didn't tell the real story. The display has great value to the museum, but it was misrepresented for so long when it was used to idealize cavalry life. It was associated with personal gain from the battle, with the idea Custer wanted to be president.

Comanche, Swearingen says, "once symbolized a terrible loss to Americans, but now he is symbolic of the conflict between Indians and whites. The horse symbolizes one of the few and the greatest of all victories the Indians ever had, and the terrible mistake made by whites. For Indians, he's a symbol of victory; everyone likes to ride a winner."

Robert Mengel, biologist at Dyche and author of *Comanche: Silent Horse on a Silent Field*, agrees that the label on the horse was bad. At the beginning of the protest, he said, when the incensed Indians gathered on the sidewalk in front of the museum, someone distributed his publication, and they were placated. Discussing the 1971 affair, he said, "motivated Caucasians came in great numbers. Some activists were idly curious. It was even akin to morbidity. The horse was associated with great deeds, dark deeds. This appeals to the psyche. It titillated them. They were like crusaders."

Murray Wax spoke to me about his role as adviser to the

Committee on Indian Affairs (CIA), explaining the encouragement he gave to the students who were upset about the display of Comanche and who took exception to his being the "last living survivor of Custer's Last Stand." He praised the wonderful cooperation of the museum administration and emphasized the fact that the affair "was very educational for the museum people." A great deal was accomplished because "instead of criticizing, the Indian students said 'here's what we want people to know about our heritage.' "

I was able to talk personally with almost all of the former CIA members, and without exception they felt gratified with the results of the protest. One remembered "When I first saw that caption on Comanche, I said 'This can't be! We can't sit by and let this happen.' It really bothered me, as it was unfair to the Indians. The whole Sioux nation survived that battle, and you put a horse up there! We told Dr. Humphrey, and we were able to rewrite the label." Another participant said

> Comanche was formerly a political-historical symbol for the importance of the Battle of the Little Big Horn as an American defeat and represented the barbarity of the Indians. It represented the idea that whites were massacred by savage Indians in the wrong. But now it's a remarkable exhibit; it spans both sides but represents primarily the Indian point of view. It features photos of Indian war leaders and quotes from them about the battle, their personal experiences in battle.

She remembers that

> before the protest at KU, several activists from AIM [American Indian Movement] made a political statement in which they threatened to liberate Comanche by force. The University of Kansas Indian students heard this and were strongly concerned that forcible liberation from the museum would bring more negative than positive results. So they decided to educate people rather than creating more negative effects.

"Then," she explained,

> we negotiated with Dr. Humphrey and convinced him to use Comanche to educate people about why the Indians in the battle were not in the wrong; they were fighting for survival. He agreed to drape it in black, and when the ceremony was held to unveil the new plaque, it was a step in educating people about the Battle of the Little Big Horn. Comanche's not a traditional symbol out of the history books but represents the legitimate concerns of the Indian people for the survival of their own culture and way of life.

One protester, a Plains Indian, said she had objected to the biased view expressed by the cavalry horse and felt it should not be on display: "The horse was dead and served no useful purpose being stuffed." She also revealed that at the time of the affair regarding Comanche, "there was a push by the university to recruit minority students—but they were recruiting everyone except native Americans. The purpose of the protest was to call attention to native Americans. We wanted to raise consciousness through Comanche."

The protest over Comanche had accomplished a great deal. Now the horse came to represent "a victory for the Indians seeking to tell their viewpoint of American history." As one writer noted, "The horse that once angered Indians" now "allows them to raise their heads in the pride of telling their side of the story." Through their complaints, Indians were able to change the horse Comanche from the battle's "lone survivor" into a symbol of the Indians' perseverance against government policy that sought to push them from their ancestral lands." According to the campus coordinator for the American Indian Movement, "Comanche [now] has a great significance to Indians," as a symbol of "the Indians' past victories and what modern Indians can accomplish." The "Indian viewpoint of history has not been written until recently," he said, "but the important thing is that it is slowly coming out" (Comanche Once Angered 1978; Comanche Stands 1978; Indians Win 1978).

The Comanche controversy was to be only the first step in initiating a series of innovations in the Indian displays at Dyche Museum. The meetings and negotiations between Indian students and museum officials which had begun with rancor over the stuffed horse were continued amicably over the next few years with the additional cooperation of faculty and students at Haskell American Indian Junior College. Interchange of ideas between Indians and whites continued and plans were formulated for alterations which would make the entire fifth-floor Indian exhibit more educational. Both museum officials and committee members felt that "besides the Comanche display, the rest of the Indian exhibit is of questionable value. . . . Many items from Indian history are hung on walls inside glass cases in the area near Comanche. Each item is labeled with a single word" and the displays are presented like "curios" (Hall 1971). (It is noteworthy that at the 1893 Chicago Exposition where Comanche was exhibited, some of these same factors were being discussed, and an effort was made to interpret native American displays in a more holistically educational manner than had been the case for the 1876 centennial [Braun 1974].)

To replace these brief identifying labels at Dyche, it was agreed that historical descriptions of the museum articles were needed to explain their purpose and meaning in the Indian culture. Following study of the artifacts, corrections would now be made for any false or misleading statements about the native American exhibits. There was concern over items such as the one labeled "ghost dance shirt," which "has very deep religious significance for some Indians." In the future, if the display of any articles proved to be offensive to any tribes, such articles would be removed. By these means, Indian displays could "serve the interests of both Indian and non-Indian people by promoting a better understanding of Indian cultures." Humphrey, as director, agreed that although museum personnel would assist with technical aspects of the new displays, exhibit changes would be directed by the Committee on Indian Affairs (Carlson and Gustin 1971a; Hall 1971).

One Committee on Indian Affairs member, a UK senior, was the first education major with an emphasis on American Indian education. Working in the museum, she acted as liaison between the museum administration and the committee; and, working with the anthropology department and the education school, she was designated to do research on the artifacts (KU Museum to Improve 1971). In this regard, faculty sponsor for the committee, sociologist Murray Wax, reported on December 8 that "things seem to be evolving splendidly," and that next semester this student "will be working with me and the staff of the Museum in redesigning exhibits," and that "the maneuver will offer course credit for her labors" (1971b).

Comanche's influence on Indian educational concerns at the university were, indeed, extended further. One of the prominent student members of the committee revealed that "a larger aim of the committee" was "to institute an Indian Studies program at K. U. No courses on Indian civilization are taught at the university. It's unbelievable," she added. "Here is a state with a wealth of Indian history from prehistory to the present century and all it had, up to a month ago, was that a horse was the 'sole survivor' of Custer's command" (Fisher 1971).

From the Comanche controversy and its peaceful resolution came a new era of understanding and cooperation between Indians and whites at the University of Kansas. Long-range plans not only called for complete redesigning of all museum exhibits relating to native Americans, but also stipulated that the Committee on Indian Affairs would annually appoint two representatives to advise the Museum Exhibits Committee. The goal for the recon-

201

structed displays was "to show how the culture of North American natives was intimately affected by the environments in which they lived, the consequent respect shown by Indians for the environment, and how the Indian cultures were affected both by the destruction of natural habitats by white man and the forced translocations of Indians to environments alien to them" (Budget Proposal KU n.d.).

It seemed that the only obstacle now remaining was monetary. The Museum Director wrote

> Nevertheless, in spite of this amiable outcome, it has been impossible to obtain the financial support necessary to move development of the Indian Hall along at anything more than a snail's pace. I would have liked to have employed a number of Indians in the Museum to work with us on the hall; a number of American Indian students feel that the level of financial support provided by the University and the federal government is totally inadequate to the needs of Indian students. In addition, it would have been wonderful if the University could have hired one or more American Indian faculty members so that Indian students might have an increased sense of recognition here at the University. From my standpoint, the progress and eventual success of the Indian Hall will depend on our having at least one more or less permanent Indian staff member in the exhibits program.
>
> None of the Indian students I know here at KU have felt that AIM was the way to go. They have felt that in the long run a reasonable, non-violent approach was much the best. At the same time, it is disappointing to note that in the University as a whole, there is seldom, if ever, any response to minority dissident groups unless there seems to be a clear threat of violence, disruption, and negative publicity. The blacks here at KU have done much better than the American Indians because frankly, I think the University administration is more afraid of blacks than of Indians. (Humphrey 1974:3–4)

Sometime after the uproar over Comanche had long since died down, I had the opportunity to talk with Museum Director Humphrey. As a central participant in the affair involving the horse, his personal thoughts and reminiscences give dimension to the story of the Indian students' protest and its consequences. The events surrounding the famous mount, he told me, "have been handed down as legend now. . . . The first meeting with the Committee on Indian Affairs," he remembers, "was heavy; we were preoccupied. We had a horse representing all that was evil about the Americans, the Anglos, including a history of broken treaties. The horse was labeled in an offensive way, for Comanche was not the 'sole survivor.' The Indians were alive. The word 'massacre' was offensive. . . . The interesting aspect of our meetings," he went on, "was that no one Indian was in charge. There was no spokesman. They all chimed in.

"When the Indians became furious about the university newspaper article about Comanche which came out while negotiations were going on," Humphrey explained, "I apologized. I responded the same day and took Comanche off public exhibition. But it seemed to me that since the horse attracted so many people to the museum, it would be good for the Indians to examine the notion of using Comanche as a symbol of past historic wrongs. They could turn it into a positive force which would foster understanding." He related that

> after the label was changed, Comanche became part of the larger scene. One Potawatomie Indian came to a subsequent committee meeting in full regalia and made the point that seeing Indian religious objects on display was offensive. Native American beliefs were against having sacred objects on exhibit. There was a strong Indian activist movement in the country at this time; AIM was confrontational at that point. The events sensitized me to things I had in the museum on Indians. I got a new awareness of their concerns about museums, the things Anglos had taken for granted. For example, on ethnographic materials, the label says "collected by ———," just like it does on the mounted birds. We should avoid this in relation to anthropological material. An item like a baby moccasin, for instance, may have been collected off a dead baby. How do we differ from the butchers in Germany?

"The Indians then got involved in planning the whole display to reflect history more accurately," the director continued.

> We hired Indian students at the museum. It was an exciting time! In working on the museum displays, a number of Indians learned they knew little about their own antecedants and culture. They had to consult anthropological literature to find out about their heritage. There had been some negative response in town to replacing the old Comanche label. And a tiny majority expressed concern over changing things in the museum in response to requests from Indians. But I was responding to reasonable requests. Eventually, I became a member of the Committee on Indian Affairs and was elected chairman one year. The effects on me were extremely important. I learned more from Comanche than the Indians did. The Comanche affair was one of the greatest learning experiences of my life.

For the Indians who participated in the events that made Comanche such an educational experience, the horse was a powerful symbol upon which many of their traditional beliefs and attitudes became crystallized. Later interviews with some of the native Americans revealed much that was going on below the surface of the Comanche controversy which was not communicated to the press or to the white authorities at the time. Underlying issues centered on the horse itself, both in life and as a museum specimen, on human relationships with animals, on contrasts in Indian and white world views, and on the clash of cultures which resulted in Custer's defeat at the Little Big Horn.

Concerning Comanche, one former protester who is "half Sioux and was raised on the reservation with a traditional background," related that

> The students involved in the controversy were products of the '60s. We were militant. The change in the sign on Comanche was a compromise. What we really wanted was for the horse to be taken away and buried. We objected to its being symbolic of one of the worst and most dishonest myths regarding the West. Comanche and the sign symbolized worship at the altar of the West that did not really exist. It epitomizes several wrong ideas regarding Indians, the Old West, cavalry, and the place of animals in society. It's sad; the poor horse is sad.
> Glorification of Comanche perpetuates the stereotypes of Indians: the massacre—poor Custer surrounded by Indians. It's like a Rand-McNally picture, wrong like whites calling Sand Creek a battle and the Custer Battle a massacre. It upholds the idea that cavalrymen were heroes and Indians villainous savages. Soldiers are pictured like John Wayne and Ronald Reagan, cowboy heroes who are definitely the strong silent type. America's worship of cowboys gives a very false picture. Cowboys like John Wayne are on liquor bottles, decorative decanters. This is along the same lines as what happened to Comanche. From primary source material about life in Custer's cavalry, it is known that Custer was not a good military man. He forced marches where he knew there was no forage for horses. He lost all of his company. He was a madman who nearly killed all of us as well as the horses. All of this is eulogized in the myth about Custer.

In conclusion, she admitted, "We're still antagonistic to the museum. It's not really patched up," and firmly repeated that "changing the sign was only a compromise, and we still want them to take Comanche away."

A former Kansas University student who had been very active in the Committee on Indian Affairs and had helped write the new label for the Comanche exhibit talked to me at length. She is half Potawatomie and half white but said "I never have felt a choice. I've always been Indian inside." Regarding Comanche, she told me

> I would rather have had the horse taken out of the museum. I suggested removing it. But after learning the horse had to stay there, I

worked with the display. The Comanche exhibit can't be moved. It would disintegrate. So we used it as a tool. Comanche was with Indian exhibits on the floor with displays of Cro-Magnon Man. It was like Indians are the next step up from cave men. We had to make changes.

The museum people were cooperative when approached about Comanche. Comanche is the most popular exhibit at Dyche. The horse is best as an educational tool, so there should be no conflict. I was present, with other members of the Committee on Indian Affairs, at the unveiling. We were successful in causing some good things to happen. The museum was receptive, and it was the beginning of a cooperative venture. When we unveiled the horse, a colonel from Fort Leavenworth wrote and said 'You are making the army sound like bad guys.' The museum people stood by us, though, and I was pleased. A white teacher six miles west of here [Lawrence] was shot at because she talked about Martin Luther King. There's still a lot of prejudice, and this is reflected in the negative comments of the colonel about the new Comanche label. I've risked my life before. Mine is one of three tribes which never signed the Indian Reorganization Act. We protested against loss of our land to whites. If they ever put the old sign with Comanche as 'sole survivor' back, I'll get all my mean relatives up here to fight it. The museum people are morally obligated not to use that label. Comanche was a symbol for students at the time of the protest. Those who were concerned with the status of Indians for the general public cared how the horse was displayed. Comanche helped the whole Indian movement. It helped in uniting us. It's one of the positive things that gave us hope. Although it's generally hard to get Indians to agree, they agreed on Comanche. We were all university students, all from different backgrounds, but we agreed.

There is a temptation to see a parallel here with the unity of the tribes at the Little Big Horn—a phenomenon said to be rare among Indians!

Another former student who had been active in the Comanche protest articulated the native Americans' anger about the original sign which had "implied the horse survived while the Indian people did not." She further commented, "Indians are still regarded as invisible unless they wear feathers. White society sees Indians as savages or bad guys, illiterate and uncultured." She explained

The sign was typical of cowboy movies, in which the hero is ambushed by six Indians, and he kills them all, on their territory. I'm disgusted with the emphasis on the frontier mentality. It makes me ashamed, and I'm angry about the glorification of pioneers. It makes me want to puke on statues of pioneers.

The Blacks raised consciousness through violence and threat of violence, and this got results for them. I thought Indian people couldn't do that. I felt we would all go our own way and not get organized. I expected we would be factionalized and individualistic, so it wouldn't happen. But when the Indian students marched on the museum, I was thrilled. Some native Americans from the reservation and some people from Haskell were involved. It was one of the few times different Indian people agreed.

I'm not much for having the horse stay here at the museum. A memorial to Custer doesn't tickle my fancy, and that seems like what it is. Comanche is with the Indian collection in the museum. Whites make a big deal of the fact that Custer rode in to kill Indians. Groups of armed men were led by a maniac who was unstable. But they followed him anyway. It was like My-Lai. The soldiers unquestioningly obeyed, even though they knew they were outnumbered. They had good enough information indicating they shouldn't have ridden in there. Following a leader in that way is not an Indian tradition. If Indian people don't agree, they go off and form another band. It really gets me. People freaked out. I think it's a terrible thing when Custer was obviously unbalanced. To glorify him and make him a hero is incredible. But it's not surprising because of the dehumanizing of the Indians. Whites lump them with wildlife and the environment.

The subject of Comanche invariably raised the issue of the natural environment, wildlife, animals, and the human relationship to them. Informants who discussed their participation in the Comanche protest and its aftermath had a great many related ideas to add on these topics. A former student who had been involved told me

The protesters wanted Comanche removed from the museum and buried because it was a violation of the horse's spirit to stuff it and put it behind glass. Christians worship Christ's shroud, nails from the crucifixion, and other material things, but to an Indian, stuffed animals are horrifying. It's a desecration of an animal's spirit. Stuffing and putting an animal behind glass is repugnant; it's a desecration, like digging up a grave.

It never dawns on people in the museum that there has been a religious violation of the spirits of those animals. Indian burial practices have something to say about relationships with animals. The dead are placed on a scaffold and birds pick the body clean. We believe after we're dead the carrion eaters have a right to our body. We lived off them, and this is a way of returning what you have taken. But when animals are stuffed, the museum is haunted with their spirits. Comanche's soul is just as lost as those souls in the Ghost Dance [at the time, a display of items pertaining to that ritual faced the Comanche display]. The dominant society wants to put Indians in a museum behind glass. They equate Indians with museum pieces—a part of nature to look at through glass.

Christians believe animals have no souls, but Indians know animals have souls and spirits. In the Indian concept of death, there is a continuing relationship with the dead, who pass into another state. Western man answers only to God, but the Indian view of the world is a circle. Spirit is in everything. If an Indian hunts a deer, he must pray and ask the deer's forgiveness; every bit of the animal is used. No form of life is more important than another. Everything belongs in the circle, and everything is required to make it function. The horse is in this circle.

The dominant society is alienated from the world of nature and animals. The growing list of extinct animals alarms us. Indians believe everything is important, that all animals are necessary to keep things in balance. Coyotes are needed to keep the plains clear. Whites fear snakes, but they have a place in the world. Whites have disturbed the balance. Ranchers hate wild horses, coyotes, and wolves, but if they let nature alone, nature would achieve balance. You don't see Indians at zoos. It's painful for us to go there. The animals are out of place; a polar bear doesn't belong in this Kansas heat.

The dominant society could learn from Indians. The animal shelter is busy here. College students get animals when they're here and abandon them when they leave. Indians wouldn't do that. My great-aunt even brought her horses into a place attached to the house, so that the heat could go out to them. Traditionally, Indians took care of horses as well as their children. Transportation depended upon them. It was a working relationship—a living, breathing, working relationship.

One native American who had been active in the protest pointed out that

For Indians, striving for harmony in life is a cultural characteristic. That's one reason the way of life at the university is difficult for people of my tribe. It's even harder for full-bloods. There's racial discrimination. When the original sign was on Comanche, Indians were considered less than rocks and weren't considered as survivors. The policy was to kill them. Either Comanche must symbolize how non-Indians conquered the Indians or how they conquered nature. Both are wrong.

Native Americans were the first ecologists. In keeping with this, we treated animals fairly. We cared for animals more in terms of what they really were.

Another of the protesters said

The label designating Comanche as "sole survivor" meant that white culture treats Indians as part of wildlife. Dehumanizing Indians was a cover up for what had been done to them. White culture views man above nature. Whites don't treat nature with respect. Indians expect to treat nature as brothers and mothers—their relatives.

A Navajo visitor who was looking at Comanche in the museum told me "Comanche should be buried. I was brought up in the Navajo tradition. When my horse died, it was buried by my father. The Indian took the horse to war. The horse was there when it was needed. It should have a proper burial out of gratitude. The same is true for this cavalry horse." Russell Means, the charismatic contemporary Sioux leader who was a founder of AIM, observed, "A horse named Comanche as the only survivor of the Custer Battle—that's a true case of poetic justice!" Means believes the horse should be buried, not stuffed. "It's disrespectful," he asserts. "Except for Lenin, they just don't do that to something that dies."

Discussing museum displays, the exhibits director at the UK Natural History Museum sees cultural discrepancies operating: "It's just like Indians can't hurry. Their values are different. Indians are spiritual, whereas we are material. Indians don't preserve things. If we hadn't done it, they wouldn't have their own artifacts. They don't take care of things like that."

The Comanche protest of the 1970s was an effort to make cultural differences educational rather than pejorative. As we have seen, it was to a large extent successful. In 1979, however, the issue of racism was still associated with the mounted horse. Once again, the trigger to antagonism was a Kansas newspaper's statement that Custer's troops were *massacred* at the Little Big Horn. In response, a native American pointed out that since historical evidence indicated Custer was defeated "soundly and fairly" by the Lakota and Cheyenne, the newspaper's assertion was "quite absurd." The writer went on to say, "However, considering that the Journal-World reflects the interests and attitudes of the Lawrence community and, ironically enough, that a horse from the Custer troop is enshrined at KU, it's all quite consistent —if deplorably so—that such tragic fictions and perverse heroes are created and sustained by such racist Kansas institutions and communities" (Thunder Hawk 1979). As recently as January of 1987, a newspaper writer who reviewed the main events of the year 1986 in Lawrence, Kansas, described the accidental flooding of Comanche and referred to the famous horse as the "survivor of the Little Big Horn Massacre" (Lawrence's Year 1987:C1). Incredibly, the 1989 spring and summer University of Oklahoma Press catalog begins the description of one new book with the phrase: "Ever since the Custer massacre on June 25, 1876."

Undoubtedly Comanche has been used, often unconsciously, in connection with unexamined ingrained attitudes, as a "racist symbol." Indeed, the cavalry horse in general once had an image in that regard. In Boniface's classic study of the cavalry, for example, the equine animal itself is credited for its role in serving man by "subduing the wilderness and its savages" (1903:1). Three years after the Little Big Horn, one writer using racist language described Comanche as "the only survivor of the Custer massacre, every man and beast save himself having been destroyed by relentless and bloody hands" (Comanche 1879). An 1891 article on Comanche referred to the Last Stand "against Sitting Bull's red devils" (Burt 1891:3). The stigma of racism does not belong only to the past but has sometimes been perpetuated in recent times through choice of words. A 1961 narrative about the horse, for example, depicts "wildly-shrieking, tomahawk-hurling braves," riding down "the pitifully outnumbered soldiers like grass, leaving no man or horse alive but the nearly-dead Comanche." After the battle, the soldiers found "the tortured bodies of their fallen comrades" (Valentry 1961:198, 199). Even in December of 1988, the *New York Times* published an article in which a writer referring to the Custer Battle used a historically inaccurate term that is prejudicial to the Indians when he stated that "Custer died in the 1876 *ambush* by the Sioux and Cheyenne." A Letter to the Editor appearing in the *Times* on January 8, 1989, strongly protested this use of *ambush* in connection with Custer's death, pointing out that the word represents a distortion of history. On January 22, 1989, another newspaper, citing the *Times* as its source, repeated the exact same phrase about Custer dying in the ambush (Egan 1988:A1; Thompson 1989:E28; Centennials Spur 1989:A20).

Comanche has not necessarily been singled out as a focus for racism; but as a large, conspicuous, well-publicized, and authentic relic of the Custer affair, he commands attention. Because of the horse's innocence—that of his species and that which accrues to him in his particular role as a servant in, not an activator of, human concerns—Comanche often acts as a foil against which the Indian's imputed "savagery" becomes more dramatic. Horses are very often perceived as "noble" in the popular mind, and this quality, combined with innocence and docility, draws much sympathy. A cavalry horse, especially a strong, obedient, and faithful one who survives a bloody battle, becomes a repository for feelings of solidarity with the soldiers' cause, a cause which at Little Big Horn has been insensitively interpreted as "civilization versus savagery." It was this image that the Indians protested.

Comanche's Indian Counterpart

It is not surprising to learn that Indian people have their own counterpart of the United States cavalry's famous "lone survivor," Comanche. This spotted horse who lived through the Battle of the Little Big Horn was ridden into that engagement by an Indian scout serving with Custer's force. The horse's story has

been recorded by Brummet Echohawk, a Pawnee, who recently
discussed the episode with me. According to him, the Arikara Indians, also called Rees, are an offshoot of the Pawnee Nation, the
split between the two having taken place about a hundred years
before the Custer disaster. The Arikaras settled in what is now
North Dakota, in the vicinity of Fort Abraham Lincoln. Because
of their common origin, the Arikaras and Pawnees had similar
languages and customs and visited each other annually to share
ceremonies and exchange songs and gifts.

Some Rees accompanied Custer in his 1876 campaign
against the Sioux and Cheyenne, acting as scouts for the U. S.
Cavalry. Three of these scouts lost their lives with Custer. Echohawk relates that the Arikara mourning rites for their tribesmen
included singing a death song followed by a warrior's song in their
honor. These songs, which are sacred and have deep meaning, are
passed down to the next generation.

> To this day, the Arikaras in North Dakota and the Pawnees in
> Oklahoma, sing a war dance song that has reference to a warrior
> and his horse. For it was sometime after the Battle of the Little Big
> Horn that an emaciated spotted horse walked into the Arikara vil-
> lage, alone. It was in the early morning when they found him.
> Scarred and showing signs of a hard journey, the horse carried an
> Army saddle intact. The reins were up as if he had just been rid-
> den. He had returned home. The Arikaras recognized him. Old-
> time Arikaras and old-time Pawnees, who knew horseflesh, have
> said that a pony will do that. Uh-tius (God) gives them a homing in-
> stinct. Recorded in an old-time Arikara and Pawnee song is: *"Asah-
> wakee Ska-rah Wah-tuh-we-cha, Keereh-putz-kee Rah-he-gooz."* The
> words in English are: Horse spotted alone has returned, Little Sol-
> dier. Its meaning is: Little Soldier's (the Ree Scout killed with Cus-
> ter at the Little Big Horn) spotted horse has returned (home) alone.
> As a full blood Pawnee, I have heard this war dance song many
> times. Our people still carry on the warrior-song tradition. A war-
> rior's song was given to me for action in the Italian campaign,
> 1943. And I know that the feeling is deep when the Arikara and
> Pawnee visit the Custer National Monument—for the last name,
> listed under Scouts, on that granite monument is "Little Soldier."
> (1964:43, 101)

Advocates of a "new American breed," the Paint horse,
point out that the spotted horse "was the Indian's favorite."
Being "especially treasured and prized," Paint horses have "always been associated with the Indian in legends, stories, songs,
and even in today's television programs." The authoritative work
on the Paint includes a retelling of Echohawk's story of "the spotted horse alone" (Haynes 1976:25–28). Though it is agreed that

the surviving Indian mount was indeed spotted, there is a conflicting idea about ownership which indicates the horse may have been ridden into the famous battle by another Indian, Bob-tailed Bull, the first of the Ree scouts to fall.

In a series of recorded eye-witness reports made by Arikara participants in the Battle of the Little Big Horn, Red Bear told of an incident he observed during the fight, when

> up the bank, through the bushes at his left downstream came the horse of Bob-tailed Bull, the reins and rope were flying, and the tail and mane floating in the wind. The horse was much frightened and ran snorting past Red Bear but a few yards away from him and Red Bear saw that the saddle was all bloody in front. Five or six white soldiers were riding through the bushes at his left, having just crossed the river. The horse of Bob-tailed Bull followed after them, and the Dakota horse he was driving dashed away after the others. (Bob-tailed Bull's saddle was an Indian saddle with a wooden frame covered with rawhide. Bloody Knife was the only one [Ree scout] with a government saddle, horse, etc.). (Libby 1920:11, 126–27)

The horse thus described as "Bobtailed Bull's big pinto" is sometimes thought to be the mount that returned home alone to the Arikara village (Connell 1984:9).

As with Comanche, one writer draws upon another. A year after Echohawk's story of Little Soldier's spotted horse appeared, a Montana newspaper carried a similar story, this time attributing ownership of the horse to the Arikara scout, Bloody Knife, who was killed at Little Big Horn beside Reno. "The pony's homing instinct was stronger than the terror of the battle or his painful wounds." The pinto made his way home alone over five hundred miles of open country, and a month after the battle he was "running with a herd of horses on the Fort Berthold Reservation." His wounds were treated, he was never again ridden, and he was honored for bravery. He took part in the celebration for returning scouts, and a Pinto victory song was composed for him (Horn 1965:7).

Factual discrepancies about ownership and type of saddle do not alter the fundamental meaning of the spotted Arikara survivor, any more than the many controversies surrounding Comanche detract from his significance. Both horses, though injured, returned to their own people and lived on. The grief that is universally felt by horsemen when one of their wounded animals falls into the hands of the enemy was long ago expressed by Cortes. During the siege of Mexico, he wrote, one of his men

fell from his mare. At once she galloped off toward the enemy, who
wounded her with arrows. She, when she saw their wickedness,
though badly wounded, came back to us. That night she died and
though we felt her death, for the horses and mares were our salva-
tion, our grief was less, as she did not die in the power of the enemy, as we had feared would be the case.

Commenting upon Cortes' sentiments, R. B. Cunninghame Graham, a dedicated horseman himself, understands the Spaniard's
joy that the stricken mare was back among comrades. He reflects
that "Cortes must have looked on the mare as a companion in his
great adventure, and was glad that the last words she would hear
were in the tongue that she had heard, and perhaps in a vague
manner understood, since the day she was foaled" (1949:24–26).

Comanche, like the spotted horse, had been wounded but
not killed by the enemy. When the museum Indian exhibits, of
which Comanche was a part, were finally renovated as a result of
student protest, the accompanying design on the walls above his
display was chosen to represent that status. The exhibits associate
who had worked on the changes and who acted as "liaison between anthropology and natural history" told me the exhibits
committee "had a hard time deciding on the symbols to use on
either side of the horse. Some wanted to copy Indian skin paintings, the yearly tribal records, but we decided abstract symbols
would be better." A painted border was designed with each motif
chosen to coincide with the exhibit below it. Three authentic patterns adapted from Lyford's book on Sioux quill and beadwork
(1984:77) were ultimately selected: one representing a "dead
man's body showing wounds and spears," one depicting "shooting-of-arrows from between the hills," and between these two,
another symbolizing "horse-killed-in-battle." The latter red and
green diamond motif was worked into a border design representing twelve horses but with only eleven killed. The twelfth is Comanche. There is one motif missing from the border above the
mounted horse display—the missing one represents Comanche
who survived (see fig. 15).

The exhibits associate told me, "We, in a sense, inherited
Comanche—a strong drawing card as far as visitors are concerned
but somewhat of a difficulty when designing exhibits. Our solution seems to have placated the Indian community—pointing out
that many Indians as well as the horse survived the battle—and
the border symbols were chosen with that in mind." One museum
employee, she said, had wanted Seventh Cavalry symbols over
Comanche's case. "But this was inappropriate on the native
American floor. The fact that Comanche is there is all that any-

body needs. During the protest, the Indians didn't want Comanche here at all. I understood their feelings. If he were telling the story of the American Indian, there was enough to tell without making that horse into a hero.

"In the early '70s, the students here were restless," she continued.

> At that time an Indian group approached the director because they found a number of the exhibits on this floor offensive. I was in sympathy, especially after listening to some of the visitors' reactions to displays. The impressions they got about Indians were unkind and untrue. People obtained no real knowledge of the situation. The old dioramas were objectionable and out-of-date. It had been twenty to thirty years since people thought that way. Mothers came with children and told them this is how Indians live. "The mommy has no clothes." We were embarrassed. Some time after the protest, I sat down with representatives from the university Indian committee. I was on the committee; I am a tiny bit Indian. An anthropologist was also present. We met and made a master plan for the fifth floor, and it developed well.
>
> The use of authentic designs representing Indian cultural groups relating to the exhibits below them was proposed. It was appropriate, for example, to put a replica of the Iroquois Covenant Belt above the display pertaining to the reservation period. The belt represents the thirteen colonies' promise to end strife with the Iroquois, to be at peace forever. Actually, it was the beginning of the move to take over more and more land.
>
> If the native American things are moved from the Museum of Natural History to the anthropology museum, this floor may be devoted just to Kansas. Comanche could be worked in at Fort Riley, with the army point of view. It would be appropriate to put the horse back in Fort Riley. They have the best cavalry museum there. But they would have to pay the bill. Comanche is the top tourist attraction in the entire state, above Eisenhower's home or anything else in Kansas.

In a conversation during one of my early visits to the museum to see Comanche, Tom Swearingen once remarked that "there's some romance to that horse, even for Indians." I happen to agree. If the relic or artifact in question were almost anything but a horse, I think it would have been removed from the museum long ago. But a horse, even a stuffed one, has its own aura of peace and harmony; and unlike almost any other element except a gun that could be mentioned as significant in the Custer Battle, it represents something of great value to each side. The horse and the gun were both gifts from whites to Plains Indian society, but the horse is at the opposite pole to the weapon, standing for life rather than death. Comanche is exempt from guilt and complicity

in Custer's actions. Thus, there is a benign neutrality accruing to
him in spite of his disputed status. The veteran cavalry horse's
symbolism proved to be not only powerful enough but adaptable
enough to survive a modern enemy onslaught.

When all the furor subsided, Comanche remained on the
fifth floor. Following the renovations in 1978, he was displayed
facing toward the Ghost Dance exhibit, which contained associated religious items including a feathered hoop and a sacred
Ghost Dance shirt. A native American praised the display as
"good and important," and felt that "such information should be
widely disseminated. A study of the Ghost Dance phenomenon,"
he noted, "is greatly relevant to the modern Indian as he stands
on the threshold of losing all cultural identity" (Rednest 1978). In
the same area, an exhibit showed life at "The Fort Sill Reservation in the 1890s." Six paintings situated in the vicinity of the
mount depicted scenes from the Battle of the Little Big Horn.
Nearby was a bronze statue of Captain Myles Keogh on Comanche and two other bronzes entitled "Indian Victor" and "The Final Moment." Some dioramas of early mankind, "the gift of the
Class of 1937 to Dyche," could be seen in the same area. Among
the exhibits was a placard with a quotation from Alistair Cooke's
America: "The White man banished the Indian to lands where no
white man could possibly survive. The Indian fooled him. He survived." Thus, though Comanche's new label did not call him a
survivor, it was perhaps the familiar theme of survival itself, more
than any other concept, that still pervaded the hall where he
stood.

Chapter 11

The Centennial and the Eighties

If we today, June 25, 1976, do not reflect upon what brought about this carnage 100 years ago, we can have no conception of the evil of man's inhumanity to man. (Harold G. Stearns, Keynote Speech, Custer Battlefield)

The native American student members of the Committee on Indian Affairs continued to meet with museum personnel for several years following the events of 1971 and 1972. Another important milestone which gave impetus for increased attention to the Comanche display was fast approaching because 1976 would mark the One Hundredth Anniversary of the Battle of the Little Big Horn. A budget request drawn up by the committee sometime during 1974 or 1975 set forth goals for making the fifth-floor Indian displays more educational, and specifies that

Included in these proposed exhibits is a set of three, relating to the display of Comanche, which highlight the Battle of the Little Big Horn, the Ghost Dance Religion, and the Massacre of Wounded Knee. These exhibits are intended to show the significance and effect of these events on the culture and history of North American Indians and to show how these epitomize the conflict of the cultures of European and [native] American men.

We hope to complete all exhibits called for in the plan in the next several years, but we are now especially interested in the three above-mentioned, because June 1976 marks the 100th anniversary of the Battle of the Little Big Horn. Thus we know that we will soon experience a marked increase in museum attendance and in publicity about Comanche. We want to be able to educate our visitors more fully about the causes and significances of all these events.

In the request, financial support was sought for the planning

215

and installation of these displays so that work could be completed by June 1976. Comanche, now designated as *"the only living animal* [italics mine] found on the Custer Battlefield when the relief party arrived two days after the battle," is cited in the proposal as "one of the most popular exhibits at the University of Kansas Museum of Natural History," and one that "has received an extreme amount of nationwide attention." Indian students would be hired to help design and install the exhibits, and in addition to Dyche Museum officials, the University of Kansas anthropologist and native Americans from Haskell would provide advice. It was hoped that there would also be representatives from Indian reservations in Kansas and from urban Indian organizations in the state. There is mention that "a decorative border of an Indian design relating to [each] exhibit" had already been found to be "a very effective, though subtle, means of communication."

Before detailing monetary needs, the final paragraph explains that

> Perhaps the most important educational function these exhibits will serve, however, is to influence the numerous persons who come to study Comanche with an eye to writing a newspaper, journal, or even book-length article about the horse and what he represents. It is remarkable how much attention the horse receives; in the last three months one book has been published in which Comanche received a full chapter, a request for another book has been received, a reporter has interviewed our staff and plans to highlight the horse in a state Fish and Game publication, and an article for a major Sunday newspaper supplement has been written. (Budget Proposal n.d.)

A few years before the Dyche Museum began to formulate plans for what was an admittedly big event surrounding its most famous and prized specimen, history once again showed that Comanche was in demand elsewhere. As early as 1969, National Park Service personnel turned attention toward the celebrated horse with hopes to bring about his presence in Montana for the event still six and a half years in the future. On November 12, the National Park Service historian wrote a memorandum to the superintendent of Custer Battlefield on the subject of the "100th anniversary of the Battle of the Little Big Horn, June 25–26, 1976." Ten ideas for use in commemoration of the centennial were enumerated. *First* on the list, which also proposed a Seventh Cavalry march reenactment and encampment, issuance of commemorative postage stamps, coins, and three different types of guns, and the invited participation of Custer descendants and "survivors of the Indian camp" or their descendants, was to "obtain the horse Comanche on a loan for the year 1976, or at least for the period May through August, 1976." Though this new projected plan to bring the Seventh Cavalry survivor back in 1976 to the site where he gained fame and immortality a hundred years before, like other proposals before it, did not come about, it is significant to note that the idea was preeminent (CBNM Files).

The University of Kansas Museum of Natural History commemorated the centennial of the Battle of the Little Big Horn in several important ways which involved the famous horse once again referred to in the press as "the sole survivor of General George Armstrong Custer's immediate command in the battle" (Museum Prepares 1976; New Exhibit 1976; Museum to Honor 1976; Museum to Commemorate 1976). The first was publication by the University Press of Kansas of a nineteen-page booklet, *Comanche.* Written by David Dary, Associate Professor of Journalism at the university, this work was the latest in the museum's Public Education Series "intended to provide popular publications on natural history for the people of Kansas." Clear and concise, the attractive booklet lived up to what Director Humphrey stated was its purpose—"to answer the many questions the museum receives about Comanche" (Museum to Commemorate 1976). Eight photographs are included, and the cover illustration is a head and neck drawing of Comanche by museum artist Tom Swearingen. Originally scheduled for release "in late June or early April" of the Custer Battle Centennial year, its actual publication date was September 3, 1976. Modestly priced and within the budget range of most visitors, the work filled an important need for material on the famous exhibit to sell at the Dyche gift shop.

Appropriately, a new museum exhibit on Comanche himself was added in honor of the centennial. Two new showcases adjoining Comanche's case were finished just in time for June 25. One contained a series of photographs showing the taxidermic process performed by L. L. Dyche on Comanche after the horse's death. The other depicted the life of Comanche as a Seventh Cavalry mount and featured Swearingen's drawing of the horse used in Dary's booklet. A further innovation was the display of a reproduction of the original note concerning the horse's death written by Samuel J. Winchester (see fig. 17), the Fort Riley farrier who cared for Comanche during his final hours. Accompanying this document in the case was a copy of a tinted photograph of Winchester with Comanche and a copy of the farrier's discharge paper.

In 1975, probably in August, these three items had been donated to the Museum of Natural History by the daughters of Samuel Winchester. Dr. Humphrey related the story of the way in which these gifts came about. One day he had received a phone call from a woman in New York who said that she had just learned Comanche was on display at the University of Kansas museum. This, she said, was of particular interest to her because she had an old trunk containing some of her father's effects, including a tinted photograph of her father standing next to the famous horse. Upon asking if the museum would be interested in having the photo, Humphrey expressed delight at the prospect, saying that if acquired, it would likely be placed on display near Comanche. Sometime later, two of Mr. Winchester's daughters came and presented the photo and the two documents to the museum. Humphrey described the affair as becoming "quite tearful at that point, partly I suppose because of the emotions connected with parting with a family treasure and partly because it was so appropriate to have the photograph and letter cared for and on display in close proximity to the horse Mr. Winchester had cared for so lovingly. It was all very touching." No wonder the museum director was affected by this unusual occurrence! For nothing could have been a more fitting centennial tribute than this original document penned so many years ago by a stricken caretaker who somehow had the prescience to feel the unique implications of a cavalry horse's death and to make a record of it which would now be preserved for all time.

As one newspaper reporter who described the new Comanche exhibits pointed out, "The Battle of the Little Big Horn is considered one of history's most famous battles. When news of the Custer battle reached the East, it cast a pall over the nation's centennial celebration in Philadelphia" (New Exhibit, Book 1976). At that time, the nation reacted with both grief for the dead cavalrymen and vengeance toward the Indians. Comanche, through the years, both in life and as a museum piece, had symbolized, for many, those two emotions. Now, in 1976, another centennial had come, and with it, many changes. As the university newspaper, quoting the new plaque on the display, duly reported on June 22, "The horse remains as a reminder of the outcome of the Indians' attempt to keep their land and way of life and the tragedy of the U.S. government's Indian policy" (New Exhibit to Encase 1976).

In 1975, when writing to a curator at the University Museum of Art in connection with his advice on the care and preservation of the valuable photo of Winchester and Comanche, Humphrey informed his colleague, "We plan to have some kind of exhibits here in relation to the centennial [of the Battle of the Little Big Horn] and I would hope that our exhibits, whatever they may be, could provide a perspective that would be useful and enlightening for Indians and non-Indians alike. In this connection," he wondered "if there might not be some possibility of collaboration among the Museum of Art, the Museum of Natural History, and the Museum of Anthropology." Humphrey expressed interest in putting together an exhibit of "various paintings and renditions of the Battle of the Little Big Horn," and of paintings, drawings, and photographs "depicting some of the Indian and non-Indian peoples of the Great Plains during the 1870s" (UK Archives).

Not all of the museum director's plans were put into effect, but some of the ideas he expressed persisted and ultimately were used in the displays. For example, portraits of certain Indians who had fought at the Little Big Horn, as depicted by Barron Brown, author of the 1935 book on Comanche, were put on exhibit. And for a time following the Committee on Indian Affairs protest, anthropology personnel from the university cooperated with the Natural History Museum on renovating the native American displays. In 1985, however, many of the Indian items were moved from the Dyche Museum to the Anthropology Museum. Exhibits formerly in proximity to Comanche, such as the Ghost Dance materials, including Sitting Bull's son's shirt, and the Reservation Life displays, were among those relocated. Also claimed by the Anthropology Museum at this time were the exhibits pertaining to the work and career of L. L. Dyche. The Natural History Museum exhibits director expressed regret over this and other changes. Most of the authentic designs, he pointed out, which had been prepared so carefully to be appropriate to the particular exhibits below them, were now unrelated to anything. For example, there had been an Eskimo design painted over the materials from Dyche's Greenland Expedition. The exhibits director feels "it's sad in some ways now, because except for the Comanche display, the correlation between designs and exhibits is all messed up."

In place of the Ghost Dance and Reservation Life displays, there is now an exhibit on the Battle of the Little Big Horn, explaining what took place as well as the events leading up to the tragedy. These exhibits, along with the pictures of some of the Indian participants, are positioned on both sides of Comanche. "These changes," the exhibits director says, "are part of changes in museum philosophy regarding the fifth floor. When the Museum Director and other personnel met, we decided to make room on that floor for traveling exhibits and temporary displays."

The exhibit on Dyche's mounting of Comanche remains, and there are explanations as to how he got his name and the way in which the museum acquired him. Three bronzes by Rogers Aston remain, including the one of Comanche and his rider (see fig. 32).

At present, museum visitors find no label accompanying the Comanche display. The text which was placed there in 1971 was removed after a period which Exhibits Director Swearingen estimates as about five years. "It was taken off somewhere between 1976 and 1978," he remembers. "At that time, it was determined that nobody would read it. The label had pleased the Indians, but it was so long and hard to read that we had no idea how many people would take time to go through it all." The associate director for membership and public relations agrees, "It was taken out because it was too long and no one read it," but dates its removal to the early 1980s. In a January 1987 conversation, the associate director indicated that a shorter version may be placed on the exhibit sometime in the future.

Another sign which once was displayed with Comanche is also absent now. This was in the form of a black "mourning drape," or wide ribbon placed over the horse's saddle, from each end of which was suspended a sign imprinted with a brief history of the mount and a copy of the famous "Orders" by General Sturgis concerning the horse. These citation tablets, as the donor called them, were made by a man from Massachusetts who sent them as a Christmas gift to the "wonder war horse" in 1968. This devoted admirer of Comanche believed that with such a "great history" the horse "should be decorated as much as possible" (UK Archives). Swearingen remembers that this item "was on the horse for several years before the 1971 uprising and was removed around that time."

In May of 1980, Comanche was the object of special interest for a group of cavalry riders representing a re-creation of a Civil War volunteer regiment, the Seventh Illinois Cavalry. Fitted with authentic uniforms and weapons from the Civil War period, the modern-day cavalrymen, whose headquarters was near Springfield, Illinois, "came to Kansas to get a look at the first cavalry fort in the U. S., Fort Leavenworth." From there they rode to Fort Riley by way of Lawrence, visiting several sites of Civil War interest and making a stop at the Dyche Museum to see Comanche. After "reining in" at the museum, much to the surprise and disbelief of passersby, they secured their horses outside and went to visit the famous cavalry horse display. After giving him "a quick inspection," they "talked about how he looked old but contented and noted that he had died with his winter coat on. They peered into the glass case, trying to find the telltale white hairs that show the 12 scars of wounds the brave horse suffered in battle. They admired his saddle and remarked that he was a gelding." Their visit, according to one reporter "had none of the intense emotion that old cavalrymen felt when Comanche died, at the age of 29, in 1891 at Fort Riley." But as the Illinois horse soldiers paid their respects to Comanche, the gap in time seemed to be momentarily bridged as one rider explained, "He's a great horse in the eyes of a cavalryman" (Haws 1980; Doll 1980; Cavalry Rides 1980).

Chapter 12

Sources, Stories, and Legends

The facts concerning Comanche are in themselves the very essence of romance. (Burton Publishing Company 1935)

A large share of the material published about Comanche's history has been drawn from Edward S. Luce's book, *Keogh, Comanche, and Custer* (1939), a source heavily relied upon by subsequent researchers of the subject. Luce had access to the "'Regimental History Seventh Cavalry,' [then] on file in Seventh Cavalry Headquarters, Fort Bliss, Texas," an advantage possessed, it appears, by no other Comanche scholar. Although the book has been much criticized for romanticism, liberties taken in interpretation, and questionable documentation, most of the details about Comanche might have been lost to history without the author's contributions.

It is evident that the former cavalryman also made efforts to obtain information about Comanche's rider from people who had direct knowledge about him. For example, when compiling his biographical material, he was in contact with Captain Keogh's friends, the Martin family of Willowbrook, near Auburn, New York. For Luce revealed to Nye that "the young lady to whom he [Keogh] was engaged, was a very strict and religious woman. If they had of been married, then General Emory Upton and General A. J. Alexander would have been Keogh's brothers-in-law." Cautioning his correspondent, "please do not let this go any further," Luce confided that Mr. E. S. Martin had told him "that he did not wish his sister to be named in the book, and I submitted my manuscript to him just a few weeks before he passed away, and he wrote me that I had 'put it very nicely.'" Luce closes his letter to the cavalry officer by "thanking you again for your very kind and complimentary remarks as to my book" (CBNM Files). In a previous letter Luce had evidenced his sensitivity to veterinarian Nye's opinion of his newly published work when he wrote: "Please be kind to me when you read the first chapter in my book when I try and describe how horses first came to America. I had hoped to 'get by' on that chapter, but now I am quaking in my boots until I hear from you" (CBNM Files).

Some of the biographical information in the book is erroneous. For example, Luce was mistaken about Lieutenant Henry J. Nowlan having been a "former comrade in arms in the Pontifical Zouaves and in the Civil War with Captain Keogh" (1939:64). Evidence indicates, in fact, that the two met for the first time on the American frontier as officers in the Seventh Cavalry. In a letter to his brother, Tom, written in 1867 from Fort Wallace, Kansas, Keogh mentioned his developing relationship with Nowlan, with whom he had become "fast friends" (NLI). The provenance of the idea about a former association between the two men is unknown because sources for Luce's statements in his book are not consistently provided. Some of his data on Comanche, of course, had to be inferred. Nothing about the horse's life during the period previous to his acquisition by the army was ever documented. Knowledge about where the animal spent his early years and the nature of his breeding must only be conjecture. It is difficult to assess whether Luce drew from his own experience in writing that "a three-quarters American and one-quarter Spanish horse possessed remarkable endurance and stamina" for cavalry service (1939:6), or whether he took this information directly from Captain Boniface's book, *The Cavalry Horse and His Pack*, in which the exact same statement appears (1903:54). In either case it could not have been accurately determined that "such was the breed of Comanche" (Luce 1939:6). It is predictable that Luce would be criticized for anthropomorphizing Comanche, especially in descriptions of the horse during the interval between Keogh's death and his rescue (1939:64). Magnussen, for example, has called "completely inane" Luce's idea of Comanche's assuming "leadership" (1974:275–76). But metaphor and so-called "fact" have a way of becoming entwined. More will be said on this issue presently.

Antedating Luce's book are two articles on Comanche which have already been mentioned. Godfrey's expanded account of *Custer's Last Battle,* dated 1908 and published by the Century Company for the forty-fifth anniversary of the battle, concluded with a straightforward narrative about the horse which had been absent from the first version (1921:37–38). As a participant in the

Battle of the Little Big Horn, Godfrey's words are naturally regarded as authoritative. Though it is safe to say that at the time of the battle he would have been unlikely to have attributed any importance to Keogh's mount, by the time of his writing of the revised version he was certainly conscious of the eminence the horse had acquired. Still, only Godfrey's final sentence about Comanche, "He still lives!" betrays any of the emotion and meaning that have engulfed the surviving animal from the first moment of his discovery.

Herbert E. Smith, as though taking up the cry from Godfrey, authored an article with the title of "Comanche Still Lives," published in 1927 in Charles Francis Roe's *Custer's Last Battle*. Unfortunately, his sources are not cited. Comanche is described as "a tall, handsome claybank gelding," and a slightly different version of his naming is given. Biographical data about the horse, including his life after the issuance of General Orders No. 7 and the acquisition and mounting of his remains by the Dyche Museum, are straightforward. But the events surrounding Comanche's discovery are too heavily charged with meaning to avoid empathetic description of the horse. Depicted as "a lone horse behaving in an unusual manner," the animal was observed by Nowlan to be "returning again and again to the field." And in five paragraphs which were published again almost verbatim in E. S. Luce's book thirteen years later (1939:64–65), Smith wrote that the horse

seemed to be seeking someone, and neighed softly, as though to call some beloved master; its bewildered eyes appeared to seek familiar faces and summon back affectionate human friends. That horse was "Comanche," sole survivor of a dark page in American military history.

What harrowing experiences befell the faithful animal! What scenes Comanche must have witnessed! What deeds of valor must have been performed that afternoon on the Little Big Horn which must forever be unknown and unwritten history! "Comanche," the only living witness, could only express by dumb actions the frightfulness of the savages' attack, and the grim stand of the troopers against what they must have foreseen as ultimate annihilation.

It is evident that in the last stages of the battle the troopers' mounts were pressed into service by the embattled soldiers as breastworks. From behind the bodies of their faithful dead and dying animals, the men had fought to the last ditch. Perhaps "Comanche," too, had interposed his heaving body between his master and the quivering arrows and leaden bullets of the Sioux.

The noble animal was dripping with blood; many crimson blotches stained his once sleek coat, and he could hardly walk. The burial party of soldiers could only guess at what "Comanche" had endured with the human heroes of the column.

He was so weak and emaciated that it was at first thought wise and humane to put him out of his misery at once. Seven bullets had pierced the animal, but yet the poor creature clung tenaciously to life.

It is not surprising, then, in the light of his personalized status that, according to Smith, once he was made comfortable on the steamer *Far West* for the journey to Fort Lincoln, and "his wounds were tended to," the horse was "nursed along, and given as much attention by the veterinaries and hospital corpsmen aboard as any of the wounded soldiers" (1927:36).

In addition to Luce's work, one nonfiction book written four years earlier also provided material which ultimately served as a source for much subsequent writing about the celebrated horse. Barron Brown's *Comanche* was published in 1935 but for many years did not become as well-known as the work by Luce. Perhaps this was because of the prominence of the latter in the field of Custer scholarship and the fact that the highly regarded bibliography of the Battle of the Little Big Horn by Fred Dustin (1939:239–51; Graham 1953: 380–405) does not include Brown's book. The more recent Custer bibliographer, Tal Luther, recorded its existence as a "high spot" but did not describe it or label it "an extremely useful work," as he termed Luce's (1972:51, 64, 80, 83). Of course, Luce included other material besides that on Comanche, and it was the appendices that "add valuable knowledge" about the regiment for which the book is especially noted by Luther. It is interesting that Luce read Brown's *Comanche,* and evidently viewed it as a rival to the book he was planning to write. In a 1938 letter, Luce indicated, "I am now prepared to start my manuscript on 'Keogh and Comanche' which I hope will be printed or rather published next year." Quite petulantly, he stated, "In checking the records against Barron Brown's book 'Comanche'—I am very sorry to say that his book is only about 25% correct." In the same correspondence, Luce told the curator of the Dyche Museum "you are at liberty to refer anyone to me for historical data on Comanche" (UK Archives).

Brown's book, unlike Luce's, is strictly a monograph on the horse. Although the author's lack of documentation for some of his material is frustrating to the scholar, there is much information contained in the work that is probably as solid as the historiography of Comanche can ever be. Of particular value are the testimonies obtained from Indian battle participants and the reprinted letters from General Scott, General Godfrey, and others with first-hand knowledge of the horse. Today, not only the scarcity of the original edition of *Comanche* but also its uniquely attractive format make the volume a book-collector's treasure. The author's drawings depicting the famous cavalry-versus-Indian clash appear on each page as a background to the text.

Brown, in a 1933 letter to Colonel O. W. Bell of the Seventh Cavalry, described himself as "primarily a portrait artist." He explained that

> while painting some of the old Custer battle survivors among the Sioux last summer I learned a good deal about the horse and at first was interested in him merely as a pictorial subject. I had planned to have an exhibit of portraits of the old surviving hostiles at Chicago this year and it occurred to me that a painting of Comanche would be interesting and worthwhile, as he was found after the battle sorely wounded, the only living thing left on that memorable field. In order to have such a picture authentic I began some research work which whetted my interest to a point where it seemed advisable to write and illustrate a small volume about the horse which would be complete and authentic. Comanche was exhibited at the World's Fair at Chicago forty years ago and I have read many newspaper clippings about the animal and have talked with and received letters from men still living who knew him both before and after the battle, including Generals Scott, Garlington, and others.

Brown's request to the colonel that his project, which he felt would be "a notable and enduring achievement," be endorsed by collaboration with the famous regiment and "the advance of a small amount of money" was "disapproved" according to a notation made on the letter by the recipient (UK Archives).

The claim of the publisher on the dust jacket that "the biography has not been fictionized" is quite accurate. Brown realistically accepted the idea that everything about the horse's life could not be known without surmises to fill the gaps. He presents the idea of "a few old-timers who claim to know" that Comanche was captured from Indians but adds that the "preponderance of evidence" does not uphold this view. "Although stories differ," he points out, "the acquisition of Comanche by the government is open to little doubt when all the evidence, added to conjecture, is taken into consideration" (1935:36). *Comanche* is a remarkable work in that the details presented about the horse's life become dramatic largely without embellishment, proving the wisdom of the publisher's statement that "the facts concerning Comanche are in themselves the very essence of romance" (dust jacket).

Like virtually everyone of his time, Brown accepted the famous mount's "only survivor" status. When a new edition of *Comanche* was issued in 1973, the foreword stated, "In many ways

Barron Brown's book is far better than either the Luce or Amaral book." What makes the work preferable, the writer claims, is that it is "completely devoid of the 'only survivor' syndrome so frequently present in other treatments of the horse" (Brown 1973:i–ii). But this statement is erroneous, for the dust jacket cover caption under Brown's drawing of Comanche reads "The Only Survivor of the Custer 'Massacre,'" and on the title page Comanche is designated "The Sole Survivor of All the Forces in Custer's Last Stand, the Battle of the Little Big Horn." The text states that "the fame of Comanche rests largely on the fact that he was the sole survivor of Custer's force," and the subtitle to the chapter entitled "Comanche at the Battle of the Little Big Horn" is "Sole Survivor of Custer's Command" (1935:22, 45).

In writing his 1961 biography of the horse, Anthony Amaral took deliberate pains to eliminate the "only survivor" designation for Comanche, subtitling his work "The Horse That Survived the Custer Massacre." (It is noteworthy that although Brown, twenty-six years earlier, had deplored the term "massacre" for the Little Big Horn, using it only in quotations and explaining that, in truth, the event was a battle and not a massacre [1935:17], Amaral retained this pejorative word.) In his text, with the objectivity that is explicitly intended to debunk legend, Amaral discloses evidence reported by those "whose works are not overly emotionally tinged" that other Seventh Cavalry horses lived through the battle (1961:30–32). He concludes that "Comanche's nearest approach to the distinction of a lone survivor is that he was the only living thing to leave the battlefield with the cavalry units which came to bury Custer and his men" (1961:32). Yet, almost incredibly, on the dust jacket flap, a description of his book still refers to "the fact that a lone horse was the only thing that survived" the Custer Battle! Thus, despite the best efforts of those who strive for strict accuracy, the lone survivor status continues to be vital to Comanche's legend.

Ostensibly, Amaral's volume represents an effort to update the work of Luce (to whom it is dedicated), not only by the use of some different sources such as *Winners of the West*, but more importantly through what the author perceives as the objective screening out of emotion and romanticism, an approach deemed worthy of the modern era. Amaral's account of the numerous persons who claimed to have found the wounded Comanche is an interesting example of the process of trying to make sense out of conflicting bits of evidence. In the last analysis, however, the treatment of this episode only demonstrates anew the necessity of ultimately having to rely not upon proof of one statement as absolute historical "truth," but of making "plausible suppositions" as to which statement is "more true to life considering the circumstances" (1961:32–41).

The study of Comanche by Dary, already mentioned in connection with the Battle of the Little Big Horn centennial, was preceded by the work of another Kansas University faculty member, biologist Robert K. Mengel. His booklet, *Comanche: Silent Horse on a Silent Field*, attractively illustrated by artist Thomas H. Swearingen, was published in the Museum of Natural History Annual for 1968 and was issued as a separate reprint the following year. Written with empathy and in language that evokes vivid images of the battle, Mengel's treatment of the "unbeautiful but leather-tough Claybank bay" is at the same time faithful to the facts available from the most reliable sources. His outline of the main events in Comanche's life rests on Brown's work, which he calls "on the whole a responsible book" (1969:3–11).

Mengel includes a brief and clear account of the Little Big Horn engagement and appropriately places Comanche in the context of that event. Stimulated by his own first-hand knowledge that the horse is the most popular of all Dyche Museum exhibits and using information gained through his visits to the Montana battlefield, Mengel was able to present an enlightening discussion of "Comanche's strange attraction and the persistent allure of the Custer battle." Two misconceptions commonly held by museum visitors—that the horse was the "only survivor" and that he had been owned by Custer—are definitively ruled out as false. The matter of "battle" versus "massacre" is made clear once and for all: the Little Big Horn was a battle, and the Washita was a massacre. With insight, Mengel was able to see Comanche as part of the Custer battle and to understand that famous battle in the light of its broad significance—as another tragic instance of the "obstinate incapacity of mankind to understand mankind" (1969:3–11).

Turning now to sources dealing with the Comanche story which are classified as fiction, it becomes evident that the legend, growing from the bare outline of what was previously known and written about the horse, developed steadily into a complex body of material which was to influence historiography of the horse even as it was influenced by it. Through the various writings about Comanche, much is revealed about perceptions of the Indian-white clash that culminated in the Battle of the Little Big Horn, the meaning of the American frontier, and the human relationship with horses. A great deal is learned, too, about the ability of a powerful symbol like Comanche, with its varying meanings for different people at different times, to influence thought and action.

The authors of creative works about Comanche based much of their plots upon historical facts that had been recorded or suggested in the nonfiction sources and embellished them with greater or lesser amounts of imaginative additions. One of these, David Appel's novel for young readers, *Comanche: The Story of America's Most Heroic Horse*, published in 1951, drew together the important existing themes of the Comanche saga and contributed some dramatic new dimensions.

Appel's book has special significance in the development of Comanche's legend. Its author contributed many elements which were permanently incorporated into the horse's mystique, and Walt Disney's movie version of the story, *Tonka*, reached a wide audience of all ages. Like Margaret Leighton's work, *Comanche of the Seventh* (to be discussed), Appel's is a juvenile novel. Yet both of these books have been used extensively as sources by later authors purportedly writing adult nonfiction and are frequently cited in Battle of the Little Big Horn bibliographies. Adults—including business and professional people—often indicate their reliance on these works for their knowledge of Comanche. One New York insurance company president wrote to the Dyche Museum, "I have just finished reading, with keen interest and deep emotion, Margaret Leighton's book, 'Comanche of the Seventh.'" Included in the letter was a request for a picture of the horse to be given as a gift to a friend who read the book with her and was also "deeply affected by the story." The remarkable influence of Appel's work, too, is demonstrated by the fact that during the 1960s it was that novelist's version of Comanche's Indian origin that museum personnel often related to correspondents (UK Archives). Because these books intended for young readers have in effect transcended their intended genre to find wide acceptance as general works in their field consulted by adults, they cannot be dismissed as worthy of only slight attention. On the contrary, they merit full consideration as vitally significant creators of Comanche's legend.

This phenomenon of adult usage, of course, does not diminish the novels' popularity among juvenile readers. Comanche, like other animal heroes, has special appeal for youngsters. For many reasons, animals occupy an extremely important role in children's literature. They are perceived as easier to relate to than people, more openly affectionate and less judgmental, and as approachable intermediaries they help youngsters to bridge the gap between their own world and that of adults. Animals and children tend to be classed in the same social group, outside the bounds of the more formidable adult sphere. A faithful horse serves not only as a friend but also as a model for ideal behavior.

In Appel's novel, as will become evident, through Keogh's mount not only is the Custer Battle explored but also wider issues such as individualism, social responsibility, loyalty, egalitarianism, and racism, as well as the conquest of nature, and the progress of "civilization" on the American continent. As an actual participant in the historic battle, who experienced its horrors and lived through it, Comanche has more credence than most animal protagonists. Most importantly, in Appel's depiction of the equine hero for young readers, the language barrier—the much lamented restriction caused by Comanche's silence—does not exist. Thus, the horse can freely and explicitly express to the reader his ideas regarding the battle, Custer and other officers, horse-human interactions, and Indian-white relationships. For Appel, Indians are closely linked to that world which only children and animals inhabit and understand—a sphere foreign to "civilized people" including adults.

Related by Comanche himself in the first person (in the tradition of Black Beauty), the novel is unabashedly sentimental. Appel portrays the horse as sagacious, a phenomenon which is not unusual for those who deal with horses, either living or symbolic. The fact that he wrote for juveniles gave the author license to emphasize the wise and all-knowing character of his equine hero, but it is by no means uncommon to find horses endowed with these qualities throughout much of standard literature. Although Comanche, with what Mengel aptly terms his "maddening muteness" (1969:8)—a limitation that all who knew him deplored—cannot answer his human associates, he *can* think. "It was agony not to be able to reply," Comanche reveals. "I inherited from my wise dam the ability to understand the language of every living thing. I can even understand the voice of the wind when it breathes snow or rain from far off." Keogh learns at the time of the great Dakota blizzard that his mount knew the bad weather was coming. On campaigns, Comanche understood the natural conditions and terrain of the plains better than the soldiers. When Custer insulted the Sioux chiefs he met with, thinking that "they could not understand him because he spoke in English," Comanche was frightened for the General, for "he should have known that uncivilized people, like horses and dogs, can sense what people are saying without having to understand each separate word" (1951:47, 103, 168, 174–75).

The intuitive powers shared by animals and "uncivilized" people, but denied to whites, are not only innate in Comanche's species, but in his particular case they are reinforced by experience as well. For in Appel's version of the story, Comanche learned a great deal about Indians because he had first belonged to them. It was White Bull, a Sioux boy, who caught him as a young wild stallion after he had left his sire's herd and who subsequently tamed and broke him for riding. Though this boy was a kind master who deeply loved his horse, Comanche soon was forcefully taken from him to become the mount of the higher ranking Yellow Bull, a warrior who mistreated him for the ensuing two years before the horse finally escaped from the Sioux camp. During this period of his life, Comanche witnessed the violence of the Sun Dance ceremony, as well as the "horrors" of scalping, counting coup on the body of a dead enemy, and horse-stealing.

At first, Comanche views the Indians as "savages." The morality and common sense of his own kind, he reflects in a spirit reminiscent of Swift's depiction of the Houyhnhnms in *Gulliver's Travels,* are far superior in many ways to these savage people's. But eventually the nobler side of the Indians' life also becomes evident. The dog who befriends Comanche at the beginning of his Indian captivity tells him, "These people are wise and brave and fierce" (1951:69). Comanche finds that, though Custer underestimates them, "they are superb cavalrymen," and that the tribesmen give very good care to their horses and never eat them. He came to understand the close relationship between people and horses, because "the Indian was as helpless without a mount as an eagle without wings." He learned from Keogh, who "through studying" knew that "before the Whites cheated them out of their land and food sources, the so-called savages were hospitable and generous." He hears reports about Custer and his "incredibly savage" white warriors who had been known to "brutally slaughter a whole village of defenseless squaws and papooses." He is referring to the Washita, an engagement in which the historic Comanche did not participate. Appel's Comanche did take part, and called it a "ruthless massacre," not a battle, a point on which "my Captain agreed." While Keogh and Benteen criticized Custer for his alleged abandonment of Major Elliott at the Washita (a matter which has been debated ever since), Comanche himself "never forgave Custer for the ruthless slaughter of those eight hundred fear-stampeded Indian ponies," and would always remember the "terrified screams of those spirited mounts" and the "wails of the squaws and boys" as they watched the soldiers kill their horses and dogs—an event which actually did take place (1951:36, 40, 45, 53–54, 57, 70, 98, 104, 155–56, 161, 163, 175).

Keogh and Comanche share insights about some of the factors that ultimately determined the outcome of the Battle of the

Little Big Horn, including strategy that emanated from certain characteristics of the major participants. Years before the Little Big Horn, Keogh discusses Custer's behavior with Comanche, deploring the official "favoritism" which had allowed the general to be reinstated sooner than the penalty resulting from his court-martial had determined. Realizing that a regimental commander with Custer's Indian-fighting experience was needed, Keogh nevertheless admits, "I detest officers who put their personal desire for prestige above their regard for the safety of their men." His words were prophetic, for on the fateful day of the final battle, Custer disregards all warnings and refuses to wait for Terry to make his attack. Though, after "three days of forced marches under the broiling sun" the general was told, "the men and horses need a rest," Custer sought "glory" for himself. His prestige was at stake; thus, for him, it was "victory at all cost." Indian warriors, Comanche reflects, though they are fearless, "exercise a certain amount of caution, the kind that Custer might well have emulated" at the Little Big Horn. Because their scouts constantly reported troop movements, the Sioux "outmaneuvered the Seventh that bloody day." Comanche points to the customary code of behavior determining that "Indians are easily and quickly satisfied with even a small victory," and their feeling that "there'll always be another day," which were responsible for the survival of Reno's and Benteen's commands at the Little Big Horn. Comanche emphasized a point not often stressed in accounts of the battle: after the destruction of Custer and his men, "even then [the Indians] were content with annihilating a few when they could easily have gone on to surround the remaining troops and destroy them all" (1951:75, 76, 147, 204).

The controversies of the famous battle are addressed through Comanche's eyes. Although Custer is admired as "all soldier" and is hero-worshipped by men such as Bob (the young recruit who once recaptured Comanche when he was free on the plains), through the horse's discussion of Keogh's assertion of responsibility for his men and horses, Custer's rashness is made clear by comparison. On one campaign, Comanche implies Custer's lack of regard for the welfare of his troops when he says "I did not mind traveling for hours without forage or water, but many of the other horses did." Riding into the last battle, when both Keogh and his horse knew they were doomed, Comanche remembered the lines from "The Charge of the Light Brigade," and knew that this time, too, "someone had blundered"—Custer. Foreshadowing the years to come when alleged cowardice and incompetence on the part of Captain Benteen, and particularly

Major Reno, would be blamed by Custer supporters for their hero's death, Comanche makes it known that when men of the Seventh felt divided loyalty for either Custer or Benteen, his beloved Keogh was a "Benteen man." When on the fateful day, Custer divided his command, sending Reno's force out alone to attack the Indian village and telling him "you will be supported by the whole outfit," Comanche heard the Major say, "Let us keep together," and felt sorry for Reno when Custer ignored his plea. As for Reno's retreat, which later evoked so much criticism, Comanche explained that "This horde of whooping, shooting Redskins —Sioux and Cheyennes—was between Reno's column and the huge Indian village, and it was a bloodthirsty horde. Reno's men did not have a chance." A wounded trooper "reported that the panicky retreat was a complete rout." Comanche later learned that Reno and Benteen "heard Custer's call for help, and even though they had their hands full defending themselves, they tried to send relief but the Redskins stopped them" (1951:104, 143, 151, 166, 201, 208, 209, 211, 217).

When, as a Sioux captive, Comanche had first encountered the smell of the Indian camp, it had been so revolting that he all but fainted. But his Indian past stood him in good stead as a cavalry mount; he never showed fright as did the other cavalry horses, particularly the Kentucky Thoroughbreds and the mules who had never been near Indians before. When his mount had received his first arrow wound in a skirmish with Comanches, Keogh had marveled at the horse's "stoical indifference to pain." As Comanche explains this trait, his master "had no way of knowing, of course, that the Comanche arrow wound was nothing compared to the bite of Yellow Bull's vicious lash" (1951:61, 84, 173–74). Indeed everything in Comanche's Indian experience seemed to fit him for what lay before him as a survivor—a horse of destiny.

White Bull's love for Comanche caused him to give the horse his own medicine bundle as a good-luck charm to protect his mount from danger. Comanche was convinced of the power of this talisman and noted that Keogh, "my Captain," never made fun of the Indians' beliefs because "he was a full-blooded Irishman and superstitious as the Indians." This power, according to Comanche, "intangible and incomprehensible to white men like Custer, but very real to Indians" explains "the fact that I am the sole survivor of the bloody battle of Little Big Horn." After his escape from the Indian camp, Comanche was protected by its mysterious power. Additionally, White Bull had made the terrible sacrifice of the Sun Dance so that Wakan Tanka would answer his prayers that no harm should ever come to his beloved horse. The young Sioux told Comanche that during his painful ordeal, "I shall pray that the wild beasts shun you and that although enemy bullets may pierce your flesh, you shall not die of the wounds." During the final battle, White Bull saw Comanche with the enemy and gave his former mount a benediction. "Go in safety," he said. "Not even the bullets of your new masters shall harm you." When Keogh and Comanche set out for the Little Big Horn campaign, the Captain wore a special gauntlet and brought along the arrowhead that had been removed from Comanche's flank after his first wounding. These, Keogh said, were "two medicine bundles" carried not to protect himself but to remind him not to commit any error which would endanger the young and uninitiated men and horses in his charge (1951:79, 80, 90, 182, 201).

The bond between horse and man is explored when Comanche explains why it was that following the battle "while the saddle and bridle were taken from the body of every other horse on the battlefield, mine were not touched." He liked to think that one of the squaws who came from the camp and saw him was White Bull's mother, who "felt the loving touch her beloved son had given me. . . . Because I lay close to him, she knew that Myles Keogh was my master. And because she knew that he must be a great warrior, she left me saddled and bridled for his long journey to the Sun" (1951:80).

Appel was able to consider both sides—Indian and white—with a considered attempt at fairness not often encountered in Comanche literature—not to mention Little Big Horn coverage in general. Ambivalence toward Indians was expressed in the novel by means of the very bad Sioux, Yellow Bull, with his sadistic nature, being set against the character of White Bull, the kindly young brave. Near the end of the Custer Battle, Yellow Bull, after shooting Comanche twice, is killed by Comanche himself. Initially motivated by the idea of preventing the fiendish warrior from counting coup on his dead master, Comanche, "with the might born of grief and hate," reared up and smashed his forefeet down on his enemy. White Bull "was one of that shrieking circle of hostiles who slaughtered Custer and his men." He survived the battle only to be sent to the reservation. "No matter how many men he may have killed and scalped, he has been amply punished by the long, living death that reservation life must mean to him," Comanche said. "There are worse things than death. I am sorry with all my heart now that White Bull did not die as he always planned to die—on the battlefield. I am even more sorry that Yellow Bull did." For "if I, like the Indians, had not been motivated by revenge and hate, Yellow Bull might well be suffering the same torture right now" (1951:88–89, 216, 217).

The dilemma of which side is preferable is ultimately decided by Comanche himself. Shortly after obtaining the horse, Keogh senses that he once belonged to Indians and allows Comanche the chance to go back to his former owners. "I know that your first master was an Indian," he told him. "And I would not blame you at all if you decide that your loyalty belongs to them. They are a great race and we have wronged them terribly. But since they wreak their vengeance on the innocent as well as on the guilty, I have taken sides against them. . . . It's all right, Clay," he said (for his name was not yet Comanche), "if you decide to cast your lot with the hostiles. Even their worst atrocities have been equalled by white men since the beginning of time. But, you see, I'm white, and I cannot sit back and let them run wild and murder." True to the code of chivalry, Keogh tells the horse, "Go and join them if that is your wish. And if we meet in battle tomorrow, let the better men win." "Without a moment's hesitation," Comanche chose Keogh, whom he now looked upon as "my own personal god," without whom even a life of freedom would mean nothing. When some white girls were rescued from Indian captivity by the troopers following the next day's skirmish with Comanches, the first thought of the youngest was not for herself. She immediately exclaimed "Oh, Lieutenant, look! Your horse has been wounded badly. See how the blood streams from his side. I'm all right. Take care of him" (1951:130–31, 139). This episode diverts attention from the "savages" and emphasizes the fact that the horse has chosen wisely and will always get prime attention from whites. Comanche, like the human former captives, was now where he belonged.

Near the end of the fateful battle at Little Big Horn, Comanche's decision is reinforced by his sight of the enemy: "Drunk with the victory of Reno's bloody repulse, the Indians swept up the valley, through the ravines and gullies—a bloodthirsty horde of Cheyennes and Sioux, shrieking war whoops and firing a steady stream of lead and arrows." The Indians were, Comanche observed, "completely out of control" and seemed "like a black, rain-swollen river," that "overflows its banks, sweeping everything before it." The warriors reminded him of the stampeding buffaloes which, many years ago when he was a three-year-old, had sent him fleeing in panic "right into the noose of the young brave, White Bull." Now, however, upon glimpsing the "ugly painted face under a flamboyant war bonnet" of his worst enemy, Yellow Bull, he felt no wish to flee but only the desire for revenge.

For men and horses alike, there was no escape "through that circle of wild, whooping savages" who "whipped their war-painted ponies forward in a mad fury." After Keogh's death, when Custer is observed making his last desperate stand "under the vengeful fury of the rampaging Sioux," Comanche loses his former animosity toward him and feels "only pity for our young commander" (1951:11, 214–15, 217).

Comanche's allegiance to the cavalry, of course, had been inevitable, once he learned compliance and was converted from a wild and defiant mustang of the plains to a tame and obedient horse. Through the process of his own conquest, he then metaphorically belonged to the "civilized" world rather than to the "wild" realm of the Indians. Early in life his mother warned him that if he were captured by Sioux and Cheyennes "you will wish you were dead." As a young horse, he rebelled against his father's tyranny by loitering behind the herd, and even then had already identified himself with the cavalry by comparing his punishment of being kicked by his sire with that of the straggling trooper's punishment—"a slow, agonizing death at the hands of Indians" (1951:16–17). The message is clear that eventually, though the brave and fearless wild Indians had their day of glory, they, too, must ultimately be conquered and subdued. Comanche, as a horse who was once free, wild, and defiant, is a more convincing symbol of the white man's conquest than would be a horse who was subservient from the beginning (see Lawrence 1985:62–63).

The fact of his having chosen the side which lost the great battle between Indians and whites fitted Comanche aptly for his preeminent role, that of lone survivor. As Appel's prologue relates, Custer had "led his valiant troopers of the Seventh U. S. Cavalry to crushing defeat—and to everlasting glory—in the valley of the Little Big Horn." But though all the men of Custer's column died, "a single creature did survive." Comanche, "one ugly, tough, plains-hardened cavalry mount came out of the holocaust alive" (1951:11).

The horse's hardiness, a major element of the Comanche legend, is a dominant theme throughout the book. Comanche possesses a "broad and capable back," and "though not a handsome animal, he was built for endurance and for rugged campaigning." As his mother told him, he "had the three qualities you must have to survive on the Great Plains: stamina, courage and good legs." These were also, Comanche learned from Keogh, "the prime requisites of a U. S. cavalry horse, especially in the Seventh." Comanche was "the 'ugly duckling' of the herd," and knew he was never handsome either as a colt or a full-grown horse. "My head and neck were too thick for the rest of my body. My legs were short and uneven." It is significant that Keogh, "when most affectionate," called his mount "you ugly brute." "Sleek looks had no place in a western regiment campaigning for weeks or months over rough terrain where water and grass were scarce." It was more important that he was "tough as nails" and that he was smart and learned readily (1951:11, 12, 13, 14, 106, 112, 144, 164).

Comanche endured through all adversities: the brutality of his sire; isolation from his own kind; dangers from coyotes, cougars, grizzlies, wolves, rattlesnakes, and prairie-dog holes; cold, snow, heat, and drought; cruel treatment by his Indian master; the harsh conditions of Custer's marches; and the various skirmishes that preceded the great Battle of the Little Big Horn. Throughout the book, Comanche is compared to the pedigreed Thoroughbred horses owned and ridden by Custer. Comanche admitted he was "nowhere near as fast," but he "could gallop without growing tired for many more hours than they could." Custer's "two beautiful, fast mounts," Vic and Dandy, "never spoke to me, and seemed to suffer excruciating agony whenever we were forced to drink from the same trough. I was not even tempted to tell them about my own family tree, which I am sure my mother could have proven was far superior to theirs." Comanche "despised their showoffishness and snobbery" and thought that "they were actually jealous because my master always made a big fuss over me and never showed the slightest interest in any of the Kentucky bluebloods, human or otherwise." Keogh declared, "I wouldn't trade my ugly Comanche for all the blood-horses in Kentucky." Although many of the cavalry mounts "looked poorly" after the 1869 campaign, the captain boasted to the quartermaster about the excellent condition of "my ugly brute." Keogh felt that horses like Vic and Dandy could not withstand exposure to hardships like the great Dakota blizzard as well as Comanche could (1951:132, 164, 165, 167–68, 174 and passim).

Not only, according to Appel, was Comanche a lone survivor, but he was also cast as a "lone wolf." Even as a young colt, he was the butt of cruel jokes and name-calling by the other young horses, who banded together against him. When, following a fight with his father, he left his herd, Comanche realized that nobody loved him and that only his mother, who had now deserted him, ever *had* cared for him (1951:15, 19). Comanche describes the sense of identification he felt with White Bull, who "became the 'lone wolf' of his herd, just as I, the ugly Claybank, became the 'lone wolf' of mine." Keogh, too, is portrayed as a solitary man for whom, Comanche said, "I was his sole confidant." Furthermore, his captain "never took leave, for he had no home in this country to visit." He spent his time off in the bachelor's quarters, "reading and studying about the Indians." Though Keogh was homesick, his mount understood, he did not return to his native Ireland because "the girl he adored died on the eve of their wedding." Thus the captain, "by his very devotion to the memory of his 'colleen,' was set apart from them [the other officers], just as I had always been set apart from other horses" (1951:15, 19, 54, 171).

Thus, through Appel's story, Comanche became an equine paragon, possessing in large measure those qualities in beast or man that were most valued on the American frontier and which are still nostalgically cherished as vital to the founding and development of the nation. Foremost of these are his unusual toughness and hardiness which, as we have seen, are his prime traits. He not only endures all hardships, but he does it patiently and without complaint, as all good frontiersmen must. The horse's legendary stoicism in the face of pain fits him for a demanding life in a harsh land. No task causes him to flinch or taxes him beyond devotion. Comanche also demonstrates integrity, and his behavior follows the chivalric "code of the West" in all matters. Even when he wanted to run away to freedom, his conscience made him ask himself "How could you leave Myles Keogh out here on this lonely plain without a mount?" It was love for Keogh, with its attendant sense of responsibility, not his willingness to be a slave, that made Comanche decide to stay with his captain (1951: 129–30).

His ugliness, as compared to the Thoroughbreds' beauty, makes Comanche represent the higher worth of the utilitarian as compared to the aesthetic, in accord with the frontier value scale. Comanche's strength is ideal for the long haul, whereas the taller and graceful blood horses only have spurts of speed for the short run. As Comanche expressed it, "Vic and Dandy were very dainty about mud" (1951:174). They are considered frivolous, with a propensity to behave badly; valued for looks and breeding, they are high strung, undependable, and lack endurance. The Thoroughbreds thus represent the aesthetic and aristocratic elements, esteemed in the Old World, where rank is important, while Comanche embodies the more pragmatic and egalitarian values of the New World, in which one is judged by the standards of work performed. They obtained their achievements by birth; he achieved his through determination, endurance, and strength. Their blue-blooded ancestors are names on pedigrees; his forefathers are noble horses from an ancient race tracing back to King

Solomon's cavalry, which explains how he, "although a wild mustang when captured, adjusted myself so quickly to life in the Seventh U. S. Cavalry." His father's descendants, when brought by the Spanish to America, were able to "race off to freedom in the wilds of the new land" (1951:14). They became the feral horses, or mustangs—the smart, tough, wily animals that were essential partners in the conquest of a continent—the "winning of the West."

Comanche's individualism, as evidenced by his "lone wolf" image, represents another trait admired on the frontier. Escaping from his father's tyranny, he had the courage to set out on his own to face the world. Yet he could not have survived without the dog who befriended him and ultimately saved his life. Friendship is necessary in a difficult world and self-reliance must be counterbalanced by solidarity. Though he belongs to the highly social equine species, Comanche never finds comradeship with his own kind. He is too much of an individualist. Other horses avoid him. He is fiercely competitive toward them and admits to "a sharp pang of jealousy" upon seeing his former master, White Bull, in battle astride "a fleet, gorgeously decorated pony." Comanche "had no feeling of hate for White Bull," but "his fleet-as-the-wind pony was my only antagonist" (1951:181–82). He turned his natural tendency for affective ties first, tentatively, toward White Bull, then, wholeheartedly, toward his kindly master, Keogh. Ultimately, there is no greater love than that he gave, for he was willing to lay down his life for his captain. Near the final moment of battle, he said "If I could have talked I would have begged him to shoot me and use my body as a shield." Ever faithful to his master's comrades-in-arms, he even tried to get to Custer's hill to "keep a bullet from Tom Custer's heart" (1951:215, 218). Thus the themes of individualism within a framework of cooperation are played out in Comanche's life as they were in the ethic of the frontier.

No creature was better suited to exalt frontier values than the cavalry horse who, in life as in legend, was an instrument and ally in the conquest of the continent. Comanche's is, in a sense, an American success story. Though ugly, abandoned, ridiculed, mistreated, and subjected to danger and hardship by both natural and human forces, he rose above all adversity to surpass those who scorned him and become a true winner. He was a unique survivor, the most famous of horses, respected, honored, and revered by devoted admirers, mascot of a bereaved regiment, pet of a shocked and grief-stricken nation, and an immortal symbol of glory in defeat.

239

It is a mistake to assume that works about Comanche intended for young audiences are not widely read and influential among adults. Fictional books in this category have frequently been consulted, as mentioned, by subsequent writers of standard (nonjuvenile) works about the famous horse and are taken seriously by many adults. This phenomenon is no doubt due, at least in part, to the absence of similar types of books addressed to mature audiences and to the unusual interest the mount has always evoked among legions of horse lovers and countless numbers of people fascinated by anything relating to Custer's Last Stand. The juvenile novels are written with an engaging style that may convince some readers that they are more authentic than the less engrossing nonfiction sources. Certain constraints, of course, apply. In Appel's story for children, Comanche remains a stallion, presumably to avoid the indelicacy of discussing his real status as a gelding—or perhaps because it is just more pleasing.

Appel, who used historical material about Comanche and the Little Big Horn as the basic outline of events for a richly imaginative book, had considerable effect upon the future lore and literature of his equine subject. The well-articulated concepts of what the horse stood for and the emotional strength of the relationship between Keogh and his mount make the book immensely appealing and give it a wider audience beyond the youthful one for which it was intended. David Dallas' 1954 booklet, *Comanche Lives Again*, for example, drew much of its data directly from Appel's book. Dallas' unreferenced work, "a stirring saga leading from Fort Riley, Kansas, to the bloody banks of the Little Big Horn," was published in Kansas and features the historical importance of the famous cavalry post in that state where Comanche once lived. The author was stimulated to write it, he said, by the "recent removal of the last of all the government owned cavalry horses from Fort Riley. . . . This marks the end of cavalry at the historic Army camp, which for a century was the traditional home of that branch of service." Dallas' theme is that Comanche symbolizes "the spirit of service that devoted men, and their equally devoted animal comrades, have given their country" (Manhattanite Writes 1954).

Dallas' work is admittedly "a fictionalized account" because it records one man's visit to Fort Riley and attributes thoughts, emotions, and conversations to that character. The first part of the narrative describes the visitor's experiences on his tour; however, at the stables, his attention is soon drawn to the pervasive memory of the fort's most celebrated former resident, Comanche. For the reader, the implication of the account of Keogh's horse which follows is, of course, that it is entirely factual because the visitor is described as an avid seeker after history who has traveled to that site to delve into America's authentic frontier past. The review of the Indian battles of the Seventh, however, is flawed by error in such instances as referring to "the Comanches of 'Black Kettle' on the Washita," when in fact the Indians were Cheyennes. Dallas has Comanche joining the Seventh at that engagement and receiving his first wound, and hence his name, there (1954:10, 11). Actually, Keogh and his mount did not take part in the Washita Battle.

In describing Comanche, Dallas picks up on the theme that "this sturdy animal was probably captured by Dakota Indians," and he introduces the odd information that this knowledge was based upon the fact that "he had the telltale hackamore halter," probably a reference to the "tie rope" that Comanche's first Indian master had placed on him in Appel's novel. Drawing directly from that novel, Dallas writes that the horse "was no prize sought by cavalry officers," with "his head and neck too thick for his body, his legs too uneven and short, . . . an unwanted ugly duckling cast in with Kentucky Thoroughbreds." In reality, judging from contemporary photos and the mounted horse himself, little of this description is true. Comanche appears to have been an attractive and well-proportioned animal. The possession of "uneven legs" by a horse would be an extreme rarity amounting to a deformity and certainly inconsistent with endurance on long marches. Yet Dallas' Comanche, adhering strictly to Appel's, has "stamina, courage and strong legs." Verbatim from Appel's novel comes Dallas's statement that "sleek looks had no place in a western regiment campaigning for weeks or months over rough terrain where water and grass were scarce" (Dallas 1954:10; Appel 1951:13).

Also taken straight from Appel are details like the name first given to Keogh's horse, "Clay," and the story of the superstitious Irishman saving the arrowhead from his mount's first wound. So, too, Keogh's image in the novel as "a bachelor, and not given to pleasurable pursuits," is retained. Referring to Comanche as "the only survivor of the Custer massacre," and noting that "one live creature: Comanche" was found on the battlefield, Dallas reinforces the concept of the horse's exclusive survival as well as the concept of the battle as a massacre. Only the description of the injured horse as having "Cheyenne arrows protruding from his body and Sioux bullet wounds in a dozen places" seems to be Dallas' own. The work ends with the often-repeated idea that since Comanche represents a life of service, freely given with "supreme

241

devotion," then "in spirit, Comanche lives on—and will live again" (1954:1, 10, 13, 14).

It was Walt Disney who ultimately made Appel's ideas come alive, inextricably embedding them into the Comanche saga for all time. *Tonka,* the 1959 Disney film version of the life of Myles Keogh's horse, "The Lone Survivor," was adapted from Appel's novel and follows its plot quite closely. Previous to becoming the central figure in this film, Comanche had appeared only briefly on the screen. Portrayed as a white charger in Thomas Ince's 1912 film, *Custer's Last Fight,* Keogh's horse returns alone to Fort Lincoln after the battle as "the silent messenger" whose wounds convey news of disaster to the wives of the cavalrymen (see fig. 18). In the 1925 revised edition of the same film, however, this dramatic scene was deleted, though Comanche was mentioned as the only survivor of Custer's force. The horse has played a minor role in at least one television program. "Have Gun—Will Travel" included a scene in which the hero, Paladin, roams over the battlefield after Custer's Last Stand. There, he encounters a claybank gelding "wounded on both sides as though caught in the cross-fire of an ambush." The 1956 film *Seventh Cavalry* included a scene in which cavalrymen, surrounded by Sioux, are saved by Custer's horse, Dandy, suddenly galloping in. The Indians are "so awed that they lift their siege and allow the men to ride away" (Dippie 1976:111, 118). Such is the power of a cavalry horse!

They Died With Their Boots On, the popular and influential 1941 film starring Errol Flynn as Custer, did not feature Comanche but did show Keogh teaching "Garryowen" to his fellow officers. It is fascinating that a 1986 Irish newspaper informs its readers that *Tonka* is "a much better film" than the Errol Flynn version, and goes on to state as fact that the subject of the Disney film, Keogh's horse, "was originally called Tonka until Keogh rechristened the animal 'Comanche.'" The writer asserts that "the film told very accurately the story of Keogh and his friendship with Captain Henry J. Nolan [sic]" (Monahan 1986). Thus in the popular mind, fiction became firmly molded into history.

Walt Disney Archives officials shared information with me about *Tonka,* including details about motivation for making the movie, publicity, and its equine star (personal correspondence 1987). *Tonka* went into production soon after the celebrated filmmaker discovered Appel's story. The foreword to the cinematic production sheet and the prologue to the movie itself reads: "The lone survivor of the historic Custer massacre was a horse. This is his story." (Thus both the horse's lone status and the term massacre are retained.) Early publicity indicated that Appel's book provided Disney with "the opportunity to retell the saga of the Little Big Horn from the Indian viewpoint." Advertisements for *Tonka* called it "The Untold Story" and "The True Story Behind the West's Strangest Legend," and theater posters billed it as "A Story of Courage and Adventure and that Violent Day when A Boy Became a Warrior! A Horse Became A Hero! and Custer Became A Legend!" A Disney staff member referred to Comanche as "an historic steed," the "counterpart in the troop of the tough old stable sergeants of the frontier post," and he saw the horse as "a foil for the nature and behavior of the men in whose life he plays a unique part."

Most reviews of the "top-budget" film with an "all-star cast" were favorable, focusing on "the drama and action along with the relationship between the boy and the horse." Any controversies over the production involved its alleged inaccurate portrayal of Custer, never the horse. In fact, Walt Disney, "an expert horseman with a great appreciation for the equine race," had viewed "thousands of horses in search of the four-legged hero to play the much-beloved cavalry horse, Comanche." Disney finally chose an eight-year-old "rugged chestnut quarter-horse" gelding for the role. Though not possessing the correct color, the movie horse did at least have a white forehead marking somewhat like the real Comanche's. Another resemblance to the cavalry steed was the horse's ultimate reward for a job well done. Following the filming of *Tonka,* its equine star, personally owned by the filmmaker, "lived the life of a retired country gentleman" at Disney's California ranch (Disney Archives).

Few viewers of any age fail to appreciate the splendid scenes depicting horse and man against a western landscape that Disney created with the new Comanche, alias Tonka. The events of Appel's book are condensed in order to make the viewer's experience of *Tonka* one of almost continual action. The opening scene shows White Bull and a companion watching a herd of wild horses being chased by older members of their tribe. White Bull quickly identifies a special young brown stallion running behind the rest as the most courageous of the herd, saying, "I think he would like to stop and fight," for "he snorts defiance at our hunters." White Bull's friend indicates that he would not want such a "big and ugly" horse, but White Bull is determined to catch the stallion for himself. Though the other boy believes the horse is too slow to keep up, White Bull knows that "he runs last to protect the little ones." Thus the horse is not only singled out for bravery but also for altruism. His special role as protector indicates rank and privilege as well as responsibility within his herd.

White Bull captures and tames the stallion, this time naming him "Tonka Wakan," meaning The Great One. Tonka is trained with the aid of a mare which the boy steals from the cavalry in order to teach his mount "what a good horse should know." Not long after breaking Tonka for riding, the pair encounter a troop of cavalrymen, headed by Keogh. The bluecoats give chase, but White Bull tells his stallion, "We will show Yellow Hair's men how a real horse runs." Tonka "ran like the wind." "It's no use," Keogh says. "We don't have anything that can follow him, let alone catch him." The captain notes "that colt runs like a frightened Comanche."

White Bull experiences a sense of identification with the wild, free spirit of his stallion, who is young like himself, and he cannot bear the thought of taking away the animal's dignity with cruel servitude. When Tonka throws Yellow Bull, who became his owner by force, the evil warrior declares "He is no good! I will have him hitched to the travois." There is a parallel here with Appel's book, in which Bob, when he first captured Comanche, had told him about the horrors of being sent to slaughter or becoming "a plow horse on a farm" (1951:101–102). These potentially degrading fates contrast to the heroic image which, in both story and film, the horse ultimately attains—for both Indians and whites.

When Tonka has been set free by White Bull and subsequently acquired by the cavalry, Keogh looks on while a corporal begins the cruel process of training. Keogh recognizes the horse as one he has seen before and is told "He's one wild bronc. He'll go down fighting like a Comanche." Keogh then realizes that this is the horse that was ridden by the Indian he chased several months ago. He promptly buys the horse, telling him, "you belong to me until death us do part." Since the mount runs and fights like one, he is named Comanche. Names are important, and on the inside back cover of the comic-book version of Walt Disney's *Tonka*, it is explained that "just as the lone survivor of the battle answered to two names, Tonka and Comanche, so did the leaders of both sides of the conflict. Until he was fourteen years old, the Indian leader was called Jumping Badger; but at that time, he earned his first coup and was given his father's name, Sitting Bull. The cavalry leader was George Custer to his troopers, but to the plains Indians he was Yellow Hair, a fighter of Indians, who had been sent to drive them from their hunting grounds" (1958). Thus each of the three protagonists—Comanche, Custer, and Sitting Bull—accepts a different role with a name change.

Shortly after acquiring Comanche and finding the good luck

talisman in his mane, Keogh oversees the horse's training. From the animal's reactions to harsh treatment, Keogh intuits some of his mount's background. There is an obvious sense of kinship between himself and the horse who is "all heart and legs," and the captain determines that he will receive only gentle handling. His new master tells him, "Comanche, I've got a feeling you took a beating you didn't deserve. But you stood up to them real good." It is an insightful moment, for the symbolism of the horse comes sharply into focus. He will be a surrogate not only for the Indians who would fight so determinedly for a lost cause, but also for the soldiers who, though losing the battle, would stand up so bravely against an overwhelming enemy force.

In the movie, White Bull is sent by the Sioux to Fort Lincoln as a scout, and while there, visits his former mount who is now in the Seventh Cavalry stable. There the boy and Keogh meet, and each acknowledges his love for the horse. Keogh, portrayed as a wise and noble peacemaker, whom White Bull admits is different from the other soldiers he has seen, escorts the young Indian safely out of the fort. White Bull tells the horse, "You have a good master, Tonka. No longer will my heart be heavy with sorrow for you." On parting, the captain tells the young Indian, "I hope there will be no trouble between your people and mine." Recognizing the horse's prior bond to White Bull, Keogh assures Comanche, "I want you to know if we meet him out there as the enemy, it was no doing of mine."

Before the boy's release, however, Custer, cast as an intense Indian-hater, interrogates White Bull, calling him a "lying, thieving, redskin." In an earlier scene, Custer had declared angrily, "We must teach these red savages who is running this country. They must learn quickly or be exterminated." And just before the final battle, when Keogh asks if Custer is making war on all Indians, even though some are still at peace, Custer replies unequivocally, "There is no way to separate the good from the bad! They've burned, massacred and pillaged. They're all bad! They must be hunted down and wiped out!" Thus, Disney addresses the ambivalence toward Indians through the characterization of Keogh, while Custer represents the extreme polarity of belief in their bad image.

As in Appel's book, Comanche kills the hated Yellow Bull (who has killed Keogh) during the Battle of the Little Big Horn, and White Bull survives. But there is a different twist to the plot, giving the movie a happier, more melodramatic ending, typical of Hollywood. White Bull does not go to the dreaded reservation as in the novel. Rather, though wounded in the fight, he regains

245

consciousness when the action is over. He crawls across the battle-field looking for Tonka, finds the stallion still alive, and the two are reunited. The boy hides as the approaching cavalrymen arrive on the scene. Seeing the wounded mount, a trooper starts to shoot "to put him out of his misery." At this, White Bull rises to his feet and cries, "No! The horse is not your enemy. I'm your enemy. Kill me." Just in time, as the trooper turns his gun on White Bull, Nowlan recognizes both the Indian and Keogh's charger, and he saves boy and horse from death.

White Bull and Tonka then recuperate at the fort. White Bull attends the ceremony held in honor of Tonka, about whom it is made known that "of all the men and horses in the Seventh Cavalry, he alone had lived through the Battle of the Little Big Horn." The famous orders about Comanche's future life of com-fort and freedom from being ridden or performing any kind of work are read to the assembled crowd by Captain Benteen. White Bull's conversion to white ways seems to have been swift and com-plete, as he stands by the stockade gate proudly dressed in a U. S. Cavalry coat and hat. During the celebration, Tonka pulls free from the trooper who held his lead rope and gallops over to his former Indian master. The boy and Nowlan both know that the horse will need exercise; so White Bull becomes the only excep-tion to the orders, being allowed to ride his beloved Tonka every day. To do this, he would have to live at the fort and thus, pre-sumably, remove himself from Sioux life.

Just before the film was released, E. S. Luce wrote to the Chicago Westerners

> Please tell the members of the Corral to be aware AND DON'T FAIL TO MISS SEEING "Tonka" a Disney film soon to be shown in your the-atres. Another writer extracted source material from my book "Keogh, Comanche and Custer," and then fictionized history, and comes out with the film as being "true history little known." It is a fictional story of Captain Keogh and his horse Comanche. Of course they have General Custer in the picture (as a selling argu-ment) and I am almost afraid to see the picture when it comes out. That will be one picture that I DO MISS.
>
> When I heard that they were going "to shoot" this picture, I, personally, pleaded with Walt Disney not to deceive the public by fictionizing American history, but to no avail. He said it "would be entertaining to the masses." There is that old hackeyed [sic] word, "Masses." Could this be subtile [sic] Communistic propaganda de-faming American History?
>
> P. S. The title name of the above Disney picture is TONKA. I believe that means BULL in the Uncpapa Sioux language, and that is exactly what it is—"BULL!" (1958a:72)

Although he strongly disapproved of the film, *Tonka,* and of the novel from which it was adapted, Luce probably looked with favor upon the next major fictional work about the famous horse. For Margaret Leighton's story for young readers, *Comanche of the Seventh,* was published in 1957 "with grateful acknowledgment to Major Edward Smith Luce" and reflects its author's reliance on Luce's book both in events depicted and in spirit. Winner of the Dorothy Canfield Fisher Memorial Children's Book Award, Leighton's popular novel was reprinted in paperback editions dated 1959, 1960, and 1972. The book still perpetuated the "only survivor" status with the subtitle "The true story of a great horse —the only survivor of Custer's Last Stand."

In *Comanche of the Seventh,* as opposed to Appel's version, Indians, except for their role of enemy in battle, play no major role in the horse's story because he is never owned by them. References to Indians lurk continuously in the background, however, foreshadowing the fateful day at the Little Big Horn. Shortly after Keogh acquires his new mount, for example, Tom Custer teases his fellow officer about riding "that Indian cayuse." Later, when the stable sergeant speaks of him as "a good, sturdy horse," Tom replies "if you favor buckskins. They look too much like Injun ponies to suit me." When Keogh's horse is turned over to the sergeant for training, the latter remarks, "He looks like something the Indians left behind." And, of course, as mentioned in Chapter 3, the horse was named not only for his "Comanche yell" when wounded, but also because his coat resembled the light bronze color of the Indian, "old Ten Bear's son," who participated in the fight on that occasion (1957:38, 48, 67, 82, 84).

Leighton's view of the Sioux and Cheyenne is far less sympathetic than Appel's. Though never owned by Indians, as a two-year-old, Comanche did come close to being captured by a young Cheyenne brave who viewed the "small golden horse" with a "greedy light" in his eyes. The buckskin colt looked to him "like the fast-running white man's horse" he had once seen, and the young brave dreamed of winning races on him. But the loop of the noose of the would-be captor "missed all but his nose" and "caught him there for a brief, painful instant before he jerked free." The colt dashed away, but "his nose burned from the harsh rope and in his nostrils was a scent that would forever after rouse terror and hatred in him—the scent of an Indian" (1957:26, 27).

Many times throughout Leighton's version of the horse's life Comanche smells Indians and responds with fear and hatred. This reaction represents an actual equine response because the olfactory sense is well-developed in horses and they are quick to make

behavioral associations. Cavalrymen who fought Indians remarked about the effect of the odor of Indians on their mounts.
One private who participated in the Battle of the Little Big Horn
reported that his horse "as soon as he smelled Indians, began to
act up badly and he could not control him." More problems arose
later, he said, when the horse "smelled Indians stronger than before." The mount also "did not like the sight of Indians" (Hammer 1976:118, 119).

Frontiersmen were familiar with the remarkable ability of
their horses to smell Indians and to become alarmed by the odor.
J. Frank Dobie claimed that "many a pioneer Texan relied on his
horses—American as well as Spanish—to give warning against
Indians" (1952:116). "The gaucho horse manifests the greatest
terror at an Indian invasion," wrote W. H. Hudson. "The gau-
chos maintain that the horses *smell* the Indians. I believe they are
right, for when passing a distant Indian camp, from which the
wind blew, the horses driven before me have suddenly taken
fright and run away, leading me a chase of many miles"
(1903:357–58). Mules have the same capacity. It was reported
that when Reno and his men, besieged by the enemy, were entrenched on top of the bluff at the Little Big Horn, some of their
mules had "run down the bluff, and the young [Indian] men
caught them, finding ammunition in the packs." But "they did
not catch all these runaways, as they would get scared when they
smelled the Indians and run back up again" (Vestal 1932:
175–76).

Comanche's ability to smell Indians is emphasized by Leighton. In at least one instance, when his rider took time out for a
swim, this capacity saves Keogh's life. The frequency with which
Comanche reacts to the odor throughout the narration (1957:27,
30, 69, 70, 81, 114, 130, 175, 180, 205–206) adds greatly to the
unfavorable image of Indians which the novel conveys. Indians
become identified with fearful creatures of the wild, so that the
dangers of the natural world to which Comanche is exposed soon
become associated not only with the horse's remarkable powers to
triumph over them but also with his fear and hatred of Indians.
When Comanche shies at, and then succeeds in pounding to death
a "monster" rattlesnake, Keogh says, "So you don't like rattlers
any better than you like Injuns?" Years later, after Sitting Bull's
death, a trooper refers to the former Sioux leader as "an old he-
rattlesnake" (1957:79, 205).

Unlike Appel, who emphasized the value Plains Indians generally placed upon horses, Leighton's negative view of the "wild
red horsemen" includes a vivid image of a warrior who "pulled

his pony in with a jerk that sent it back on its haunches." In one fight, cavalrymen observe the Indians "flogging their ponies," one of which soon stumbled and fell, spilling its rider. No kindly boy like White Bull appears to gently claim and tame the horse he loves. Rather, his counterpart, an unnamed Cheyenne brave who attempted to lasso the horse, wants the animal not for its bravery or any kinship he feels with it, but merely for vanity, to get the attention of girls. Horse stealing, for Leighton, is shorn of its cultural context and meaning, being just the "favorite of all sports to an Indian buck" (1957:5, 27, 69, 71, 148).

Leighton's linguistic use of animal imagery and words with connotations of being uncivilized when describing Indians helps to articulate the ethos expressed throughout the novel. Indians are "Injuns," "bucks," "red devils," "savages," "scalp-hungry warriors," or "stupid fools." An individual brave may be called a "poisonous varmint" or a "barbaric" figure. Indians "swarm about" with "complaints and demands," are "uppety," "ornery," and are described as "frothing at the mouth" when angry. They slyly plot to obtain guns. It is necessary for the army to "clean them out"; but "exterminating" them brings "a howl from soft-hearted civilians back East" (1957:64, 65, 66, 82, 147, 148, 156). The 1957 novel is starkly out of keeping with the more empathetic tenor of the approaching 1960s and harks back in spirit to an earlier time of unquestioned assumptions about racial differences and unequivocal good guys and bad.

Following Luce, Leighton's Comanche is "one quarter Spanish, three quarters American." His father is a "fine blooded animal" from Kentucky; however, his great endurance is traceable to his "mustang blood." He is an ordinary colt, "only a little stronger boned than average." As a youngster, his good chest and legs are first noted by the rancher who rounds up his herd. He soon becomes known as "sensible," "lively and willing," "quick and sure on his feet," and possessed of "tremendous stamina." He is far stronger than Keogh's other mount, Paddy, who "soon gave out" under harsh conditions and is more durable and more highly valued by his master than "all the thoroughbreds in Kentucky." Keogh knew from the first that he "wouldn't have much of a show against a long-legged, blooded horse" like Tom Custer's, but his horse would be best "for a short stretch over rough ground." He is versatile enough to be as good in a buffalo hunt as in a battle. Keogh praises his mount for knowing "how to rustle for yourself," when feed was scarce. Comanche could gnaw on cottonwood bark, which, Keogh remarks, is "an Injun cayuse's trick." But it is clear that the horse had learned this from "an old mustang pony" before joining the army, not from former Indian experience to which Appel's story traces it (1957:2, 4, 19, 33, 34, 67, 103, 110, 116, 135, 150).

Though Comanche is not quite an "ugly duckling" for Leighton, he is far from outstanding in looks. Tom Custer says of the group of horses among which Comanche was purchased that they are "good average critters, but there's hardly an officer's charger among them." The sergeant quotes an old saying indicating that "buckskins come tough, and that they'll outlast a lot of better-looking animals on a long march over rough country." Although in preference to another mount with "real style" who "looks like an officer's mount," Keogh, the archetypal horseman, chooses the buckskin as "a bit of nice horseflesh," he makes it clear that "a horse's color is the last thing to judge him by." Rather, he explains to the troopers who look to him as an "expert judge" of horses: "His head and the way he carries it, the look of his eyes, his shoulders and chest and barrel, the length and line of his back, the legs, the long springy pasterns and the feet under him—look at those things first. Take my word for it, the buckskin's a bit small, but he's the best-made horse of the lot." And, though a veteran stable sergeant sees Comanche as a "small dull colored brute," yet "he seems like a well set up animal." Something about the horse's eyes and ears make the man prophesy "You're not showy, but I reckon you'll be all the mount a soldier could want, either on a long, hard march or in a tight place" (1957:38, 39, 40, 41, 47–48).

Sometimes, there is a parallel drawn between Comanche's toughness and Custer's remarkable endurance. As soon as he had been captured, Comanche was found to be "sturdy, high-spirited and tireless." As a cavalry mount, even when grazing was poor, his "energy and spirit never flagged." His ability to get along when food was scarce made him known as "a regular old campaigner." Likewise, it was said of Custer "a little hardtack's all *he* needs to keep going." The General possessed a limitless physical strength that often made him set a pace too rapid for his men to match. "Nothing ever tires him," the troopers said, as he was "built out of rawhide and steel springs, not flesh and blood." He "don't feel cold or heat like anybody else." The "driving energy" of his leadership is praised, and General Sully is unfavorably compared to Custer, "the superb and dashing horseman." Major Reno's "indecisive leadership" contrasts to Custer's verve and boldness. Although "not prudent," and somewhat of a "glory-hunter," General Custer knows no fear and is always in the thick of the fight. Ultimately, however, it is Dandy, the handsome

Thoroughbred who always prances, that is Custer's true counter-part, a mount more appropriate than Comanche to his restless, impetuous nature. The little bay could not learn to walk, and for most men, his trot was too hard a gait for a long march. "He'll either wear himself out or wear out the man who rides him," Keogh had observed when first seeing the horse. But "the danc-ing bay," Keogh later thought, might be just the mount for Cus-ter. "What else but a horse that'd shake the teeth from any lesser man in a day's march would suit our dashing leader so well?" (1957:33, 88, 89, 90, 95, 115, 116, 118, 166).

Following the Luce tradition, Custer is a true hero for Leighton, who also wrote *The Story of General Custer* and *Bride of Glory*, biographies of the General and his wife. Custer is portrayed as magnanimous, extending chivalrous behavior even to defeated enemies. For example, Monaseta, like most of the other Indian women taken prisoner at the Washita, was "so surprised by the good treatment given all the prisoners that she seemed to hold no grudge even against the soldiers who had killed so many of her kinsmen." One of the most fascinating aspects of *Comanche of the Seventh* is the author's bringing together of the central figures of two of the most pervasive Custer legends—Monaseta, the Chey-enne woman believed by many people to have been the General's mistress, and Comanche, the steed who was famous for endur-ance. Monaseta acted as a guide for the Seventh Cavalry, and as Leighton tells it, the squaw's "eyes grew even brighter" when they rested on Comanche. "*He* is a fine horse," she said. "The Hunkpapa Sioux have a horse like that. He is a sacred horse and he always leads the processions around the council fire. He is rid-den in war by their bravest chiefs. Many bullets have struck him but they cannot kill him because his medicine is strong and he has the heart of a warrior."

Though Comanche reacted to her Indian odor with fear and recoiled from her "dark, reaching hand," Monaseta did not seem surprised or offended. "Yes, he is a chief's horse," she said. Later, when the Seventh was stationed in Kentucky and Comanche re-ceived his "third wound in the line of duty" in a "skirmish with bootleggers," the horse "made his usual quick recovery." Keogh recalled Monaseta's words, asking his mount to remember what "that little Cheyenne squaw said about the sacred horse the Hunkpapa Sioux had that led the processions around their coun-cil fire. He was supposed to be bullet proof and she thought you looked like him. . . . Are you maybe related to that animal, Co-manche?" After the Battle of the Little Big Horn, in trying to de-termine how Keogh's horse had managed to survive, the question is posed "Could the horse be bullet proof, like the one the Hunk-papa Sioux had in their camp long, long ago?" (1957:113–114, 149, 150, 192).

The simple outline of a meeting between the Indian woman who once loved General Custer and the horse who survived the famous battle is in fact described in Miller's *Custer's Fall*. In that book, written from data provided to the author by Indians including some who took part in the battle, there is a description of Monahseetah, followed by her child, the "little light-haired Yellow Bird," wandering over the field with her aunt after Custer's force had been wiped out. Passing by "the carcasses of some seventy cavalry horses and two Indian ponies," she noted

> A few live horses still limped downhill toward the river, their wounds obvious even at a distance. The women needed only a glance to assure them that the hopelessly injured animals were not worth bothering with.
> Another horse stood head down, unable to move. Under the dust and blood, he appeared to be a claybank gelding—he was later identified as Comanche, Keogh's mount, supposedly the only living thing left on the field. His saddle had twisted under his belly and Monahseetah thought for a moment of taking the gold-edged blue saddle blanket. But it was mostly spoiled by bloodstains. Yellow Bird shouted at the horse and threw an earth clod his way, yet the animal would not move over. (1957:168–69)

Returning to Leighton's work, Keogh, as in most other accounts, is portrayed in the novel as the romantic "wild Irishman" who is said to "know horseflesh" and who "can always seem to get everything there is from his mounts." Major Elliot (as Leighton spells it) tells Tom Custer that "Keogh's a good horseman, as good as any in the Seventh except perhaps your brother." The new element in this story is that when Tom notes the average quality of the group of horses from which Keogh bought Comanche, he supposes "Keogh's broke again," in keeping with his reputation for not being able to hold onto his money. Elliot reveals that this is true, for Keogh, he says, "told me that the army cost price of ninety dollars is all he can afford at the moment" (1957:39).

Of far more interest than this rather banal episode of his horse's purchase is the fact that in the novel Keogh is the only person who voices real empathy for the Indians. When orders come for a campaign against the Sioux, which means a showdown with the leader of the hostiles, Sitting Bull, Keogh exclaims, "To tell the truth I don't blame the old savage for preferring the free-roaming life of the wild Indian to begging and starving around the agencies. Faith, I'd choose the same myself if I were he" (1957:163). It seems that Keogh, alone among Seventh Cavalrymen, has been led to this frame of mind through his ennobling relationship with his remarkable mount. Metaphorically, through the intercommunication between horse and rider, Comanche is a unique bridge to empathy and understanding few others can share. Appropriately, as the tragic Custer Battle comes to a close, Keogh's horse is the only element of peace amid the violence. For though "Indians galloped their ponies jubilantly over the battlefield, while others scalped, stripped and pillaged" the dead, they passed the wounded horse many times "but did not harm him further nor try to drive him away." "He is too badly hurt to be useful to us. See, he bleeds from many places," they said. "He is a faithful horse. Let him stay beside his master. His master was a brave chief" (1957:196).

Thus the wounded horse, in a pattern familiar from Appel, once again became the object of a benediction upon a bloody field —for the enemy as well as for his own people. Leighton records that after discovering Keogh's mount alive, the Seventh Cavalrymen "touched him gently, reverently. They looked with pity and wonder at his wounds, and spoke to each other in hushed tones almost as though they were in church." Then "men who had endured the long ordeal of the battle and held their emotions in check through all that time now felt tears flowing without restraint and without shame. 'Good old Comanche!' they said, over and over again." Comanche had now fulfilled the destiny that had not been foreshadowed by his ordinary appearance as a colt—that his name "would some day ring in men's ears like a trumpet call carrying wild echoes of glory and defeat and eternal mystery." So sacrosanct did Comanche become after the famous Orders No. 7 were issued, according to the novel, that a recruit who was about to throw a clod of dirt at him was warned just in time, "Look out! That's Comanche, you fool! Hitting him would get you a court-martial just as quick as striking any other officer" (1957:2, 199, 203).

Leighton's novel, based upon the material about Comanche recorded by Luce, crystallized the psychological and spiritual impact of the equine survivor as well as chronicling the events of his life the way they might have occurred. Except for Keogh's spurt of empathetic identification with the foe, the narrative proceeds strictly from a perspective typical of the times it portrays, in which the whites are right and the Indians are wrong. Implacable to the end, the author depicts even the tragic Wounded Knee episode in terms which imply that hostile Indians were to blame: it happened because "Big Foot, another Sioux Chief, started to make trouble." And the Indians' belief in the Ghost Dance religion is made to seem ridiculous (1957:205–206).

Comanche of the Seventh portrays a much less anthropomorphized horse than was true of the hero of Appel's book. Keogh's mount for Leighton is flesh and blood cavalry horse—gelded and branded, an exceptionally hardy and tractable animal who accepted life as it came. The author's skillful affect of realism, in fact, has contributed to the rather remarkable acceptance of her novel at times as though it were nonfiction. For example, although David Dary acknowledged that there are several legends concerning Comanche's naming, he took from Leighton (1957:84) the details of the version he believed most likely. He describes Keogh holding his horse's head and talking to him quietly while the farrier treats the wound, and cites a trooper's announcement that when the arrow struck, the animal made a noise like a Comanche (Dary 1975a:4; 1975b:7; 1976b:70–71). At least two other instances in print illustrate direct usage of Leighton. Evan S. Connell, author of a recent best-selling book on Custer and the Little Big Horn, refers to the juvenile novel as a source. He relates the traditional story of Comanche's first wound and states, "In a popular story by Margaret Leighton, *which is reasonably factual* [italics mine], a trooper called McBane tells Keogh that he saw the arrow strike" (1984:296). In 1976, when sculptor Rogers Aston created a bronze of "Captain Myles Keogh on Comanche" for the centennial, a pamphlet, *Keogh, Comanche and the Little Big Horn*, accompanied each statue. In detailing Comanche's life, Aston states unequivocally that the horse "was captured by rancher Clem Bates and his sons in Indian Territory near the Texas line." Yet Clem Bates and his son, Bart, who catches Comanche and begins to gentle him, as well as his brother Billy, are *fictional* characters from Leighton's story, not historical persons! Such instances indicate much about the historiography of the celebrated horse, and how it developed.

It is not surprising that Comanche, because he lived through the battle, has appeared in fiction as a means of escape for a human survivor (Dippie 1976:67). Perhaps, because "the facts concerning Comanche are in themselves the very essence of romance," history and legend are entwined more inextricably in the case of the famous horse than is true for some other subjects. Yet "Comanche is immortalized, not through fairy tales nor legend, but through records from known pens, his story told by living witnesses" (Comanche 1911). As Brian Dippie has aptly pointed out, "Comanche's story is the most popular of the Custer legends possibly because it is basically true" (1976:149n). Of course, he is referring to truth as a set of historical facts. Legends have their own form of "truth," in another sense, for they express beliefs and perceptions that are of value to people and which articulate important cultural and societal concepts. More will be said on this subject in the final chapter in summing up the meanings attributed to Comanche, past and present. Now, a look at some art works, sculptures, poems, and songs about the horse reveals the ideas of their creators who, to a greater degree than prose writers, are granted license to romanticize and construct imaginative and moving images.

Chapter 13

Art, Poetry, and Song

Comanche, the brave horse, you gave your all.
(Bandy and Horton)

Artists, sculptors, poets, and creators of song lyrics, as well as historians and novelists, have turned their attention to Comanche. From various vantage points, these portrayers of the horse have given expression to different aspects of the meanings attributed to him, both during his life and after his death.

Art

Most of the popular and well-known artistic renditions of the Battle of the Little Big Horn are centered upon the area of the Last Stand, now called Custer Hill. Since these works do not show the portion of the field where Keogh died, they do not include Comanche. But there are some paintings, drawings, and sculptures that have contributed a visual dimension to Comanche's legend. As is true of all artists, their particular depictions of the famous horse and the phase of his life each chose to perpetuate reveal much about the viewpoints of the creators.

Regarding his work "He Screamed Like a Comanche," Thomas H. Swearingen explains that he painted the horse as he might have appeared in 1868, when Keogh rode him during a skirmish with Indians "in the territory that is now Oklahoma." In the background the artist has shown the wagon train which had been under attack by Indians and was rescued by the cavalry. Comanche is depicted as a spirited charger, with neck arched, ears forward, and tail held high. Keogh raises his rifle to shoot, while his mount has already been hit by an arrow embedded in his right hip (see fig. 23). This was the arrow wound which, according to legend, was responsible for the horse's name. "Comanche" may have been chosen because the injury was sustained in a fight against Comanches, as suggested by Luce (1939:27), or Keogh's mount may have made a sound like a "Comanche yell" when hit, as described by Leighton (1957:84). Dary's article, "The Horse That Got Its Name from an Indian Yell" (1975a), for which Swearingen's oil painting was specifically created, incorporates Leighton's version.

A watercolor by William Nelson shows Comanche just at the close of the Battle of the Little Big Horn. The horse, with the saddle still in place and the bridle reins hanging down, lowers his head and stands guard over the body of his dead master. In the background, mounted Indian warriors are just leaving the scene. A print of this painting, given to the Museum of Natural History at the University of Kansas in the early 1970s, is now displayed near the Comanche exhibit. Noted Montana artist J. K. Ralston sketched Comanche following the battle as a gaunt figure, reflecting the terrible ordeal he has endured. His head hangs down and blood drains from his nose. Two arrows are lodged in his hindquarters. The saddle is twisted and dangles from his body, and the bridle is missing. He bears the brand US on his left shoulder. Another similar sketch by Ralston (1968) depicts Comanche facing slightly toward the viewer. A third arrow, with a broken shaft, is embedded in the horse's neck. A bird, probably a magpie, perches on his withers. In the foregound, just above Comanche's drooping head, lies a rifle (see Upton 1975:87, 98).

Ernest L. Reedstrom's two drawings (1970, 1971) also show Comanche as he might have been immediately following the battle. Wounds are plainly visible and blood drips from his nostrils. The broken bridle and the saddle, twisted and hanging under the horse's belly, appear as described to Luce by Peter Wey (Luce 1939:65). In the earlier of the two versions (see Reedstrom 1970:cover), dead soldiers' bodies are visible, one with arrows protruding. Though obviously injured, Comanche's head is up, his ears are forward, and he is moving ahead, though painfully. In Reedstrom's later drawing, the horse is far more dejected, with eyes sunken and lids half closed, his ears tilted sideways in the position typical of an ailing animal. The naked body of Keogh lies under the horse's nose (see fig. 24). Stark realism, especially in the second rendition, sets these two works apart from others on the subject, and imparts hopelessness, an overwhelming sense of the unmitigated horror of the battle's aftermath.

A painting by Charles O. Kemper (1973) also portrays Comanche after the battle. The bridle and saddle are as described previously. But the horse is shown turning his neck and slightly lowering his head, focusing his alert eyes upon something on the ground. His ears are turned a bit to the side, as though listening intently. Signs of the violent battle are not prominent in comparison to the commanding figure of the horse. A pair of bare legs sticks out from a corpse hidden by a clump of sagebrush, an arrow shaft is visible in the grass, and a trooper's hat with a bullet hole in it is evident in the foreground. No blood or wounds are visible on Comanche's body, and he appears unsullied. He is still a forceful figure whose endurance has clearly allowed him to transcend the carnage (see fig. 26).

Pat Hammack's (1979) watercolor, too, depicts Comanche at the end of the battle but shows him as a healthy animal with bridle and saddle intact. The mount stands over his fully clothed prone master. One set of reins drops down as though gripped in Keogh's left hand, according to legend. Above this scene is a head portrait of the captain, taken from a photograph (see fig. 27). Obviously the work is intended to illustrate the bonding between horse and man, and it demonstrates only that aspect of the story. "Silent Horse on a Silent Field," an oil painting by Thomas H. Swearingen (1969), captures Comanche at the close of the battle in a much different way (see fig. 28). Rising up in the foreground with his finely chiseled head held high and with ears pricked forward at attention, Comanche looks into the distance as if transfixed by a sublime call or vision. The horse seems to have transcended defeat and death. Though one bridle rein is broken, the saddle and pack are intact, in apparent readiness for his rider. The horse's injuries are hardly visible, and he exudes energy and spirit. Time and place are established by the background in which a few mounted Indians can still be seen riding off over "Custer Hill." A dead horse and trooper lie nearby. The artist explained that his painting "shows the clouds coming in during the sunset of evening. The colors in the clouds are blues, reds, and yellows to represent the cavalry colors, the Indians, and the blood spilled by both sides on that day. The grass was short and sparse due to the dry weather."

As a sequel to his oil painting, Swearingen drew a pencil sketch, "Bringing Water from the River," illustrating the scene described by a participant who said that when the men who were burying the dead discovered Comanche, he was too weak to stand and some of them rode to the river to bring water for him in their hats. In portraying this event, the artist said that he studied the terrain near where the horse may have been found, in order to depict it accurately. The burial party can be seen at work in the background near the foot of the hill where Custer made his Last Stand (see fig. 25).

"Comanche!" an original oil painting by Hildred Goodwine (author's collection), appears on the cover of this book. In Goodwine's portrayal, a great deal of expression is evident in the horse's face as he lowers his head to the ground and seems to use all his senses in searching. An arrow is embedded in his body just below the withers, and blood streams from the wound. His saddle is twisted and his bridle is missing. Yet the horse, whose color and markings are depicted accurately, retains a noble grandeur. An Indian lance protrudes from the ground near the wounded mount, and the American flag still flies in the distance on Custer Hill. In this skillful and sensitive artistic rendition Comanche bridges the two enemy realms—red and white—and stands as victor. A somewhat different version of this painting hangs in the Cowboy Art Room of the Wall Drug Store in South Dakota.

In discussing her depiction of the famous mount with me, Hildred Goodwine said

> As a painter of horses, I was familiar with Comanche's story, and knew that when found, he was standing hurt and not feeling well. I thought about how he would look at that time. In painting portraits of horses, I try to make the viewer understand what that horse is thinking, because they think just like we do. In my portraits, I try to capture the horse's disposition and temperament. Before painting Comanche, I went to the Custer Battlefield and made my background look like that. It's a sad place, but I stayed away from putting in too many dead people.

Mrs. P. A. Haynes, with her work "The Empty Saddle" (1891), done in India ink, chose an episode from the period of Comanche's retirement for illustration. Here, Keogh's horse, saddled and bridled, takes his place between two mounted officers in his role as the symbolic "riderless horse" during a Seventh Cavalry full-dress parade. Since the artist could well have seen Comanche, it is regrettable that the distinguishing white star on his forehead was omitted (see fig. 29). Jeanne Mellin's more recent painting of Comanche as a "Morgan Gelding" (1966) is set in a similar context. It reveals a beautifully conditioned Comanche without his white markings and with a typical Morgan conformation and large expressive eyes. All his accoutrements are in place as he is proudly led by a trooper during an occasion when, as the ceremonial riderless mount, he is led on review for the Seventh Cavalry. Numerous uniformed mounted cavalrymen stand at attention to watch the horse parade by (see fig. 30).

In 1987, James E. Connell painted a vivid action-packed work entitled "Get Comanche!" In this scene, mounted Indian warriors are chasing and attempting to lasso the riderless Seventh Cavalry mount who gallops furiously, headlong toward the viewer. The horse, strong and vigorous and as yet unwounded, eludes his pursuers. The artist has depicted the mount as chestnut in color with a white blaze rather than with Comanche's true color and markings. The painting is owned by John M. Carroll, who believes it appeared on the cover of an English pulp magazine (see fig. 31). Comanche is, of course, illustrated in the books and pamphlets written about him. Barron Brown's drawing of the horse for the dust jacket of his monograph (1935) is a head study which, strangely for one so interested in details about the horse, shows none of his individual characteristics. Rather the head is drawn short and wide, with a blocky muzzle and nondescript features. The enlarged "kind eye" which horsemen attribute to special mounts is the only distinguishing trait. A head study drawn by Swearingen for the cover of Dary's 1976 pamphlet is a more accurate likeness, having been based upon a contemporary photograph of Comanche. Appel's and Leighton's books and Walt Disney's *Tonka* contain numerous illustrations depicting the events in their respective texts.

Two bronze sculptures of Comanche were created around the time of the Little Big Horn centennial. The one by Rogers Aston features Keogh mounted on Comanche during the Battle of the Little Big Horn (see fig. 32). The horse is shown at an extended gallop, and the rider shoots his pistol straight ahead. An arrow pierces the ground beneath them. In the artist's own words, his studies led him to see Keogh as a "courageous and dedicated cavalry officer" and Comanche as a "brave and determined mount." Thus he molded them as a dynamic pair at a moment of intense concerted action. Juan Dell's bronze figure of Comanche, on the other hand, stands alone, wounded, after the battle, his head drooping. Her sculpture in the first ten castings included an arrow protruding from the horse's hip and two arrows piercing the ground nearby. But after John Carroll told her that he believed the arrows represented an inaccuracy, the subsequent bronzes, he said, were produced without that feature (personal communication 1988).

On display in the museum at Custer Battlefield National Monument is a statuette of Comanche encased in plexiglass. Orval Coop made this twelve-inch-high carving of the mount out of cottonwood and then painted it, after studying the Comanche exhibit at the University of Kansas. In a description of his work, Coop mistakenly refers to the horse as belonging to the "Morgan breed." There are also some smaller works depicting the famous horse. A statue of a dun-colored Comanche with several bloody wounds and two arrows piercing his left hip was molded from clay by an unidentified artist. Real horsehair, much lighter-hued than Comanche's, was used for the mane and tail of this six-inch-tall mount. The saddle has slipped under the horse's belly and the bridle is broken, with the bit dangling (see fig. 33). Additionally, Tom Bookwalter, a creator of miniature military figures, has produced an accurate likeness of Keogh on Comanche galloping over the sagebrush, with the rider ready to fire his pistol and an arrow shaft visible in the foreground (author's collection).

Poetry

Like the artists and sculptors, the poets who chose Comanche as a theme focused on certain aspects of his life and legend. The verses written about the horse are testament to his diverse meanings and popular appeal, and they reflect the sense of identification with the horse that many people felt. As was the case with some of the artists who depicted the Little Big Horn, certain well-known poets who wrote about the battle did not include references to Comanche. Famous and/or popular and prolific poets who dealt with Custer and the battle, such as Walt Whitman, Joaquim Miller, John G. Neihardt, Henry W. Longfellow, John Greenleaf Whittier, Ella Wheeler Wilcox, Captain Jack Crawford, and Arthur Chapman, fail to mention the surviving mount whose presence would have added a dramatic element to their verse.

Some of the poems about Custer and/or the battle, however, do contain meaningful references to Comanche. "The Custer Mystery" by artist-poet J. K. Ralston raises the themes of the horse's status as a survivor and the animal's silence:

> There's one we know came through the fight,
>   Though all the others fell.
> That's old Comanch', the buckskin light,
>   Survived that breath of hell.
> He's one who could have told us right,
>   But he would never tell.

Francis Brooks' poem, "Down the Little Big Horn," published in 1898, devotes five lines to Keogh's mount who waits in vain for his dead rider:

> A single steed in the morn,
> Comanche, seven times hit,
> Comes to the river to drink;
> Lists for the saber's clink,
> Lists for the voice of his master.

Written for the 75th anniversary of the Custer Battle and published in the *Denver Post*, Catherine E. Berry's "Look Past the Stars" emphasizes the finality of the tragedy with the lines:

> No man was left to tell the story then.
> Comanche, tired, aimless mount, alone
> Still stood to serve the troop.

"The Second Departure of Custer" by Mary Boynton Cowdrey mentions only that as the expedition marches out from Fort Abraham Lincoln toward the Little Big Horn, "A captain spurs Comanche's sides." Here the poet depends upon the reader's prior knowledge of the horse who later would become famous as the "only survivor," in order to produce her effect of foreshadowing the tragic fate that awaits the cavalrymen of Custer's command. In contrast, Vaun Arnold, who composed "To the Last Man," uses Comanche effectively as a dramatic climax to his poem:

> Seek in all history some epic story
> Dwarfing what Custer has wrought!
> Back from that valley a bleeding Comanche,
> Only one charger was brought!

Poems that are devoted specifically to Comanche emphasize some of the main themes of his life and legend. William V. Wade, probably after he saw the horse at Fort Lincoln in 1877 (Dippie 1978:232), and was moved to write a verse addressed to "Old Commanche" in which he urged the animal to

> Tell us of that dreadful day,
> Tell us of that bloody fray,
> . . . .
> When Custer led his
> troopers on
> To doom. All but you.

But Comanche, even though he is the "only one who survived that awful day," cannot provide what "All of us would love to know." For his "mute tongue can never tell" about the battle.

G. T. Lanigan composed a stirring poem entitled "Old Comanche" which was published in the *United States Army and Navy*

Journal in 1878 without giving credit to the author. The poet emphasized Comanche's special status with the lines

> Honor to Keogh's charger!
> Only his flashing eye
> Saw the Three Hundred fighting—
> Saw the Three Hundred die!

And rather eloquently recognized the bond between cavalryman and mount:

> The horse is part of the soldier:
> He mixed his blood with theirs.

Grief for the fallen rider is expressed in the vain wish

> But, oh, to see the Captain
> Upon his back again.

John Hay's poem, "Miles Keogh's Horse," was first published in *The Atlantic Monthly* in 1880. It appears in Luce's book (1939:70–71) and has been reprinted quite often. The author, an American statesman who served as ambassador to Great Britain as well as secretary of state, stresses the fact that Custer's men were outnumbered at the battle and places some of the blame for their defeat on Congress:

> Three hundred to three thousand!
> They had bravely fought and bled;
> For such is the will of Congress
> When the White man meets the Red.

He describes the horse's survival:

> Of all that stood at noonday
> In that fiery scorpion ring,
> Miles Keogh's horse at evening
> Was the only living thing.

The significant element in this work is that it relates Sturgis's order to later events. After explaining this document which established Comanche's retirement status, the poet notes that the order will be appreciated by future generations as long as

> the love and honor of comrades
> Are the soul of the soldier's creed.

Hay then goes on to assert that at a time when the army is the object of unjust criticism, Sturgis' order

> Shall prove to a callous people
>   That the sense of a soldier's worth,
>   That the love of comrades, the honor of arms,
>   Have not perished from the earth.

Thus Comanche represents not only the bond between horse and rider, but the soldier's loyalty to his comrades as well.

The poem "Comanche" by Mrs. Minnie E. Carrel was published in *Winners of the West*, June 24, 1926, to honor the fiftieth anniversary of the Custer defeat. After using nature imagery to evoke the desolate wildness of the area where the battle had occurred, the poet notes that

> Not a breath of life was stirring,
>   Where had passed that dreadful fray.

But then a dramatic discovery is made:

> There a sorrel horse is standing,
>   Bending o'er a form so still.
>   'Tis Comanche o'er his master,
>   The only life to greet the day,
>   Keeping there his lonely vigil,
>   As the long hours crept away.

The wish that the horse could "tell us of the horrors of that night" is accompanied by a description of his wounds and his search for Keogh. The enduring mount is addressed as "Faithful Comanche," the "lone survivor of the Big Horn" who is "enshrined in memory"

> Not because your feet were fleeter,
>   Nor was it for your form more grand,
>   But that you were always faithful
>   To the one who held command.

James H. McGregor, who penned a very different verse, "Comanche," once served as superintendent of the Rosebud and Pine Ridge Sioux Indian reservations (McGregor 1945:viii). Unlike most other poets of the time, he knew many Sioux Indians personally, and expressed sympathy with their cause:

> History will give them credit:
>   In this battle, they were in the right.
>   Custer was hunting them down,
>   And of course was expecting a fight.

McGregor believed "history honors a race that fights bravely to survive." He wrote that Comanche

Alone survived the Indians' fire.
  About it, he had nothing to say.
He was pastured near an army post,
  Close to the white man's might,
And to his dying day
  He was the hero of that fight.
But if you'd attended a gathering
  Only of the Sioux,
You would have discovered immediately
  They had their heroes too. (1945:49)

The controversy about moving the mounted horse to Fort Riley prompted Robert E. Haggard to argue for keeping Comanche at Lawrence with a poem, "Comanche," published in the *New York Herald Tribune* in September 1948.

What would Comanche, given to the keeping
Of modern cavalry, have felt to see
Platoons of armored motorcycles sweeping
The praise of his time, unfenced and free?
The chill of more than simply terror
Would have benumbed his blood. His quaking flanks
And snorting nostrils would have shown the error
Of linking him with highly mobile tanks.

His was the day of fair haired reckless Custer
Of Sitting Bull and wild Rain-In-The-Face
Of yelping Sioux and troopers quick to muster
For fun or fight, and these were out of place
Where no fast horses were, nor bugle peals . . .
What tie has he with cavalry on wheels?

A copy of this poem was sent to Chancellor Malott at the University of Kansas by a person who knew it would be important to the chancellor's espoused cause of keeping Comanche at the university rather than surrendering him to Fort Riley. The cover letter stated that the poem "shows that someone senses the incompatibility of Comanche with modern cavalry, General Wainwright to the contrary, notwithstanding" (UK Archives).

The *Little Big Horn Associates Research Review*, Spring 1972, published a colloquialized and empathetic verse, "Talk t' Me," by Ben Mayfield, focusing on a desire to hear the horse speak.

Talk t' me Commanche—'bout that you know so well
You're the only livin' critter whut's ever been to Hell.

The poet expressed respect for the horse who has passed through such a terrible ordeal:

I kin' smell yer ev'ry fear and feel yer every woe
I takes me cap right off t'you—ol' buddy of Keogh—

It is appropriate that Comanche not only be rewarded with good treatment during his life, but also in the afterlife:

If they ain't no horses heaven—they're makin' one for you
Endless fields o' clover and hay wavin' in your own green coulee.

In 1975, a verse, "Commanche," by Audrey J. Hazell, was published with Frank Mercatante's reprint of Charles King's *Custer's Last Battle*. Detailing the high points of the life of the horse, the poet asserts that the mount had "done his best," and "stood his ground." He was "restored to health," and took his place as "second commander of the regiment." Finally,

Like other old, old soldiers
Came his time to fade away.
At Fort Meade in 1890,
Commanche had his final day.

He "still lives" in the town of Lawrence;
He's standing without his rider
At the University of Kansas,
Commanche, the sole survivor.

"Comanche" by Gary Gildner (1979:156–57) has a fresh viewpoint and a different tone from the previous works, depicting a prosaic and disillusioned, rather than a heroic horse. The poem is written in the words of Comanche himself after he had become a museum display, reflecting back upon his life, death, and preservation.

They think I like it here, I guess,
Stuffed and boxed in glass in Kansas
but I don't. I don't like being
saddled up and never watered, never fed
or let to rub against a tree. And I don't
like my ears pricked up by wires, man
there isn't anything to *hear*.

For almost fifteen years after Custer bit
the dust, I had a pleasant deal at Riley—
Got to walk around the Fort and jaw
with Korn the blacksmith, got my eats
and rubdowns, dropped my apples
where I pleased—and all I had to do
was lead the regiment in fancy marches
now and then, draped in mourning

—thanks to Col. Sturgis who had made a speech
concerning Bloody Tragedy and Special Pride
and Desperate Struggle. God and it was hot
and women cried, but anyway, because I didn't fall
at Little Big Horn, Sturgis gave this order:
no one rides or works me.

Fine. No more Keoghs kicking in my guts
("rugged" Capt. Myles Keogh owned and rode me),
no more massacres and thirsty drives—
just me and gentle Korn and swishing flies,
and eventually a decent death.
But look at me, I lived to thirty-one, a tasty age,
And then they shot me full of nothing.

"Comanche! Oh Comanche!: A Narrative in Verse" was written and published in pamphlet form by F. A. Lydic in 1982. This
biographical poem, containing sixty-seven stanzas, details the life
of Keogh's mount, using Dary as its main source. The poem portrays Comanche as

Myles Keogh's peerless steed!
Paragon example of
The wiry mustang breed!

The themes of the horse's plainness and endurance emerge, for
when Keogh bought him

His comrades may have smiled,
Because the "clay-bank" gelding,
Was far from beauty's child.
Keogh did not select him,
For beauty or for grace,
But for stamina to stand,
An army campaign's pace.

After recounting the horse's saga, the poet tells him

Your tale is far from dead.
It lives today in Kansas,
Upon Mount Oread.

He adds that Comanche has become the "deathless symbol" of
the Seventh Cavalry," and closes with the wish

May you be found standing there
At the final "tick" of time.

Lydic was a riverboat man on the Mississippi for over twenty years and, hence, has a special interest in the role of the steamer *Far West* in the Custer story. A few stanzas telling about Comanche's journey aboard this steamer are included in his poem, "The *Far West*'s Race with Death." The reader learns that

> Besides the wounded troopers,
> A battle stricken horse,
> Was brought aboard the steamer,
> Upon that water course.

and that the animal received treatment along with the men, as

> Aboard the river steamer,
> Comanche's wounds were dressed.
> The Seventh's troopers held him,
> As comrades of the rest.

Thus the verses about Comanche communicate the commonly felt compassion and empathy for the ordeal of the silent horse who survived the Custer Battle. Prominent themes in the poems are Comanche's stamina, his faithfulness to his rider, and his bond with his former comrades which brings him honor and allows him to become a surrogate for the expression of grief for the dead cavalrymen. Some of the poets made factual errors which are found in other literary forms dealing with the subject— i.e., referring to sabers being used at the Little Big Horn, reporting the wrong number of fatalities, and citing an erroneous date and place of death for the horse. But the poems transcend such details to attest to the depth of emotion evoked by Comanche and to suggest the surviving cavalry horse's symbolic role in articulating the pathos and glory of Custer's Last Stand.

Songs and Their Composers

Bolder Than an Eagle's Heart

Comanche has been the inspiration for music, as well as poetry. "Tonka," the theme song composed especially for the Disney film, provides a fitting backdrop for the exploits of its equine hero. Songwriter George Bruns, who created the "pulsating, rhythmic melody," explains, "Walt asked us to come up with a very stirring song, one that would typify the spirit of the Sioux and Cheyenne. I believe we did exactly that" (Walt Disney Archives). Comanche is depicted in lyrics written by Gil George as brave, strong, and wild, as well as swift. The heroic horse who is able to span two opposing cultures is extolled through metaphors from nature—the wind, the oak tree, a lightning storm, sounds of thunder, autumn leaves, stars, wind, and an eagle's heart. Though the horse in art and literature often represents a symbolic bridge between people and nature (Lawrence 1985:194–97), in the lyrics of "Tonka," the horse is portrayed as belonging completely to the realm of nature. There is no mention of human mastery or indeed of human intervention of any kind. The song thus places the horse above the hostilities that exist between the two warring cultures that claim him. He transcends all petty human concerns, and, like wild nature itself of which he is a part, stolidly endures. The ballad leaves no doubt that Tonka is the "great one."

Grazing Forever Where the Wild Grasses Grow

Duane Valentry, a writer who has published accounts of the Battle of the Little Big Horn, as well as several articles about Comanche, in various magazines and newspapers, has also created a song about the famous cavalry horse. She composed both the music and the words of the piece, which is entitled "Comanche." Regarding her ballad, which she "wrote in the '60s or '70s," Valentry says, "I always felt close to Comanche," and "sang his song hundreds of times." She remembers that "when I sang it along with my guitar (hoofbeats and all) those listening more than once called it 'moving,' 'stirring,' with some even moved to tears."

Upon first learning the story of Comanche, Valentry "thought it was thrilling—and surely must have been for those soldiers who came upon that hideous field of dead and mutilated to find *a living creature*. And Comanche was a pampered pet from then on. I thought it would make a good song and it has." On the subject of replacing Comanche's label in 1971, Valentry had definite objections. "The change of reading by his remains makes me mad. Although I've written from the Indian side I don't have much feeling for it in this case, anyway, not after reading about the Indian squaws' mutilation of the wounded and dying on the battlefield, which was some of the horror that shocked the nation when the troops came on the scene" (personal communication 1987).

Like many of the poets and writers on the subject, Valentry is mindful of the frustration resulting from Comanche's silence. In one article she asks, "What happened that day, Comanche? You were there. What happened at the Battle of the Little Big Horn? . . . Did the yellow-haired 'Boy General' ride his men into a death trap, sacrificing them for glory? Or was he a brilliant leader

"Tonka." Words: Gil George. Music: George Bruns. © 1958 Walt Disney
Music Company.

outnumbered and outmaneuvered?" But, she notes, "Comanche
never told." More than most writers on the Little Big Horn, Valentry focuses attention on the horses. In an article entitled "The
Horses Died First," she says of the cavalry mounts: "Most of them
were prized, and some were loved, by the men who rode them."
She speculates about what the feelings of the troopers must have

been near the end of the battle, when the decision to "shoot their own mounts in order to form a hurried breastwork" was made. "With Indian bullets and arrows pounding into their mark all around, there was no time for farewell between horse and soldier —only the hasty pointing of a gun and the shot fired—a sacrifice that, in the end, was to be useless after all" (1966:20).

Keogh, she writes, especially "loved the plain army horse on which he had ridden into battle that fateful day," and Comanche

had returned his affection and later mourned for the master who was killed in the battle which the mount alone survived. Valentry believes that as the Custer Battle drew to a close, "It is doubtful, when the troopers shot their horses in order to fire those Springfield one-shot guns over them, that reckless Major Keough [sic] did so. Keough was far too fond of his chestnut bay, Comanche, bought by the army for $90 for his personal use, the horse that had bravely carried him through other Indian skirmishes, the

272

Words and Music by Duane Valentry. Used by permission.

horse he loved." It was out of respect for Comanche's dead master that the famous army order was given that no one would again ride him. The veteran cavalry horse became "an honored and celebrated army mascot until his death many years later, forever a reminder of the tragedy of the Seventh and of the fact, often forgotten, that in war, horses as well as men pay a terrible price" (1959:58; 1966:22).

Duane Valentry has graciously provided the lead sheet for her previously unpublished song about the brave horse, Comanche, and his life of glory in the world beyond.

DUANE VALENTRY
4121 CALLE JUNO
SAN CLEMENTE, CA. 92672

Running Wild and Free

Les and Sandee Orestad wrote and recorded twelve songs about Custer and the Little Big Horn included in an album released in 1987. One ballad, "Comanche," details the horse's life, following Luce's biography. It begins when the horse was "born on the open prairie," continues through his acquisition by the army, his purchase by "a big strong man, Myles W. Keogh," his naming for bravery, his discovery after the battle as he "stood alone," the "lone survivor of the Seventh," through his retirement during which he "lived a good long time." The song's refrain, not surprisingly, is "Brave horse of the Seventh Cavalry!" At the end, the lyrics declare that Comanche is now "Running wild and running free." So the faithful mount has come full circle —born in freedom and returning to freedom. He has gone from wild to tame, and back to wild, living out the transformations that are characteristic of the equine species. He thus recapitulates the history of the American mustang, who, though descended from countless generations of Old World domesticated stock, successfully adjusted to the feral state on the western plains. Comanche, like many other steeds, has become a symbol of freedom.

Comanche, the Good Soldier, Who Fought Hard and Tried

It was on April 10th, the anniversary of the date of issuance of General Sturgis' Orders No. 7, that I arrived in Nashville, Tennessee, to meet Frances Bandy, composer of the popular 1960 ballad "Comanche (The Brave Horse)." Fran herself reminded me "this was the day Comanche got his honors." I had long admired the song and looked forward to meeting its creator. Fran arrived at the appointed time, bringing me a gift of the Johnny Horton record that included her song and some fragrant purple irises, the state flower of Tennessee. We spent an unforgettable day and evening together, sharing a spontaneous friendship. When we parted, Fran said "You're special," and that expressed the way I felt about her—and the song she had created.

Months before, I had contacted Fran with the help of the Country Music Foundation Library and Media Center in Nashville. An official from that organization had written in response to my inquiry about "Comanche" that Fran Bandy "as it turns out wrote the entire song and only put Johnny Horton's name on it since he agreed to record it." Fran responded immediately to my letter, expressing pleasure in my appreciation of "Comanche," the song which, she confided "has a special place in my heart." She said she was "very interested and honored" by the prospects of an interview with me.

"I wrote 'Comanche,' " Fran told me, "at about the time when Johnny Horton was doing his best things. I was beginning to write songs, and this was my second or third song. Johnny Horton was interested in historic things, and I was open for something historic." She happened to be looking through an issue of *Coronet* magazine, she recalled, and read the article "The Lone Survivor" (Greenspan 1956:158). The article inspired her to write a song. She composed the song, put it on tape, and brought it to the Hi-

Lo Music Company. When Johnny Horton was contacted, he asked if it were a true story; Fran responded that it was. She vividly remembers Johnny Horton playing the song back to her on the telephone, with the hoofbeat accompaniment that sounded so appropriate.

Discussing the factors that motivated her to write the song about a horse, Fran said

> Animals play such an important part in a person's life and survival, yet how little honor, kindness, and loyalty they get in return! Animals have contributed so much to people's happiness. They give unselfish and undemanding love. Children need them. When I was little, we lived in the country and I had a wonderful spotted pony called Lady. I also had a small white dog, Trixie, that I loved. When Trixie died, my father buried her in the old family graveyard. In the spring, I remember buttercups growing on the grave, and I was so close to that dog that I still cry when I see buttercups, or even white hair. It's a sad thing when animals die. When my father killed a hog on our farm, I hid under the bed, with my fingers in my ears. I couldn't kill chickens or other animals. An animal has so much intelligence. But no matter what they're thinking, they can't tell you about it. The Maker has limited them in this way.

"I'm interested in making a study of animals which are outstanding for one reason or another," Fran said. She continued

> When I read about Comanche, I thought of what the horse must have felt. I had to imagine what a horse would think and feel, and what the situation was like around it. I'm a sensitive person, and I express my own emotions when I write a song. I paint a picture. You have to work hard to express it right. Sometimes you think you have expressed it well, but people don't get the idea; then you have to "re-express" it. You want to make sure another person would understand it. You must feel what the horse felt, to write the song. Songs express how I would feel under a certain set of circumstances or how another person or an animal feels.

Speaking about the famous battle, Fran said

> Comanche did his duty, and I wanted to tell his story. I feel sorry for both sides in the Battle of the Little Big Horn. The Indians were trying to survive, and the white man was trying to prevent it. People were taking their land. One songwriter once asked me, "Why would anyone write a song about that horse?" Later, I found out this man was married to an Indian, and that's why he felt this way. At the Little Big Horn, as in any other war, people were following their ruler. It might or might not reflect a person's own views. In World War II, we were taught to hate, but I don't feel animosity toward any human beings. They have no control over what they did. Our boys did what they had to do.

Animals and human beings both do what they have to do for survival. There's a strong instinct for survival. Animals are brave by choice as well as by instinct. When tested, human beings have more fearless instincts than they think. That horse, Comanche, was there because someone led it there. I've always wondered why, after two days, it didn't stray from the immediate battleground, out of fear. Any battle is tragic, especially that one at the Little Big Horn. Comanche had bravery, or else he would have jumped or run into the bushes when the battle began. He was very brave not to run away. The odds were against him that day.

"So many people," Fran noted, "take credit for what other people or animals do. The general takes credit in a battle, and people forget about the little guy and the animals that contribute. In the same way, songwriters are the least-known people in show business. They don't get the credit. The one who sings the songs gets the credit."

Bandy's sense of her own close association with Comanche's story reflects an almost universal feeling. The theme of personal identification with the wounded but heroic horse is a compelling one, shared not only by lyricists and poets, but by multitudes of others who, through the years, have demonstrated interest in and admiration for the Seventh Cavalry horse. Bandy's central focus is bravery, whereas Valentry's is immortality, a theme recurrent in poetic images of Comanche's heavenly reunion with his master. As is true of the fiction writers and poets, each of the lyricists in turn expresses certain facets of Comanche's complex existence and meaning.

In the songs as in the poems, descriptions of unspeakable suffering and carnage, and the horse's ability to rise above these conditions, often take on religious overtones and impart a kind of sacredness to the lone equine survivor. More than any other figure or symbol of the celebrated battle, the "battle-scarred and torn" but still living horse becomes the perfect representation of the tragic clash of cultures at the Little Big Horn. For ironically, the Indians' overwhelming victory over Custer's force turned out to be a precipitating cause of their own ultimate destruction, whereas the army's utter defeat brought in its wake total victory over the foe. In an analogous way, Comanche, a fighter on the side which lost, is nevertheless a winner through his own remarkable survival against the odds. Bandy's characterization of Comanche as "a good soldier" who "gave your all" expresses the mighty effort that is required in order to triumph in the face of such a horrifying disaster.

To this day in the national consciousness, Custer and the

men of his command are known for their undying courage in fighting to the end at their "Last Stand" on the hilltop, even though outnumbered and surrounded. So, too, the Sioux and Cheyenne, declaring "it is a good day to die," are remembered for rallying all the power they possessed to oppose the white civilization, though undoubtedly mindful that it would inevitably engulf them. Metaphorically, Indians, troopers, and especially the brave Comanche who "alone" was able to surmount the catastrophe, stand for all people—as inspiration to take up arms against our own difficulties and meet life's woes with the same calm tenacity and grace as the deathless wounded horse, whose "deeds did speak loud" as the silent "symbol of bravery at the Little Big Horn."

Frances Bandy generously provided the words and music of her song for inclusion in this book, and they are reprinted here with the kind permission of Knox Phillips, Hi-Lo Music, Inc.

COMANCHE
(The Brave Horse)

Words & Music by
Francis Bandy & Johnny Horton

1. The battle was over at Custer's last stand, and
(2. Though) you are silent, your deeds did speak loud, if your

taps were sounding for all the brave men. While
buddies could see you I know they'd be proud. The

one lone survivor wounded and weak, Com-
symbol of bravery at the Little Big Horn,

anche, the brave horse lay at the Gen-'ral's feet.
poor ole Com-anche, battle-scarred and torn.

Chorus

Com-anche, you've fought hard, Com-anche, you tried. You

were a good soldier, so hold your head up high.

Even the greatest sometimes must fall; Com-

anche the brave horse, you gave your all. 2. Though all.

© Copyright 1960 by Hi-Lo Music, Inc. and Magic Circle Publishing Co., 706 Union, Memphis, TN All rights reserved.

"Comanche," by Johnny Horton and Frances Bandy. Hi-Lo Music, Inc., used by permission.

Chapter 14

Comanche's Appeal and Meaning

> The moment of survival is the moment of power. . . . All
> grief is insignificant measured against this elemental triumph.
> . . . The essence of the situation is that he [is] unique. (Ca-
> netti 1973:227)

The concept of Comanche as the legendary "sole survivor" of
Custer's Last Stand has persisted from the time of the horse's discovery through the present day. The exclusive status of Keogh's
mount has been eloquently defended by many writers over the
years. A typical statement on the subject was written forty-eight
years after the horse's rescue: "The only authentic sole survivor
of the tragic battle of the Little Big Horn, connected with Custer's company was 'Comanche' an honored horse. . . . To detract
from 'Comanche's' distinction is unworthy and leaves a chapter in
history that is misleading." The authors conclude: "There may
have been many who served in 1876 with honor, and with records
unofficially attached to their passing away to the bugle call of
eternity, but careful search of the records of that bloody catastrophe will bear out the statement that 'Comanche' was the sole survivor of Custer's last battle" (Brown and Willard 1924:221–22).

Even today, in spite of Indian protest during the 1970s and
in the face of frequently cited historical proof to the contrary,
Comanche's niche in fame is firmly carved as "the only survivor"
of the Seventh Cavalry's famous battle with Indians. In a recent
publication describing Disney programs on cable television, for
example, Keogh, White Bull, and the horse are pictured in a scene
from the film—with the caption "The Lone Survivor of the Little
Big Horn: TONKA" (A Winter Festival 1986–87:back cover).
The image promises to be more pervasive, for the newly released

videocassette of *Tonka* is now so popular that "we just can't keep it in stock," one big New York dealer recently told me.

As pointed out in Chapter 12, even when writers have made a deliberate effort to avoid the designation of uniqueness for Comanche's survival, somehow this quality just will not be denied, and almost invariably surfaces, as though out of the collective unconscious. Discussing the horse, Evan S. Connell asks why "the legend persists of a lone survivor." Responding to his own question, he states naively, "It is as reasonable to ask why the myth of Custer's long hair persists when there is no doubt that on the campaign his hair was short. He expected to be in the field several weeks and long hair collects dirt." But, "nevertheless at the climactic moment General Custer must have flowing locks. So it is with Keogh's horse—the one survivor" (1984:295–96). Thus in effect, by viewing Custer's hair only in a pragmatic light and thereby dismissing the whole issue of its potent symbolism, the writer begs the question of analysis of the sole survivor concept—a theme also charged with deep significance.

Psychologically, it makes sense that if there is only *one* individual who survives after a great calamity, then the risks and dangers involved in that event must be assumed to have been very great indeed. As soon as more than one survivor is conceptualized, however, the degree of risk is perceived as much lower. There is no question that the uniqueness of the condition of survivorhood vastly increases the importance of its object. Exclusivity is a vital component of the special status accorded to a survivor. By channelling all the emotion evoked by survival to one creature, instead of diffusing the feeling among many, it is far stronger and productive of a more powerful symbolic attribution. Thus Comanche is not just a horse with remarkable endurance, but becomes the paragon of endurance.

The fame of the lone equine survivor, of course, cannot be separated from the epic grandeur and pathos of the Little Big Horn. Comanche is very much a part of the perpetual popular appeal of the flamboyant, brash, romantic, and heroic image of General George Armstrong Custer and of the men he led to doom and immortality on a Montana hillside. Deeply entrenched in legend is the mistaken idea that the entire Seventh Cavalry, rather than just Custer and his immediate command, was wiped out in the great battle. The total annihilation of a battalion is, of course, the very epitome of glorious tragedy. Symbols do their work precisely and well. Referring to Comanche as "the sole survivor" not only discounts Indians and other cavalry mounts who lived through the engagement, as well as several alleged canine survivors, but more significantly, reinforces the dramatic misconception that no man of the exalted regiment lived.

There have been many human claimants for the status of sole survivor among participants of Custer's Last Stand. It has been said, in fact, that "had all the bogus 'last survivors' only been ranged with Custer in that fight, his troops would probably have outnumbered the Indians against whom they fought" (Comanche and the Custer Fight 1939). Douglas W. Ellison, who studied the case of the best-known purported survivor, Frank Finkel, places the number of claimants more conservatively at "well over a hundred" (1983:5). Curley, a Crow scout who served with the Seventh, was for a time mistakenly regarded as a survivor. In reality, though, he was hired as a guide in locating the Sioux, not as a soldier, and he did not remain with the regiment during the fight.

At the very heart of the unusually intense popular appeal of the Battle of the Little Big Horn is the mystery of the episode. Countless Custer Battle buffs have told me that fascination with the enigma is responsible for their profound interest in the subject. This intrigue explains why the question of survivors is so crucial for dedicated Custer enthusiasts. A journalist who interviewed members of the Little Big Horn Associates (an organization whose purpose is to study the Battle of the Little Big Horn and the life and times of George A. Custer) concluded "the unknowns about the Last Stand seem to be as fascinating as General Custer himself." "Custer fans" told him, "There's such an element of mystery and excitement about Custer. . . . There's a veil of mystery around the whole thing." The classic remark on the subject which most vehemently expresses the attachment that buffs show to the concept of an unanswerable mystery (obviously overriding any deeper concerns) came from the man called by the Associates "the Dean of Custer Scholars." Dr. Lawrence Frost, author of numerous Custer books, told the interviewer, "Thank God there weren't any survivors!" (Richards 1985; Horn 1987).

Recent archaeological finds at the Little Big Horn may help to put in place some pieces of the puzzle but never in the same way that a survivor would have. Commenting on the results of the excavations in the *New York Times*, the superintendent of the Custer Battlefield National Monument explained that "part of the renewed interest [in the area] may be because a greater understanding of the site only deepens the mystery surrounding the battle. From the time Custer rode into Medicine Tail Coulee until the bodies were found, we still don't know anything about what happened. . . . And it's the mystery about what really happened, the mystery of it all, that keeps bringing people back to this place." A response in disagreement with this statement was soon published. A firm letter to the editor pointed out that "The hundreds of Sioux who defeated Custer knew what happened, and years later several who were still alive told the story of that fateful day." The writer went on to cite sources where such documentation can be found (Peterson 1986:A18; Weiss 1986:A22).

As Soubier points out, "there were no army survivors in the five companies under Custer's immediate command, and it is this lack of official witnesses which forms the basis of much of the Custer mythology, and in turn, Comanche's aura. The Custer buff stands glassy-eyed before the mounted hide muttering 'if he could only speak!' Since many Indian accounts of the battle exist, the implication is that the testimony of an Army horse would be more credible than an Indian's" (1970:3). The mystery surrounding the Custer Battle that makes it so intriguing is enhanced by its "only survivor," who, lacking speech, could never destroy the fascination generated by the enigma. Swearingen expressed this mystique when he wrote that after many years of study about Comanche, "I know one thing for sure: the reason he is such an important, enchanting beast is that we really don't, and won't ever know all the real, actual details" (UK Archives).

Even one of the legendary dogs that lived through the battle is associated with mysterious information, forever lost to history. A big black dog was reportedly seen by Indians escaping after the fight, "just as the last white man went down." It was first spotted "running around among the horses with a bundle of papers tied to its collar," before it finally "took off north." Indians chased the animal for twenty miles, but "could neither catch nor kill it," and "then lost track." Thus the content of those papers, which might have held the key to some of the battle's enigmas, "remains one of the unsolved mysteries of the west." Nor was any information provided by "Smoke," a terrier who had been rescued from the battlefield where his Indian master had been killed and adopted into the family of Captain Eugene Gibbs (Echoes of Custer's Last Fight 1912; Canine Survivor 1910; Smoke 1910).

The only survivor to gain widespread acceptance and to have stood the test of time, however, is Comanche who, though also mute, has been able to communicate in many ways. Ever since the time of the Custer Battle, when the impact of the totality of the tragedy was enhanced by the existence of a lone survivor, reasons have been sought for Comanche's seemingly miraculous escape from death. Many explanations have been proposed for his mysterious tenacity for life. Among these have been his color, because buckskin horses are believed to be more resilient, or his breeding, since mustang blood confers toughness. The quality of invulnerability gives a supernatural or magical quality to the horse, raising the question of his possible protection through the luck of a charmed life, or by means of a special talisman, vow of sacrifice, or prayer. And assumptions have been made that such great strength as Comanche's could only come from a former harsh existence as an Indian mount, inuring him to the harrowing experiences that would have destroyed an ordinary cavalry horse.

In his treatise on the horse in history, Basil Tozer notes that some cavalrymen have observed that "a wounded horse gives in at once, that he seems to have no heart" (1908:105). But Comanche, wounded many times in his cavalry duties, was a notable exception. It is Keogh's mount's unusual endurance which prompted one writer to begin his narrative about Comanche by stating, "This is not the story of [a] horse's devotion to his master, but of a horse who came to honor through his own endurance" (Reid 1952:139). Comanche's endurance is a very important part of his image, both in reality and legend, and is always emphasized in descriptions of him at all stages of life. Pain did not prevent him from attaining the military ideal of stoicism. After the battle, when the soldiers found that "Comanche was alive to greet them," it was noted that "like a good warrior he stood erect and strove to be alert" in spite of his wounds (Only Survivor 1926). In his old age, Comanche was still exceptionally hardy. Seventh Cavalry Captain P. W. Wey described what the regimental veterinarian considered "a remarkable feat" of endurance. The 28-year-old mount "made an overland march with the regiment in 1887 from Fort Meade, D. T., to Fort Riley, Kansas," a distance of "approximately 900 miles," and he "accomplished this without apparent fatigue, covering as high as 25 to 30 miles per day" (1926:433). Comanche was characterized as possessing that "courageous spirit so often found in patricians of the human race," a quality "not found in the ordinary cavalry horse" (Benninghoff 1935:69).

It is said that the "gallant bay will never 'fade away'" for he is "part of our national heritage" and stands for "the courage and character of 'old soldiers who never die'" (Epperson n.d.). People identify strongly with Comanche's extraordinary endurance. As the one living creature in Custer's command that even the victorious Indians did not destroy, the horse redeems the Last Stand from total disaster and is a metaphor for hope in the face of defeat. As Custer's hilltop fight came to represent the universal human condition of being surrounded by a sea of troubles, so Comanche's survival symbolizes a triumph in the struggle against life's woes and difficulties.

Although Comanche was not considered a fast horse, the speed that he might have acquired on the day of the battle as a result of his devotion to his dead rider has been cited as a reason for the mount's survival. "There are many stories about how the Sioux who annihilated Custer and his men tried to capture Commanche but the beast would not be taken by the warriors who slew his master." The writer goes on to say that "a huge mural, which shows the Sioux trying to run down Commanche, adorns a wall at the service club at the veterans hospital at Ft. Meade" (Morrell 1949). I was able to find that mural in the recreation hall of the hospital, but it turned out to be a portrayal of three Indians chasing a white horse. Bear Butte, a Black Hills landmark, and two Indian villages appear in the background. The only label on the work reads "5th Cavalry, 1943." Probably the mistaken identification is related to an article published two years earlier in a Black Hills newspaper in which Comanche was cited as "a white horse" (Custer's Massacre 1942). The provocative idea that Comanche survived because the Indians could not catch him is vividly depicted in the painting "Get Comanche!" owned by John Carroll, as described in Chapter 13 (see fig. 31).

Comanche's feat of endurance at Custer's Last Stand is generally attributed not to a particular set of circumstances intrinsic to the battle itself, but rather to the horse's own individual strength—his will to survive and his physical stamina. Though Comanche's own qualities were essential, interaction with his rider, in all probability, had contributed to his survival. "Faithfulness and fortitude" were the twin virtues represented by Comanche (Benninghoff 1935:70). Reports of the discovery of Comanche after the battle often indicate that he was found standing near Keogh's body. One account details that "he watched by his master's body, although wounded in a dozen places, for days and nights, and when the rescuers came there he stood, gaunt, starving, wounded, but faithful to the dead man" (Owen 1926; Sole Survivor 1926). Many writers on the subject make a close association between a strong bond of devotion with Keogh and the horse's remarkable survival. The theme of fidelity between horse and rider is an almost invariable element in the Comanche saga. Although the particulars of his life before the great battle, along with details about his color, breeding, birthdate, and place of origin, may be argued, his loyalty to his rider is seldom questioned. And Keogh, with the typical Irishman's "eye for a horse," is always portrayed as having an especially close relationship with his mount.

Illustrating the correlation between Keogh's bond to his

horse and Comanche's survival is the report stating "some Indians say [the horse] broke away and ran, but the more popular version is that, his master being unable to consider the thought of taking the life of the beast who had served him so well, dismounted and, giving the animal a stinging blow with his sword, drove him away and turned his unprotected front to the foe." Comanche then "dashed over the steppe," and "the Indians, being on foot, made way rather than meet death beneath his hoofs" (He's Joined 1891). There is also a story told in later years by Little Soldier, a Sioux Indian who as a boy had fought at the Little Big Horn. In answering the question "why did Comanche live when the other 276 horses were killed and why wasn't he taken by the Indians?" Little Soldier related that near the end of the battle, the white soldiers "killed their mounts to serve as cover from behind which they fired. However, Keogh retained his mount for emergency duties." Little Soldier's

> version is that Custer followed the ridge when Captain Keogh, with his detachment, turned down a narrow ravine and went toward the water. They were driven back and as they arrived at the summit Captain Keogh halted and gave the command to dismount, kill the horses and get behind them and fight. Every horse was killed but Comanche which Keogh was riding. The Captain kneeled between Comanche's front legs and shot from under his breast. Every man was killed, Keogh had two bullet wounds in his body but he died gripping the bridle reins tightly in his hands. It was the Indian's regard for the Spirit that saved Comanche. He had no fear of Keogh alive but Keogh dead and holding his horse was something different. Every other man was stripped, scalped, and mutilated except General Custer, which was in line of their usual respect for the commanding officer. But Captain Keogh was not touched, the crucifix was not taken from his neck, he was not scalped.
>
> Little Soldier was a boy of 17 when he went into that battle with Chief Gall and admitted that he was sorely in need of a horse but opined that, "No Indian would take that horse when a dead man was holding the rein." (Charles 1941:4; Corpse Saves Comanche 1941)

Evidently this tradition of respecting the unity between a horse and rider in this way was not always observed. Dewey Beard, a Sioux warrior who participated in the Battle of the Little Big Horn, stated in a 1935 interview that the "soldier chief" the Indians called "Long Hair" (Custer), had died "with the reins of his horse's bridle tied to his wrist. It was a fine animal, a blaze-faced sorrel with four white stockings [Vic]. A Santee named Walks-Under-the-Ground took that horse" (Miller 1971:38).

Stressing Comanche's partnership with Keogh, Luce wrote

that following Keogh's death, "It is not at all improbable that for two days he stood faithful watch over his beloved master, nuzzling him, trying to awaken him, hoping that his rider was only sleeping as he had so often seen him do on many hard and tedious marches" (1939:64). Both Smith and Luce wrote of the horse: "Returning again and again to the field, he seemed to be seeking someone and neighed softly, as though to call some beloved master. His bewildered eyes appeared to seek familiar faces and to summon back the affection of human friends" (Smith 1927:36; Luce 1939:64). It is true that in some instances a faithful horse will stand guard over its master and rouse him in time of danger (Hudson 1903:355).

Many present-day readers, lacking close and prolonged contact with horses, consider such descriptions to be romantic exaggerations. Total mechanization of modern life and the relegation of horses to recreational purposes that generally provide, at most, short and infrequent periods of interaction between horses and people have obliterated our understanding of the potential for such behavior. Yet it is possible, given the number of hours that Keogh spent alone with his mount in garrison, and particularly on expeditions, that Comanche might have reacted in a manner like that described.

Indeed, strikingly similar behavior, showing the "mutual friendship" and "close and affectionate relationship between the soldier and his horse" was recorded in a diary kept by a British cavalryman who fought in a 1794 campaign.

> A soldier would as soon see his comrade killed as his horse; and that the horse has an equal regard for, and knowledge of his master, will be seen in the following fact, which though in some measure a contradiction of what has been observed of a horse returning to his troop, when his rider is dismounted, yet it nevertheless shows equal sagacity in the animal. A dragoon being shot in a skirmish on the borders of a wood, was left behind by his own party, they not having it in their power to carry him off, on account of the numbers of the enemy who were coming up, and as he fell from his horse when he received the ball, his comrades concluded that he was dead, which was actually the case. A patrol coming by the place about two days afterwards, discovered the body, with the horse feeding by it, and which the poor creature had never quitted, as was plainly seen by the grass being eaten close within a few yards round the body. When they buried the corpse on the spot, the faithful animal seemed to show great reluctance to come away without his master, frequently turning his head and neighing, as if wishing his dead master to come and mount him; this was an old horse that had lived with one rider many years. (Lamb 1938:193–94).

After Keogh's death, as Luce describes it, "Comanche was now riderless. Captain Keogh had taught him leadership, and now he was in supreme command, the last living remnant of the 'Second Balaklava' " (1939:64). As previously mentioned, Luce has been criticized for this statement alleged to be "completely inane" and worthy of the "cavalry rebuttal"—"Horseshit!" (Magnussen 1974:275–76). It is easy, so many years after the event, in our mechanized age, to dismiss Luce's words on the grounds of romanticism. What exactly did Luce, a former cavalryman himself, mean by "leadership" and "command" as they related to a riderless horse? As is evident to a person who has spent a lifetime closely interacting with horses, a skilled and concerned horseman —as Keogh seems to have been—working in relationship to a responsive horse—as Comanche must have been—would bring out the best capacities in that animal. Through a dynamic interrelationship of man and horse through eight years, reinforcement of the finest equine capabilities would undoubtedly occur. It follows that Comanche would have acquired a kind of presence, a set of qualities that would indeed distinguish him through the possession of confidence, a strength that combined both physical and nonphysical qualities. In a horse, this trait is called "heart," and characterizes a mount who will give the extra measure of effort to carry out whatever task he is asked to perform. There is a sense of "do or die" in such an animal, for he will often accomplish nearly impossible feats to comply with the will of his rider.

The point that Luce makes has also to do with the unity between man and mount. Comanche and his rider shared a sense of identity, which is not an uncommon phenomenon. Comanche now seems to represent his fallen rider and, by extension, his dead comrades-in-arms as well. Luce's interpretation places heavy emphasis on the horse being the "last living remnant" of the regiment and compares the heroic "Last Stand" with the "Charge of the Light Brigade," where brave cavalrymen were also outnumbered. The idea of leadership seems to imply that there was a dead man and a living horse. The torch was passed to the only part of that man's self which still existed.

A true cavalryman, like any keen horseman, knows that horses demonstrate a remarkable plasticity enabling them to adapt their behavior to the particular rider and situation at hand. Comanche's long experience on the frontier as the mount of Captain Keogh had undoubtedly inculcated the qualities that meant he would not panic even under the worst of circumstances, and this contributed to his ability for survival. "Leadership," then, refers to the tenacity Comanche showed in living, enduring as a survivor in the context of utter chaos and destruction, defying the death and ugliness of his surroundings, embodying the only known contrast to and relief from the grief and shock of those who first encountered the grisly evidence of the Custer tragedy. As a discovered and identified living element that had once been in close partnership with those cavalrymen now dead, his quality of endurance has given Comanche the metaphorical "supreme command." Even Luce's account of the wounded horse's actions during the interval following the battle until he was found on or about June 27 is likely correct. The idea of Comanche's going to the stream to "slake his ever-increasing thirst," and making his way "with careful step between the bodies of the fallen troopers and horses" has ethological authenticity, for horses have the ability to find water sources under such conditions and do refrain from treading on objects like bodies whenever possible.

There is, in fact, evidence to support the probable existence of an affective relationship between the Captain and his horse. Keogh's Irish heritage likely predisposed him to a special interest in horses, and it is assumed he had a quality called "the Irishman's inherent way with a horse" (Watson 1983:15). His letters, as mentioned in Chapter 5, contain references to his mounts, suggesting a more than routine concern for them. An undated note written to him by Anthony Keogh about the condition of a horse, Paddy, obviously represents a reply to an inquiry made by Myles about the animal (author's collection). A fellow cavalryman who served with him in the Civil War remembered that Myles Keogh "rode a horse like a Centaur" (Allen 1898:227), a quality which, at a time when everyone rode horses, implies a dynamic interaction with the mount rather than a mechanical sense of mastery. His written documents reveal Keogh as a romantic, brooding, sometimes melancholy person—lonely, or at least tending to be a "loner." An 1863 letter to Tom indicates, "I have too few real friends in this world," and in numerous letters on file at the National Library of Dublin, he repeatedly reveals a deep loneliness. Referring to his parting with his brother, he admitted in 1867 "I am no happier today than I was then, and I feel that the strife is very much all the happiness I shall probably have." An 1869 letter indicates that "I never propose to form any ties and the future is so uncertain that I often feel a great deal cast down," and that "life is monotonous." In 1867 he wrote that the only thing besides "raising of our flagstaff tomorrow" which relieves his boredom is "the great event" of "my dog Spot having seven little puppies." From Willowbrook in New York in 1868, he indicated he was shipping "five dogs by rail" to Kansas.

Individuals with such temperaments and concerns often (though by no means always) show a tendency to form close bonds with animals, and it is not too far-fetched to postulate that the long hours spent with his horse and their sharing of experiences would foster such a relationship. If the recorded anecdotes of Comanche's continuing to carry his master even when wounded in several early skirmishes are authentic, then such stoical behavior would certainly have endeared the mount to the man whose life depended upon him.

It is true that as the Custer Battle drew to a close and the cavalrymen were overwhelmed, many shot their horses for protective breastworks. As noted previously, Keogh did not do this. So there may be truth in the idea that the regard in which his master held him was an influential factor in preserving Comanche's life. The mount's strength and willingness to obey Keogh, too, may have kept that officer alive longer than would otherwise have been the case. Indian testimony led David H. Miller to believe that Keogh may have been the last man of Custer's detachment to be killed (1957:154). As previously mentioned, evidence indicates that Keogh was mounted on Comanche until the end, for the burial party observed from the nature of the rider's and the horse's wounds that the same bullet hit them both and they went down together (Luce 1939:60). Thus a circumstance that would appear to be the stuff of legends is in this case historically documented.

Consideration of the possible strong attachment between Keogh and Comanche inevitably raises the issue of just what was the nature of the usual relationship between cavalryman and horse. If one can generalize at all, this is an important and intriguing question, yet seldom if ever has it been pursued in any depth. A reader must search, and search almost in vain, for references to specific information about human-horse relationships in books devoted to the cavalry—regardless of the era in which they were written. Tactics, battle histories, accoutrements, uniforms, and arms occupy page after page, chapter after chapter. The living, sentient animal that was part of the human/horse unit and affected the battle's outcome was largely ignored. Perhaps the writers were merely ignorant of the horses' role. Undoubtedly their customary outlook, molded by society and culture, was anthropocentric. Or it is possible that the subject would have been overwhelming in its emotional ramifications, once it was raised. It may be that the debt to a nonhuman creature was simply too great, the acknowledgment of it too psychologically costly. At any rate, the topic of what the cavalryman thought about and felt toward his mount rarely receives a sentence in most standard cavalry books before the subject is closed. So the issue has been one which, if not considered taboo, was treated rather as nonexistent than as unimportant.

If people think about the cavalryman's relationship to his horse, or when they are pressed to do so, their perceptions reflect more about themselves than about their knowledge of the topic. Those disillusioned with the feeling aspects of life, who are detached from meaningful experience with animals and nature and who tend to view the world pragmatically, say that the cavalry horse was considered more or less as a tool, held without regard except as a necessary object for exploitation. One writer referring to Civil War conditions mentions "the ingrained cavalry tradition that cavalry horses were as expendable as paper plates are now" (Gray 1977:250), and of course this may have been true for vast numbers of soldiers. Some people, however, often erroneously dubbed "romantic" or idealistic, whose temperaments allow projected empathetic understanding of what might have transpired between man and mount, or those whose own experiences have included close bonds with animals, feel that there indeed was in *some* cases a kind of "love" between a cavalryman and his horse.

"Love" is in quotation marks because much of the problem intrinsic to this controversy arises from the broad range of linguistic meanings in this overused word. Naturally, love for a cavalry horse would not generally include components of protective pampering or indulgence as toward a true "pet" or animal companion that is not utilitarian. But that does not exclude solicitous respect for the animal, caring for it sincerely but at the same time doing so within the bounds of its understood use and purpose. Mutual dependency, which gives rise to deep affective attachments, could well have been responsible for close man/mount relationships in the cavalry.

I have argued that the treatment given to their horses by certain Indians which appears callous or cruel by different cultural standards arises out of the tribesmen's own self-image as tough and hardy and their respect for animals who are able to exist independent of human care and concern (Lawrence 1985: 49–51). So it probably was also true of the cavalry soldier that his own life of hardship, which subjected him to danger and discomfort, would predispose him to expect from his horse-partner comparable stoicism and physical endurance. "Coddling" was not a component in his attitude toward himself, his comrades—or his horse.

There are some instances where light shines through the shadows to illuminate the question of horse and man in the Seventh Cavalry. Jacob Horner, a trooper of Company K who did not participate in the Custer Battle because he was without a horse at the time, provided several interviews about his cavalry experiences which were later published. He related that after his discharge, he learned one day that the Seventh was encamped near his home. He drove out to the area "to see the boys. I also wanted to see my old horse." He had no trouble picking out the mount from a herd of one hundred. "I spent considerable time patting him and I was sorry when the time came to leave." Horner stated that

> The cavalrymen grew very fond of their horses and spent a great deal of time caring for them. The name of each horse was inscribed over his stall. The owners delighted in foraging for special treats for their animals. Each horse appeared to have a personality of its own.

Some horses, Horner pointed out, were difficult to handle, being prone to nip or kick. He had been glad when one mount whose "dancing, prancing gait when traveling with other horses in formation" had "caused him considerable grief" was condemned. After that, he chose a "fine sorrel pacer" with a very comfortable gait. When "women at the fort fell in love with the horse," he had to complain in order to stop officers' wives from being allowed to ride it. When asked for his own estimate of Custer, Horner noted that "most of the men did not like him. He was too hard on the men and horses" (Johnson 1949:26–27).

Sergeant Charles P. Windolph, who was with Benteen's troop at the Little Big Horn, died in 1950, the last surviving participant of the famous battle. From first-hand interviews, his story was published. Recalling one of his cavalry marches, Windolph said

> We'd make two or three stops every day to water and feed our horses, and cook our own meals. Each man would look after his own horse, and we'd usually give him a little exercise and a good rubdown. All troop horses were geldings, though once in a while an officer would have his own privately owned mare.
>
> A trooper thought a lot of his mount, and a cavalryman would have to be pretty mean who wouldn't take good care of his horse. If we got a good chance we'd steal a little extra oats or hay for our individual mounts. My horse at this time was named Pig. That wasn't his real name, but I called him that because nothing could keep him from rolling in a mud hole when he was being watered, after we'd come in from a long ride. He was fast and he could show his heels to most of the horses in the regiment. I thought a lot of him but the army condemned him after we'd been in the Dakota country a year

or two. . . . Two or three years after the army sold him, I saw him in a contractor's six-horse team in the Black Hills. He looked so poor and abused, I'd have bought him from the contractor but I didn't have the money. I went up to him and petted him. He knew me all right. He nickered and looked at me as much as to say, "Come on, please, Charlie, get me out of here." I had ridden old Pig thousands of miles, and more than once he saved my life. I pretty near cried when I saw him that time in the Black Hills. (Hunt 1947:9–10).

Former Seventh Cavalryman John Ryan related that "On many occasions, I have shared my rations with my horse, and have even crept around in the night to pilfer a little forage for him" (1912). Ryan wrote that upon obtaining his discharge six months after the Little Big Horn Battle

> I went to the stable and gave my horse a thorough good grooming, an extra feed of oats, patted him on the neck and said goodbye. If it had not been for that horse I would not be here today to write this story. I rode him ten years on every skirmish, engagement and campaign that Custer was on while lieutenant colonel of the Seventh Cavalry.

He added, "I felt as if I had the blues when leaving the company of old friends whom I had served with for 10 years, and especially my horse." Ryan evidently followed the fortunes of his mount, for he noted: "I afterwards learned that the horse was taken by Major G. Tilford of the Seventh Cavalry, and used for some years afterward" (1980:191, 192).

As described in Chapter 1, Godfrey, whose gray Indian pony found upon the battlefield was obviously treasured, had called to the animal using the Indian word for "friend." And Infantry Captain Walter Clifford, who arrived at the scene of Reno's fight after the battle, showed empathy for a badly injured Indian pony who laid his head on his own horse's rump, "looking straight at me, as if pleading for help." He spared the horse "the lingering agony that must follow if left to himself" by shooting it (Burdick 1940:54). The event was important enough to document in some detail, even in the presence of the overwhelming amount of human suffering and death which was encountered.

Evidence of attachment to their mounts on the part of Seventh Cavalrymen comes from the words of the men themselves and from their diaries. Because it required changes in the assignment of horses, General Custer's 1869 order about "coloring" of the troops under his command, already referred to in Chapter 2, was extremely disturbing to some of the affected men. Captain

Benteen, for example, was furious when he "found that Custer had taken away his 'fine mount of horses' in a little exercise called *coloring the horses.*" This European cavalry tradition meant that the horses were arranged within the regiment by color and by company, with each company riding horses of the same color. Benteen was particularly resentful that Custer had initiated the change which would put the men on unfamiliar horses "at the beginnings of the severest campaign that ever cavalry underwent"—the winter campaign planned by General Sheridan. Benteen, who "had gone to extraordinary lengths to obtain the best possible horses for his own company, was penalized in effect by the change" (Mills 1985:156–57).

Captain Albert Barnitz also indicated his sharp disapproval of the plan in his journal for November 10, 1868:

> General Custer is requiring all the company commanders to exchange horses, so as to secure a uniformity of colors in each company. I have bitterly opposed the scheme, but must comply, I suppose. All my old horses were well trained, and very carefully trained, and the men were much attached to them, and now, just as we are to march on the campaign, every thing is to be turned topsy turvy!—There is much dissatisfaction among the men, in consequence which will result in numerous desertions hereafter. Had the change not been insisted upon until after the campaign, and just as we were going into garrison, it would have been far better.

Two days later Barnitz wrote

> General Custer has ordered that all my chestnut colored horses I have in all, shall be placed upon one end of my picket lines, and shall all be formed together at the head of the column on a march! This will necessitate the breaking up of the squads, as at present organized, or necessitate a reissue of my horses, and will cause renewed dissatisfaction. . . . Have felt very indignant and provoked all evening in consequence of General Custer's *foolish, unwarranted, unjustifiable* order with regard to the new horses, which will necessitate the placing of them together, whereas they should be scattered among the old horses, and in the front rank, (as well as the rear rank) where no recruit nor uninstructed horse ought to be! . . . I am thoroughly *disgusted* and *disheartened.* (Utley 1977:204–205)

Peter Thompson, a participant in the Battle of the Little Big Horn, also recorded his perception of a cavalryman's relationship to his horse. Thompson was a member of Company C, Seventh Cavalry, and would have died with Custer's command but for the fact that his horse collapsed prior to the Last Stand. (The animal's exhaustion, in one newspaper account, was blamed on "faulty shoeing" [Faulty Shoeing 1926].) Thompson wrote a manuscript entitled "The Experiences of a Private Soldier in the Custer Massacre" which was first published in serial form in 1913–14, and later appeared in the book *Black Hills Trails* (Brown and Willard 1924). In 1974, *Peter Thompson's Narrative of the Little Bighorn Campaign 1876* was published with editorial comments and analysis by Daniel O. Magnussen.

According to his record of events, Thompson managed to join the Reno and Benteen commands on the hilltop late in the day of June 25. Of this experience he wrote

> By the time we had everything arranged, the sun was going down. We all knew that the Indians never fought after nightfall. We thought we would have time enough to fortify ourselves before the light of another day appeared. But in the meantime several accidents happened which helped to make it a serious matter for us. We saw that our horses and mules were beginning to drop quite fast, for they were in a more exposed position. This is very trying to a cavalryman, for next to himself, he loves his horse, especially on a campaign of this kind. (Magnussen 1974:188)

In a reference note for Thompson's statement about a cavalryman's love for his horse, Magnussen writes

> Not according to the record—most cavalrymen hated their mounts and resented having to take care of them. Hollywood has added to the legend of the cavalrymen loving their horses. Most Westerners, as a matter of fact, do not have a high regard for the horse, other than as a "work animal," whereas Easterners regard horses in an entirely different light. In Chapter 4 of this manuscript, Thompson refers to his horse as a "restless brute," hardly indicating any "love" for him. (1974:189)

Several important points must be made in regard to these editorial assertions. First of all, Thompson is the cavalryman, not the editor, and it is hardly feasible that this soldier who actually experienced the human-horse relationship of cavalry life would be under the influence of a "legend." Although it could, of course, be true that some cavalrymen hated and/or resented their horses, Magnussen cites no reference for this belief. Additionally, the statement about Westerners and their horses is far too sweeping a generalization to have validity. It is not clear just what categories of people he includes as Westerners. If by this he means cowboys, there is just as much evidence for their love of their horses as for the opposite feelings. Many western ranchers and cowboys *do*, in fact, have a high regard for their horses, though admittedly some do not. This subject is extremely complex, requiring more than a lifetime of study, and several books, not just a paragraph, in order to even begin to obtain insights. It certainly *is* true that Easterners and Westerners view horses differently, but the different perceptions are not simply stereotypes of opposite feelings toward the animals (see Lawrence 1982, 1985; Bennett 1969:172–203).

In support of Thompson's alleged lack of love for his horse, Magnussen cites the cavalryman's reference to his horse as a "restless brute." This is fallacious reasoning, for the designation has been taken out of context. Thompson described the situation he experienced in camp on the evening of June 23, at the end of a very long march. "Custer seemed tireless himself and seemed to think his men were made of the same stuff," the private wrote, and explained.

> It was a hard sight to see men, who have been roused out of their sleep at half past three in the morning; not only once but day after day, sleeping in their saddles; and lucky indeed was the man who had a quiet and steady horse that allowed the luxury of a sleep while travelling. I often took a nap in this way although my horse was a very restless brute. (Magnussen 1974:93)

Thus, in reality, Thompson considered himself relatively fortunate in having a mount that allowed him to sleep *often* in this manner. In this light, Thompson's comment seems only a minor complaint, at worst. Of even more importance is the fact that Thompson in several instances uses the term "brute" when he actually expresses sympathy for a horse. For example, he relates, "I looked back and saw my comrade Watson trying to get his horse on its feet. The poor brute had fallen and was struggling to gain an upright position. . . . Finally the poor animal gained his feet with a groan." And again, describing the conditions when Major Reno's command was in "a flat bottomed ravine," Thompson noted, "The Indians were pouring a shower of lead into us that was galling in the extreme. Our horses and mules were cuddled together in one confused mass. The poor brutes were tired and hungry" (Magnussen 1974:121, 186).

It is relevant to recall that in Appel's sympathetic portrayal of Keogh as a man who loves his horse beyond anything in life, the captain twice, obviously out of affection, uses this word when he calls Comanche "You ugly brute, you," and asks the quartermaster "What do you think of my ugly brute?" (1951:144, 164). Though Appel was writing fiction, this example shows the author's use of brute in a teasing way that denotes emotional attachment. Interestingly, the keen horseman W. H. Hudson also used the term to designate an animal which was the object of positive feelings, when he wrote, "When I was thirteen years old I was smitten with love for a horse I once saw—an untamable looking brute, that rolled his eyes, turbulently, under a cloud of black mane tumbling over his forehead. I could not take my sight off this proud, beautiful creature, and I longed to possess him with a great longing" (1903:352). Evidently in an earlier time, the word brute had none of the derogatory meaning which the cynical Magnussen assigns to it. Rather it seems to have been almost a synonym for "animal."

When I began asking people associated with horses what the word brute meant to them, no one felt it had a negative connotation. Some said it signified power, strength, or dominance. A farrier who spends twelve hours a day, six days a week, with horses asserts that the term brute applied to a horse "refers mainly to its large size. It would be a big horse. It would also imply that the horse was bold or was inclined to be somewhat pushy." In no way did he feel that it was an unflattering word or that using it implied lack of regard for the designated horse. For another person brute signifies "being in command." This is ironic, in light of Magnussen's note that Luce's idea of Comanche taking command is "inane."

Whether or not cynics accept it, however, people who live constantly and closely with horses have documented instances when their mounts have taken command. This is exemplified by horses who, without any human direction, are known to bring their riders home through raging blizzards or who carry injured or incapacitated people back to safety. I personally know of instances in which a horse has refused to proceed into a passage through which the animal itself could easily go but which by doing so would injure the rider. A. F. Tschiffely, who made an arduous ten-thousand-mile ride in two and a half years, beginning in 1925, wrote of his experiences and explained, "I say 'we' although I was traveling without human companionship, for—after all—my two faithful horses did most of the hard work, and if it hadn't been for their instincts and thinking I should have come to grief on more than one occasion." He related one instance in which

> the horse I was riding refused to go a step further, and the more I tried to urge him on the fussier he became. When I finally used my spurs he reared up and snorted, but still refused to go forward. Luckily an Indian who spoke Spanish appeared on the scene and told me that I was on the very edge of a dangerous mud hole. How the horse sensed the danger is really mysterious, for there were none of these mud holes in his native regions. He probably saved my life, anyway. (1955:449)

General Custer's widow, Elizabeth Bacon Custer, who showed considerable interest in horses throughout her life, had accompanied her husband whenever possible during much of his military career. She authored several books about her army experiences and also lectured about them. In November of 1891, Mrs. Custer gave a presentation entitled "Life on the Western Plains" for a New York City audience, focusing on her own observations about the soldier's bond to his horse. According to a contemporary newspaper report

> Her talk was principally of the cavalry, naturally. She told of the trooper's love for his horse, citing individual instances of devotion, and declaring that in moving regiments of cavalry under recent orders, by which horses are not moved, but are allotted to the new regiment, a man will often transfer to the new garrison, thus severing connection with a whole regiment of comrades for the sake of retaining his old mount. (Life on the Western Plains 1891)

In 1889, on the occasion of the death of her husband's horse, Dandy, who had been with the pack train at the Little Big Horn Battle and was later shipped to her in Monroe, Michigan, Mrs. Custer's eulogy appeared in the hometown newspaper. In cavalry life, she noted, "Our horses were such intimate companions on the plains that we found ourselves as anxious to be *en rapport* with them and understand their humor as those of our friends beside whom we rode." Though some mounts could be "sulky or wilful or stubborn," Dandy's only fault was his gait, a "dancing trot." The General's relationship with the horse was vividly depicted:

> Imagine any one awakening in the gray dawn to the sound of reveille in a cavalry camp, and, after an ice cold bath, a lukewarm breakfast, stepping shrinkingly forth into chilly drizzle that the troopers declared had "come to stay." What if all about were silent or dulled by the damp, was it not everything to be met by the dancing motion of a pair of nimble heels, and the softest, most affectionate eyes, while the head turned to rub itself against the arm or shoulder of one the animal loved? Let the elements do their worst —and they attempt every vagary on the plains—that indomitable will and sunny disposition of Dandy's triumphed over everything. (1890:326-27)

Thirteen years earlier, in August of 1876, Mrs. Custer had received a letter from Seventh Cavalry Major Marcus A. Reno written "on the part of the officers" of her husband's regiment which provides insight into the soldiers' appreciation for the sharing of experiences between mount and man. Reno informed the widow that the horse, Dandy, was being sent to her. He wrote

An expressed wish of yours having reached us to have the horse "Dandy" ridden by the Genl. so many years he is shipped in this boat to Monroe, Michigan, through the care of Lt. Burns, to you, from the surviving officers of the Regt. at the head of which, his beautiful form was seen thro' so many hard marches and expeditions. (author's collection)

Similarly communicating a cavalryman's high regard for horses, E. S. Luce, writing to Colonel Nye in 1941, asked for the veterinarian's expert advice in interpreting the skeletal evidence he had discovered in several "horse cemeteries" on the Custer Battlefield. Nye felt the horses in question had been buried "possibly at the time the men were buried at the main monument." The two corresponded in detail about the horse bones, but the important point was that in his original letter on the subject, former Seventh Cavalryman Luce noted, "In those days the men thought just as much of their horses dead or alive as they did of human beings and it struck me then as being very sentimental to bury horses" (CBNM Files).

Not every cavalryman experienced a close relationship with his horse but evidence indicates that many of them did. In a book published in 1865, a cavalryman wrote, "The condition of our poor horses sometimes in winter is such as to make any heart susceptible of pity feel the most profound sorrow. . . . In actual campaign both men and horses must suffer, but do not let us cavalry people make our only friends—our horses—suffer unnecessarily." American cavalrymen, he asserted, are "natural riders, and soon become good horsemen. They quickly learn how to take care of horses. This is particularly the case where the men become attached to their animals, and make pets of them. I have known many a soldier to sit up half the night in order to get a chance to *steal* a feed for his horse. This venial offense is forgiven generally by the officers. . . . No man can be a good cavalry officer unless he is continually on the alert looking out for the welfare of his horses" (Brackett 1965:162, 163, 164, 165). There is no indisputable evidence that Keogh and Comanche shared a bond of fidelity and mutual affection, but it is a probability, given the characteristics of each and the circumstances of life that paired them. Keogh was certainly regarded as an excellent cavalryman.

Anthropologists employ ethnographic analogy to study ways of life that no longer exist, using insights gained from studies of the modern counterparts of a people to shed light on how their existence might have been in vanished times. Since no cavalrymen are now available to reveal that life, I made the nearest approximation to them through an in-depth study of urban mounted po-

299

licemen and their horses. Although differences exist, there are enough similarities between the contemporary mounties who spend their working day with an equine partner and the cavalryman to allow some extrapolation of data.

My extensive field work with the mounted police reveals that many contemporary troopers are indeed bonded to their horses. Daily routines in which they work together with their mounts for long periods of time, and which involve commonly shared risks, dangers, and travail, give the majority of men a sense of solidarity with their horses. Mutual dependency and the experience of acting as a unit lead to affective relationships between man and horse. A trust is built from which both animal and rider draw confidence. This is the main reason, according to mounted policemen, that they insist upon the "one rider-one horse" rule insuring exclusivity of mounts in their unit. Once a mountie's relationship with his horse has developed, he holds a strong proprietary attachment to the habitual partner which enhances the effectiveness of each man-horse team. Exclusivity is considered vital, and each man takes great pride in his particular interaction with his own animal which insures that the horse's behavior is far superior when he rides it than when another officer does so (see Lawrence 1985:161–64). Not only does another mountie fail to experience harmonious interaction with another man's horse, but even by riding such a horse occasionally without communicating with it in the same way, may "spoil" the horse and damage future interaction with its regular rider. The cavalry horse, like the police horse who has participated in such a partnership, will outdo itself—pushing far beyond the performance of an animal without this bonding. It is likely, from what is known and surmised, that Keogh was that kind of man, and Comanche was that kind of horse.

Adaptability exhibited by changing behavior with different riders is an equine trait frequently noted by those who work closely with horses. It is now well-known from the results of therapeutic horseback-riding programs for the mentally and physically handicapped that horses have remarkable capacities to adjust their behavior for a particular rider. Such differences in interaction with one rider as compared to another demonstrate the horse's capability for individual experience which, under the right circumstances, can lead to bonding. The sensation of riding, as one keen horseman who spent the early part of his life in the saddle each day from dawn to dusk describes it, means that a horse is "not a mere cunningly fashioned machine" which sustains us; but a something with life and thought, like ourselves, that feels what we feel, understands us, and keenly participates in our pleasures. Take, for example, the horse on which some quiet old country gentleman is accustomed to travel; how soberly and evenly he jogs along, picking his way over the ground. But let him fall into the hands of a lively youngster, and how soon he picks up a frisky spirit! Were horses less plastic, more the creatures of custom than they are, it would always be necessary, before buying one, to inquire into the disposition of its owner. (Hudson 1903:352)

In the case of Custer's war horse, Dandy, whose fieriness and dancing gait were known throughout the Seventh, an opposite transformation took place when he was sent home and given to the General's father. As Elizabeth Custer described it, she begged her father-in-law, who was then over seventy, to let an officer "at least ride him around the block" before the older man mounted his son's spirited horse. "He yielded, and off Dandy tore through the quiet streets to the amazement of the town. . . . It is my belief," Mrs. Custer revealed, that the horse "had been studying up his future master. He let him mount leisurely and seemed instantly to tame down in gait and manner." Thus "from the life of a gay, dashing cavalry steed he dropped into a steady going family horse" (Frost 1986:163–64).

Of the reciprocal relationship between cavalrymen and mounts in battle, a participant of an earlier time wrote

In an engagement the horses show as great courage as it is possible for a man to show; and when restrained from partaking of the glories and honors of combat, they show the utmost impatience and ardour, on hearing the sound of cannon, drums and trumpets, in a manner truly expressive, by pawing the ground, erecting their ears, snorting and foaming, in a manner which proves them to be possessed of the highest courage. When the trumpet sounds the charge, it would be nigh impossible for the most experienced riders to hold them in; but they rush instinctively into the thickest of the enemy, preserving at the same time the most regular order and each animal seems to vie with the other in procuring for his rider honour and fame by every means in his power, of which this noble beast seems to partake in equal degree with his master; and though apparently impelled by a fierceness ungovernable, yet in the hands of a skilful equestrian, he is as gentle as a lamb, and obeys every touch of the reins or sound of his master's voice, with the most cheerful alacrity. (Lamb 1938:193)

Bucephalus, the horse of history's most celebrated cavalryman Alexander the Great of Macedonia, was acquired by the future leader when, as a boy, he alone succeeded in riding the wild and rebellious mount that had defied the expert horsemen of his

301

father's kingdom. The two formed a partnership that lasted to the end of the horse's life. An incident from the annals of Alexander's military conquests documents the bond between horse and rider. Of Bucephalus it was related

> In former days he had shared with Alexander many a danger and many a weary march. No one ever rode him but his master, for he would never permit anyone else to mount him.
>
> In Uxia, once, Alexander lost him, and issued an edict that he would kill every man in the country unless he was brought back—as he promptly was. (Plutarch 1980:257–58; Arrian 1986:282–83)

According to military historian John Keegan, "Alexander commonly rode another horse to the edge of battle, mounting Bucephalus only for the fray, another ingredient of his theatricality" (1987b:48). Thus the practice that Keogh is believed to have followed in changing to Comanche just before the Battle of the Little Big Horn dates back to an ancient cavalry tradition. Besides the practical benefits of such a maneuver in both instances, it certainly emphasized the importance of the special relationship between man and mount.

The great horseman R. B. Cunninghame Graham wrote in the preface of Tschiffely's book, which was dedicated to the two horses that shared the author's long wilderness journey, "I have always held that the distinction some people make between instinct and reason is false, and that all animals reason and that all men have instinct" (Tschiffely 1933:v). In contrast to such people who lived intimately with horses and have experienced the sensitivity and intelligence of the equine animal, and particularly its adaptability, a recent writer on the subject of General Custer's horses inexplicably generalized that

> Serious students of equine behavior know that everything a horse does is governed either by habit or by instinct. Contrary to what many believe, a horse has no reasoning power. All of the incidents or circumstances in which horses are said to have displayed intelligence can be explained or traced to their having been trained by repetition. A habit has been developed by constant repeated training of an act or reaction to an instinct. (Frost 1986:28)

It would be hard to find a better example of the need for referencing. Just who are these anonymous "serious students," and what is the source of their data? Inexplicably, as the book goes on to reveal, if Lawrence Frost, as the Custers' biographer, believed this statement, the subjects of his works certainly did not. The strange incongruity of the view Frost expresses is brought sharply

302

into focus in later chapters of the same book, both by statements made by the author himself and by those he cites as quotations from the Custer family and other involved observers.

The reader finds, for example, in this same book a statement by Mrs. Custer that when ridden while hunting buffalo, "Dandy knew that the only way to bring an animal down was by sending the fatal shot behind the forequarter. . . . The bridle did not need to be touched, so clever was the horse in getting into favorable position for firing." Custer's mount is said to have "put on little proud peacock airs." The General wrote that on a demanding 1873 expedition, Dandy "seemed to realize the difficulties of the route, and although permitted to run untethered, he followed me as closely and carefully as a well-trained dog." In bad weather, Dandy "learned with the other horses to scrape snow from the ground in the river valleys, and, failing this, gnawed the bark from cottonwood trees." He had an "indomitable will," and was "full of good cheer." He loved and played with dogs, and "was capable of showing more affection in the few mute ways left open to him than people who have the human voice and expressive features at their disposal." He enjoyed the hunt, pursued game with "unflagging pertinacity," and "made such demonstrations of delight over the preparations for the chase he grew almost human." Dandy "begged for a run," and "evinced by every motion that he was born to lead." He could "show appreciation" for human company, and was seen "affecting coltish airs and pretending timidity, which was purely fictitious," making a "pantomime of sham fright." He "knew the step of his master," and when near death, "met suffering as bravely" as in his "old soldiering days." Custer's other mount, Vic, once "evinced joy and gratitude" when rescued. And Comanche, true to the often repeated story, "adored" his master, Korn, and "followed him everywhere like a pet dog." The old horse, according to his caretakers, "lost interest in life" when Korn died (Frost 1986:129, 142, 146, 154, 158, 159, 160, 161, 165, 166, 167, 201, 240).

Though some of these descriptions may be exaggerations, they are not entirely out of the realm of possibility, according to the latest findings in the scientific study of equine behavior. To corroborate my own knowledge and experience in the rapidly expanding field of horse behavior and cognition, I consulted with other authorities—some of the world's leading professional ethologists. They showed unanimity in total disagreement with the paragraph in which Frost states that "everything a horse does is governed either by habit or by instinct" and in sharp criticism of its absolute terms and sweeping generalizations. It was called "irresponsible." Summarizing the experts' responses, university scholars now believe that social affiliations of horses with their own kind and with other species "show great qualitative features, including systems which evidently call for intellectual function. Such behaviors could not be governed solely by instinct or habit." Horses "show use of knowledge," including "intellectual way-finding." There is "evidence of cognitive ability," and in certain instances, the accomplishment of horses' work "calls for good judgment and quick anticipation." At one university, workers have recently obtained "visual evidence" strongly suggestive of the equine thought process. At another university, experimenters found that equine "speed of learning is impressive." Horses could master a new movement in three trials, showing "a faster rate of learning new tasks than many children." In highly schooled horses, "intuitive leaps of learning" have occurred. The ideas expressed in the paragraph by Frost reflect the anthropocentric bias characteristic of our culture, and, as one behavioral specialist pointed out, "such thoughtless statements inhibit the advancement of scientific inquiry and the understanding of animals" (personal communications; see acknowledgments).

The subject of the paragraph by Frost is well worth considering, for it represents a curious instance of a writer molding the nature of a species for his own purpose in order to explain an incident that might otherwise detract from Custer's reputation. Equine "habit" or "instinct" is alleged by Frost to be the basis for an episode in which Custer's horse, Don Juan, while taking part in an 1865 "Grand Review" parade, plunged and bolted in a short "wild dash" during which he was out of his rider's control. This event involving the colorful Civil War hero received much publicity, and some people claimed that the General actually staged the event to draw attention to himself. Others, like Frost, attribute Don Juan's behavior to conditioning the animal received during training as a race horse (1986:28–30). The truth about this controversy can never be known, but the important point now is that a certain manipulated view of horse behavior is put forth by Frost mainly in order to insure that nothing would denigrate Custer's legendary horsemanship and character. As explained earlier, the remainder of the book which follows the paragraph actually contradicts the ideas presented about the equine species' lack of intelligence. This example demonstrates once again the fascinating way that horses are utilized to substantiate certain viewpoints and "pro or con" opinions about the principal participants in the Little Big Horn drama (see Chapter 3).

Horses such as the famed Clever Hans, who ultimately received recognition for being able to give answers to mathematical questions not by computation as originally claimed but through perception of his mentor's minute cues which were all but indiscernible to human onlookers, are unusual, but nevertheless real. Only about four decades after the Custer Battle, a World War I soldier observed the acute discriminatory powers of the army mounts: "Many horses seemed to know the difference between enemy and friendly planes. One black polo pony used suddenly to stop, toss her head, and begin to stamp and neigh—sure enough five minutes later, enemy planes would appear overhead. When our planes flew past, she ignored them and carried on feeding" (Cooper 1983:34).

Evidence shows that horses are not only capable of behavior far more complex than mere instinctual response, but that they interact with people and bond with their riders in very meaningful ways. As a former cavalryman described the rapport between soldiers and their horses, "On campaign, riding and tending the same horse for months on end, sleeping in the open only a few yards behind the picket lines at night, and suffering the same privations, the soldier came to regard his horse as almost an extension of his own being" (Brereton 1976:128–29). Another cavalryman explained the human-horse relationship in these terms: "Reflect for a moment on one military advantage which [horses] gave, and to which the machine can offer no parallel. Every man, however humble, who rode in the ranks of a cavalry regiment, had an independent command, consisting of one living creature, his horse. The successful command of any living creature depends largely upon sympathy, an emotion which plays no part in the control of a machine" (Wyndham 1979:112, 143).

The determination with which military establishments tried to preserve cavalry units despite technological progress that made them obsolete is a phenomenon that sprang from deeper roots than mere nostalgia for the past. Evidently the chivalric code, with its "old ideals of personal combat and honorable death," and the "true cavalry spirit which scorns mathematical calculations" were difficult to relinquish. According to one authority, the reluctance to do away with horse soldiers "may now be seen as a last desperate effort to withstand the depersonalization of war" (Ellis 1986:54–56). Horsemen have long been known as the noblest of soldiers, and this is due in large measure to the prevalent concept of horses as noble creatures and to the age-old bond between riders and their mounts.

After a long history of close interaction with people, the capability of horses for responsiveness to and rapport with their human partners is a truth embedded in the human psyche which has become an archetype in enduring myths. In particular, this theme is articulated in classic battle epics, for the fate of a war horse is so emphatically entwined with that of its rider. In Homer's *Iliad*, the bonding of steeds to warriors finds timeless and dramatic expression. Achilles lent his two fine horses, Xanthus and Balius, to his friend Patroclus to draw his chariot on the Trojan battlefield. When Patroclus was killed, the two horses were deeply grieved by the loss of their beloved driver.

> Far from the conflict, the horses of Achilles had been weeping ever since they learnt that their charioteer had been brought down in the dust by the murderous Hector. Automedon, Diores' stalwart son, did all he could with them: he lashed them repeatedly with his whistling whip, he coaxed them, and he cursed them freely; but the pair refused either to go back to the ships and the broad Hellespont or into the battle after the Acheans. Firm as a gravestone planted on the barrow of a dead man or woman, they stood motionless in front of their beautiful chariot with their heads bowed to the earth. Hot tears ran from their eyes to the ground as they mourned for their lost driver, and their luxuriant manes were soiled as they came tumbling down from the yoke-pad on either side of the yoke. (Homer 1986:327–28)

Later, when the funeral games for Patroclus were held, Achilles spoke of his horses.

> I and my splendid pair will not compete; they are in mourning for their glorious driver. How kind Patroclus was to them, always washing them down with clean water and then pouring olive-oil on their manes! No wonder they stand there and grieve for him. Their manes are trailing on the ground and in their sorrow they refuse to move. (Homer 1986:419–20)

Because of close relationships with people, other instances of equine grief are recorded in legend, for "as the horse exults by neighing over the good fortune of the hero who rides him, so he not only becomes sad, but sheds real tears when his rider is about to meet with misfortune." Caesar's horse, for example, is said to have "shed tears for three days before the hero's death" (De Gubernatis 1872,I:349–51).

The Wounded Horse

It is not surprising that, following Keogh's death, Comanche was often portrayed as a bereaved figure, capable of grief and unwilling to forsake his dead master. He himself was badly wounded, though there is little agreement as to the nature and extent of his injuries. For many reasons, his wounds took on great significance and made him the object of much interest and sympathy as well as speculation during his lifetime and into the present. Even today, museum visitors often want to see and count his scars. "Certain people become caught up with the scars," the exhibits director says. "They look for areas where bullets passed through, and want them to be still visible." One admirer wrote of Comanche, "The scars of Battle still show on his coat, every cicatrix a Badge of Honor" (UK Archives).

From the earliest moments after Comanche's discovery, the number of wounds he had sustained was specified—usually varying from four or five to the most common, seven, and up to ten or twelve, or even twenty in one account. One newspaper reported that "Comanche was found on the field of carnage with scarcely a spot on his body that was free from wounds inflicted by Indian bullets and arrows. . . . When Comanche was raised to his feet his wounds bled so profusely that the soldiers tore up the clothes of some of their brave comrades who had fallen a few hours before and stanched the flow of blood" (Progress of Fort Riley 1890). Leighton, in a children's novel about General Custer, numbered Comanche's wounds at twenty-eight (1954:179), a phenomenon specially noted by at least two later writers. Magnussen calls attention to it as one of the "weird tales" that developed about Comanche (1974:275). Connell notes that "a book for bloodthirsty juveniles presents the poor beast skewered twenty-eight times" (1984:296). (That either writer would consult a fictionalized work for children is in itself fascinating.)

Most accounts, however, including Chandler's history of the Seventh Cavalry, mention seven wounds, a number which, of course, corresponds to Comanche's regiment (not to mention "General Orders No. 7"). On a deeper level, the designation may reflect the tradition that seven has always been a meaningful, magical, and sacred number in human thought. From antiquity, "certain numbers, particularly those between one and thirteen," have "had peculiar power. . . . Four, which was once of great importance as a symbol of unity, endurance, and balance, seems to have left few traces on everyday superstition, but seven is almost everywhere thought to be lucky, or at least, significant." Seven occurs frequently in folklore. Seven is considered holy in many religions and is an expression of totality in the Bible. The number seven denotes perfect order, completeness, wholeness, perfection, security, safety, and rest. It is a number of "exceptional value." Most importantly in the present context, "it is the symbol of pain" (Cirlot 1983:233; Cooper 1978:117; Matthews 1986:170–71; Radford and Radford 1974:249).

Following Keogh's death, Comanche's condition was described in terms that proved to be prophetic of the way the horse was to be regarded forever afterward, as his legend grew and developed. Some accounts of finding Comanche express the idea that his wounds impart to the horse a sacrificial and quasi-religious quality. "With blood dripping from his many wounds he consecrated that battlefield." Perhaps Comanche "had interposed his battle-scarred body between his master and the arrows and bullets of the Sioux. When he was discovered, he was still dripping blood—many crimson blotches stained his shaggy coat, and he could hardly walk" (Luce 1939:64, 65). Association of sacrifice, blood, and consecration with the surviving animal all indicate the way that religious overtones quickly crept into the accounts of Comanche. Farrier Korn's description of finding Comanche "bleeding, dying," includes the impression of supernatural intervention, for "not a leaf stirred, not a blade of grass moved. The very voice of nature seemed hushed into awful silence. . . . The silence seemed to grow more oppressive" (1936:4). Thus nature itself was stilled as though in honor of the wounded horse.

Hushed silences and muted voices characteristically used in the presence of the supernatural have been associated with Comanche from the first. For many people, the Custer Battlefield immediately became "sacred ground" because of the heroic deaths of so many men who left no human being alive to speak for them. Comanche, as "the sole survivor," became symbolic of the deep emotions evoked by the soldiers who fell there, and of men too young to die, fighting bravely to the end against overwhelming odds. Comanche's wounds, his blood that was shed as part of defeat, made him a participant in battle but also a larger-than-life figure standing alone as a source of solace in the aftermath of the bitterness of war. He became a metaphor for near-religious veneration to a grieving country which, in a never-to-be-forgotten military engagement, had been deprived of some beloved heroes whom it had formerly believed invincible, and had also lost the great national confidence in the belief that its soldiers could always triumph over the "savages" which were enemies of the expansion and progress of "civilization" and the superiority which was attributed to Euro-American values.

Throughout the remainder of his life, Comanche was regarded with admiration and awe. The strict command that he should never again be ridden or called upon to do any work and the order that there should be no restraints on his freedom conferred upon him an almost sacred status that any deviation from orders would profane. As a cavalryman described Comanche's special status, "Major Reno's command cared for him as if he had been human," and after recovery Comanche "never [again] suffered the indignity of serving in ranks" (Ultimus 1928:258). The statement that Captain Keogh "was the last man that ever mounted" the horse bespeaks an inviolable tie to the hallowed dead. After Comanche's own death, the preservation and care of his remains and the establishment of his position in the museum as a cherished relic reinforced the honor accorded him in life. Robert Ege, an ardent Custer admirer, wrote that "Comanche's remains are now *enshrined* at the University of Kansas" (1966:32). Flag wavers, badge wearers, and uniform devotees have a special attraction to the horse. The desire to stand before him, to touch him, or to own a piece of his hair evidences his unusual power as a physically embodied symbol. A Custer Battle buff who recently saw the horse called him "a sacred piece of history that was luckily preserved for posterity." Visitors today who travel to the Dyche Museum because of special interest in Comanche's stuffed remains still tend to speak in hushed tones when in the vicinity of the display.

An unusual aura of reverence has surrounded Comanche from the first moment of his discovery two days after the battle when he was found by the soldiers designated as a burial party for their comrades killed at the Little Big Horn. It is customary that human dead are accorded a certain sanctity as soon as they have given up life. Thus the deceased are transformed into "hallowed dead," more especially if they died for a patriotic cause. Few people, however, are respectful or in awe of a dead horse. But it is understandable that a live horse, one who, though sorely wounded, rises up unexpectedly out of the overwhelming carnage of such a scene, would achieve the hallowed status.

Preoccupation with Comanche's wounds dramatizes the bloodiness and finality of the Last Stand in which there were no human survivors of the command. The more severely wounded the animal, the greater the perceived risks of the battle. The closer he came to death, the more remarkable and miraculous becomes his survival. His battle-scarred body speaks of his unusual strength and endurance. It must be remembered that

> The Seventh cavalry's claim to renown is certainly unusual, if not wholly unique; generally a command is remembered because of some brilliant victory. This one is remembered because of an overwhelming defeat. Around this defeat the organization's whole history practically centers, perhaps because it was at once profoundly tragic and highly melodramatic. (Richeson 1930:5)

Comanche's fame is inextricable from defeat. He, like his fallen comrades, was severely wounded. But unlike theirs, his wounds were not fatal. His survival made him a bridge between the dead and the living. He was identified with those who had been killed by the enemy, and yet he represented hope because, although not unscathed, he still lived. Solicitude was accorded to Comanche which could not be given to the fallen men. The horse was an extension of them, their mute surrogate. His suffering became important to a wounded nation, a people shocked beyond belief by the unexpected defeat of its favorite military regiment and the death of a hero once believed invincible. As one man who visited the surviving mount at Fort Lincoln in 1878 described the care the animal had received following the battle: "Never was invalid nursed more tenderly than Comanche. No royal monarch nor martyred president was cared for with profounder medical and surgical skill" (Burt 1891:3).

Sefton

As horses weep for their lost masters, so do people weep also for stricken horses. Comanche, even today, is often the focus of a remarkable outpouring of feeling—a sense of empathetic identification—not just from artists, poets, and lyricists, but from many others as well. As one man recently expressed it, "I've often thought about what Comanche went through. It was cold at night after the battle and he was alone. And to think the men may have been near him but didn't find him until later!" Another person noted, "It was a very hot, dry summer on the plains the year of the Little Big Horn campaign. But that night after the battle, a little rain shower fell to dampen the dust. Maybe mother nature shed a tear. It must have been a relief to the suffering horse to feel the rain."

A wounded horse can still elicit strong and widespread reactions. In 1982, a modern counterpart to Comanche, a British horse named Sefton, demonstrated that not only national, but even worldwide, concern is evoked by a horse badly wounded by the enemy. Sefton's story, with its similarities to Comanche's, is relevant to the present discussion, shedding light as it does on people's reaction to a courageous horse who endures and surmounts grave injuries to become a powerfully ennobling force in human affairs.

A mount of the Queen's Household Cavalry, Sefton, a black gelding with a white blaze and four white socks, was carrying out routine ceremonial duties in London's Hyde Park on July 20, 1982. Tragedy struck that morning, when four cavalrymen and seven horses were killed by the explosion of a bomb deliberately set off by the IRA (Irish Republican Army). The surviving men and horses received injuries of varying degrees of severity. Among the horses seriously injured was the nineteen-year-old Sefton, whose thirty-eight wounds, including a severed jugular vein, made his condition the most critical of the surviving mounts.

On the same day in Regents Park, seven infantrymen—members of a band of the Royal Greenjackets—were killed by a similar explosion. In spite of the human deaths and injuries, the media focused on the horses and chose Sefton as the central symbol of "the outrage," as the event was soon labeled. A prominent Irish journalist, documenting IRA acts of terrorism, commented on the overwhelming attention directed to the horses: "Curiously, it was the bomb that claimed the lives of animals as well as people that created the greatest controversy of the period." The bombings "killed and maimed a number of horses, which seemed to create as great an outrage both in England and Ireland as the deaths of the soldiers. . . . I happened to be in London the week after the explosions. People were still laying wreaths on the spot in Hyde Park where the horses were killed, but I saw no signs of activity in Regents Park where the bandsmen were blown up." The "TV pictures, nightly it seemed, carried pictures and reports of the surviving horses' condition, giving these greater prominence than the medical bulletins for the surviving soldiers" (Coogan 1987:646–47).

The gallant Sefton's fight for life and his subsequent recovery following surgery elicited a degree of sympathy rarely encountered. The progress of his healing held the people of the nation, as well as those of many foreign countries, spellbound. Brigadier Gerald D. M. Landy, OBE, who was closely associated with the whole Sefton affair, told me, "People become irrational over horses. They're not human, but people attribute human feelings and understanding to horses which they don't have." The officer then related incidents of his personal interaction with Sefton. "That horse really loves acclaim," he revealed. "He loves being the center of attention. One day I was patting him and feeding him mints, and then I turned to talk to a person next to me. Sefton grabbed my hand, very gently but firmly, and brought it back to him. He wanted my attention again, and knew how to get it. He has a great personality, a very strong personality, and that was an important factor in his recovery. He was determined he would survive." The genial Brigadier paused for a moment, and we both smiled at a simultaneous moment of insight. I did not say anything, but he voiced it: "All right, I'm convinced! I was wrong!"

Once again, as in Frost's paragraph about "instinct" previously discussed, here was a typical expression of the bias of culture dictating against the existence of animal mental and emotional experience, repeated by rote but actually disbelieved in the face of pragmatic evidence to the contrary.

The army officer went on, "The horse became a symbol of great bravery. Though he suffered agonizing physical pain when his body was filled with metal from the bomb, it was Sefton's resolution that he was not going to let it get him down that enabled him to survive. He took it with discipline and dignity. The terrorists who did such a sorry, sordid thing in that vicious, cowardly act, miscalculated, for Sefton remained serene through it all."

Following the disaster, news spread that the horse's courage was the trait which allowed him to recover from his dreadful wounds. Like Comanche, until the tragedy, "Sefton had been just another troop horse, but the events of that day made his name a household word for all that is good and courageous." A painting of the "brave and defiant horse" was auctioned to benefit families of the victims, and many thousands of cards, plates, and pendants made from it were sold. Readers of the many letters addressed to "brave Sefton" or "that brave horse" found it hard to remain dry-eyed. People prayed for his recovery. Gifts for Sefton and the other equine convalescents, including a quarter of a million polo mints, poured in, and get-well cards received were "thick as confetti. . . . 'Cheat the bastards,' one of them exhorted him, 'live!'" Two days after the bombing, "Sefton was already a name that brought waves of affection to the heart and tears to the eyes" for Londoners. After his recovery, when Sefton appeared at the Horse of the Year Show, one "could see pocket handkerchiefs spreading through the stands." The "sobbing was contagious and quite unashamed" (Greenwood 1983:11, 73, 88, 89; Watson 1983:5, 94, 99, 104).

When J. N. P. Watson, the author of a book about Sefton, was asked to justify the occupation of the limelight by a wounded horse instead of the human victims of the bombing, he explained that compassion had been aroused primarily for the horses partly because of the "'dumb creature' syndrome. When animals, who are without sin, are the victims of men's cruelty, there is a collective sorrow, a tenderness of a special brand, a sense of shame and a passion for revenge." The men "had incurred the hatred of the IRA by being soldiers," but "the horses were not carrying the soldiers by choice," and by any standards were innocent. The writer voiced some of the perceptions that were influential for Comanche's image as well. The larger the wounded animal, the greater may be the degree and volume of its pain. And because "horses do not scream in agony, do not yelp like dogs or howl like cats when they are hurt, they have little outlet for their feelings. So, all the more must we humans weep for them." Eye-witnesses at the bombing reported that after the explosion there was "a silence so absolute it chilled the mind and the senses. . . . Not one horse made a single sound. No Whinnying. No snorting." In attempting to understand why witnesses to the carnage could "never erase the pathos from their memories," Sefton's biographer asks: "Was that because animals are so devoid of malice, so impeccably innocent, so undeserving of involvement in the quarrels of man, yet so vulnerable to his cruelty and hatred? Perhaps it was because the noble horse, of all the domestic creatures, is so unstinting in his duty, so full of fortitude, so silent in his agony, that when he suffers it makes man ashamed for the human race?" (Watson 1983:9, 89, 90, 92, 94).

From the very first moment following Sefton's injury, intense effort was expended to save him. Major Noel H. Carding, the veterinarian who tended him and performed the surgery, told me "a corporal who was nearby put his fist into Sefton's neck wound to close the vein. Otherwise the horse would have died before he got to me." We discussed the perplexing question of why the horses received more publicity than the men who had been injured or killed. He said "Although we lost four men in Hyde Park, and some others were injured, none of our men were maimed. In Regents Park, seven men were killed, and the injuries of the surviving men were worse; they were badly maimed." He thought the families must have felt badly about the attention to the animals, but this was never expressed. The wife of an army veterinarian who had been close to the event and knew the mother and widow of one of the dead cavalrymen confided, "We feel guilty about the amount of sensationalism and so much fuss about the horses, but the families didn't complain. They didn't seem to resent it, but we felt sad for them." Brigadier Landy, who is in charge of the Army Benevolent Fund, addressed this issue.

> There were mixed reactions on the part of the public. Some civilians outside of the army thought it was wrong to make such a fuss about horses. At the other extreme were people who felt all the money donated for the horses should be given strictly to animal charities. One irate person wrote in to express the hope that all the money sent in for Sefton would be spent on him. But Sefton will be well looked after for the rest of his days, and could never use all that money, anyway. The funds raised through Sefton were used for the families of the soldiers who were killed, so they benefited

from the attention the horse drew. They were not resentful. People seized upon the horse and identified with it. They could be more openly emotional about a horse. Sefton provided a focus for the public to express wholesome feelings and to condemn those who could do such a despicably cruel thing.

Brigadier John Spurry, the army veterinarian who tends Sefton in his retirement, spoke about the fact that "mounted policemen report that people never hurt the horses. They go after the riders but never the animals, because there is usually a built-in instinct against hurting horses. But the IRA broke this code. The people in this country made a terrific outcry because they love horses. Sefton is an outlet for their attachment to animals."

Another aspect of the superabundant attention given to the horse is that "perhaps we cannot bear to hear about the death of the soldiers or even those who did not die but were maimed or wounded, and the public at large instead fastened its attention on a dumb animal who survived" (Greenwood 1983:73, 79). By diverting attention from grief, as well as by its own presence, an animal possesses a remarkable capacity to heal. Emanuel Custer, the bereaved father who had lost three sons, a son-in-law, and a nephew at the Little Big Horn, identified his son's surviving mount with his dead loved ones, and said of Dandy, "I don't know how I could have lived without that horse. He's been a comfort to me for thirteen long years." Elizabeth Custer called the horse her father-in-law's "anchor," a beloved link to the past (Frost 1986:151, 163, 166, 167). For the many people who viewed Comanche as a near-sacred object, such a process must have operated in assuaging some of the pain of an overwhelming personal and national loss. The equine survivor became an object for the transference of their suffering in much the same way as he had first served in that role for General Sturgis. As the man whose famous orders transformed the Seventh Cavalry equine survivor into a revered celebrity, he was also a grief-stricken father who had lost his only son with Custer's force. Understandably, the horse he honored as the "only living representative of the bloody tragedy" was meaningful beyond words.

Identification with Sefton's courage, dignity in suffering, and will to survive was strong, reflecting qualitatively similar reactions to those elicited by Comanche. The modern-day audience, of course, because of the media channels available a century later, was much larger and more widespread. With his worldwide fame, "Sefton's model of character and courage has been an inspiration to millions." After a ten-year-old amputee and cancer victim visited the horse, "her morale soared." She said Sefton's example of how to pull through gave her the will to recover too. The plight of the wounded horse evoked comparisons with people. Some pointed out that it was only "yellow-bellied" humans who "fussed over their ailments." Animals are "philosophical, stoical, intrepid," and "the most worthy examples for mankind to emulate." Admired for being resilient when most horses would have succumbed, Sefton evoked renewed patriotism and came to epitomize a nation's contempt for its enemies. He represented the "valorous and noble character of the war-horse" of the past. It was said that Sefton's recovery pays tribute to the sacrifice that all good soldiers make. He was "the modern personification of all his fellows who suffered and died in the service of men," the recipient of an overdue debt of gratitude to mankind's "best, most faithful, longest serving friend, servant and ally." Sefton "had instantly become the symbol through which shock and horror were to change into pride and hope," and by proving that cruelty and hatred cannot win, he stood for "the triumph of good over evil" (Cooper 1983:12; Greenwood 1983:9, 13, 16, 58, 73, 87, 90; Watson 1983:94, 102, 105).

The IRA attackers elicited special disgust because of the irony that the stricken Sefton, like nearly all Household Cavalry horses, had been born and bred in Ireland, where "that vivid grass country and the genus equus are practically synonymous." It had been assumed that man's inhumanity to man might be expected, but never malice toward horses from the Irish, who had always held the animals in high regard. Traditionally the home of fine horses and skilled horsemen, Ireland was, too, Keogh's native land. Other themes in Sefton's and Comanche's sagas reveal common threads. The British horse represented a "success story," at first an unpromising individual, but "full of life and vigor," who overcame obstacles and made good through his own character and spirit—a prominent element in the Comanche legend. Also, Sefton formed close bonds with human associates as it is probable that Comanche did. Every soldier and his mount at Hyde Park on the fateful day were, like the Seventh Cavalry captain and his steed, known for the "centaur-like co-ordination of horse and trooper." Sefton's rider, for whom the horse demonstrated obvious affection, was, like Keogh, wounded in the leg during the attack, the boot of the Household cavalryman showing "four ugly holes where the nails had pierced the man's leg." This trooper, injured and half-conscious, still held the bleeding Sefton and was the first sight that caught the eye of the commanding officer when he arrived at the scene of the bombing (Greenwood 1983:12, 13, 68, 70; Watson 1983:10, 21, 24, 27, 69, 74, 88, 92).

Souvenir hunters requested the metal surgically removed from Sefton's body, a nail from his shoe, and, as with Comanche, coveted strands of the brave animal's mane. At the Household Cavalry barracks, one of the nails projected into his flesh by the bomb was mounted "as a symbol of this cowardly and cruel act," just as the Keogh of legend preserved an arrowhead that had wounded Comanche. After recuperation Sefton, like Comanche, was "spoiled" by permissive treatment, and "took on the mantle of a film star" for admirers and the press. Many well-wishers declared no one should ever get on his back again, and urged "Don't imprison him in a stable! Let him roam free!" He now has been given his freedom, "the greatest gift you can give a horse," according to his former rider, and enjoys an exceedingly comfortable life in retirement, in which his nonwork status is strictly enforced. At the farm where the retired Household Cavalry mount still resides, "any member of the staff who dares to mount a horse, even for a snapshot, invites instant dismissal." Sefton, like Comanche, is visualized as partaking of the afterlife when he dies (Greenwood 1983:9, 63–64, 79; Webb 1987:37; Watson 1983:62, 100).

On a recent visit to the Home of Rest for Horses, where Sefton is spending his retirement, it was easy to tell which stall belonged to the hero. Crowds were gathered around the door where he reached his head out to accept the offerings of carrots, apples, mints, and sugar lumps brought by admirers. "That's the famous one!" people in the group were saying. And several were exclaiming to companions, "*That* is a very brave horse!" No one was surprised that I had come all the way from the United States to visit him.

In addition to the reputation for bravery, there were other similarities with Comanche. "Although hundreds of people ask for Sefton to open a show or fete," the director of the rest home explained, "and many charities want him, we always say no. We keep him here, where people can visit him." The brigadier in charge of the Army Benevolent Fund told me "We don't want him to be a peep show." So it was once reported of Keogh's mount: "Enterprising showmen have from time to time endeavored to secure Comanche for exhibition purposes, but the authorities have invariably refused to disturb his well-earned rest" (Comanche Dies 1891).

Both horses had earned a life of undisturbed comfort through the feeling of admiration their courage had inspired. The extent of the solidarity of feeling they engendered is shown by their undisputed status of "idle honor" in retirement. In 1876, a newspaper reporter wrote of the "old soldier," Comanche, that "his honorable wounds should require that he be placed on the retired list with full pay" (*Chicago Times* August 20). An 1879 account of the horse who "has been honored by military distinctions" includes the discerning statement that he is "pensioned on luxury and sentiment" (Comanche 1879). The wording of newspaper clippings from 1888 and 1890 reveals the national interest in and sentiments regarding Comanche's retirement. The celebrated horse was newsworthy as "the only horse ever pensioned by Congress." Regarding this "horse in the United States army on the retired list drawing a pension," it was revealed that "His pension is sufficient to cover his transportation wherever he goes and to pay for his forage. He is cared for by a man detailed for that duty, and who does nothing else. He is saddled, bridled, and equipped and led out for inspection, yet no one dares to sit in his saddle." There is "a standing order that anyone who elevates himself to 'Comanche's' back shall be at once court-martialed and summarily dealt with" (The Only Survivor 1890; An Equine Pensioner 1890). The simplest statement was the most revealing: "It transpires that there is a horse on the pension roles. It was a participant in the battle of the Little Big Horn, where Custer was killed. Many a man who draws a pension can show no such good record" (It Transpires 1890).

A newspaper reported that the first pension case involving the Battle of the Little Big Horn to come before Congress was one to increase the pension of the widow of First Lieutenant Porter. Mrs. Porter, "a confirmed invalid," then received "$16, which is the main support of herself and her child," and it was recommended that "the pension be increased to $30 per month." The article goes on to reveal "As yet, nothing has been done by Congress for General Custer's widow" (The First Pension Case n.d.). Using the case of Comanche's honored status under the famous orders of her father, Nina Sturgis Dousman argued, "how much more, I feel, should the cause of the National Indian War veterans appeal to all, when even an Indian War veteran horse was considered worthy of such care and attention." Through reference to the famous horse, she drew attention to the needs of "those brave Indian War veterans who have given their youth, their strength and prime, not only to their country's defense, but to its development and growth through the progress of civilization made possible by their service" (1926:7). In 1934, the Indian War veterans' publication, *Winners of the West*, published complaints from "Real winners of the West" who "fought off the Indians from the lands your parents settled on" that they received only "$13 per month," while the settlers for whom they cleared the way grew

317

rich (Werel 1934). That there seemed to be no bitterness regarding the attention to Comanche is revealed in a 1947 letter from an Indian War veteran's widow, whose husband had "joined the army when he heard of the Massacre" of General Custer and his men. Mrs. Anna Vertrees Kincaid wrote (in part) to the Commandant of Fort Riley (and also to the chancellor of the University of Kansas),

> I was glad to note in the Sunday Kansas City Star, of your interest in the Indian War Relic—the remains of Comanche—the horse that Gen. Custer was riding when the Indians killed him and all the men with him.
>
> Our nation does not honor the Indian War Vets and their dependents as they do other War Vets. Our Legislators last session, voted a 20% increase for all War Widows except the Indian War Widows. We should receive more than the Spanish War Widows for they are young enough to help with their living expenses. 64 years ago today I married James B. Kindcaid[.] He was discharged in 1881 having enlisted in August 1876. . . . I have his discharge! "Excellent— Good Habits, Reliable and thoroughly trustworthy."

The letter from the cavalryman's widow closed "Well I am glad they are honoring the Horse that was in the Indian war if they do not Honor the ones that cared for the Indian war Veterans, when they passed away from their suffering" (UK Archives).

Thus both Sefton and Comanche seemed to be elevated above the concerns of people, as they had become the focus of powerful feelings, thoughts, and emotions evoked by the violent events that made them famous. Recently, a psychologist has done research which shows that in any situation, the presence of an animal makes the context less threatening to people (Randall Lockwood personal communication 1988). Certainly the two horses brought a sense of comfort and healing to their respective populations. Both Comanche and Sefton embody societal values that have complex roots and are not readily explainable in terms of single causes. Shedding some light on Sefton's fame as a "Horse of Destiny," John Oaksey points out that "money has never been the only measure" of the value people attribute to horses. On the same day that the IRA bombing took place, he explains, "an Anglo-Irish syndicate paid four and a quarter million dollars" for a single thoroughbred yearling. But even if that colt "grows up to win an Epsom Derby he will never attract one hundredth part of the sympathy and admiration which, in the months that followed the Hyde Park outrage, centred around an old black horse called Sefton whose stoic courage made him such an appropriate living memorial to its victims" (Greenwood 1983:11). He could have been speaking, too, for an earlier counterpart of the London mount, a brave wounded survivor who also represented his fallen comrades, Myles Keogh's Comanche.

Comanche's Enduring Image

Serving as an emotional outlet to assuage the nation's grief and as an antidote for the shock of the sudden deaths of men for whom there had been no time for farewells, Comanche gave to the Custer tragedy a necessary finality, a vital sense of closure. The Last Stand had a beginning—and, in the surviving horse, an end. In the words of David H. Miller, who chronicled Custer's defeat through use of Indian testimony, the famous battle was a story that extended "from the soldiers' killing of the Indian boy at dawn to the discovery of Captain Keogh's horse, Comanche, in the final chapter" (1957:vii).

Feelings evoked by the surviving horse have always been inseparable from those evoked by the battle that he survived. If Custer's cavalry had been victorious, the dashing leader would have no doubt earned his share of fame, yet the battle itself would involve none of the mystery, intrigue, and enduring appeal that have surrounded it. And, if the Seventh Cavalry had won, few would have ever heard of Comanche. Even one white survivor of Custer's command would have usurped the horse's fame and left him no niche in history.

Other Seventh Cavalry mounts who may have lived through the battle were no rivals for Comanche. Equine survivors of other military engagements, even an authentic "sole survivor," draw little attention. After the total annihilation of Captain William J. Fetterman and his detachment at the hands of Sioux warriors led by Crazy Horse in December 1866, an eye witness arriving on the scene made a report. He found "every man killed" and "nothing that had life left but a gray horse, Dapple Dave of Co. C 2nd Cavalry, the only horse left on the battle field being shot with both bullet and arrow, all the other horses were captured by these Indians" (Guthrie 1932:716). Like Comanche, Dave had lived through a bloody "massacre," but there the similarity ends. No honors or special status for the gray have been recorded. Neither was there much mystery about the Fetterman Fight or disagreement about its leader, known to be overconfident and headstrong, who had ignored his superior's warnings only to be decoyed, with his eighty men, into a fatal trap. The name of the rider of Dapple Dave was not even noted.

There was, too, an equine survivor of the "terrible massacre of 1862, when the Sioux of Minnesota killed nearly a thousand people on the frontier." A band of farmers and their horses were rounded up to fight the Indians, and in a two-day battle "quite a number of the amateur soldiers had been killed or wounded, and every one of their horses, with a single exception, had been shot dead and their bodies were dragged into a pile to serve as a barricade. This exception was an 8-year-old bay mare, owned by a Hennepin County farmer. Not a bullet had touched her. Instinct seemed to have led her to 'lie low.' After serving through the campaign she was returned to peace and the plough on her owner's land" (Comanche Dies of Old Age 1891).

As he is not the only battle survivor, Comanche is also not the only military horse whose remains were preserved for display after death. Winchester, the mount ridden by General Sheridan in almost every engagement from 1862 until the close of the Civil War, was described by the general as "an animal of great intelligence and of immense strength and endurance. . . . I doubt if his superior as a horse for field service was ever ridden by anyone." When Winchester died in 1878, his body was mounted and presented by Sheridan to the Museum of the Military Service Institute, Governor's Island, New York, and was later transferred to the Smithsonian Institution, where it now stands (Winchester 1980). Robert E. Lee's beloved gray horse, Traveller, "survivor of many a fierce battle," and "one of the most fearless of war horses ever to be honored in history," who lived to lead his master's funeral procession, was first buried near the Confederate leader. Exhumed years later, the skeleton now stands in the Washington and Lee Museum, "an eternal memorial to [Lee's] gallantry" (Peterson and Smith 1961:160–61). Stonewall Jackson's Civil War charger, Old Sorrel, was exhibited after death for twenty-one years at state and county fairs and is now at the Soldier's Home in Richmond, Virginia (Ballantine 1964:271).

In a 1958 memorandum to the chief of military history in Washington, the commanding officer of Fort Riley suggested that one or both of "the last two remaining Cavalry horses, Gambler and Chief," then retired and stabled at the fort, "who are well advanced in years and will probably pass on to their reward within the next year or two," be mounted for display in the Fort Riley Historical Museum following their demise. The officer's reply indicated that there were no provisions for raising money and "no military funds that could be used" for this purpose, and the plan was never carried out. An admirer of Comanche expressed his disapproval of the proposed preservation of Chief, who "had nothing but routine Drill and Service," and who "was no war veteran." To bring this horse to the museum with Comanche, he said, "would have completely destroyed the Historic Value of Comanche" (UK Archives). Some horses whose fame is not military have been preserved. Among these is Trigger, the horse of whom owner Roy Rogers said, "I just couldn't put the old fellow in the ground," with "the worms and everything," and who still rears up in his famous pose at a California museum. The celebrated rodeo bronc War Paint is on display in Pendleton, Oregon (Morgan and Tucker 1984:97–98; Sipchen 1987).

Comanche's deeply entrenched fame as America's most celebrated horse continues to overshadow that of all other steeds. His preeminence is exemplified by the persistent tale of his alleged burial in New York. Myles Keogh developed a close friendship with the Throop Martin family of the Willowbrook Estate near Auburn, often visiting their home and ultimately being buried in their cemetery lot. The acquaintance had developed through Keogh's Civil War companion, General Andrew J. Alexander, who married a Martin daughter. Alexander had a favorite war horse, the Black Sluggard, whom he rode in many battles. Though wounded many times, the reliable mount "ever displayed a courage and indifference to danger," that endeared him to the general. In 1864, because of his affectionate feelings for the horse whom he wished to "hear no more the cannon's loud roar, and the bursting shell," he shipped the faithful animal back to Willowbrook to live a life of ease and special privileges in retirement somewhat like those enjoyed by Comanche. When the horse died in 1877, he was buried in the vicinity of Willowbrook (Manion 1986:1–3). Later in the same year, Keogh's remains were reinterred in an Auburn cemetery. A local newspaper in 1951 reported that "Colonel Keogh's horse," who survived the Custer Battle "was brought to Auburn and retired to pasture at Martin's point wher[e] he lived to a ripe old age" (Many Events 1951). According to John S. Manion, many people in Auburn, at least as recently as 1967, believe that Comanche was buried at Willowbrook. Custer Battle buff Bruce Liddic has "heard stories many times from the people of Auburn about how Comanche was buried at Willowbrook. One old man even remembered seeing the horse's tombstone near the lower house" (personal communication 1988). It is easy to understand how the confusion with another horse resulted in this locally popular legend. The Black Sluggard, though he was an equine war hero, never attained the fame of Comanche, and through the surviving Seventh Cavalry mount's tie to his master, Comanche became associated with the area where Keogh was buried.

321

Years before, the preoccupation with burying the faithful mount near his master was evident in a Kansas newspaper article indicating that Comanche was "soon to receive a military burial beside the Custer Monument where are buried the bones of all the soldiers killed in the battle." According to the erroneous report, "arrangements are being made to disinter the bones of the horse from where they now rest at Old Ft. Lincoln and to have them reburied at the monument." Although he had been "buried with full military honors" following his death, "men of Troop I will be detailed to give old Comanche another, and final, burial. . . . Because of their pride in the old horse," the article reveals, Troop I had become "the 'crack' troop of the regiment" (Honor For A War Horse 1913).

The legacy of Keogh's bond with his mount was perpetuated by the heirs of the Seventh's tradition. While he lived, Comanche was a revered link to the past. After his death, the horse's memory still connected former cavalrymen to old times. Theodore Goldin expressed this nostalgic association when he wrote in his 1921 letter about Comanche: "Trusting you will pardon this uncalled for letter and attribute it to my love for the old horse, the old service and in the interest of history" (UK Archives). For men of a later generation who figuratively took up the regimental guidon, Comanche's remains still served as a rallying point, symbolizing the spirit of the Seventh and solidifying the camaraderie between Little Big Horn scholars like E. S. Luce, Colonel Nye, Colonel Graham, Dr. Kuhlman, R. G. Cartwright, and George Osten. They delighted in the experience of vicarious participation in a bygone era, whether it was shared in correspondence, get-togethers, or visits to the battlefield. Former cavalryman Luce had direct ties to the Little Big Horn through personal acquaintance with battle participants Godfrey, Varnum, Edgerly, and Hare, and Nye had many times talked with Varnum. Luce and Nye each wrote of their uncanny feeling of "a certain 'nearness' of the troops and Indians," a sense of actually being "in the midst of those stirring scenes," when visiting Custer Battlefield. Luce's enthusiasm for participation made him confide to Nye in 1940, "I would die happy if only I could get that position [Curator of the Custer Museum] if but for one day." Twenty years later he reflected on the years in which his dream had been a reality. Following a 1960 reunion with fellow Custer Battle buffs he wrote, "all agreed that the years of from 1941 to 1955 were the fifteen 'golden years' of our lives." A "'certain something' about this Custer history" had "brought so many wonderful people together in a lasting friendship." The "Garryowen Esprit du Corps" of the Seventh Cavalry was a "germ" they had caught "that lasts through a lifetime" (CBNM Files). As the quintessential representation of the bond between cavalrymen and their mounts, Comanche was the thread that tied together all their nostalgic sentiments.

In an attempt to unlock the battle's mysteries, Luce consulted Nye about the significance of horse bones discovered in a "cemetery" at Custer Battlefield, about horseshoes found there, and about the details of a typical cavalry horse's stride and gaits, the timing of cavalry marches, and the possible influence of equine disease upon the disastrous 1876 expedition. By reference to the objects of their common affection, Luce tempted Nye to visit him at Custer Battlefield headquarters in 1943: "You won't feel lonesome for the 'chevaux,' as I am forever chasing Indian horses and ponies out of this area" (CBNM Files). Luce and Nye always wrote of Comanche as though he were alive, and they never gave up hope that he would someday be on display at the battlefield. Nye, in his paper "What of Comanche," lamented that "[Comanche's] day and the heroic times he represented are gone," and drew attention to the alleged neglect of the "earthly remnant of this great animal." The "proper and fitting solution" was to locate him in the Custer Battlefield Museum where "all the relics and mementos of that day are available. What more suitable action, what more appropriate ending to a gallant career, than to place the mounted Comanche in the place of honor in that Museum. Let Comanche return to the field of his greatness!"(n.d. (a):3).

Comanche in life and after death represents the highly charged meanings of the Little Big Horn. Beginning with his discovery after the battle, he has evoked emotions which enable people to relate in a meaningful way to the tragedy of the Custer defeat. Fourteen years after the Little Big Horn, Captain Charles King wrote, "Bleeding from many wounds, weak and exhausted, with piteous appeal in his eyes, there came straggling into the lines some days after the fight Myles Keogh's splendid sorrel horse Comanche. Who can ever picture his welcome as the soldiers thronged around the gallant charger? To this day they guard and cherish him in the Seventh" (1890:386). The connection between horse and men was expressed no less clearly and eloquently seventy-five years later by a man who could only "stand in imagination before [Comanche's] glass stall." He was "shaken by the strong feeling that this moving exhibit evokes," and said, "I salute the old ⌐laybank charger within in reverential tribute to the memory of the gallant and heroic men who rode to their death in the service of their Country by the bank of the Little Big Horn River almost one hundred years ago" (Farnum 1965).

Comanche's fame generally remains inextricable from the image of the "fighting Seventh" and its leader. Custer and his cavalry have become one of the foremost symbols of the conquest of the American continent known as the "winning of the West." The general's heroic status has depended, in large measure, upon his role in subduing the wild land—spearheading the advance of civilization and furthering the progress of Manifest Destiny. Comanche's biographer, Brown, extended this symbolism to the cavalry mount when he wrote, "Comanche belongs to the University of Kansas, but he belongs, too, to the whole country and is identified with all that is best in our military annals and the conquest of our West." He goes on to identify the horse not only with westward expansion, but with patriotism and pioneer virtues: "My researches, and the long and close study of the famous horse which are condensed in the little book have made a better man and a better American of me. I wish that I and a lot of other people had the same self-possession, devotion to duty, courage, sense of obedience, and as few faults as had the noble animal" (UK Archives). He extolls the equine species' role in "our growth up from savagery" and ends with a tribute to Comanche as a "personification of faithfulness and fearlessness, a symbol of the conquest of a great continent," who "will always live as long as valor and the dreams of high achievement live in the hearts of men" (1935:16, 77). A writer reporting the death of the "gallant steed that was with General Custer at the fateful Little Big Horn massacre" called Comanche a reminder "for future generations of men" of "one of the saddest of all the many massacres by the merciless aborigines." Though he was "but a horse" he served his country well, and "from his back many brave blows were struck for the preservation of the lives and homes of frontier settlers" (Old Comanche Dead 1891b).

Horses were the instruments which made possible the penetration into the American wilderness and settlement there, and they were the vital force in vanquishing nature and the roving tribes of Indians that stood in the way of the white advance. The horse has been, from ancient times, an archetypal symbol of man's conquering force. The taming and riding of the equine animal represents domination over nature, and the figure of a man on horseback has throughout history been a sign of conquest. Power and aggressive force have long been associated with the mounted man, whose advantages over a pedestrian foe were proven to be overwhelming. For implicit in the horse-rider relationship is the fact that the rider has already mastered the horse, and dominance over the animal may be seen as setting the stage for further conquest (see Lawrence 1982:134).

Custer's reputation as a hero, as Paul Hutton has pointed out, undergoes changes in correlation with the views of society concerning the American frontier that are prevalent at a given time. When perceptions of the natural world and of Indians living in harmony with it began to include appreciation, rather than being viewed strictly as objects for exploitation and conquest, the glory formerly accorded to Custer began to fade. The development of American social conscience (with consequent feelings of guilt regarding injustices toward Indians) and the rise of the environmental movement caused Custer and other figures of the frontier to become "demythologized." This process is epitomized in *Tonka*, where Custer is depicted as a crazed and "vain racist," and the General's "image had fallen so low that even Walt Disney, as great an upholder of traditional heroes as the movie factories ever produced, turned on him" (Hutton 1976:37–45).

Media coverage of the recent Iran-contra scandal demonstrated that Custer's reputation is no better in the 1980s. One newspaper reporter described Lieutenant Colonel Oliver North's plan for a "last stand for the contras" as his "very own secret Little Big Horn scheme." North's scheme, it was alleged, "smacked of the mentality of the now thoroughly discredited George Armstrong Custer, whose headstrong, disastrous, they-died-with-their-boots-on bravado form of generalship produced the perfect military failure in American history: the 7th Cavalry's last stand at the Little Big Horn" (Johnson 1987:A23).

Comanche, however, has never fallen from grace along with Custer. Known after the battle as "the hero of his regiment," the mount has maintained that status for over a hundred years. Unlike human Little Big Horn participants, alive or dead, Comanche can be unequivocally admired. No one weighs his actions in battle to determine if they were wise or foolish or judges his bravery or cowardice. In the modern world where force is still measured in horse power and horse sense is a high compliment, he continues to make an ideal hero. As a cavalry mount in *Tonka*, he, and even his rider who is seen as wiser and more humane by association with so fine an animal, far from inheriting Custer's tainted status, retain nobility. As an integral part of Plains Indian life, and as a part of nature, the horse itself has been exempt from blame. During the Indian protest of 1970 and 1971 at the University of Kansas, anger was not directed at Comanche, but rather at the way he was symbolized. One of the former student protesters who discussed Comanche told me, "Horses are very important to Plains tribes, especially in my culture—I'm Kiowa and Comanche. Even now at ceremonial giveaways, horses are given as gifts. Because of our regard for horses, I thought it was unfortunate to have a stuffed horse on display. The horse should have been buried. It was moth-eaten and pitiful, and it showed poor taste to display it. But museums are museums, you know." Since the equine animal possessed value and meaning within each of the two cultures which clashed at the Little Big Horn, neither side has shown animosity toward Comanche himself. Horses, in any case, sustain a far more durable image than human heroes and are seldom "debunked."

As humankind's working partner since earliest times, the horse has occupied a uniquely elevated status in human society, in peace as well as in war. By providing transportation and traction, this powerful species opened up new worlds for human beings, not only by expanding the physical realm, but by enlarging horizons bringing mental and spiritual enrichment as well. The sharing of motion and rhythm with another creature was a unique dimension of human experience. The merging of bodies and of wills between mount and rider provided a complementarity leading to bonding of a different order from that of other human-animal relationships. Although, paradoxically, often victimized by exploitation and abuse, the horse has quite generally been held in high esteem and considered the noblest of all animals. Because of the close interrelationship with people that existed, many societies established a taboo against eating horse flesh, and it is undoubtedly the only animal whose consumption was specifically prohibited by papal decree (Harris 1985:96–97). Even after the advent of the machine age, horses continue to be cherished as leisure-time partners in recreation, sport, and spectacle.

The horse adapts well to a feral existence independent of human intervention, as exemplified by the Spanish mounts who once attained freedom and reverted to the wild in the American plains and became mustangs. Although each individual is wild and must be tamed and trained in order to be useful for human purposes, yet once mastered, it willingly does man's bidding to a remarkable degree. As a species, the horse is a peaceful herbivore, whose natural defense is flight from disturbance or danger. Brereton notes that the horse is by nature timid, and not normally aggressive, "preferring discretion to valour" (1976:6). Yet so adaptable is the equine animal that it will go into the most terrifying battles as a faithful ally, lending its power and strength to the leadership of the rider, to become the symbol of war itself. Hudson recognized this "noblest kind of brute courage" when he wrote, "The very horses that fly terror-stricken from the smell of an Indian will, when 'maintained by a man,' readily charge into a whole host of yelling savages" (1903:359, 361). The well-established dominance hierarchy inherent in equine social order may explain how "a cavalry charge can be held together with very little effort by the human rider or driver who assumes the position of the stallion" (Clutton-Brock 1981:86). Horses are an innately gregarious species, and the accepted explanation of their intimate relationship with people is that the social nature of the animals allows them to respond to human beings as they would ordinarily react to dominant members of their own species. It is this capacity which makes horses able to respond as acutely as they do to human mastery.

The dual nature of the horse—emanating from the wild, to which it can readily revert, yet partaking of the tame realm, to which it is easily transformed—is also exemplified in its peaceful nature which throughout history has been so ironically molded into an instrument of war. The animal's peaceful nature reflects the species' vulnerability and its symbolic innocence. Left to itself, the horse will flee from disorder and conflict, yet it will submit to the domination of a physically less powerful master. The fact that military mounts had no choice in partaking of the enmity between armies is often lamented by those who empathize with war horses. "What was our share in the sinning, that we must share in the doom?" the horses ask of their master who "sold us into hell," as articulated by a poet (Bates 1929).

Just as the time of nonviolence will come, according to the Bible, when swords are beaten into ploughshares, horses often take on the imagery of a bridge to peace. Sefton and the other mounts wounded in the London bombing were a strange contrast to the pandemonium around them, as described by a witness. "The surviving horses, pouring blood from jagged flesh wounds, looked oddly peaceful as they were led back to the stables" (Watson 1983:91). Valued by both sides in a cavalry battle, horses are warriors without enmity and represent a kind of "common ground" between opposing armies. Many soldiers at the Washita Battle, for example, deplored Custer's shooting of approximately eight hundred Indian ponies. And cavalryman Jacob Horner, who participated in a movement against the Sioux in October 1876 when "orders had been given to take all horses and ponies found in possession of the Sioux," left a touching vignette of a group of Indian youths who were herding ponies. "Horner recalls how the boys cried when they learned their ponies were to be taken from them." On this expedition, two thousand such ponies were "rounded up, driven to Bismarck and shipped East" (Burdick and Hart 1942:18–19). A native American writer notes the horse's aura of neutrality when describing the capture of one hundred and fifty of another Plains tribe's mounts by his people. It seems odd, a warrior reflects, that "two sleeps ago these horses were content to belong to the Crows. Now they were Pikuni [Blackfeet] horses and seemed equally content. There was something about this easy changing of allegiance that made him almost envy the horses. As long as they weren't harmed, as long as the grass was long on both sides, they would live in peace" (Welsh 1986:34). It is this same spirit that stimulated the growth of the legend of Comanche's dual ownership by Indians and whites which reached its zenith in *Tonka*. With relative ease, the same horse who lived as an Indian pony could become a cavalry mount. And the identical tranquil horse, mounted in a museum, could take on the mantle of a "racist symbol" or become transformed into a powerful representative of Indian victory and accomplishment. In like manner, throughout the literature of the Little Big Horn controversy, both fiction and nonfiction, it is evident that Comanche is as easily used to express hatred for Custer as he is instrumental in expressing admiration for him.

Horses often take on the symbolism of regeneration, and in many traditional worldwide customs and rituals, they stand for fertility and the cycle of renewal on earth (see Lawrence 1985:183–84). Horse sacrifice in many cultures was practiced to insure fruitfulness. And in Greek mythology, out of the place where the hoofs of the winged horse, Pegasus, touched the ground, a fountain of water burst forth (Barloy 1974:79; Howey 1958:139). In more recent times, out of the devastation caused by atomic explosion came a legendary "bald charger, blind and without a mane, which the survivors of Hiroshima claim to have seen roaming among the ruins of their city" (Barloy 1974:81). According to ancient tradition, shearing a horse's mane and tail denotes grief following bereavement (see Plutarch 1980:329). The absence of the Hiroshima horse's hair represents not only burns caused by radiation, but is a sign of mourning. The charger has been maimed by blindness so he does not see the desolation around him. The fact that he is alive symbolizes hope for rebirth. So also Comanche partakes of the image of regeneration, both in fact and in metaphor. It was reported that after the Custer Battle, "the soldiers leaped at a chance to save one life—man or beast—from among the still forms that dotted the plains." For upon the field "every inch of which had been contested with frenzied desperation and courage, not a single other thing was found that had the breath of life." Though "not a soul survived to tell the tale, . . . Comanche remains to connect the living with the dead" (Comanche 1879; Burt 1891; Horse Survived 1926). Thus Comanche rises from the scene of carnage, a living being surrounded entirely by death—the one element which the Indians, even in their greatest victory at Little Big Horn, did not destroy.

Life and death seemed to be simultaneously represented by the celebrated equine survivor. After his recovery, Comanche's most important role under Sturgis's orders was to be paraded with the regiment on all ceremonial occasions. At those times, Keogh's mount was bridled, saddled, and draped in mourning, according to cavalry custom, with empty boots in the stirrups facing backward. This old tradition of the riderless horse being led in a military funeral or ceremonial procession dates back to primitive belief that the dead officer's "ghost needed to ride to heaven." The boots were "fixed backward in the stirrups because it was thought ghosts wore their feet backward" (Walker 1983:411).

Comanche encompasses many oppositions—the living and the dead, Indian and white, civilization and "savagery," animals and people, the mute and the voiced—and links the horse age with the machine age. Horses have a poignant power to recall the past and to evoke nostalgia. In the present era, when technology has removed us so far from the simpler times which were lived to the natural rhythmic pace of hoofbeats, countless numbers of people still go to Dyche Museum to see its most famous display. Almost all of them stand before the glass-encased horse, at least for a few moments, in awe and silence. Their thoughts and feelings are as varied as the knowledge and viewpoints they bring with them. Because Comanche is a cavalry mount, many observers turn their attention to his associates, the men who died for their country in the line of duty. If the visitor holds a belief that the cause the soldiers died for was wrong, there is still the idea that the soldiers who performed their duty deserve to be honored. Bringing to mind the Indian enemy that Comanche fought, some will think of a just but losing cause and a vanished way of life. Many will consider only the white Anglo-European's destiny to rule a continent.

If I were to hold my own protest and to create a new label for Comanche, I would enlarge the focus of the display. I would compose it to make the horse's remains stand as a symbol for the immeasurably great contribution that his species and other animals have made to human life and welfare, in peace as well as in war. It is important to write the placard to place the Battle of the Little Big Horn within a larger frame of reference, the clash of cultures on the Montana slopes being one part of the totality of tragic human conflicts and conquests. Comanche would challenge and protest the right of the strong to oppress the weak, the injustices that are worldwide in scope, and the universal barbarity of war.

The suffering of Comanche and other cavalry horses under conditions of violence they did not create is a reminder of humankind's domination over and ruthless persecution of the innocent in the quest to exert control over the earth. The battle-scarred horse should articulate the idea that we must revise the aggressive attitudes toward nature and animals that have proven so destructive. As a horse held in high regard, a revered human partner, he expresses the interconnection between all forms of life that must be recognized and honored before it is too late. Comanche, as a being who once lived on the brink of the age of technology, represents a bygone era of dependency upon animals, but he can speak to the times that must adopt fresh attitudes of sharing the earth with all creatures, a new interdependency that is vital to our own continued existence. The famous survivor should once again become "a learning experience," but on a larger scale appropriate to current world problems. For in the last analysis, if humankind itself is to survive, it must be clear that contemporary instruments for armed conflict, the tanks and bombs which have supplanted the cavalry mounts, are, like the war horse, "a vain hope for victory" which "by its great might . . . cannot save" (Psalms 33:17).

References

Adams, Jacob
   1965   *A Story of the Custer Massacre.* Carey, Ohio: Robert G. Hayman.
Albert, Paul
   1941   The Romance of the Western Horse. *Western Horseman,* vol. 6, no. 3 (May–June): 12–13, 38–45.
Alderdice, Gary
   n.d.   *The World's Best Horseracing Book Ever.* Hong Kong: Lincoln Green.
Allen, Theodore F.
   1898   Yesterday, The Reminiscences of Theodore F. Allen. *Journal of The United States Cavalry Association,* March: 227–28.
Amaral, Anthony
   1961   *Comanche: The Horse That Survived the Custer Massacre.* Los Angeles: Westernlore Press.
Appel, David
   1951   *Comanche: The Story of America's Most Heroic Horse.* New York: The World Publishing Co.
Arrian
   1986   *The Campaigns of Alexander.* New York: Penguin Books.
Atkinson, Major B. W.
   1909   Two Horses and a Mule. Unidentified magazine (CBNM Files).

The Backlog
   1950   South Dakota Natural Resources Bulletin.
Badger, Reid
   1979   *The Great American Fair: The World's Columbian Exposition and American Culture.* Chicago: Nelson Hall.
Baldwin, Nita
   1934   Another Friend of Comanche. *Winners of the West,* vol. 2, no. 4: 1.
Ballantine, Bill
   1964   *Horses and Their Bosses.* New York: J. B. Lippincott.
Barloy, J. J.
   1974   *Man and Animals: 100 Centuries of Friendship.* New York: Gordon & Cremonesi.

Bates, Katharine Lee
1929   The Horses. In *Animal Lover's Knapsack.* New York: Thomas Y. Crowell Co.

Beals, Carleton
1942   Kansas at the World's Fair. *Kansas* Magazine: 19–24.

Beecher, Elizabeth
1959   *Walt Disney's Tonka.* New York: Golden Press.

Benedict, Burton
1983   *The Anthropology of World's Fairs.* Berkeley: Scolar Press.

Bennett, John W.
1969   *Northern Plainsmen.* Arlington Heights, Illinois: AHM Publishing Corp.

Benninghoff, Cornelia
1935   "Comanche" of the Cavalry: The Endurance of a Horse. *Our Dumb Animals*, May.

Billings, John S.
1974 (first pub. 1871)   *Report on Barracks and Hospitals and Chapter on "Arrow Wounds" from Circular No. 3.* New York: Sol Lewis.

Billy: Last Survivor of Custer Massacre Passes Away
1900   *Saratoga Sun.* April 12.

Bird Douses Old Warhorse Comanche
1986   *Wichita Eagle-Beacon.* March 18.

Boniface, Captain Jno. J.
1903   *The Cavalry Horse and His Pack.* Kansas City, Missouri: Franklin Hudson Publishing Co.

Bourke, John Gregory
1891   *On the Border with Crook.* New York: Charles Scribner's Sons.

Brackett, Albert G.
1965 (first pub. 1865)   *History of the United States Cavalry.* New York: Argonaut Press.

Brady, Cyrus Townsend
1904   *Indian Fights and Fighters.* New York: Doubleday, Page & Co.
1916   Captain Yates' Capture of Rain-in-the-Face. *The Teepee Book*, vol. 2, no. 6.

Braun, Judith Elise
1975   *The North American Indian Exhibits at the 1876 and 1893 World Expositions: The Influence of Scientific Thought on Popular Attitudes.* Master's Thesis. Washington: George Washington University.

Brereton, J. M.
1976   *The Horse in War.* New York: Arco Publishing Co.

Brill, Charles J.
1938   *Conquest of the Southern Plains.* Oklahoma City: Golden Saga Publishers.

Brininstool, E. A.
1925   *A Trooper with Custer.* Columbus, Ohio: The Hunter-Trader-Trapper.
1952   *Troopers with Custer.* Harrisburg: The Stackpole Co.

Bronson, O. W.
1907   Comanche. *Outdoor Life*, vol. 19 (April): 345–46.

Brown, Barron
1935   *Comanche: The Sole Survivor of All the Forces in Custer's Last Stand, The Battle of the Little Big Horn.* Kansas City, Missouri: Burton Publishing Co.

1973   *Comanche* (with a new preface and introduction, and the inclusion of *Marching with Custer* by Elwood L. Nye). New York: Sol Lewis.

Brown, Dee
1971   *The Fetterman Massacre.* Lincoln: University of Nebraska Press.

Brown, Jesse, and A. M. Willard
1924   *The Black Hills Trails.* Rapid City, South Dakota: Rapid City Journal Co.

Budget Proposal
n.d. (1974 or 1975)   University of Kansas Museum of Natural History.

Burdick, Usher L.
1940   *Tales from Buffalo Land.* Baltimore: Wirth Brothers.

Burdick, Usher L., ed.
1949   *David F. Barry's Notes on "The Custer Battle."* Baltimore: Wirth Brothers.

Burdick, Usher L., and Eugene Hart
1942   *Jacob Horner and the Indian Campaigns of 1876 and 1877.* Baltimore: Wirth Brothers.

Burt, William
1891   He Saw Comanche. *The Junction City Union.* November 21: 3.

Cameron, William E., et al.
1893   *World's Fair.* Chicago: Chicago Publication & Lithograph Co.

Campbell, James B.
1894   *Campbell's Illustrated History of the World's Columbian Exposition.* Chicago: N. Jul Co.

Canetti, Elias
1973   *Crowds and Power.* New York: Continuum.

Canine Survivor of Custer's Last Battle Is Buried Here
1910   *Detroit Free Press.* May 29.

Carlson, Sally, and Richard Gustin
1971a   Comanche Out of Action. *University Daily Kansan.* November 10.
1971b   New Comanche Exhibit Unveiled. *University Daily Kansan.* December 3.

Carroll, John M., ed.
1974   *The Benteen-Goldin Letters on Custer and His Battle.* New York: Liveright.

Catlin, George
1876   *Illustrations of the Manners, Customs, and Condition of the North American Indians.* 2 vols. London: Chatto & Windus, Piccadilly.

Cavalry Rides Tuesday
1980   *Lawrence Journal-World.* May 5.

Cavalrymen Fed Beer to Wounded Horse
1965   *The Mountaineer.* July 16.

Centennials Spur Indian Outcry
1989   *Providence Journal.* January 22: A20.

Chandler, Melbourne C.
1960   *Of Garryowen In Glory.* Annandale, Virginia: The Turnpike Press.

Chard, Thornton
1940 Did the First Spanish Horses Landed in Florida and Carolina Leave Progeny? *American Anthropologist*, n.s., 42:90–106.

Charger, Samuel
1928 A Chronology of the Sioux Indians from an Early Period. *Sunshine Magazine*, vol. 9, no. 8: 304.

Charles, Tom
1941 Why Comanche Survived. *The Graduate Magazine*, December: 4.

Cheney, Roberta Carkeek
1984 *Names on the Face of Montana.* Missoula, Montana: Mountain Press Publishing Company.

Chew, Peter
1976 Morgan Horses: Brave, Unchanging All-Purpose Breed. *Smithsonian*, vol. 7, no. 5 (August): 44–53.

Chief: Commemorative Ceremony
1968 June 1. Fort Riley, Kansas.

Children's Bookshelf
1963 *The Kansas Teacher*, vol. 71, no. 1 (February): 45.

Circlot, J. E.
1983 *A Dictionary of Symbols.* New York: Philosophical Library.

Clark, Robert H.
1947 Clings to Famed Relic. *Kansas City Star*, September 11: 14.

Clutton-Brock, Juliet
1981 *Domesticated Animals from Early Times.* Austin: University of Texas Press.

Comanche
1879 *The Animal World*, vol. 10, no. 118 (July): 1.

Comanche
1926 *The Cavalry Journal*, vol. 35, no. 144 (July): 432–34.

Comanche: Diary of a War-Horse
1966 *Kansas!* Kansas Department of Economic Development. Third Issue: 10, 12, 13.

Comanche and the Custer Fight
1939 *Kansas City Star.* January 17.

Comanche Back in Dyche Museum
1941 *The Graduate Magazine*, May.

Comanche Dies of Old Age
1891 Unidentified newspaper clipping, Kansas City. November 11.

Comanche Faces Battle Again!
1953 *University Daily Kansan.* September 29.

Comanche Gets Bid
1947 *The Graduate Magazine*, December: 7.

Comanche into Storage until Museum Is Rebuilt
1934 *University Daily Kansan.* January 12: 1,3.

Comanche Not in Trim
1939 *Kansas City Times.* January 17.

Comanche Now in New Dispute
1970 *University Daily Kansan.* September 26.

Comanche Once Angered Indians
1978 *Olathe Daily News.* January 10.

Comanche—Only Survivor of the Big Horn
    1911   *Historia Quarterly* (Oklahoma Historical Society), vol. 2, no. 2.
Comanche Returns
    1941   *The University Daily Kansan* (February 13).
Comanche Stands for Indians Too
    1978   *Wichita Beacon.* January 9.
Comanche to Gallop Again in Disney Movie
    1956   *University Daily Kansan.* October 26.
Comanche, Weary of Fighting, Needs Rest
    1953   *University Daily Kansan.* October 21.
Comanche's Last Stand
    1947   *Newsweek*, vol. 30, no. 11 (September 15): 25.
Comanche's Last Stand at K. U. Draws Indian Fire
    1970   *Kansas City Star*, September 29.
Connell, Evan S.
    1984   *Son of the Morning Star.* San Francisco: North Point Press.
Coogan, Tim Pat
    1987   *The IRA.* Glasgow: William Collins & Co.
Cooper, J. C.
    1978   *An Illustrated Encyclopaedia of Traditional Symbols.* London: Thames & Hudson.
Cooper, Jilly
    1983   *Animals in War.* London: William Heinemann.
Corpse Saves Comanche
    1941   *University Daily Kansan.* October 2.
Craig, Major Gen. Malin
    1926   Four-Footed Soldiers Get in Book of Remembrance. *Kansas City Times.* November 26.
Custer, Elizabeth B.
    1885   *Boots and Saddles.* New York: Harper & Brothers.
    1890   *Following the Guidon.* New York: Harper & Brothers.
    1876   Washington correspondent of the *Cincinnati Gazette.*
Custer's Massacre
    1942   *Rapid City Journal.* June 26.
Custer's Pants Join Famed Comanche at KU Museum
    1955   *Lawrence Journal-World.* December.

Dadd, George H.
    1854   *The Modern Horse Doctor.* Boston: John P. Jewett and Co.
Dallas, David
    1954   *Comanche Lives Again.* Manhattan, Kansas: Centennial Publishing Co.
Darwin, Charles
    1868   *The Variation of Animals and Plants under Domestication.* 2 vols. New York: Orange Judd & Co.
Dary, David
    1975a   The Horse That Got Its Name from an Indian Yell. Sunday Magazine of the *Kansas City Star.* June 22: 1–4.
    1975b   Comanche. *Kansas Alumni*, Fall: 5–9.
    1976a   *Comanche.* Lawrence: University of Kansas.
    1976b   Comanche of the Little Bighorn. *Horse and Horseman.* vol. 4, no. 6 (August): 70–81.

Davis, Col. George R.
　　1893　*The World's Columbian Exposition, Chicago, 1893.* Philadelphia: P. W. Ziegler & Co.

De Gubernatis, Angelo
　　1872　*Zoological Mythology.* 2 vols. New York: Macmillan & Co.

Dill, W. A.
　　1939　Kansas University News Bureau Release. January.

Dippie, Brian W.
　　1976　*Custer's Last Stand: The Anatomy of an American Myth.* Missoula: University of Montana.

Dippie, Brian W., ed., in collaboration with John M. Carroll
　　1978　*Bards of the Little Big Horn.* Bryan, Texas: Guidon Press.

Dobie, J. Frank
　　1952　*The Mustangs.* Boston: Little, Brown and Co.

Dobie, J. Frank, Mody C. Boatright, and Harry Ransom, eds.
　　1965　*Mustangs and Cow Horses.* Dallas: Southern Methodist University Press.

Doll, Julie
　　1980　Cavalry Unit Tours City Sites. *Lawrence Journal-World.* May 5.

Donnelle, A. J., ed.
　　1889　*Cyclorama of General Custer's Last Fight.* Boston: Cyclorama Co.

Dousman, Nina Sturgis
　　1926　General Orders No. 7. *Winners of the West.* (August): 7.

Downey, Fairfax
　　1941　Charger On A Stricken Field. *Adventure,* vol. 105, no. 5 (Sept.): 47–55.

Dustin, Fred
　　1939　*The Custer Tragedy: Events Leading up to and Following the Little Big Horn Campaign of 1876.* Ann Arbor, Michigan: Edwards Brothers.
　　1941　Notes on Col. Elwood L. Nye's Paper, "Marching With Custer." Unpublished manuscript.

Dyche, L. L.
　　1893　Mounting of Large Animals. *Scientific American,* October: 234–35.

Echoes of Custer's Last Fight
　　1912　*Toledo Times.* December 15.

Echohawk, Brummett
　　1956　The Best Horse I Ever Rode. *Western Horseman,* vol. 21, no. 1 (January): 27, 47–48.
　　1964　The Spotted Horse Alone. *Western Horseman,* vol. 29, no. 8 (August): 43, 99–101.

Ediger, Theodore A., and Vinnie Hoffman
　　1955　Some Reminiscences of the Battle of the Washita. *The Chronicles of Oklahoma,* vol. 33, no. 2 (Summer): 137–41.

Edwards, Ralph
　　1934　The Horse Comanche. *Winners of the West,* vol. 11, no. 4 (April): 3.

Egan, Timothy
　　1988　Old West's Centennial Effort: Hail Indians (and Custer, Too). *New York Times.* December 13: A1.

Ege, Robert
 1966   Legend Was a Man Named Keogh. *Montana, The Magazine of Western History*, vol. 16, no. 2 (Spring): 27–39.
Ellis, Horace
 1909   A Survivor's Story of the Custer Massacre on American Frontier. *Journal of American History*, vol. 3, no. 2: 227–32.
Ellis, John
 1986   *The Social History of the Machine Gun.* Baltimore: Johns Hopkins University Press.
Ellison, Douglas W.
 1983   *Sole Survivor: An Examination of the Frank Finkel Narrative.* Aberdeen, South Dakota: North Plains Press.
Epperson, Hoss
 n.d.   *Comanche.* Fort Bliss, Texas: U.S. Horse Cavalry Association.
An Equine Pensioner
 1890   *Chicago Sunday Tribune.* October 26.
Escaped the Massacre: Comanche, Captain Keogh's Steed, at the Fair
 1893   *Chicago Inter-Ocean.* July 12: supp. 7.

Famous "Comanche" and His Latest Tail
 1936   Unidentified newspaper.
Farnum, George R.
 1965   The Saga of a United States Cavalry Horse. *Reverence for Life Magazine*, vol. 50, no. 7 (September): 1–2.
Faulty Shoeing of Horse Saved His Life at Little Big Horn Battle
 1926   Unidentified newspaper.
Feudin' and Fussin' over Comanche
 1947   *The Graduate Magazine*, October: 16.
Finerty, John F.
 1970 (first pub. 1890)   *War Path and Bivouac: The Big Horn and Yellowstone Expedition.* Lincoln: University of Nebraska Press.
The First Pension Case
 n.d.   Unidentified newspaper (CBNM Files).
Fisher, James J.
 1971   Cavalry Horse Now Tells Indians' Story. *Kansas City Times.* Dec. 2.
Flocking to Things Historical
 1979   *Kansas Alumni*, vol. 77, no. 5 (February): 5.
Frazer, Bob
 1960   Only One of Famed Cavalry Horses Remains. *Junction City Union.* May.
Frazer, Robert W.
 1972   *Forts of the West.* Norman: University of Oklahoma Press.
Fredriksson, Kristine
 1985   *American Rodeo: From Buffalo Bill to Big Business.* College Station: Texas A & M Press.
Friswold, Carroll
 1968   *Frontier Fighters and Their Autograph Signatures.* Los Angeles: Westernlore Press.
Friswold, Carroll, ed.
 1964   *Marching with Custer* by Elwood L. Nye. Glendale, California: The Arthur H. Clark Co.

Froissard, Jean, and Lily Powell Froissard
    1980 *The Horseman's International Book of Reference.* London: Stanley
    Paul.

Frost, Lawrence A.
    1976 *General Custer's Libbie.* Seattle: Superior Publishing Co.
    1986 *General Custer's Thoroughbreds.* Mattituck, N. Y.: J. M. Carroll
    Co.

Fry, James B.
    1892 Comments by General Fry on the Custer Battle. *The Century
    Illustrated Monthly Magazine,* vol. 43, no. 3 (January): 385–87.

General Custer's Pants Given Museum by Former Sheridanite
    1955. *Sheridan Press,* November: 2.

Ghent, W. J.
    1934 The Horse, Comanche. *Winners of the West,* vol. 2, no. 4
    (Feb.): 1.

Gildner, Gary
    1979 Comanche. In *The Poetry of Horses,* comp. William Cole. New
    York: Charles Scribner's Sons.

The Globe Gets Double-Crossed
    1939 *The Atchison Daily Globe.*

Godfrey, Calvin Pomeroy
    1934 General Edward S. Godfrey. *Ohio Archaeological and Historical
    Quarterly,* vol. 43, no. 1 (January): 61–98.

Godfrey, Edward S.
    1892 Custer's Last Battle. *The Century Illustrated Monthly Magazine,*
    vol. 43, no. 3 (January): 358–84.
    1921 *General George A. Custer and the Battle of the Little Big Horn.*
    New York: The Century Co.
    1925 One of Custer's Troopers Tells of Days on Warpath. *New
    York Times.* August 16.

Graham, R. B. Cunninghame
    1949 *The Horses of the Conquest.* Norman: University of Oklahoma
    Press.

Graham, W. A.
    1926 *The Story of the Little Big Horn: Custer's Last Fight.* New York:
    The Century Co.
    1953 *The Custer Myth: A Source Book of Custeriana.* Harrisburg: The
    Stackpole Co.

Graham, W. A., ed.
    1951 *The Official Record of the Reno Court of Inquiry.* 2 vols. Pacific
    Palisades, California: privately printed.
    1954 *Abstract of the Official Record of Proceedings of the Reno Court of
    Inquiry.* Harrisburg: The Stackpole Co.

Gray, John S.
    1977 Veterinary Service on Custer's Last Campaign. *The Kansas
    Historical Society Quarterly,* vol. 43, no. 3 (Autumn): 249–63.

Green, Ben K.
    1974 *The Color of Horses: The Scientific and Authoritative Identification
    of the Color of the Horse.* Flagstaff, Arizona: Northland Press.

Greenspan, Bud
    1956 The Lone Survivor. *Coronet,* vol. 40, no. 5 (September): 158.

Greenwood, Jeremy
1983 *Sefton: The Horse for Any Year.* London: Quiller Press.
Grisham, John
1953 Missouri Gets In a Claim. *Kansas City Star.* October 17.
Guthrie, John
1932 The Fetterman Massacre. *Annals of Wyoming*, vol. 9, no. 2: 714–18.

Haines, Francis
1971 *Horses in America.* New York: Thomas Y. Crowell Co.
Hall, Mike
1971 Indians Question "Sole Survivor" Status of Horse. *Topeka Capital-Journal.* November 14.
Hammer, Kenneth
1966 The Glory March: A Concise Account of the Little Bighorn Campaign of 1876. *The English Westerners' Brand Book*, vol. 8, no. 4 (July): 1–6.
1972 *Men With Custer: Biographies of the 7th Cavalry, 25 June, 1876.* Fort Collins, Colorado: The Old Army Press.
1980 *The Glory March.* Custeriana Monograph #7. Monroe, Michigan: Monroe County Library System.
Hammer, Kenneth, ed.
1976 *Custer in '76: Walter Camp's Notes on the Custer Fight.* Provo, Utah: Brigham Young University Press.
Hanson, Joseph Mills
1909 *The Conquest of the Missouri.* Chicago: A. C. McClurg & Company.
Hardin Wants Comanche and Fight to Be Put Up by Kansas Students
1939 *Helena Independent.* January 19.
Harris, Marvin
1985 *Good to Eat: Riddles of Food and Culture.* New York: Simon and Schuster.
Haws, Dick
1980 Modern Cavalry Pauses for a Salute to an Old Campaigner. *Kansas City Times.* May 7.
Hayes-McCoy, G. A.
1965 *Captain Myles Walter Keogh, United States Army 1840–1876.* Dublin: National University of Ireland.
Haynes, Glen
1976 *The American Paint Horse.* Norman: University of Oklahoma Press.
He Is Properly Cared For!
1953 *Lawrence Journal-World.* October.
Henderson, Sam
1985 Those Fabulous Horses of George Armstrong Custer. *The Western Horse*, vol. 4, no. 2: 34–37.
Hennessy, Maurice N.
1973 *The Wild Geese: The Irish Soldier in Exile.* Old Greenwich, Connecticut: The Devin-Adair Co.
He's Joined His Command
1891 *The San Francisco Examiner.* November 22.

Hoig, Stan
  1976   *The Battle of the Washita.* Garden City, New York: Douᵇ'eday & Co.
Holcombe, A. A.
  1881   Army Veterinary Medicine. *American Veterinary Review*, 5 (November): 335–49.
Homer
  1986   *The Iliad.* New York: Penguin Books.
Honor For A War Horse
  1913   *Kansas City Star.* January 12: 9A, col. 1.
Hope, C. E. G., and G. N. Jackson
  1973   *The Encyclopedia of the Horse.* London: Peerage Books.
Hopf, Alice L.
  1977   *Wild Cousins of the Horse.* New York: G. P. Putnam's Sons.
Horn, Don
  1987   Notes from the Chairman. *Little Big Horn Associates Newsletter*, vol. 21, no. 7: 2.
Horn, Miles (White Crow)
  1965   "The Pinto"—Battle's Other Equine Hero. *The Billings Gazette.* June 20.
Horse Survived Custer Disaster
  1926   *Washington Star.* June 27.
Howey, M. Oldfield
  1958   *The Horse in Magic and Myth.* New York: Castle Books.
Hudson, W. H.
  1903   *The Naturalist in La Plata.* New York: E. P. Dutton & Co.
Humphrey, Philip S.
  1974   To Milton D. Thompson. May 16.
Hunn, Frank
  1950   Editorial. *Sturgis Tribune.* January 19.
Hunt, Frazer and Robert
  1947   *I Fought with Custer: The Story of Sergeant Windolph, Last Survivor of the Battle of the Little Big Horn.* New York: Charles Scribner's Sons.
Hutton, Paul A.
  1976   From Little Bighorn to Little Big Man: The Changing Image of a Western Hero in Popular Culture. *The Western Historical Quarterly*, vol. 7, no. 1: 19–45.

Indians Win "Battle" Over Stuffed Horse
  1978   *The Christian Science Monitor.* January 20: 17.
Inman, Henry
  1891   A Veteran War Horse. *Topeka Daily Capital.* November 12.
It Transpires That There Is a Horse on the Pension Roles
  1890   *Savannah, Georgia, Times.*

Johnson, Haynes
  1987   Oliver North's Very Own Secret Little Big Horn Scheme in Nicaragua. *Providence Journal–Bulletin.* June 20: A3.
Johnson, Robert Underwood, and Clarence Clough Buel, eds.
  1956   *Battles and Leaders of the Civil War*, 3 vols. New York: Thomas Yoseloff.

Johnson, Rossiter, ed.
1897, 1898   *A History of the World's Columbian Exposition* (Vols. 1 & 2: 1897; vols. 3 & 4: 1898). New York: D. Appleton & Company.
Johnson, Roy
1949   *Jacob Horner of the Seventh Cavalry.* Bismarck: The State Historical Society of North Dakota. Reprint from *North Dakota History,* vol. 16, no. 2 (April).
Jones, Bob
1964   Horse's Problems Continue Even after Death. *University Daily Kansan.* February 13: 6.

Kansas and Kansas History
1939   *Kansas City Times.* January 25.
Kansas Can Keep Custer's Pants but Local Kiwanians Want His Horse Back in Montana
1955   *Lewistown Daily News.* November 23.
Kansas "U" Editor Says "No" to Hardin Comanche Plan
1939   *Helena Independent.* January 23.
Keegan, John
1987a   *The Face of Battle.* New York: Penguin Books.
1987b   *The Masks of Command.* New York: Viking.
King, Captain Charles
1890   Custer's Last Battle. *Harper's New Monthly Magazine,* vol. 81, no. 483 (August): 378–87.
Korn, Gustave
1936   The Custer Battle. *Winners of the West,* vol. 13, no. 2 (January 30): 1–4.
K. U. Gets Comanche Back in Shape
1986   *Lawrence Journal–World.* May 11.
K. U. in Gallant Stand to Rescue Comanche
1953   *Topeka Daily Capital.* September 30: 22.
K. U. Museum Given Top Tourist Ranking
1978   *Lawrence Journal–World* (November 24).
K. U. Museum Has Display of Battlefield Articles
1947   *Kansas City Star.* September 7.
K. U. Museum in Dark on "Comanche" Petition
1970   *University Daily Kansan.* September 29: 8.
K. U. Museum to Improve Comanche Exhibit
1971   *Lawrence Journal–World.* November 17.
KU's Dyche Museum Ranked Number One State Attraction
1978   University of Kansas Division of Information. November 21.
Kuhlman, Charles
1940   *Custer and the Gall Saga.* Billings, Montana: privately printed.
1951   *Legend into History.* Harrisburg: The Telegraph Press.
1972   *Massacre Survivor! The Story of Frank Finkel—A Trooper with Custer at the Little Big Horn.* Fort Collins, Colorado: The Old Army Press.

Lamb, A. J. R.
1938   *The Story of the Horse.* London: Alexander Maclehose & Co.
Lamb, Harold
1979   *Alexander of Macedon.* Los Angeles: Pinnacle Books.

Last of Custer's Officers Goes to Join Comrades
  1936 *San Francisco News.*
Last Stand Survivor Popular Dyche Exhibit
  1950 *University Daily Kansan.* October 2: 2.
Lawrence, Elizabeth Atwood
  1982 *Rodeo: An Anthropologist Looks at the Wild and the Tame.* Knoxville: University of Tennessee Press.
  1985 *Hoofbeats and Society: Studies of Human-Horse Interactions.* Bloomington: Indiana University Press.
Lawrence's Year in Review
  1987 *Lawrence Journal-World.* January 1: section C, p. 1.
Leighton, Margaret
  1954 *The Story of General Custer.* New York: Grosset & Dunlap.
  1957 *Comanche of the Seventh.* New York: Ariel.
Libby, O. G.
  1920 *The Arikara Narrative of the Campaign Against the Hostile Dakota June 1876.* Bismarck: North Dakota Historical Collections, vol. 6.
Life on the Western Plains: An Interesting Talk by Mrs. Custer
  1891 *New York Times.* November 7: 8, col. 6.
Lockwood, John C.
  1923 Comanche, the Sole Survivor of Custer Massacre, Once Pet of Seventh Cavalry Regiment. *University Daily Kansan.* October 1.
Luce, Edward S.
  1939 *Keogh, Comanche and Custer.* Privately printed.
  1958a Letter. *Westerners Brand Book* (Chicago), vol. 15 (November): 72.
Luce, Edward S., ed.
  1958b The Diary and Letters of Dr. James M. De Wolf. *North Dakota History*, vol. 25 (April–July).
Luther, Tal
  1972 *Custer High Spots.* Fort Collins, Colorado: The Old Army Press.
Lydic, F. A.
  1981 *The Far West's Race with Death.* Joliet, Illinois: privately printed.
  1982 *Comanche! Oh Comanche!* Joliet, Illinois: privately printed.
Lyford, Carrie A.
  1984 *Quill and Beadwork of the Western Sioux.* Boulder, Colorado: Johnson Publishing Co.

McClernand, Edward J.
  1969 *With the Indian and the Buffalo in Montana, 1870–1878.* Glendale, California: The Arthur H. Clark Co.
McCoy, Alvin S.
  1947 Vie for a Custer Relic. *Kansas City Star.* August 31.
MacEwan, Grant
  1973 *Sitting Bull: The Years in Canada.* Edmonton: Hurtig Publishers.
  1978 *Memory Meadows.* Saskatchewan: Western Producer Prairie Books.
McGregor, James H.
  1945 *Wigwam Smoke.* Cynthiana, Kentucky: The Hobson Book Press.

Magnussen, Daniel O., ed.

1974 *Peter Thompson's Narrative of the Little Big Horn Campaign, 1876.* Glendale, California: The Arthur H. Clark Co.

Mallery, Garrick

1893 *Picture-Writing of the American Indians.* Tenth Annual Report of the Bureau of Ethnology to the Smithsonian Institution, 1888–89. Washington: U.S. Government Printing Office: 25–822.

Manhattanite Writes Fort Riley History

1954 Unidentified newspaper clipping, Fort Riley files.

Manion, John S.

1986 Concern for a Dead Horse, or The Legend of Comanche's Burial at Willowbrook. Privately printed.

Many Events of Historical Interest Remain Alive in the Monuments and Inscriptions of Fort Hill

1951 *Citizen Advertizer,* Auburn, New York. May 31.

Marquis, Thomas B.

1933 *She Watched Custer's Last Battle: Her Story Interpreted in 1927.* Privately printed.

Maslowski, Karl

1978 Horse Surviving Custer Massacre Turns Up in Museum in Kansas. *The Cincinnati Enquirer.* November 26.

Matthews, Boris

1986 *The Herder Symbol Dictionary.* Wilmette, Illinois: Chiron Publications.

Mayhew, Edward

1872 *The Illustrated Horse Doctor.* Philadelphia: J. B. Lippincott & Co.

Medley and Jensen

1910 *Seventh Cavalry, United States Army.* Denver: Williamson-Haffner Co.

Meketa, Ray

1984 *Hidden Treasurers of the Little Big Horn.* Douglas, Alaska: Cheechako Press.

Mellin, Jeanne

1961 *The Morgan Horse.* Brattleboro, Vermont: The Stephen Greene Press.

Mengel, Robert

1969 *Comanche: Silent Horse on a Silent Field.* Lawrence: University of Kansas.

Merillat, Louis A., and Delwin M. Campbell

1935 *Veterinary Military History of the United States.* 2 vols. Kansas City, Missouri: Haver-Glover Laboratories.

Merington, Marguerite

1950 *The Custer Story: The Life and Intimate Letters of General George A. Custer and His Wife Elizabeth.* New York: The Devin-Adair Co.

Midway Types: A Book of Illustrated Lessons about the People of the Midway— World's Fair 1893

1894 Chicago: The American Engraving Co.

Miller, David Humphreys

1957 *Custer's Fall: The Indian Side of the Story.* New York: Duell, Sloan and Pearce.

1971 Echoes of the Little Bighorn. *American Heritage,* vol. 22, no. 4 (June): 28–29.

Miller, William B. E., and Lloyd V. Tellor
   1885   *The Diseases of Livestock.* Philadelphia: H. C. Watts & Co.

Mills, Charles K.
   1985   *Harvest of Barren Regrets: The Army Career of Frederick William Benteen.* Glendale, California: The Arthur H. Clark Co.

Mohr, Erna
   1971   *The Asiatic Wild Horse.* London: J. A. Allen & Co.

Monahan, John
   1986   The Colonel From Carlow Who Died With His Boots On. *The Carlow Nationalist*, June: 17.

Montana In Bid For Comanche
   1953   *Manhattan Mercury-Chronicle.* September 29, 1953.

Montana Sets Sights on Comanche
   1953   *Lawrence Journal-World.* September 29.

More of the Story of Comanche, Survivor of the Custer Battle
   1932   *Lawrence Journal-World.* January 13: 10, c. 1–5.

More Shots at Old Comanche
   1953   *Kansas City Star.* September 28.

Morgan, Hal, and Kerry Tucker
   1984   *Rumor.* New York: Penguin Books.

Morrell, Warren
   1949   *Through the Hills.* Sturgis, South Dakota. July 22.

Mulford, Ami Frank
   n.d. (first published 1878)   *Fighting Indians in the 7th United States Cavalry.* Corning, New York: Paul Lindsley Mulford.

Museum Gets Request from Illinois for a Hair from Comanche's Mane
   1950   *University Daily Kansan.* March 16.

Museum Prepares Comanche Exhibit
   1976   *Lawrence Journal-World.* June 21.

Museum to Commemorate Little Big Horn and Horse
   1976   *Russell Daily News* (Kansas). June 25.

Museum to Honor Custer's Battle with Exhibit, Book on Comanche
   1976   *Colby Free Press Tribune* (Kansas). June 24.

New Exhibit, Book Concerns Comanche
   1976   *Council Grove Republican* (Kansas). June 23.

New Exhibit to Encase Little Big Horn Relic
   1976   *University Daily Kansan.* June 22.

New Town Named Comanche
   1909   *Great Falls Tribune.* July 21: 1.

Nye, Elwood L.
   1941   Marching with Custer. *The Veterinary Bulletin*, vol. 35, no. 2 (April): 114–40.
   n.d.(a)   *What of Comanche.* Unpublished manuscript.
   n.d.(b)   *Cavalry March.* Unpublished manuscript.

Old Comanche Dead
   1891a   *Bismarck Daily Tribune.* November 13: 1.

Old Comanche Dead
   1891b   *Junction City Union.* November 14: 3.

Old Comanche in the Place of Honor at K.U.
   1921   *University Daily Kansan.*

An Old Friend of Comanche Finds Him in K.U. Museum
    1931   *Kansas City Star.* April 30.
An Old Timer Dead. The Last Survivor of the Custer Massacre Died
    Yesterday
    1900   *The Daily Sun-Leader.* Friday, March 23.
Old Timer Who Was Near the Last Stand of General Custer Sends Co-
    manche's Real Story.
    1921   *University Daily Kansan.*
One Horse Survivor of the Little Big Horn
    1934   *Winners of the West*, vol. 2, no. 2 (January): 6.
The Only Survivor
    1890   *Chicago Tribune.* September 12.
Only Survivor of Custer's Last Stand
    1926   *Columbus, Ohio, Dispatch.* June 25.
Otis, George A.
    1871   *Arrow Wounds: A Report of Surgical Cases Treated in the U.S. from
    1865 to 1871.* Circular No. 3. Washington: U.S. Government Print-
    ing Office.
Owen, Ida May
    1926   From the Fort to the Field of Annihilation. *The Bismarck Capi-
    tal.* June 24.
Owens, Harry J.
    1983   Another Survivor of the Custer Battle. *True West*, vol. 30, no.
    5 (May): 12–15.
The Owner of Comanche Rides out of the Past
    1930   *The Kansas City Star.* December 21.

Partoll, Albert J., ed.
    1939   After the Custer Battle. *Frontier and Midland*, vol. 19, no. 4
    (Summer): 277–79.
Peterson, Florence K., and Irene Smith
    1961   *A Cavalcade of Horses.* New York: Thomas Nelson & Sons.
Peterson, Iver
    1986   110 Years after Custer's Defeat, Mystery Lives On. *New York
    Times.* June 26: A 18.
Peterson, John M.
    1981   W. Harvey Brown and K.U.'s First Buffaloes. *Kansas History*,
    vol. 4, no. 4 (Winter): 219–26.
Pittenger, Peggy Jet
    1967   *Morgan Horses.* New York: A. S. Barnes and Co.
Plummer, Alexander, and Richard H. Power
    1909   *The Army Horse in Accident and Disease.* New York: Military
    Publishing Co.
Plutarch
    n.d.   *Plutarch's Lives.* New York: The Modern Library.
    1980   *The Age of Alexander.* New York: Penguin Books.
Pohanka, Brian
    1986   Myles Keogh. *Military Images*, vol. 8, no. 2 (September-Octo-
    ber): 15–24.
Pride, W. F.
    1926   *The History of Fort Riley.* Fort Riley, Kansas: privately printed.

Progress of Fort Riley
1890   *New York Times.* September 26.

Radford, E., & M. A. Radford
1974   *Encyclopaedia of Superstitions.* London: Book Club Associates.
Rednest, Fred
1978   Ghost Dance Exhibit at KU Soon. *The Indian Leader*, January.
Redskins Attack, Want Comanche Moved
1970   *Manhattan Mercury.* September 30.
Reedstrom, E. L.
1970   The War Horse. *Research Review*, Little Big Horn Associates, vol. 4, no. 4 (Winter): 1–5.
Regnary, Thomas
1953   Letter to the Editor. *University Daily Kansan.* November 2.
Reid, Marshall
1952   *Horses and Dogs of Great Men.* New York: The McBride Co.
Report of the Kansas Board of World's Fair Managers
1894   Topeka: Hamilton Printing Co.
Richards, Bill
1985   This Unlikely Hero Is Attracting Crowds to Site of Last Stand. *Wall Street Journal.* August 30: 1, 7.
Richeson, Voorheis
1930   Seventh Cavalry. *Winners of the West.* April 30: 5–6.
Riley, Peg
1971   Horse Comanche Survives Little Big Horn, Students. *University Daily Kansan.* October 7: 1.
Russell, Don
1970   *The Wild West.* Fort Worth: Amon Carter Museum of Western Art.
Rutter, Mary
1964   Strange Tale of Little Big Horn Survivor. *Kansas City Star.* June 25.
Ryan, J. C., ed.
1966   *Custer Fell First.* San Antonio: The Naylor Co.
Ryan, John
1980   *General Custer Among the Indians.* Bryan, Texas: privately printed by John M. Carroll.
Ryan, John, Captain
1912   Custer's Last Fight. *The National Tribune.* Washington, D.C. January 4.
Rydell, Robert W.
1984   *All The World's A Fair.* Chicago: University of Chicago Press.
Rydjord, John
1982   *Indian Place Names.* Norman: University of Oklahoma Press.

Sandoz, Mari
1953   *Cheyenne Autumn.* New York: McGraw-Hill Book Company
1966   *The Battle of the Little Big Horn.* New York: J. B. Lippincott Co.
Schneider, George A., ed.
1977   *The Freeman Journal: The Infantry in the Sioux Campaign of 1876.* San Raphael, California: Presidio Press.

Schultz, Floyd
1939   Comanche—A Loyal Horse Helped Set a Tradition. *The Times.* Clay Center, Kansas. March 2.
Schuyler, Randy
1974   KU Promoted by Early Professors. *University Daily Kansan.* February 21: 1, 5.
See a Frail Comanche
1939   *Kansas City Times.* January 19.
Self, Margaret Cabell
1946   *The Horseman's Encyclopedia.* n. p.: A. S. Barnes and Co.
Shannon, Tom
1953a   Old Stud Replies: Montana Horse Claims Kansan Letter a Fake. *University Daily Kansan.* October 26: 8.
1953b   Student Makes Offer to Help in Horse Theft. *University Daily Kansan.* November 10.
Sheridan's Horse on Exhibition
n.d.   Unidentified newspaper (CBNM Files).
Shultz, A. L.
1953   Send Custer's Horse to Montana? *Topeka State Journal.* September 29.
Sibrava, Frank E., and Nelson Ober
n.d.   Echoes of Garryowen. Unpublished manuscript.
Sipchen, Bob
1987   Paying Homage to Roy Rogers. *Providence Sunday Journal.* December 20: A 6.
Sketch of the Family History of the Keoghs or Kehoes
n.d.   Carlow, Ireland.
Smith, De Cost
1949   *Red Indian Experiences.* London: George Allen & Unwin.
Smith, Herbert E.
1927   Comanche Still Lives. In *Custer's Last Battle* by Charles Francis Roe, ed. Robert Bruce. New York: National Highways Association.
Smith, John Stewart
1953   Letter to the Editor. *University Daily Kansan.* October 29.
Smoke: A Story of The Custer Massacre
1910   *Chicago Inter-Ocean.*
Snyder, Leonard
1951   Comanche Still Lives. *Western Horseman,* vol. 16, no. 10 (October): 13, 35–36.
Sole Survivor of Custer Massacre Dead
1891   *Bismarck Daily Tribune.* November 13: 3.
Sole Survivor of Custer's Fight
1926   *Chicago Inter-Ocean.*
Soubier, L. Clifford
1970   *L'Affaire Comanche or Flogging A Dead Horse.* Unpublished manuscript.
The Spirit of Comanche (name withheld by request)
1953   Comanche's Spirit Sets Forth Case. *University Daily Kansan.* Oct. 9.
State University
1891   *Topeka Daily Capital.* November 11: 8.

Stewart, Edgar I.
1980   *Custer's Luck.* Norman: University of Oklahoma Press.
Stewart, Edgar I., and Jane R. Stewart, eds.
1957   *The Field Diary of Lt. Edward Settle Godfrey.* Portland, Oregon: Champoeg Press.
Stewart, George R.
1985   *American Place Names.* New York: Oxford University Press.
Stir over Comanche
1939   *Kansas City Times.* January 16.
Stocking, George
1985   *Objects and Others: Essays on Museums and Material Culture.* Madison: University of Wisconsin Press.
Sullivan, P.
n.d.   The Custer Massacre. Unidentified newspaper, Boston (CBNM Files).
Summer Reading
1953   *Rapid City, South Dakota, Daily Journal.* July 19.
Survives Massacre But Not Dyche
1939   Unidentified Kansas newspaper. January 17.
Survivor of Little Big Horn Becomes Prey of Frozen Bird
1986   *The Sioux City Journal.* March 20: B5.
Swergal, Edwin
1949   Keogh and Comanche. 2 parts. *The Milwaukee Magazine,* July and August.

Taunton, Francis B.
1967   The Man Who Rode Comanche. In *Sidelights of the Sioux Wars.* London: English Westerners Society. Pp. 70–78.
Thomas, De Ann
1986   Comanche Back under Saddle Again. *University Daily Kansan.* June 11.
Thompson, Daniel Q.
1989   Letter to the Editor. *New York Times.* January 8: E28.
Thunder Hawk, Cal
1979   Comments about Custer: Letter to the Editor. *Lawrence Journal-World.* July 7.
Tozer, Basil
1908   *The Horse in History.* London: Methuen & Co.
The True Tail of Comanche by Son of Comanche
n.d.   Unpublished manuscript.
Tschiffely, A. F.
1933   *Tschiffely's Ride.* New York: Simon and Schuster.
1955   Ten Thousand Miles in the Saddle. In *Man Against Nature: Tales of Adventure and Exploration,* ed. Charles Neider. London: Weidenfeld and Nicolson. Pp. 443–51.
Turner, Frederick J.
1894   *The Significance of the Frontier in American History.* Annual Report of the American Historical Association 1893. Washington: U. S. Government Printing Office.
Turner, John Peter
1950   *The North-West Mounted Police 1873–1893.* 2 vols. Ottawa: King's Printer and Controller of Stationery.

TV Spurs Interest in K.U.'s Comanche
 1959 *Topeka Capital.* February 22.
Twardy, Chuck
 1986 Famed Comanche's All Wet. *Lawrence Journal–World.* March 17.
Tyler, Bill
 1939 Comanche Legally Belongs Here; Stabled in Hoch. *University Daily Kansan.* January 13.

Ultimus
 1928 Some Famous War Horses. *The Cavalry Journal,* vol. 37, no. 151 (April): 253–58.
Upton, Richard, ed.
 1975 *The Custer Adventure.* Fort Collins, Colorado: The Old Army Press.
Utley, Robert, ed.
 1972 *The Reno Court of Inquiry: The Chicago Times Account.* Fort Collins, Colorado: The Old Army Press.
 1977 *Life in Custer's Cavalry: Diaries and Letters of Albert and Jennie Barnitz, 1867–1868.* New Haven: Yale University Press.

Valentry, Duane
 1959 Comanche Never Told. *This Day,* June: 58.
 1961 Comanche. *The Quarter Horse Journal,* vol. 13, no. 6: 198–200.
 1966 At the Little Big Horn: The Horses Died First. *The Blade Sunday Magazine.* June 10: 20–22.
Van de Water, Frederic
 1934 *Glory-Hunter: A Life of General Custer.* New York: Bobbs–Merrill Co.
Vestal, Stanley
 1932 *Sitting Bull: Champion of the Sioux.* Boston: Houghton Mifflin Co.

Wagner, Glendolyn Damon
 1934 *Old Neutriment.* Boston: Ruth Hill, Publisher.
Waldman, Charley W.
 1964 *Early Day History of Sturgis and Fort Meade in the Beautiful Black Hills of South Dakota,* volume I. Sturgis, South Dakota: privately printed.
Walker, Barbara G.
 1983 *The Woman's Encyclopedia of Myths and Mysteries.* New York: Harper & Row.
Walker, Stella A.
 1953 *In Praise of Horses.* London: Frederick Muller.
Walt Disney's *Tonka*
 1958 New York: Dell Publishing Co.
Warhorse and Weasels
 1952 *Newsweek,* vol. 39, no. 2 (January 14): 50.
Watson, J. N. P.
 1983 *Sefton: The Story of a Cavalry Horse.* London: Souvenir Press.
Wax, Murray
 1971a Comanche's Stand: To the Editor. *University Daily Kansan.* October 15.

1971b   Report to Robert M. Mengel. December 8.
Webb, Christine
1987   A Home for Heroes. *Woman.* March 27.
Weiss, David
1986   Hundreds Live To Tell of Custer's Defeat. *New York Times.* July 10: A 22.
Welsh, James
1986   *Fools Crow.* New York: Viking Penguin.
Werel, F. M.
1934   The Real Winners of the West. *Winners of the West,* vol. 11, no. 4 (April 30): 3.
Wey, P. W.
1926   Comanche. *The Cavalry Journal,* vol. 35, no. 144. (July): 432–34.
Wheeler, Homer W.
1925   *Buffalo Days.* Indianapolis: Bobbs-Merrill Co.
Whitman, S. E.
1962   *The Troopers.* New York: Hastings House.
Whittaker, Frederick
1876   *A Complete Life of General George A. Custer.* New York: Sheldon & Co.
Wilmsen, Steven
1986   Soaked Comanche Is Nearly Dry. *The Lawrence Journal–World.* April 30.
Winchester: General Philip H. Sheridan's War Horse
1980   Bulletin from Public Inquiry Mail Service, Smithsonian Institution.
A Winter Festival of Fine Family Programs Coming to the Disney Channel
1987   *The Disney Channel Magazine.* December 7, 1986–January 17, 1987.
Wister, Owen
1972   The Evolution of the Cow-Puncher. In *My Dear Wister: The Frederic Remington–Owen Wister Letters.* Palo Alto: American West Publishing Co.
Wood, William R.
1927   Reminiscences. In *Custer's Prelude to Glory: A Newspaper Accounting of Custer's 1874 Expedition to the Black Hills,* eds. Herbert Krause and Gary D. Olson. Sioux Falls, South Dakota: Brevet Press: 271–72.
Worcester, Don
1986   *The Spanish Mustang.* El Paso: Texas Western Press.
Wyndham, Colonel The Hon.
1979   1940: In Retrospect. In *The World's Greatest Horse Stories,* ed. J. P. N. Watson. New York: Paddington Press, pp. 112, 143–44.
Wyoming Notes
1900   *Wheatland World.* March 30.

Zacherle, Col. George H.
1976   Letter to the Editor. *Little Big Horn Associates Newsletter,* vol. 10, no. 12 (December): 23.

Index

351

286; memorial service for (1986), 93; portrayal of, in fiction and film, 230–55; reinterment of, 90; relationship with Custer, 83; will of, 89–90; wounds of, 90, 94, 290

Korn, Gustave, 22, 62, 75, 105, 107, 108, 131, 267, 303, 308

Kuhlman, Charles, 63, 67, 68, 92, 132, 322

Label on Comanche display. *See* Sign on Comanche exhibit

Language barrier. *See* Silence of Comanche

Leighton, Margaret, novel by, 53–54, 229, 247–52, 253–54, 257, 260

Little Big Horn Expedition, 57–73

Lockwood, John C., 76–77, 186–87

Lone survivor, Comanche as. *See* Sole survivor, Comanche as

Luce, Edward S., 20, 54, 67, 74–75, 82, 92, 112, 171–72, 176, 246–47, 249, 251, 253, 257, 287, 288, 289, 322, 323; book by, 82, 112, 132, 133–34, 135–36, 222–25; as Custer Battlefield superintendent, 134, 135, 151, 322; efforts of, to move Comanche to Custer Battlefield, 112–13, 132–36, 138–39, 142–43, 151–52, 153–54, 162; opinion of, about Brown's book, 225; opinion of, about *Tonka*, 246–47; and Seventh Cavalry records, 20, 56, 74–75

Markings of Comanche, 47, 48, 49, 259; adage concerning, 74, 81; symbolism of, 49

Massacre, use of the term for the Custer Battle: by Amaral, 227; by Dallas, 241; discussed by Mengel, 228; in 1891, 324; by grandson of Dyche, 190; Indians' objection to, 188, 189, 193, 198, 202, 204, 208–9; in 1989, 208; in 1987, 208; in 1947, 142; in 1979, 208; in original sign on the Comanche exhibit, 188; in *Tonka*, 242; at World's Columbian Exposition, 117

Mengel, Robert, 178, 192; publication by, about Comanche, 46, 198, 228

Meotzi. *See* Monahseetah

Mercy killing: of cavalry horses, 79; of Indian pony, 28, 293; proposed, of Comanche, 78, 81, 96

Monahseetah, 52, 251–52

Monaseta. *See* Monahseetah

Morgan (breed of horses), Comanche as, 43–44, 261

Mounted policemen, relationship of, with horses, 299–300

Mounting of Comanche, 111–14

Mourning: Comanche draped in, 107–8, 117, 329; contemporary counterpart of Comanche draped in, 93, 328; by Sturgis, associated with Comanche, 105–6

Museum display: changes in, 22–23; purpose and function of, 22–23; techniques of, 115–17, 125–28; value of Comanche as, at Custer Battlefield, 152–54, 160–61, 162–64, 168–69

Museum of Natural History, University of Kansas. *See* Dyche Museum

Mustang, 19, 40, 42–43, 47, 48, 236, 239, 249–50, 267, 275, 284, 326

Mystery regarding Custer's Last Stand, 19, 282–83, 319, 322–23

Naming of Comanche, 20, 52–54, 241, 244, 246–47, 254, 256–57, 275

Nap (horse alleged to be a survivor of the Custer Battle), 34

Nature: Comanche's understanding of, 230; metaphors from, associated with Comanche, 264, 269; stilled in honor of Comanche, 308

Neglect, alleged, of mounted Comanche, 132–33, 135–36, 138, 139, 148, 155–56, 157–58, 323

Nowlan, Henry J., 75, 87, 89–90, 92, 107, 108, 109, 113, 114, 223, 224, 242

Nye, Elwood L., 63–64, 65–70, 71, 100, 132, 134–35, 139, 146, 222–23, 322, 323; attitude of, toward horses, 69–70; cavalry march of, 67; interest of, in Comanche, 70, 168–69, 323; paper of, on Comanche, 323; view on Custer of, 70

Only survivor. *See* Sole survivor, Comanche as

Ownership of Comanche: by Keogh, 39; mistakenly attributed to General Custer, 29, 41, 111, 116, 159, 168, 170, 171, 178, 179, 195, 228, 318; prior, attributed to Indians, 181, 186–88, 226, 230–31, 235, 284, 328; report of, by Tom Custer, 39; report of, by U.S. Government, 39; report of, by Troop I, 39

Paddy (Keogh's horse), 54–55, 249, 289

Elizabeth Atwood Lawrence holds a V.M.D. from the University of Pennsylvania School of Veterinary Medicine and a Ph.D. in Cultural Anthropology from Brown University. An associate professor in the Department of Environmental Studies at Tufts University School of Veterinary Medicine, Dr. Lawrence has written a number of articles on human-animal relationships and is the author of *Rodeo: An Anthropologist Looks at the Wild and the Tame* and *Hoofbeats and Society: Studies of Human-Horse Interactions.*

The manuscript was edited by Connie Bracken. The book was designed by Elizabeth Hanson. The typeface for the text is Baskerville. The display type is Pyramid. The text is printed on 50 lb. Glatfelter paper. The cloth edition is bound in Holliston's Roxite B grade cloth.

Manufactured in the United States of America.